Writing Effective Career Statements
有效撰寫英文職涯經歷

By Ted Knoy
柯泰德

Illustrated by Chen-Yin Wang
插圖：王貞穎

Ted Knoy is also the author of the following books in the Chinese Technical Writers' Series（科技英文寫作系列叢書）*and the Chinese Professional Writers' Series*（應用英文寫作系列叢書）：

An English Style Approach for Chinese Technical Writers
精通科技論文（報告）寫作之捷徑

English Oral Presentations for Chinese Technical Writers
做好英語會議簡報

A Correspondence Manual for Chinese Technical Writers
英文信函參考手冊

An Editing Workbook for Chinese Technical Writers
科技英文編修訓練手冊

Advanced Copyediting Practice for Chinese Technical Writers
科技英文編修訓練手冊進階篇

Writing Effective Study Plans
有效撰寫英文讀書計畫

Writing Effective Work Proposals
有效撰寫英文工作提案

Writing Effective Employment Application Statements
有效撰寫求職英文自傳

This book is dedicated to my wife, Hwang Li Wen.

近年來，台灣無不時時刻刻地努力提高國際競爭力，不論政府或企業界求才皆以英文表達能力為主要考量之一。唯有員工具備優秀的英文能力，才足以把本身的能力、工作經驗與國際競爭舞台接軌。

柯泰德先生著作《有效撰寫英文職涯經歷》，即希望幫助已有工作經驗的求職者能以英文有效地介紹其能力、工作經驗與成就。此書是柯先生有關英文寫作的第九本專書，相信對再度求職者是進入職場絕佳的工具書。

元培科學技術學院　校長

林進財

Table of Contents

Foreword

Professional writing is essential to the international recognition of Taiwan's commercial and technological achievements."The Chinese Professional Writers'Series" seeks to provide a sound English writing curriculum and, on a more practical level, to provide Chinese speaking professionals with valuable reference guides. The series supports professional writers in the following areas:

Writing style

The books seek to transform old ways of writing into a more active and direct writing style that better conveys an author's main ideas.

Structure

The series addresses the organization and content of reports and other common forms of writing.

Quality

Inevitably, writers prepare reports to meet the expectations of editors and referees/reviewers, as well as to satisfy the requirements of journals. The books in this series are prepared with these specific needs in mind.

Writing Effective Career Statements is the fourth book in The Chinese Professional Writers'Series.

Writing Effective Career Statements（《有效撰寫英文職涯經歷》）爲「應用英文寫作系列（The Chinese Professional Writers'Series）」之第四本書，本書中練習題部分主要是幫助國人糾正常犯寫作格式上的錯誤，由反覆練習中，進而熟能生巧，提升有關個人職涯描述的英文寫作能力。

　　「應用英文寫作系列」將針對以下內容逐步協助國人解決在英文寫作上所遭遇之各項問題：

A.寫作型式：把往昔通常習於抄襲的寫作方法轉換成更積極主動的寫作方式，俾使讀者所欲表達的主題意念更加清楚。更進一步糾正國人寫作口語習慣。

B. 方法型式：指出國內寫作者從事英文寫作或英文翻譯時常遇到的文法問題。

C.內容結構：將寫作的內容以下面的方式結構化：目標、一般動機、個人動機。並了解不同的目的和動機可以影響報告的結構，由此，獲得最適當的報告內容。

D.內容品質：以編輯、審查委員的要求來寫作此一系列之書籍，以滿足讀者的英文要求。

Introduction

This writing workbook aims to instruct students with work experience on how to write career statements in order to sum up their professional development and current directions. The following elements of an effective career statement are introduced: expressing interest in a profession; describing the field or industry to which one's profession belongs; describing participation in a project that reflects interest in a profession; describing academic background and achievements relevant to employment; introducing research and professional experiences relevant to employment and, finally, describing extracurricular activities relevant to employment.

Rather than merely listing one's personal information and previous achievements (which are often found in a resume), an effective career statement reflects an applicant's ability to demonstrate his or her language capabilities within a confined space. More importantly, an effective career statement can elucidate the way in which one's academic and professional interests would benefit the company at which one is seeking employment; one's anticipated contribution to a company if employed there, and one's acquired knowledge, skills or leadership qualities that are relevant to employment.

Each unit begins and ends with three visually represented situations that provide essential information to help students to write a specific part of a career statement. Additional oral practice, listening comprehension, reading comprehension and writing activities, relating to those three situations, help students to understand how the visual representation relates to the ultimate goal of writing an effective career statement. An Answer Key makes this book ideal for classroom use. For instance, to test a student's listening comprehension, a teacher can first read the text that describes the situations for a particular unit. Either individually or in small groups, students can work through the exercises to produce a well-structured career statement.

簡　介

　　本書主要教導讀者如何建構良好的英文職涯經歷。書中內容包括：1.表達工作相關興趣；2.興趣相關產業描寫；3.描述所參與方案裡專業興趣的表現；4.描述學歷背景及已獲成就；5.介紹研究及工作經驗；6.描述與求職相關的課外活動；7.綜合上述寫成英文職涯經歷。

　　有效的職涯經歷描述不僅能讓再度就業者在企業主限定的字數內精準的描述自身的背景資訊及先前工作經驗及成就，更關鍵性的，有效的職涯經歷能讓企業主快速明瞭求職者如何應用相關知識技能及先前的就業經驗結合來貢獻企業主。

　　書中的每個單元呈現六個視覺化的情境，經由以全民英語檢定為標準而設計的口說訓練、聽力、閱讀及寫作四種不同功能來強化英文能力。此外，本書也非常適合在課堂上使用，教師可以先描述單元情境而讓學生藉由書中練習循序在短期內完成。

Elements of a successful career statement

Look at an example of an effective career statement:

Long-term health care management has fascinated me since undergraduate school, during which, I received hospital training in social welfare services. This invaluable training allowed me to effectively respond to a diverse array of problems. For instance, I once delivered medicine to an elderly individual infected with tuberculosis. The poor living environment of this individual living in such dire circumstances shocked me. Following this experience, I began to focus on the long-term health care sector in Taiwan, eventually leading to my successful completion of a graduate degree in this field.

According to World Health Organization (WHO) statistics, Taiwan has been an "aging society" since 1993. However, the island's health care sector for long-term care does not have an equitable standard, neither in service nor in service fees. This explains my interest in investment within the long-term care sector. I ultimately aspire to become a health care manager capable of adopting commercial management practices in non-profit organizations. Not only an essential and effective strategy, such an application is a global trend. While majoring in Healthcare Management during undergraduate school and conducting graduate level research in Business Management, I attempted to understand theoretical and practical applications between commercial and non-profit organizations. These studies exposed me to a diverse array of seemingly polar topics, in which I searched for their possible relationships in a practical context. As your company is renowned for its strong organizational culture and management structure, I firmly believe that working in your company would allow me to fully realize my career aspirations.

Governments worldwide strive to provide their residents with a stable and prosperous environment. With its rapid economic progress in recent decades, Taiwan is striving to build upon its industrial and technological prowess while, simultaneously, establishing a sound social welfare system. According to numerous investigations, developing a country's social welfare system represents not only the level of development for that country, but also the ability to forecast the prosperity or decline of that country in upcoming decades. As a renowned leader in the long term healthcare sector, your company has impressive organizational objectives, combined with a strong management structure and diversity of training courses. This strong organizational commitment is reflected in the high quality services that you provide to your customers. As a member of your corporation, I hope to actively participate in your company's external affairs. Individuals working in this position need to closely interact with other organizations and customers. My work experience and solid academic background will enable me to comprehend and familiarize myself with all of the commercial practices of this corporation and professional field in a relatively short time.

For instance, my abundant experiences from administrative work while in the military service and extracurricular activities in the student association during university will definitely be a plus towards my ability to orient myself with my new responsibilities at your company. My familiarity with several analysis methods in the decision science field, as learned during graduate school, is another strong asset that I bring to your company. I can apply such methods more flexibly after securing employment in a non-profit organization such as yours. Moreover, my previous academic and work experiences will enable me to more clearly explain analysis results so that the company can reach management decisions efficiently.

My strong commitment to the marketing profession is demonstrated by my graduate school research in identifying effective demographic variables to develop a deterministic and stochastic model so that growth trends in the long-term health care sector can be accurately forecasted. In addition to confirming the ability of the forecasting model to evaluate precisely how the weight of early population and the demand for long-term care health care resources are linearly related, the results of my graduate school research also helped clarify how demographic variables affect the growth rates in the long-term healthcare sector. Policymakers in the social welfare sector and business investors heavily rely on accurate forecasting reports that predict market demand to devise finance-related policies in the health sector and develop inventory projects. Your organization's great working environment, combined with the impressive number and diversity of training courses to maintain the competitiveness of your employees in the market place, would definitely ensure the continual development of my professional skills as well as benefit the living standard of your customers.

My graduate degree in Business Administration at Yuanpei University of Science and Technology provided me with specialized curricula that aimed not only to strengthen my knowledge of modern business practices and English writing skills for publishing my research findings, but also equip me with the necessary skills to significantly contribute to the workplace. My diverse academic interests and strong curricular training reflect my ability not only to see beyond the conventional limits of a discipline and fully comprehend how the field relates to other fields, but also to possess strong analytical and problem-solving skills. My graduate level research focused primarily on quantitative aspects of decision science and statistical science. These scientific disciplines involve a diverse array of analysis, qualitative, and quantitative methods, as well as complex mathematical models. The most challenging task is to comprehend and explain those results completely. Owing to my academic interests and curricular training, I learned how to analyze problems, find solutions, implement those solutions, and report those results clearly both in writing and orally, through approaches which I learned how to develop my thoughts through logical reasoning concepts taught in class. Although quantitative science and academic research are often approached independently, my course loading and frequent oral reports in graduate school allowed me to appreciate the need for harmony among collaborators to achieve goals successfully.

Managers always encounter the most difficult question: "How can I identify the best decision or project to implement given the numerous options available?" Graduate school has equipped me with much knowledge, skills and logical competence to effectively address workplace challenges. Among which include the methods and skills taught in Business Research Science (i.e., logical reasoning ability), Quantitative Aspects of Decision Science (i.e., ability to construct qualitative, quantitative and mathematical models), Statistical Science (i.e., analytical ability), English Writing (i.e., professional communicative skills), Business Administration (i.e., finance, marketing, technology and human resources), as well as participation in professional societies (i.e., communicative skills, interpersonal relations, and leadership qualities). Moreover, the ability to integrate and explain seemingly polar concepts to those outside of my field of expertise was invaluable training for a situation in which I will often encounter in your workplace: to provide sufficient details to managers to enable them to make management decisions based on that information.

Following university graduation, I joined the army as a commissioned officer. I was initially responsible for handling administrative work involved monthly in the physical examinations of six thousand new soldiers out of a large squadron of around ten thousand military personnel. In this capacity, I was directly responsible to a general. The environment provided me with many opportunities not only to coordinate with experts in diverse fields, but also to familiarize myself with how a large-scale organization operates. These valuable experiences enabled me to comprehend how slogans, mission statements, and corporate strategies can be transformed into action plans.

My second job responsibility was managing the activities of nearly 160 soldiers in a platoon. Blending my previous experiences with the task at hand, I not only realized how students lack experience in adopting different models and operations in medium-sized and large-scale organizations, but also comprehended why basic level employees often become discouraged with management methods that are neither inapplicable in actual business practices nor innovative. Administrators in these organizations have various management styles and ways of implementing tasks. For instance, large-scale organizations tend to emphasize legal procedures, but lack flexibility and efficiency. Whereas medium-sized organizations focus on a leader's personality and style, they lack sufficient resources and support. The above experiences instilled in me solid management concepts and strong communication skills.

After retiring from the professional military service of nearly four years, I served as a research assistant in the Society of Emergency Medicine, R.O.C., which allowed me not only to see the connection between theoretical knowledge and actual business practices, but also to realize how results from academic investigations can influence governmental medical policies.

During university, my campus life was filled with participation in student associations. I was actively involved in the student activity center (SAC) for three years. SAC was largely responsible for coordinating the administrative activities of sixty-five student associations at Chungtai Institute of Health Sciences and Technology, such as distributing the funding for extracurricular activities from the school administration, coordinating personnel and use of equipment and facilities, consulting with other campus associations, and sponsoring large-scale activities. At SAC, I was in charge of furnishing and operating stage lighting and acoustics for extracurricular activities. This position offered me ample opportunities not only to come into contact with individuals from diverse backgrounds, but also become more receptive to the occasionally opposing priorities of different organizations. In addition to strengthening my managerial and communication skills, I served as a student association leader, in which I cooperated with the governmental sector in holding small-scale activities. This position not only advanced my organizational skills and ability to handle unforeseeable circumstances, but also made me a perseverant and punctual individual. Professional and extracurricular activities have definitely made me more efficient in performing academic tasks. For instance, holding conference meetings to facilitate collaboration is an essential communication medium in daily work despite its occasional tediousness and inefficiency. Effectively using time in conference meetings reflects my thorough understanding of the importance of teamwork while actively pursuing a common goal that will strengthen our knowledge skills and expertise. I attach a particular importance to the necessity of understanding the merits and limitations of various methods in a business enterprise to attain a clearly defined objective. In addition to a solid academic background, a good manager should have strong communicative, organizational and management skills. Confident of possessing these qualities, I look forward to contributing to your corporate family.

Not necessarily in the following order or that of the above example, a successful career statement comprises the following elements:

A Expressing interest in a profession 表達工作相關興趣

1. Stating how long one has been interested in a particular field or topic 描述專業興趣所延續的時間

2. Describing the relevance of one's interest to industry or society 描述興趣與產業及社會的相關性

3. Stating how one has pursued that interest until now 描述興趣形成過程

4. Stating how finding employment related to one's interest would benefit the applicant and/or the company 描述興趣與工作的配合對勞資方都有利

B Describing the field or industry to which one's profession belongs 興趣相關產業描寫

1. Introducing a relevant topic with which one's profession is concerned 介紹業界所關心的相關主題

2. Describing the importance of the topic within one's profession 強調主題的專業性

3. Complimenting the company on its commitment to excellence in this area of expertise 讚美公司對專業的自我期許

4. Stating anticipated contribution to company in this area of expertise if employed there 所期望對公司的專業貢獻

C Describing participation in a project that reflects interest in a profession 描述所參與方案裡專業興趣的表現

1. Introducing the objectives of a project in which one has participated 介紹此方案的目標

2. Summarizing the main results of that project 概述該方案的成果

3. Highlighting the contribution of that project to the company or the sector to which it belongs 強調該方案對公司或部門的貢獻

4. Complimenting the company or organization, at which one is seeking employment, on its efforts in this area 讚美公司對業界的專業努力

D Describing academic background and achievements relevant to employment 描述學歷背景及已獲成就

1. Summarizing one's educational attainment 總括個人的學術成就

2. Describing knowledge, skills and/or leadership qualities gained through academic training 描述學術訓練所獲得的技能及（或）領導特質

3. Emphasizing a highlight of academic training 強調一個學術訓練的特定領域

4. Stressing how academic background will benefit future employment 強調學術背景對未來求職的利處

E Introducing research and professional experiences relevant to employment 介紹研究及工作經驗

1. Introducing one's position and/or job responsibilities, beginning with the carliest position and ending with the most recent one 介紹個人歷年至今所任工作職位

及職責

2. Describing acquired knowledge, skills and/or leadership qualities 描述個人所獲得的知識、技能及（或）領導特質

F Describing extracurricular activities relevant to employment 描述與求職相關的課外活動

1. Introducing an extracurricular activity in which one has participated 曾參加的相關課外活動介紹

2. Highlighting the acquired knowledge, skills or leadership qualities that are relevant to employment 強調和求職相關的已有知識、技能或領導特質

Unit One

Expressing interest in a profession

表達工作相關興趣

Vocabulary and related expressions 相關字詞

theoretical knowledge 理論知識
expertise 專門技術
independent research 自主性做研究
career path 求職路徑
knowledge-based skills
以知識為主的技能
career aspirations 職業熱誠
refine 精練
employed 被雇用
actualize 實施
implement 工具
advancement of ……的進展
valuable assets 有價資產
conducive 有益的
national health insurance system
全民健保

transformed 使改觀
living standards 生活水準
innovations 創新
crucial 重要的
rapidly evolving 快速發展
employment opportunities 求職機會
medical technology 醫學科技
purify 純化
characterize 描繪……的個性
potential 可能的
exposed 暴露
case studies 個案研究
senior thesis 大四畢業前論文
information technology 資訊科技
posed 呈……姿勢
stems 由……造成

feasible strategies 可行的策略
competitive 競爭的
unique 獨特的
organizational culture 組織文化
consulted 商議
practices 練習
strives 努力
professional aspirations 專業熱誠
necessitating 使成為必要
aggressive 具侵略性
alleviate 緩和
intensely competitive 高度競爭的
biotech sector 生化部門
human relations 人類關係
intrigued 好奇的
essential 必要的
excellent learning environment
絕佳的學習環境
one's intended meaning
某人意欲表達的意思
incidence 影響
grasp 理解
limitless 無限制的
potential applications 可能的應用
learning module 學習模組
on the rise 上升中
human immune system 人類免疫系統
instituted 創立
recent emergence 近來顯現
integrate 合併
deduction 扣除
monthly income 月收入
entitled 給予……權力
outpatient or admissions services
門診及住院病患服務
Industrial Technology Research Institute
(ITRI) 工業技術研究院

seemingly 似乎地
unlimited 有限制的
conveniently 方便地
accessed 接近
peruses 仔細研究
novel management concepts 新的管理觀念
research capabilities 研究能力
competent 有能力的
unforeseeable obstacles 無可預知的障礙
distinguish 區別
collaborators 共同研究者
congenial 一致的
exciting challenges 令人興奮的挑戰
beneficial results 有利的結果
generate 產生
wholeheartedly 全心全意地
endeavor 努力
prevalence 流行
enrolled 登記
human civilization 人類文明
previous ways of thinking 先前的思考方式
management principles 管理原則
practical work experience 實際的工作經驗
solid determination 堅定的決心
management level position 管理階層職位
reputed 有名的
excessively 過度地
straining 拉緊
formulating 公式化表示
indicator 指示
monitor 監視
financial strain 財政緊張（拉緊）
encouraged 受到鼓勵的
specialization 專門化
fraction 小部分
scientific and technological breakthroughs
科技突破性發展

Susan

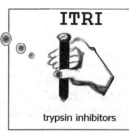

ITRI

trypsin inhibitors

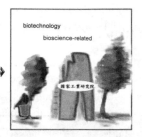

biotechnology

bioscience-related

Tom

YUST

information technology

Business Management

Internet

Tom

Mary

某某大學

Hospital Management

NIH

organizational culture

Chang Gung Memorial Hospital

A Write down the key points of the situations on the preceding page, while the instructor reads aloud the script from the Answer Key.

Situation 1

_____

_____

_____

Situation 2

_____

_____

_____

Situation 3

_____

_____

_____

B Oral practice I

Based on the three situations in this unit, write three questions beginning with **What**, and answer them. The questions do not need to come directly from these situations.

Examples

What have Susan's recent research interests provided her with?

A sound theoretical knowledge of medical technology

What area does Susan hope to apply her professional and academic knowledge?

A biotechnology or bioscience-related career

1. _____

_____

2. _____

_____

3. _____

_____

C Based on the three situations in this unit, write three questions beginning with *How*, and answer them. The questions do not need to come directly from these situations.

Examples

How did Tom's interest in information technology stem from his contact with this field in undergraduate computer classes?

His interest in information technology

How has the Internet helped Tom cut down on expenses when exploring his research interests?

By cutting down on expenses that he might otherwise spend on textbooks or other literature

1. _____

_____

2. _____

_____

3. _____

_____

D Based on the three situations in this unit, write three questions beginning with *When*, and answer them. The questions do not need to come directly from these situations.

Examples

When was Mary first exposed to hospital management?

During undergraduate school

When did Mary become aware of how novel management concepts can be applied in a practical setting?

While consulting a hospital administrator on the various practices adopted in daily operations

1. _____

   _____

2. _____

   _____

3 _____

   _____

E Write questions that match the answers provided.

Examples

Where did Tom acquire much valuable research experience?

Through graduate studies in the Institute of Business Management at Yuanpei University of Science and Technology

How long have telecommunications and related consumer products intrigued Tom?

Since high school

What is Mary committed to?

Strengthening her research capabilities

1. _____

_____

The importance of hospitals establishing feasible strategies for remaining competitive

2. _____

_____

Many exciting challenges

3. _____

_____

Chang Gung Memorial Hospital

F Listening Comprehension I

Situation 1

1. What have Susan's research interests allowed her to develop?

    A. a sound theoretical knowledge of medical technology

    B. advanced expertise in conducting independent research

    C. a research plan

2. Where are there potential employment opportunities?

    A. Industrial Technology Research Institute

    B. the hi tech sector

    C. in the rapidly evolving medical technology field

3. What is Susan confident of?

    A. her ability to design and implement a research plan

    B. her ability to contribute significantly to the advancement of Taiwan's medial sector

    C. her ability to conduct experiments to purify trypsin inhibitors from seeds

4. What has Susan become familiar with?

    A. acquiring a sound theoretical knowledge of medical technology

    B. designing and implementing a research plan

    C. the demands of her chosen career path

5. Where would Susan like to begin a biotechnology or bioscience-related career?

    A. Industrial Technology Research Institute

    B. Taiwan's medical technology sector

    C. the rapidly evolving medical technology field

Situation 2

1. What Institute did Tom study at for his graduate study?

A. The Computer Institute

B. The Institute of Business Management

C. The Institute of Information Technologies

2. What does Tom occasionally peruse at the bookstore?

A. The Internet

B. career magazines

C. the latest technology magazines

3. Where would Tom like to work?

A. ABC Corporation

B. Yuanpei University of Science and Technology

C. the bookstore

4. What has helped Tom cut down on expenses?

A. reading magazines in the bookstore

B. using the Internet

C. using the latest computer programs

5. Why is almost everyone eager to learn how to use the latest computer programs and acquire as many knowledge-based skills as possible?

A. Because ABC Corporation provides an excellent environment not only to actualize one's potential in a career,

B. because information technologies have definitely transformed living standards globally, as new innovations seem to appear daily

C. because the Internet provides seemingly unlimited information that can be conveniently accessed anywhere

6. What is Tom's major information source?

A. textbooks or other literature

B. the bookstore

C. the Internet

Situation 3

1. What position is Mary seeking?

    A. a nursing one

    B. a management one

    C. a medical technology one

2. What has Mary become aware of?

    A. beneficial results that she can generate

    B. how to become a more competent professional

    C. an individual hospital's needs

3. As a researcher, what does Mary strive to do?

    A. to distinguish herself from other collaborators while remaining congenial and approachable

    B. to consult hospital administrators on the various practices adopted in daily operations

    C. to establish feasible strategies for hospitals to remain competitive

4. What has Mary spent considerable time to learn about?

    A. Changes in Taiwan's national health insurance system

    B. the unique organizational culture of hospitals and research related topics

    C. how to apply novel management concepts in a practical setting

5. Where was Mary first exposed to Hospital Management?

    A. graduate school

    B. Chang Gung Memorial Hospital

    C. undergraduate school

21

G Reading Comprehension I
Pick the word or expression whose meaning is closest to the meaning of the underlined word or expression in the following passages.

Situation 1

1. Susan's recent research interests have not only provided her with a <u>sound</u> theoretical knowledge of medical technology, but also allowed her to develop advanced expertise in conducting independent research.

   A. noise

   B. flawless

   C. blemished

2. Susan's recent research interests have not only provided her with a sound theoretical knowledge of medical technology, but also allowed her to develop <u>advanced</u> expertise in conducting independent research.

   A. progressive

   B. fundamental

   C. preliminary

3. Susan's recent research interests have not only provided her with a sound theoretical knowledge of medical technology, but also allowed her to develop advanced <u>expertise</u> in conducting independent research.

   A. nonprofessional

   B. amateur

   C. proficiency

4. In pursuing these interests, she has acquired many professional skills to become <u>familiar</u> not only with the demands of her chosen career path, but also with potential employment opportunities in the rapidly evolving medical technology

field.

A. routine

B. oblivious

C. ignorant

5. In pursuing these interests, she has acquired many professional skills to become familiar not only with the demands of her chosen <u>career</u> path, but also with potential employment opportunities in the rapidly evolving medical technology field.

A. curiosity

B. vocation

C. inquisitiveness

6. In pursuing these interests, she has acquired many professional skills to become familiar not only with the demands of her chosen career path, but also with <u>potential</u> employment opportunities in the rapidly evolving medical technology field.

A. unattainable

B. improbable

C. latent

7. In pursuing these interests, she has acquired many professional skills to become familiar not only with the demands of her chosen career path, but also with potential employment opportunities in the rapidly <u>evolving</u> medical technology field.

A. stagnant

B. unfolding

C. dormant

8. As for the <u>specifics</u> of her research involvement, Susan has conducted experiments to purify trypsin inhibitors from seeds and characterize the trypsin

inhibitor assay.

   A. survey

   B. overview

   C. details

9. As for the specifics of her research involvement, Susan has conducted experiments to <u>purify</u> trypsin inhibitors from seeds and characterize the trypsin inhibitor assay.

   A. cleanse

   B. smudge

   C. blacken

10. As for the specifics of her research involvement, Susan has conducted experiments to purify trypsin inhibitors from seeds and <u>characterize</u> the trypsin inhibitor assay.

   A. avoid

   B. describe

   C. avert

Situation 2

1. Tom's interest in information technology <u>stems</u> from his first contact with this field in undergraduate computer classes.

   A. arrives

   B. originates

   C. to reach a particular place

2. The Internet especially <u>fascinates</u> him, with its ability not only to provide seemingly unlimited information that can be conveniently accessed anywhere, but also to help him cut down on expenses that he might otherwise spend on textbooks or other literature.

A. tire

B. captivate

C. weary

3. The Internet especially fascinates him, with its ability not only to provide <u>seemingly</u> unlimited information that can be conveniently accessed anywhere, but also to help him cut down on expenses that he might otherwise spend on textbooks or other literature.

A. secluded

B. concealed

C. apparently

4. The Internet especially fascinates him, with its ability not only to provide seemingly <u>unlimited</u> information that can be conveniently accessed anywhere, but also to help him cut down on expenses that he might otherwise spend on textbooks or other literature.

A. restricted

B. infinite

C. insular

5. The Internet especially fascinates him, with its ability not only to provide seemingly unlimited information that can be <u>conveniently</u> accessed anywhere, but also to help him cut down on expenses that he might otherwise spend on textbooks or other literature.

A. feasibly

B. inaccessible

C. inopportune

6. The Internet especially fascinates him, with its ability not only to provide seemingly unlimited information that can be conveniently <u>accessed</u> anywhere, but also to help him cut down on expenses that he might otherwise spend on

textbooks or other literature.

A. entered

B. blocked

C. prohibited

7. Although the Internet is his information source, Tom occasionally <u>peruses</u> the latest technology magazines at the bookstore.

A. skim

B. glance

C. scrutinize

8. Information technologies have definitely <u>transformed</u> living standards globally, as new innovations seem to appear daily.

A. constrained

B. converted

C. restrained

9. Information technologies have definitely transformed living standards globally, as new <u>innovations</u> seem to appear daily.

A. relapse

B. regressions

C. creations

10. This fact explains why almost everyone is <u>eager</u> to learn how to use the latest computer programs and acquire as many knowledge-based skills as possible.

A. enthusiastic

B. appalled

C. dreaded

Situation 3

1. Mary was first <u>exposed to</u> hospital management during undergraduate school,

where she read many hospital management-related case studies in preparation for her senior thesis.

A. sheltered

B. made aware of

C. protected

2. Mary was first exposed to hospital management during undergraduate school, where she read many hospital management-related case studies in preparation for her senior thesis.

A. conjecture

B. dissertation

C. assumption

3. Changes in Taiwan's national health insurance system have posed serious challenges for hospitals, requiring that they employ skilled management professionals.

A. presented

B. profusion

C. trade

4. Becoming aware of an individual hospital's needs has shown Mary the importance of hospitals' establishing feasible strategies for remaining competitive.

A. irrelevance

B. significance

C. inconsequential

5. Becoming aware of an individual hospital's needs has shown Mary the importance of hospitals' establishing feasible strategies for remaining competitive.

A. impractical

B. useless

C. viable

6. Becoming aware of an individual hospital's needs has shown Mary the importance of hospitals' establishing feasible <u>strategies</u> for remaining competitive.

　A. josh

　B. tactics

　C. jest

7. Additionally, frequently coming into contact with hospitals has allowed her to spend considerable time to learn about their <u>unique</u> organizational culture and research related topics.

　A. mundane

　B. ordinary

　C. incomparable

8. For instance, she once <u>consulted</u> a hospital administrator on the various practices adopted in daily operations.

　A. argued with

　B. discussed with

　C. debated with

9. Such experiences made her aware of how <u>novel</u> management concepts can be applied in a practical setting.

　A. unique

　B. typical

　C. commonplace

10. Moreover, Mary is <u>committed to</u> strengthening her research capabilities.

　A. in disagreement with

　B. opposed to

　C. devoted to

H Common elements in expressing interest in a profession include:

1. Stating how long one has been interested in a particular field or topic
2. Describing the relevance of one's interest to industry or society
3. Stating how one has pursued that interest until now
4. Stating how finding employment related to one's interest would benefit the applicant and/or the company

In the space below, express your interest in a profession.

_____

_____

_____

_____

_____

_____

_____

Unit one

Expressing interest in a profession
表達工作相關興趣

1. Stating how long one has been interested in a particular field or topic
   描述專業興趣所延續的時間

2. Describing the relevance of one's interest to industry or society
   描述興趣與產業及社會的相關性

3. Stating how one has pursued that interest until now
   描述興趣形成過程

4. Stating how finding employment related to one's interest would benefit the applicant and/or the company
   描述興趣與工作的配合對勞資方都有利

Look at the following examples of expressing interest in a profession.

◎Although deeply interested in computers since childhood, I gradually became interested in a medical career out of empathy for the seemingly endless number of people who seek medical examinations in a hospital to alleviate their illnesses. This career aspiration has persisted until now, with my recent completion of a Master's degree in Medical Imagery from Yuanpei University of Science and Technology. I remain ever optimistic that medical science and related technologies can cure ill patients and ensure that they receive the highest quality of preventive healthcare. Moreover, I am confident of my ability to pursue a research career in this area and, in doing so, significantly contribute to society. Your organization would provide me with such an opportunity.

◎My deep interest in this profession manifested itself in a recent collaboration to measure the infarct field range with an order of severity level. Based on those results, patients suffering from an acute infarct stroke can now receive the accurate radiation dosage for treatment. I firmly believe that writing an integral diffusion mode map for acute infarct stroke patients requires taking advantage of the latest software programs, in which different maps appear directly for different diseases. In doing so, clinical physicians can precisely understand the nature of all kinds of disease diffusion in the brain, thus increasing the effectiveness of clinic evaluations and curative treatment. Taiwan currently lacks technology professionals who are proficient in the use of such advanced instrumentation. I eventually look forward to the opportunity of collaborating with medical instrumentation manufacturers in developing software programs to treat acute infarct stroke patients. Such applications would not only benefit those patients, but also expand the quality of medical services that your hospital provides. If I am successfully employed in your organization, your hospital would offer me comprehensive training and challenging experiences that would greatly enhance my professional skills. In addition to your solid training for radiological technologists, your hospital offers an attractive salary and benefits package that I am drawn to.

◎Having recently completed my master's degree requirements from the Institute of Biotechnology at Yuanpei University of Science and Technology (YUST), I hope to bring my technical expertise and extensive laboratory experience to a renowned biotech firm such as yours. My graduate school research focused on microbal and molecular aspects of living creatures, with my master's thesis examining the role of *Vibrio parahaemolyticus* in food production, as clarified by molecular biotechnology procedures. Among the related molecular biotechnology procedures and areas that I became proficient in included pulsed-field gel electrophoresis (PFGE), polymerase chain reaction (PCR), multiplex PCR, and drug sensitivity analysis. Graduate school research also exposed me to molecular epidemiology-related topics. Before I entered graduate school, my undergraduate studies in the Food Science Department at YUST instilled in me a fundamental knowledge of molecular biotechnology, food composition, additives analysis, chemistry analysis, microbial development, enzyme separation, determination of food enzyme activity, food processing and dietetics. In addition to acquiring a basic knowledge of medicinal applications, I received First Aid certification from the Red Cross, which oriented me on pertinent medical procedures. Therefore, I bring to your company a unique background in Biotechnology and Food Science, disciplines that will prove to be valuable to any research effort that I belong to.

◎A vocational arts course I enrolled in as a junior high school student sparked my interest in electronic devices. Becoming aware of how electronic devices significantly impact our daily lives motivated me to diligently study electronic circuits. High school allowed me to acquire fundamental knowledge of electronic devices, including electronic circuitry packaging, electronic parts, theoretical fundamentals of electronic circuitry, television maintenance, transceivers, radio operation, as well as amplifier packaging and maintenance. During that period, I also obtained much information on the structure and theory of IC digital circuits, tube structure theory, and circuitry design. This early training explains why I majored in Electronics Engineering in both junior college and university. Since 1990, I have worked as a dosimetrist in the Radiation Oncology Department at Chang Hua Christian Hospital. Given my interest in radiation oncology and radiation dosimetry, I attended many symposia held by other hospitals or medical societies. At work, I have been responsible for quality assurance of treatment machinery, dose calculation and radiotherapy treatment planning. Additionally, I passed a rigorous nationwide examination to become a licensed primary radiation protector. I am especially interested in thoroughly understanding all aspects of measuring the proper radiation dose. As a graduate student in the Institute of Medical Imagery at Yuanpei University of Science and Technology, I strived diligently to attain advanced knowledge skills in medicine to enhance the quality of radiation therapy. An effective way of achieving this goal was to attend several domestic and international symposia, which as a manager in the Radiation Oncology Department, I am required to do in order to more effectively handle personnel matters and communicate effectively. I firmly believe that your hospital will find my above academic and professional training to be a valuable asset in your highly respected organization.

◎Devotion to a career requires compassion, sincerity and determination. Much of my devotion to a career in nursing goes back to childhood, when I helped my parents take care of my younger brother and sister. Another memorable experience was when I took care of a patient up until I started nursing school, where I first became fully aware of life and death issues that severely ill patients must confront. Nursing school provided me with many valuable training opportunities, such as when I worked in the Emergency Care Department of Chang Gung Memorial Hospital for three years Following marriage, I took a break from the hospital for three years. I have worked in the emergency care department of a hospital for nearly ten years. Accidents frequently occur that affect the operations of an emergency ward. For instance, a train accident occurred in Ying ger during the summer of 2002, resulting in the admission of fifteen patients to our emergency ward. The following summer, a bus accident on the national highway resulted in twenty patients admitted to our hospital as well, which was followed by another train accident in Ying ger last September. These large-scale accidents required that I work closely with other emergency personnel in the hospital to carry out the missions of our medical community. From my early nursing experiences to my current work as a professional nurse in an emergency care department, I have actively engaged in many efforts that required critical care of patients. Among those included responding to the devastating Chi Chi earthquake that hit Taiwan on September 21, 2000, setting up a medical station at San Xia Da Bao River, and counteracting the deadly SARS virus in our hospital environment. While my job often requires me to respond to many unforeseeable circumstances, I remain fascinated with the dynamics of my profession owing to the deep sense of satisfaction that I have in helping others. From a recruitment advertisement on the Internet, I learned that your hospital is looking for a new supervisor in the emergency care department. Fully understanding that your hospital hopes to operate an emergency care department that can coordinate its efforts with emergency medical network in Taipei, I am confident of my ability to handle such administrative tasks, especially in light of my solid nursing experience and management skills.

◎My recent research has focused mainly on culturing microorganisms and conducting related clinical experiments that require a foundational knowledge of molecular biology. I was especially fascinated with a study involving the natural transformation of Helicobacter pylori in relation to transposon shuttle mutagenesis and expression proteins. I slowly began to realize how biotechnology encompasses many disciplines, such as information science, statistics and molecular biology to name a few. I also learned how to perform computer analyses in efficiently handling experiential results, such as compiling statistics to assay experimental tends and to determine the significance of those results. Spending considerable time in studying whether horizontal DNA transfer is associated with antibiotics resistance and genetic diversity in Helicobacter pylori fostered my patience and resolve to significantly contribute to this specialized field of scientific research. In particular, while realizing that genes are essential for natural transformation in Helicobacter pylori, I learned how to utilize culture bacteria, determine DNA sequence, extract expression proteins and assay their function. Further expanding my research capabilities requires that I pay particular detail to each experimental step and identify potential problems before they arise, even if it requires spending more time on a particular task than originally planned. Doing so involves consulting with other researchers, especially those in the microorganism inhere field. My gradual maturation as a proficient researcher during graduate school will hopefully prove to be a valuable asset in your laboratory, allowing me to contribute significantly to any of your team's research efforts.

◎My deep concern since childhood over a world inflicted with many diseases has transformed me into a medically conscious individual. As evidence of the lack of researchers investigating viruses in Taiwan, viruses such as SARS and influenza virus (H5N1) inflict the island's inhabitants. Out of concern how viruses can endanger an individual's health, I researched the Epstein-Barr virus during graduate school. While Epstein-Barr virus infects a large portion of the human population, most carriers remain asymptomatic. Epstein-Barr virus is a human herpesvirus associated with several human cancers, including Hodgkin's lymphoma, Burkitt's lymphoma or nasopharyngeal carcinoma. Nasopharyngeal carcinoma (NPC) is especially prone to appear in Asia. As demonstrated in a related investigation, Epstein-Barr virus latent membrane protein (LMP) 1 is an oncogene. In addition to providing me with a solid background knowledge of biotechnology, my research of Epstein-Barr virus-related topics instilled in me the desire to become an academic researcher. This diverse education not only strengthened and broadened my solid knowledge base, but also further enhanced my sensitivity towards various medical issues. These are hopefully assets that your research institute is looking for.

◎While developing an interest in microorganisms and fermentation procedures, I also became deeply interested in living creature techniques, such as activating and keeping microorganisms, using for mass production, fermenting enzymes to produce pure bacteria, handling DNA samples and separates, as well as mastering techniques such as RCR. I also spent considerable time in understanding the manufacturing technologies involved for the biotech industry, whether it be for developing health foods or examining diseases as efficiently as possible. The more time spent in studying living creature-related procedures and pertinent industrial related research made me realize how much I need to know in order to full grasp the concepts of this field. As a member of your organization, I hope to contribute to your creative efforts to develop biotechnology products for commercial purposes. The food science division within your company will provide me an advanced understanding of the health food sector as well as enable me to perform food poison examinations for marketing purposes. I am confident of my ability to contribute to the professional image of your company.

◎My current research interests have focused on investigating macrophage-related topics. While investigating the function of macrophage in the development of a zebrafish embryo, I adopted microinjection technology to delete a gene that is associated with the macrophage function. In addition to providing me with advanced technical expertise and knowledge skills that will be invaluable for the workplace, hopefully at your research institute, this research allowed me to acquire strong analytical skills and practical laboratory experiences that will enable to further excel in the biotechnology or medical technology profession. During this period, I fostered a particular interest in medical knowledge, especially hematology, microbiology and molecular biology. In addition to my graduate school background, I am also a licensed medical technologist, having worked in a hospital two years ago. This exposure allowed me to acquire valuable clinical experiences in the medical technology field. With my above background, I feel equipped to serve as a researcher in biotechnology or medical technology-related fields, areas that your research institute is renowned.

◎Encompassing many topics such as diagnosis and radiotherapy, medical imagery has enthralled me since junior college. My strong interest resulted in the recent completion of a master's degree in this discipline. As evidence of the importance of medical imagery in medicine, physicians diagnose whether patients have a particular illness based on examination results, followed by a decision on what therapy those patients should receive. In addition to providing precise information on a patient's condition, a concise medical image can avoid unnecessary examinations and treatments. Recalling my first contact with medical imagery, I felt that it was more than just interesting, but almost magical. When scanning an image for patients, I can use image processing to create a concise image that will ensure an accurate diagnosis. Additionally, owing to the potentially large variation of a medical image, processing programs require only a two dimensional image to produce a three-dimensional one. With the extensive applications of medical imagery, the ability to design a reliable image processing system in order to simplify and make an examination as accurate as possible can elevate the quality of treatment and reduce overhead costs, ultimately elevating a hospital's reputation. I bring to your organization abundant experiences in the medical imagery field.

◎Having immersed myself in the radiation field for quite some time, I am especially interested in researching biology-related topics. A recent research effort I participated in involved experimenting with immunoflurochemistry stain and comfocal microsopic procedures in a hospital laboratory in Chunan, northern Taiwan. Despite my extensive academic and work experience in the radiation field, I am increasingly drawn to biotechnology, which is undoubtedly an emerging global trend in the new century. Its emergence reflects an increasing emphasis on health, as evidenced by an increasing elderly population worldwide. To become proficient in this area, I must acquire further laboratory experience. Overall, my diligent study in the radiation technology field has made me more patient and attune to minute details when conducting independent investigations, an attribute which I believe that your organization looks for in research staff.

◎I have aspired to become a medical professional since childhood, explaining why I completed my junior college diploma and bachelor's degree in the Department of Radiotechnology at Yuanpei University of Science and Technology, and eventually a Master's degree in Medical Imagery from the same institution. In addition to my academic work, I acquired many practical working experiences, as evidenced by my obtaining professional licenses in diagnosis radiation, radiotherapy, nuclear medicine and radiation protection. Given my strong academic background and numerous work experiences, I hope to gain employment at your hospital owing to your commitment to excellent medical image processing as well as advanced PACS instrumentation. In addition to my technical expertise, I am also interested in enhancing my management proficiency within your organization.

◎While cancer ranks as one of the leading causes of mortality in Taiwan, advanced technologies are constantly adopted in treatment machinery in order to treat this disease as effectively as possible. When using machinery from ^{60}Co to Linac, treatment time is reduced as the photon efficiency and energy increase. As computer technologies continuously progress, 3D computer planning systems are developed to execute intensity modulated radiation therapy (IMRT). Such systems can reduce the after effect and increase the dosage to reduce the tumor size during radiation therapy. While studying electronic engineering during my undergraduate study, I became proficient in maintaining instrumentation, particularly those in the hospital laboratory as I often repaired malfunctioning machinery. I have always enjoyed the sense of satisfaction when I can repair an electronic device without any assistance. I have thus tried to combine this talent of repairing malfunctioning instrumentation with my knowledge of how to more effectively care for cancer patients. This explains why my research heavily emphasizes the study of radiation physics and medical imagery. I believe that your institute will find this unique combination as a valuable asset to any research effort that your staff undertakes.

◎Having fascinated me since high school, bioscience encompasses a diverse spectrum of related subjects, including biology, physiology, biochemistry, virology, and medical imagery. Especially fascinated with medical imagery, I am intrigued with how this discipline has enabled me to more thoroughly understand complex phenomena found in daily life. For instance, a medical image can diagnose many maladies, including tumors, cancer and numerous other physiological conditions. These maladies can be diagnosed through a diverse array of disciplines, including blood velocity brain wave, sonography, and radiology. I am especially concerned with how the latest computer programs can save a patient's lives. Your medical organization would definitely provide me with the opportunity to further pursue my professional interests.

◎Although the general public is alarmed over potential radiation harm, carefully controlled amounts of radiation can benefit humans, such as in medical treatment or for industrial use. For instance, tumor treatment occasionally requires extremely high dosage amounts to eliminate a tumor. Thus, radiation security is essential to decreasing the likelihood of unnecessary radiation injuries to both patients and technical personnel. This field of research has definitely equipped me with the necessary practical and theoretical skills to become an accomplished medical physiologist that can contribute to a patient's well being and maintain radiation security simultaneously. I believe that your organization offers an excellent environment to further pursue this career path.

◎My recent completion of a Master's degree in Medical Imagery Technology at Yuanpei University of Science and Technology attests to my commitment to pursuing a related research career. While attempting to understand the nature of a tumor in a patient, I devoted my graduate study into investigating the role of radiotherapy in eradicating tumors. Results of my research have contributed to ongoing efforts to more effectively treat patients with tumors. I am determined to devote myself to investigating how radiation therapy on tumors can facilitate patient recovery; this area of research has received increasing attention in recent years. Working in your hospital would hopefully allow me not only to pursue some of my above research interests, but also to contribute to the overall welfare of those patients seeking therapeutic treatment.

◎Commercial development planning has enthralled me since I took part in a business management training course sponsored by the Council of Labor Affairs. I also focused on development planning in medical industry while studying in the Department of Healthcare Management at Yuanpei University of Science and Technology (YUST). These experiences instilled in me the confidence to undertake a career in development planning. Taiwan currently faces a dilemma in consumer purchasing habits, with an increasing number of individuals switching from pharmacies to merchandisers when purchasing health foods and even medical products. This trend reflects consumer's tendency towards one-stop shopping over merely purchasing specialized products quickly from a convenient location. Given this dilemma, local pharmacies incapable of enhancing their business performance will lose their competitiveness and eventually close. My recent research thus focused on how local pharmacies can maintain their competitiveness, in which I identified the primary business factors involved and then developed a management strategy model. Working in your organization would give me a practical context for the direction in which my career is taking.

◎ Science-related curricula have fascinated me since I can remember, eventually leading to my successful completion of a Master's degree in Business Management from Yuanpei University of Science and Technology (YUST). With my bachelor's degree in Hospital Administration at Chia Nan University of Technology, I have majored in Hospital Administration for seven years (including junior college). In a related focus, my graduate school focused on marketing in the healthcare sector. The health care sector in Taiwan is extremely competitive, with patients free to choose from an array of hospital-related services. Patient dissatisfaction may cause individuals to select another hospital. According to recent statistics, the cost of attracting a new patient is equivalent to that of maintaining five existing ones. I am especially interested in making strategic decisions aimed at bolstering a hospital's competitiveness. In particular, my undergraduate and graduate studies have fostered my interest in statistics, logical reasoning, hospital information systems and medical marketing. The strong graduate curricula at YUST equipped me not only with the academic fundamentals necessary for a career hospital management, but also with the workplace skills to meet the rigorous challenges of this exciting field. Securing employment at your hospital would definitely allow me to fully realize my career aspirations.

◎My fascination with finance can be traced back to undergraduate school, in which an economics course aroused my curiosity in acquiring more knowledge. With Taiwan's recent entry in the World Trade Organization, the recent deregulation of Taiwan's market will provide a diverse array of financial services, thus necessitating that domestic companies possess a high level of financial expertise in global markets. I am especially interested in those financial aspects that can enhance companies' global competitiveness. Having devoted myself to developing computer information systems for over a decade along with considerable time spent in researching data mining applications in information science for the finance sector, I developed a particular interest in integrating concepts from these two fields and, then, applying them to the recently emerging financial sector in Taiwan. These two ingredients are definitely crucial to my ability to fully realize my career aspirations, hopefully at your company. Your company is an undisputed leader among financial institutes in Taiwan. Renowned for effectively dealing with unforeseeable emergencies and enhancing customer services, your company has established a vision, which deeply impresses me. Moreover, I am attracted to your company's advanced financial information system for analyzing business transactions models, a system which will equip me with the competence to more significantly contribute to your organization's excellence in marketing.

◎The teaching profession has strongly interested me since childhood because educators can closely interact with the younger generation. While eager and occasionally moody, students have summer and winter holiday vacations to break up the monotony of academic work. Hoping to teach in the near future, I chose the radiography discipline owing to it uniqueness and relevance in modern society. I especially enjoyed a course in Radiology Physics during university. Exactly what is radiation? Radiation produces a wave length that causes some materials to produce physical, chemistry reactions and increases the efficiency of biological activities. Radiation was discovered in 1895. Geissler developed the tube (vacuum space) with voltage, in which the first film was photographed for his wife. Moreover, radiation is increasingly used in industry and medicine. For instance, industrial materials can be evaluated for amounts of radiation. Furthermore, in medicine, radiation is often used in physical examinations and therapy, e.g., radiation diagnosis, radiation therapy, and nuclear medicine. Radiation-related technologies have definitely enhanced people's lives immensely. Working within your organization would allow me to fulfill my dream of teaching others and benefiting others through radiation technology-related research.

◎My current research focus is on cell signal transduction, which I am extremely interested in owing to its complexity. I am especially interested in a commercial attempt to manufacture a DNA chip. Specifically, I studied the DNA chip manufacturing process, as well as attempted to understand more about DNA applications. My current research interests have involved investigating cellular DNA mutation and its potential role in leading to diseases. Within this topic, I am especially interested in human DNA sequencing research. This topic plays a critical role in establishing and implementing a human DNA gene bank. In this area, I plan to analyze either inherited or gene defective diseases. More specifically, a slight amount of mutation nucleic acid can be analyzed and compared in search for a mutation protein that causes an innate or acquired gene defective disease. Your organization would provide me with the opportunity to further pursue my research interests in this area and, in doing so, significantly contribute to Taiwan's rapidly growing biotech sector.

◎While studying Marketing as an undergraduate student at Yuanpei University of Science and Technology, I became intrigued with topics related to the marketing of emergency-oriented products and services. I am particularly interested in evaluating the post SARS situation to compile relevant data into a consumer-oriented administrative database system in order to fully understand consumer/supplier relations. Thus, I wish to further my knowledge through graduate studies on interactive marketing research, which is a timely topic for the recently emerging sector aimed at resolving inequalities in healthcare services for invalids. Your organization would provide me with such an opportunity to pursue this professional interest.

◎Disputes over medical treatment have intrigued me not only because they are interesting, but also because physicians and patients experience similar medical treatment problems. I am especially fascinated with diagnosing and treating medical problems owing to their interesting nature. Additionally, many events concerning medical treatment have occurred in recent years, especially how to use and inject a curative. Treating medical problems is a major concern in daily life. With many events in Taiwan related to treating medical problems, local hospitals still lack knowledge on how to distinguish between different diseases or maladies. Also, many patients are not exactly sure how to use curatives properly. Proper instruction on how to use a curative from a physician or nurse would help prevent unnecessary hazards. Additionally, physicians and nurse must have specialized medical knowledge skills to carefully diagnose patients' illnesses. Most domestic drugs have English language instruction for proper usage. However, if the drug contained instruction in Chinese for its proper use, then the likelihood of filling a faulty prescription would decrease, thus ensuring safety in dealing with curatives. Given my above interests, I am especially attracted to your company owing to its commitment to providing quality medical healthcare.

◎Despite working in the information sector, I majored in Electrical Engineering at university. Nevertheless, I am fascinated with business management-related topics. To more fully understand how information technologies increasingly can enhance business management, I recently completed a graduate degree in Business Administration at Yuanpei University of Science and Technology (YUST). Additionally, I worked on developing information systems for nearly a decade, thoroughly familiarizing myself with computer technology and semiconductor processes. The strong research fundamentals acquired from my work experience prepared me for advanced study on how information systems can assist managers in making the optimal decision. My subsequent graduate level research centered on how to apply mathematical calculations, such as use of gray and fuzzy methods, to simulate business decisions more effectively. As for developing an expert information system to achieve such an objective, I studied diligently to understand lot dispatching, entity feedback systems and cost accounting information systems. I am particularly interested in how to make an accurate, effective, and efficient database system. Thus, I wish to further my knowledge not only on Business Management-related topics, but also on mathematical calculations for use in real time control, marketing and decision making. If employed in your organization, I am confident that you would offer me comprehensive training and challenging experiences that would greatly enhance my professional skills in the above areas.

◎Exposure to research early on in my academic studies fostered my interest in graduate study and a biotechnology-related research career. I also frequently attend research symposiums to clarify my research direction and to prepare my experimental methodology. My gradual maturation as a proficient researcher will hopefully prove to be a valuable asset in your laboratory, allowing me to contribute significantly to your company's product development efforts.

◎Human resource management (HRM) intrigued me while I was pursuing a bachelor's degree. This discipline includes the study of organizational, culture, employee education, training and development research. Fascinated with the dynamics of this field, I am actively engaged in this area of research. Many Taiwanese businesses have attempted to strengthen their knowledge management skills in recent years by applying them to human resource management. Doing so would directly or indirectly contribute towards an organization achieving its maximum value. By adopting personnel management practices, a company can effectively control or reduce operational costs. In this area, I hope to significantly contribute to your organization.

◎Particularly fond of science-related curricula, I have always enjoyed performing new experiments involving those subjects. This interest led to my successful completion of a bachelor's degree in Hospital Administration at Chia Nan University of Technology. However, a bachelor's degree did not equip me with all of the skills necessary for the workplace, explaining why I subsequently pursued a master's degree in Business Administration at Yuanpei University of Science and Technology to further my knowledge of healthcare management research. Having recently completed this degree, I look forward to working in a governmental institution such as yours to further enhance my management proficiency skills.

◎Having dreamed of becoming a scientist since childhood, I acquired a bachelor's degree in Biochemistry and Microbiology from Yuanpei University of Science and Technology and, later, a master's degree in Biotechnology from the same university. The opportunity to work at your company would provide me with an excellent environment not only to fully realize my career aspirations, but also allow me to apply theoretical concepts taught in graduate school to a practical work setting.

◎Students undoubtedly aspire to attend university in order to broaden their horizons and pursue professional interests. Having received a bachelor's degree in Radiology Technology, I became highly interested in diagnostic images, especially image processing. To continually upgrade my professional skills, I learned how not only to interpret medical images, but also to perform computer programming. Furthermore, I intend to become more proficient in processing medical images for patients in diagnostic values. Doing so would allow me to increase the accuracy of diagnosis. I subsequently acquired a graduate degree from the Institute of Medical Imagery at YUST. Magnetic resonance imaging (MRI) has enthralled me since undergraduate school, allowing me to grasp theoretical and practical concepts related to this discipline as well as future trends. Working in your company would enable me to further pursue my research interests so that I could more fully understand the practical implications of what I have studied for several years.

◎I received a bachelor's degree in Chemical Engineering from National Taipei University of Technology, with the intention of entering either the chemical engineering or the electronics industry as an R&D engineer. However, the departmental curriculum at university sparked my interest into various directions. I became interested in medical imagery and radiotherapy in tumors, especially for curative purposes. Several years of academic study have left me with the deep impression that study is more than not just for securing employment. This motivated me to adopt a more meaningful strategy towards learning, especially how different fields can be integrated and further my knowledge of science. Working for your organization would offer many opportunities to view firsthand how such an integration occurs at the product development level.

◎I have long been intrigued by medical science. Building upon my solid academic training and relevant work experiences, I completed a master's degree in Medical Imagery. This effort encompassed absorbing enormous amounts of information. With education as a life long pursuit, I hope to significantly contribute to Taiwan by applying what I have learned in the classroom and laboratory. While preparing to enter graduate school, I concentrated on medical science-related topics. Despite my insufficient background in medical technology. I was able to compensate for my shortcomings through diligent study of seemingly polar disciplines. Your organization offers an excellent environment for me to continually upgrade my knowledge skills while, at the same time, contribute to your corporate goals.

◎ While optimistic that individuals can achieve their career aspirations, I have always dreamed of a world free of illness. As a medical technologist, I must remain abreast of the latest medical machinery and how to operate them properly. Restated, medical machinery must be in optimum condition to function properly. While lacking sufficient knowledge of computer programs in such machinery, I realize that I need to improve upon this area. With the increasing importance of computers in daily life, I am fascinated with how the Internet has impacted all aspects of modern medical technology as well. To compensate for my limitations in this area, I recently completed a Master's degree in Medical Imagery. A medical image can diagnose many maladies, especially tumors, cancer and numerous other physiological conditions. These maladies can be diagnosed through a diverse array of disciplines, including blood velocity, brain wave, sonography, and radiology. I am especially concerned with how the latest computer programs can save patient's lives. To do so, I need to integrate such programs with the Internet and related technologies, thus favoring the patient outcome immensely. Therefore, I believe that your company offers an excellent working environment to pursue a research career in the intensely competitive medical sector.

◎I am fascinated with how radiation protection impacts all aspects of radiation incidents. This fascination resulted in my successful completion of a master's degree in Radiological Technology with a concentration in radiation detection from Yuanpei University of Science and Technology. Taiwan's news media constantly reports on public apathy and selfish pursuits of self-interest, such as in stories on radiation leaks and how they endanger or frighten nearby residents. Taiwan lags behind other developed countries in handling and disposing radiation contaminated waste. Previously, such contaminated waste was disposed of without restraint; Taiwan also lacked manpower to protect the general public from potential disasters. During this period, many illegal proprietors even used radiation-contaminated materials to construct buildings. Subsequently, my graduate school research focused on how to detect radiation limits and offer effective protection in order to decrease the likelihood of potential accidents. Your company's solid reputation in tackling radiation-related problems explains why I am eager to join your organization.

◎The recently emerging medical imagery field focuses on adopting image processing to store images in order to replace films. Computer technology not only makes the images clearer, but also more accurate, thus allowing physicians to diagnose patient's problems more reliably. I am highly interested in this field. Life becomes unpredictable when individuals become ill and must be sent to a hospital. A series of thorough physical examinations are necessary for a physician to accurately diagnose a particular illness. Precise and clear medical images are thus essential. My successful completion of a Masters degree in Medical Imagery enabled me to strengthen my knowledge expertise in this field. Working in your hospital would hopefully allow me not only to pursue some of my above research interests, but also to contribute to the overall welfare of patients seeking therapeutic radiology treatment.

◎Radiation technology has rapidly progressed in recent decades. Whereas knowledge of radiation oncology was lacking more than a decade ago, computerized recombination has greatly added to our knowledge of this area. Computerized recombination allows not only for treatment planning of three-dimensional radiation therapy, but also development of advanced procedures for intensity modulated radiation therapy. My work in the Radiation Therapy Department has been personally fulfilling for me.

◎I have aspired to become either a physician or medical professional since childhood, explaining why I enrolled in the Radiology Technology Department of Yuanpei Junior College in 1992. Even after receiving a junior college diploma, I felt that my fundamental knowledge skills were still inadequate and, thus, started working on my bachelor's degree in the Radiology Technology Department of the same institution in 1999. The strong research fundamentals acquired during my undergraduate years prepared me for the stringent demands of a hospital. For instance, upon graduation, I started working in the Radiology Department of the Veterans General Hospital in Taipei. During this period, I further developed my interest in nuclear medicine and subsequently decided to pursue a master degree in this field so that I could find employment opportunities beyond that of a radiology technician. Given my above academic and professional experiences, I look forward to working in an organization such as yours to continually refine my professional skills.

◎Having immersed myself in the radiation field for quite some time, I recently completed a master's degree in Medical Imagery. Given my strong interest in researching biology-related topics, biotechnology is definitely an emerging global trend in the new century. I majored in Radiotechnology during undergraduate school, a discipline belonging to the clinical medicine profession. When occasionally asked to define what radiation is, I reply that this energy form can be found throughout the human body. Therefore, researching how radiation occurs inside the human body is a highly useful topic for those in the clinical medicine profession. Your organization's commitment to providing quality health care, especially for individuals undergoing radiological therapy, explains why I am eager to join your corporate family.

◎Undergraduate school sparked my interest in microbiology in relation to food science. In line with this interest, I served as a research assistant at both Academia Sinica and Tri-Service General Hospital. However, feeling that my knowledge skills in this area were still lacking, I successfully completed a master's degree in Biotechnology. With my recently acquired degree and strong desire to significantly contribute to Taiwan's biotechnology sector, I look forward to working in a globally renowned company such as yours.

◎My interest in researching microbiology and genome-related topics stems from undergraduate school, where I studied gene transfer, genetics, and biotechnology. My graduate studies at the Institute of Biotechnology at Yuanpei University of Science and Technology furthered my interest in pursuing a career in biotechnology research. In addition to my competence in the laboratory, my graduate school research focused mainly on infarction and immunity, especially how to sterilize and identify bacterial virulence. As knowledge is infinite, I must study a lifetime to remain abreast of the latest developments in this field. I believe that your company offers a unique environment in which I can continually refine my knowledge expertise of biotechnology.

◎My strong academic background in science explains why I am interested in researching molecular biotechnology-related topics. This interest led to my successful completion of a master's degree in this field. Recent biotechnology developments in Taiwan have led to the application of biological methods to diverse areas, including (1) genetic engineering, (2) cell fusion methods, (3) bioreaction technologies that encompass fermentation methods, enzyme technology, and bioreactors, (4) cell culture methods, (5) gene recombination, (6) embryo transplantation methods and nucleus transplantation methods. To remain abreast of the latest technology trends, my research currently focuses on cell fusion and cell culture methods, especially for human cell signal transduction. The opportunity to work in your company would provide me with an excellent environment not only to fully realize my career aspirations, but also allow me to apply theoretical concepts taught in graduate school to a practical work setting.

◎Biochemistry and biotechnology have long intrigued me. The careful selection of which methods to adopt and enforce in order to ensure that the best decision is made is what will make me a successful biotechnologist. This explains why I successfully completed a master's degree in Biotechnology. I would like to build upon my solid academic training and relevant work experiences in order to pursue a career in biotechnology. With my strong interest in biotechnology, I hope to use my knowledge of biology and assay methods to contribute to efforts to diagnose diseases, especially for control and community medicine. My interest in biotechnology extends beyond the classroom. An orientation seminar held at the Industrial Technology Research Institute (ITRI) further sparked my interest in this field, leading to my decision to acquire further knowledge skills in graduate school. Given my particular interest in researching cancer-related topics, I look forward to working in your medical center, which has distinguished itself with its innovative therapeutic treatment strategies.

◎Performing research requires substantial resources and effort. Research can be a tedious, monotonous and tiring process, explaining why I have a strong support group of close friends whom I can go to whenever I become frustrated with bottlenecks in my research that I occasionally encounter. Moreover, I have a strong personality and must constantly encourage myself to remain resilient. My research focuses on *E.coli, Staphylococcus aureus* and *Psedomonas aeruginosa*. This entails culturing bacteria, determining colony-forming units (CFU) and the bacterial growth curve, accumulating statistics and extracting bacterial plasmids, DNA and RNA. Despite the complexity of these tasks, my academic advisor in graduate school ensured me that I would succeed if I attempted to simplify my research tasks as much as possible as well as remain open to the latest knowledge skills in science and technology. Doing so requires that I spend much time not only in study and research, but also in consultation with my graduate school advisor. I firmly believe that your medical organization would provide me with the opportunity to further pursue my professional interests.

◎My exhaustive literature review on cancer-related research enabled me to understand its mechanisms and subsequent impact. In particular, I am interested in investigating the immunology system of a human diagnosed with cancer. Equipped with my academic knowledge of microbiology and biotechnology, as well as practical training at the Industrial Technology Research Institute, I aggressively apply my knowledge skills to this research field. Having acquired considerable knowledge skills of biotechnology, I can adeptly apply my knowledge skills to practical situations. With this commitment, I am determined to devote myself to a career in biotechnology, hopefully in your company's reputed product development division.

◎Study in food science since junior college at Cha-Yi University up until completion of a master's degree in Biotechnology at Yuanpei University of Science and Technology has allowed me to full grasp molecular biology and biotechnology-related topics. Since graduate school, I have continued to delve into those topics to more clearly identify my research interests. Science and technology are continuously advancing, with agricultural developments to reach a new milestone. Restated, biotechnological applications will significantly transform agricultural production.

Biotechnology has played a vital role in agriculture for thousands of years, with fermentation technology as a typical example. Your company's commitment to developing state-of-the-art product technologies in this field explains why I am eager to join your research staff.

◎Modern biotechnology has focused on molecular biology, genetic engineering, and transduction, which involve the genetic substances of living organisms. Rather than depending only on simply breeding or fermentation procedures, agricultural production in the future will increasingly depend on biotechnology innovations such as genetic transduction to elevate living standards. This explains why, following my recent completion of a master's degree in biotechnology, I continued to investigate related topics. In many aspects, biotechnology is highly promising for increasing the quality of life. Graduate school built upon my solid research fundamentals acquired during undergraduate school, especially in food processing for biotechnology applications. While food and humans are inseparable, food processing has already reached its peak in Taiwan. I am thus interested in how the biotech industry can increase the competitiveness of the domestic food science sector. Therefore, I hope to continually upgrade my technology skills in this field in order to significantly contribute to the development of healthy foods. The biotech industry has evolved out of commercial development of living creature techniques by combining research results with the desire to commercially develop product technologies. Given my above interests, I feel equipped to serve as a researcher in biotechnology or medical technology-related fields, areas that your research institute is renowned.

John

civilization

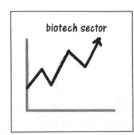

biotech sector

Lisa

chilldhood

human relations

Business Management

GHI

work experience

Jerry

1995

NHI

hospital

健保卡

financial
strain experienced

I Write down the key points of the situations on the preceding page, while the instructor reads aloud the script from the Answer Key.

Situation 4

_____

_____

_____

Situation 5

_____

_____

_____

Situation 6

_____

_____

_____

J Oral practice II

Based on the three situations in this unit, write three questions beginning with *What*, and answer them. The questions do not need to come directly from these situations.

Examples

What does John hope to eventually to do in order to achieve his professional aspirations?

Obtain a doctorate degree in a related field

What area does Susan hope to apply her professional and academic knowledge?

A biotechnology or bioscience-related career

What is on the rise?

The incidence of human cancer

1. _____

   _____

2. _____

   _____

3. _____

   _____

K Based on the three situations in this unit, write three questions beginning with *How*, and answer them. The questions do not need to come directly from these situations.

Examples

How was Lisa totally challenged in her previous ways of thinking?

Through a management course in which she enrolled during her senior year at university

How did Lisa learn to grasp management principles more fully?

By her work experience after she received undergraduate and graduate level training

1. _____

_____

2. _____

_____

3. _____

_____

L Based on the three situations in this unit, write three questions beginning with *Why*, and answer them. The questions do not need to come directly from these situations.

Examples

Why was Taiwan's national health insurance scheme instituted in 1995?

To integrate insurance and medical treatment throughout the island

Why do Taiwanese pay only a small fraction of the entire cost of health-related expenses?

Because they are entitled to hold an insurance card for hospital outpatient or admissions services

1. _____

_____

2. _____

_____

3. _____

_____

M Write questions that match the answers provided.

Examples

Why is Jerry interested in formulating an indicator?

To monitor the financial strain experienced by a hospital

What is Mackay Memorial Hospital's specialization?

In providing quality medical services

What portion of hospital services do Taiwanese residents pay?

Only a small fraction of the entire cost

1. _____

_____

That his professional interests match Mackay Memorial Hospital's specialization
in providing quality medical services

2. _____

_____

A valuable service

3. _____

_____

Many individuals excessively using medical treatment resources

N Listening Comprehension II

Situation 4

1. Why does John hope to eventually obtain a doctorate degree?

A. to contribute significantly to society

B. to discover new scientific applications

C. to achieve his professional aspirations

2. What is John's research interest in?

A. cancer and the human immune system

B. biotechnology

C. human civilization

3. How does John hope to contribute to society?

A. to alleviate the suffering of those with diseases

B. to discover new scientific applications

C. Both A and B

4. What has recently emerged as a significant area of scientific development?

A. cancer and the human immune system

B. biotechnology

C. the intensely competitive biotech sector

5. What is on the rise?

A. biotechnology

B. human civilization

C. the incidence of human cancer

Situation 5

1. What did Lisa do after completing undergraduate school?

A. continue to research human relations

B. grasp management principles more fully

C. look for a management level position in a reputed company

2. What does Lisa believe is essential?

A. pursuing a Master's degree in Business Management

B. finding one's own unique way of communicating

C. finding the most effective way to communicate one's intended meaning

3. When did Lisa enroll in a management course that totally challenged her previous ways of thinking?

A. during her senior year at university

B. while pursuing a Master's degree in Business Management

C. after completing undergraduate school

4. When did Lisa decide to pursue a Master's degree in Business Management?

A. after completing undergraduate school

B. while looking for a management level position in a reputed company

C. while enrolled in a management course

5. What does Lisa believe has little value without work experience?

A. theoretical knowledge

B. undergraduate and graduate level training

C. human relation

Situation 6

1. How can all Taiwanese residents participate in the health insurance scheme?

A. by integration of insurance and medical treatment throughout the island

B. by paying only a small fraction of the entire cost

C. by the deduction of a certain amount from their monthly income

2. Why is Jerry interested in formulating an indicator for Taiwan's national health insurance scheme?

A. to provide quality medical services

B. to monitor the financial strain experienced by a hospital

C. to use medical treatment resources excessively

3. What has led to many individuals' excessively using medical treatment resources?

A. an increase in monthly premium costs

B. payment of only a small fraction of the entire cost

C. integration of insurance and medical treatment throughout the island

4. When was Taiwan's national health insurance scheme instituted?

A. 1994

B. 1995

C. 1996

5. What is the result of many individuals' excessively using medical treatment resources?

A. an increase in monthly premium costs

B. entitlement of all Taiwanese residents to hold an insurance card for hospital outpatient or admissions services

C. a strain in the National Health Insurance system's finances

O Reading Comprehension II
Pick the word or expression whose meaning is closest to the meaning of the underlined word or expression in the following passages.

Situation 4

1. The <u>prevalence</u> of many diseases increases as human civilization progresses.

   A. elimination

   B. existence

   C. eradication

2. The prevalence of many diseases increases as human civilization <u>progresses</u>.

   A. stagnates

   B. decelerates

   C. advances

3. For instance, the <u>incidence</u> of human cancer is on the rise.

   A. disappearance

   B. occurrence

   C. increase

4. With his research interest in cancer and the human <u>immune</u> system, John hopes to participate in a learning module where he can work further on this fascinating topic.

   A. protection

   B. invasion

   C. inhibition

5. With his research interest in cancer and the human immune system, John hopes to participate in a learning <u>module</u> where he can work further on this fascinating topic.

A. caution

B. advice

C. course

6. With the recent <u>emergence</u> of biotechnology as a significant area of scientific development, his expertise gained at graduate school will hopefully enable him to contribute significantly to society as he strives to discover new scientific applications.

A. retreat

B. appearance

C. reclusion

7. With the recent emergence of biotechnology as a significant area of scientific development, his <u>expertise</u> gained at graduate school will hopefully enable him to contribute significantly to society as he strives to discover new scientific applications.

A. ineptness

B. incapability

C. proficiency

8. To achieve his <u>professional</u> aspirations, John hopes eventually to obtain a doctorate degree in a related field.

A. novice

B. crackerjack

C. amateur

9. To achieve his professional aspirations, John hopes eventually to obtain a doctorate degree in a <u>related</u> field.

A. pertinent

B. polar

C. opposing

10. As scientific and technological <u>breakthroughs</u> are made daily, biotechnology appears to have limitless potential applications, necessitating the aggressive research efforts.

    A. cycles

    B. repetitions

    C. innovations

Situation 5

1. Human relations have <u>intrigued</u> Lisa since childhood.

    A. fascinated

    B. dulled

    C. pooped out

2. Each individual has his or her own <u>unique</u> way of communicating.

    A. collective

    B. singular

    C. communal

3. Finding the most effective way to communicate one's <u>intended</u> meaning is essential.

    A. replicated

    B. imitated

    C. original

4. Finding the most effective way to communicate one's intended meaning is <u>essential</u>.

    A. unimportant

    B. critical

    C. irrelevant

5. Lisa's <u>fascination with</u> this endeavor led her to continue to research human

relations after completing undergraduate school.

A. intrigue with

B. boredom of

C. tolerance of

6. A management course in which she enrolled during her senior year at university totally challenged her previous <u>ways of thinking</u>.

A. anger towards something

B. antipathy towards something

C. attitude towards something

7. During that period, she decided to <u>pursue</u> a Master's degree in Business Management.

A. run away from something

B. go after something

C. prevent something from occurring

8. Her work experience after she received undergraduate and graduate level training increased her <u>desire</u> to grasp management principles more fully.

A. avoidance of

B. lack of intention

C. intention

9. Her work experience after she received undergraduate and graduate level training increased her desire to <u>grasp</u> management principles more fully.

A. relinquish

B. acquire

C. relegate

10. <u>Theoretical</u> knowledge has little value without work experience.

A. hypothetical

B. reasonable

C. actual

Situation 6

1. Taiwan's national health insurance scheme was <u>instituted</u> in 1995 to integrate insurance and medical treatment throughout the island.

   A. abolished

   B. established

   C. bankrupted

2. Taiwan's national health insurance scheme was instituted in 1995 to <u>integrate</u> insurance and medical treatment throughout the island.

   A. separate

   B. distinguish

   C. combine

3. All Taiwanese residents <u>participate in</u> the health insurance scheme, by the deduction of a certain amount from their monthly income.

   A. refrain from

   B. join in

   C. abstain from

4. All Taiwanese residents participate in the health insurance scheme, by the <u>deduction</u> of a certain amount from their monthly income.

   A. withdrawal

   B. multiplication

   C. addition

5. They are thus <u>entitled</u> to hold an insurance card for hospital outpatient or admissions services, paying only a small fraction of the entire cost.

   A. avoided

   B. prevented

C. allowed

6. They are thus entitled to hold an insurance card for hospital outpatient or admissions services, paying only a small <u>fraction</u> of the entire cost.

   A. partial

   B. whole

   C. comprehensive

7. This health insurance <u>scheme</u> provides a valuable service, especially for those in poverty and for the elderly.

   A. detour

   B. place

   C. plan

8. This health insurance scheme provides a valuable service, especially for those in <u>poverty</u> and for the elderly.

   A. wealth

   B. destitution

   C. prosperity

9. This health insurance scheme provides a valuable service, especially for those in poverty and for the <u>elderly</u>.

   A. adolescents

   B. middle aged people

   C. old people

10. However, an increase in monthly premium costs has led to many individuals' <u>excessively</u> using medical treatment resources, straining the system's finances.

   A. insufficiently

   B. exorbitantly

   C. inadequately

Unit Two

Describing the field or industry to which one's profession belongs

興趣相關產業描寫

Vocabulary and related expressions　相關字詞

Green Silicon Island 綠色矽島
swift 快速的
severely 嚴格地
lacks 缺乏
integration 整合
access 接近
state-of-the-art technologies 最高級科技
exported 出口
brand recognition 品牌識別
abroad 在國外
international appeal 具國際吸引力
renowned 有名的
outstanding 傑出的
asset 資產
collaborative 合作的
product development effort 產品發展成果

innovative 革新的
securing employment 安全的環境
practical context 實際的背景
scope 範圍
disciplines 紀律
medical applications 醫學上的應用
restrict 限制
hectic pace 忙亂的步調
consumption 消耗
nutritious 有營養的
therapeutic treatments 治療
prognostic factors 預後因子
radiological technology 放射科技
pharmaceutical 製藥的
medical imaging 醫學影像
reputation 名聲

range 排列

emerged 出現

recent global trends 最新全球流行趨勢

ideal working environment
完美的工作環境

over a decade 超過十年

modify 修正

practical operations 實際的運行

gone online 上網

ergonomic 人類工程學

consumer demand 消費者需求

solid academic background
堅固的學術背景

devoted oneself to 把自己奉獻給……

persists 堅持

academia 學術界

technological capabilities 技術能力

corporate profits 公司利潤

obstruct 障礙

societal progress 社會進步

expended 花費

as evidenced by 由……可證明

highly respected 高度受尊敬的

easily distinguishing 可容易辨別的

constantly strives 不停的努力

clinical department 醫療部門

maturation 成熟

proficient researcher 精練的研究者

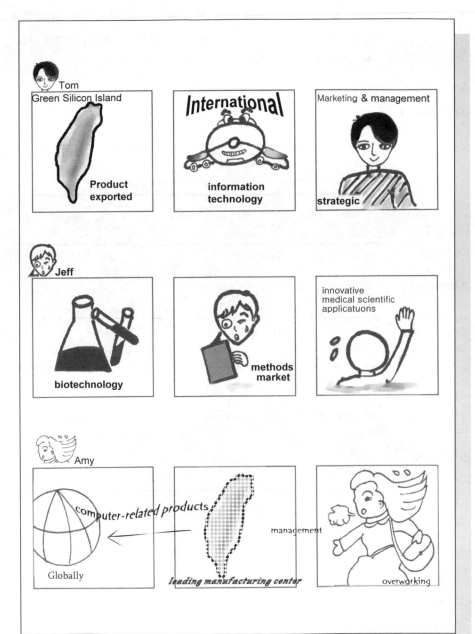

A Write down the key points of the situations on the preceding page, while the instructor reads aloud the script from the Answer Key.

Situation 1

_____

_____

_____

Situation 2

_____

_____

_____

Situation 3

_____

_____

_____

B Oral Practice I

Based on the three situations in this unit, write three questions beginning with **How**, and answer them. The questions do not need to come directly from these situations.

Examples

How has Taiwan positioned itself as "Green Silicon Island"?

Following its swift industrial development in recent decades

How did DEF Corporation become a leader in the information technology sector?

Owing to its state-of-the-art products and services, as well as outstanding product research and technical capabilities

1. _____

_____

2. _____

_____

3. _____

_____

C Based on the three situations in this unit, write three
    questions beginning with ***What***, and answer them.
    The questions do not need to come directly from
    these situations.

Examples

What has emerged in Taiwan in recent years?

Biotechnology

What prevents Taiwan from keeping up with recent global trends in research and

development?

It severely lacks biotechnology professionals with management backgrounds.

1. _____

   _____

2. _____

   _____

3. _____

   _____

D Based on the three situations in this unit, write three questions beginning with **Why**, and answer them. The questions do not need to come directly from these situations.

Examples

Why is staff often unable to complete their tasks effectively?

Because analyzed information is typically insufficient

Why do most Taiwanese strive to work efficiently?

Because they grow up in such a competitive environment

1. _____

_____

2. _____

_____

3. _____

_____

E Write questions that match the answers provided.

Examples

When does Amy hope to further her expertise in this area?

Following her completion of a graduate degree in Business Management and several years of work experience in the information sector

What is Amy confident in her ability to do?

Pursue a research career in this field

1. _____

_____

Methods of upgrading information systems to suit Taiwan's unique manufacturing processes and management culture

2. _____

_____

A globally leading manufacturing center

3. _____

_____

Imported information systems

F Listening Comprehension I

Situation 1

1. What does Taiwan's information industry severely lack?

   A. scientific, technological and societal advances

   B. international marketing and management personnel

   C. outstanding product research and technical capabilities

2. What has recently emerged in Taiwan as an important area of research?

   A. the information industry

   B. international marketing and management

   C. the integration of IT with marketing or management science

3. What will definitely make Tom an asset to any collaborative product development effort?

   A. his ability to remain open and does not restrict himself to the range of his previous academic training

   B. his expertise developed in graduate school and his strong academic knowledge and practical skills

   C. his willingness to become to become a member of the DEF corporate family

4. What aspect of DEF Corporation is Tom especially interested in?

   A. how marketing and related management departments make strategic decisions

   B. its state-of-the-art products and services

   C. its outstanding product research and technical capabilities

5. Why have few of the products from have been exported from the Taiwanese information sector been exported abroad?

   A. Few Taiwanese products have brand recognition abroad

   B. Many information sector personnel in Taiwan lack international marketing and management backgrounds

C. Both A and B

Situation 2

1. What can Jeff contribute to ABC Corporation if employed there?

A. new applications, methods and market sectors in Taiwan

B. the development of innovative medical scientific applications

C. his research capabilities and professional knowledge

2. What prevents Taiwan from keeping up with recent global trends in research and development?

A. lack of research capabilities and professional knowledge

B. lack of innovative medical scientific applications

C. severe lack of biotechnology professionals with management backgrounds

3. What has emerged in Taiwan in recent years?

A. biotechnology

B. innovative medical scientific applications

C. professionals with management backgrounds

4. What would an ideal working environment allow Jeff to do?

A. create new applications, methods and market sectors in Taiwan

B. enhance his research capabilities and professional knowledge

C. contribute to the development of innovative medical scientific applications

5. What does Taiwan's biotech sector have the potential to do?

A. integrate seemingly polar disciplines

B. develop medical applications

C. keep up with recent global trends in research and development

Situation 3

1. What has been much discussed recently?

A. methods of upgrading information systems

B. death due to overworking

C. Taiwan's unique manufacturing processes and management culture

2. What does an excellent system depends on?

A. information technology

B. the appropriate consideration of management issues

C. both A and B

3. How does Amy hope to further her expertise?

A. by pursuing a research career in Business Management

B. through employment in a globally renowned corporation

C. by contributing significantly to society

4. What is typically insufficient to help staff to complete their tasks effectively?

A. analyzed information

B. a globally leading manufacturing center

C. experienced information technology personnel with management experience

5. Who strives to work efficiently?

A. Amy

B. information technology personnel

C. individuals who grow up in such a competitive environment

G Reading Comprehension I
Pick the word or expression whose meaning is closest to the meaning of the underlined word or expression in the following passages.

Situation 1

1. Taiwan has <u>positioned</u> itself as "Green Silicon Island" following its swift

industrial development in recent decades.

A. replaced

B. displaced

C. placed

2. Taiwan has positioned itself as "Green Silicon Island" following its <u>swift</u> industrial development in recent decades.

A. detained

B. rapid

C. retarded

3. Besides scientific, technological and societal advances, international marketing and management are <u>essential</u>.

A. fundamental

B. trivial

C. dispensable

4. However, Taiwan's information industry severely <u>lacks</u> international marketing and management personnel.

A. requires

B. requests

C. replenishes

5. However, Taiwan's information industry severely lacks international marketing and management <u>personnel</u>.

A. protestor

B. claimant

C. staff

6. The <u>integration</u> of IT with marketing or management science has recently emerged in Taiwan as an important area of research.

A. immunity

B. segregation

C. combination

7. The integration of IT with marketing or management science has recently emerged in Taiwan as an important area of research.

A. materialized

B. receded

C. declined

8. Although the Taiwanese information sector has access to state-of-the-art technologies, few related products have been exported. Moreover, few Taiwanese products have brand recognition abroad.

A. exit

B. admission

C. depart

9. Although the Taiwanese information sector has access to state-of-the-art technologies, few related products have been exported. Moreover, few Taiwanese products have brand recognition abroad.

A. rudimentary

B. advanced

C. basic

10. Although the Taiwanese information sector has access to state-of-the-art technologies, few related products have been exported. Moreover, few Taiwanese products have brand recognition abroad.

A. depreciation

B. demotion

C. acknowledgment

Situation 2

1. While biotechnology has <u>emerged</u> in Taiwan in recent years, the island severely lacks biotechnology professionals with management backgrounds, preventing Taiwan from keeping up with recent global trends in research and development.

    A. stopped

    B. curtailed

    C. commenced

2. While biotechnology has emerged in Taiwan in recent years, the island <u>severely</u> lacks biotechnology professionals with management backgrounds, preventing Taiwan from keeping up with recent global trends in research and development.

    A. strictly

    B. flexibly

    C. malleable

3. Biotechnology has the <u>potential</u> to integrate seemingly polar disciplines to create new applications, methods and market sectors in Taiwan.

    A. deadlock

    B. consequence

    C. possibility

4. Biotechnology has the potential to integrate seemingly <u>polar</u> disciplines to create new applications, methods and market sectors in Taiwan.

    A. opposing

    B. similar

    C. resembling

5. Biotechnology has the potential to integrate seemingly polar <u>disciplines</u> to create new applications, methods and market sectors in Taiwan.

    A. occupations

    B. careers

C. fields

6. Taiwan's biotech sector has the potential to <u>develop</u> medical applications.

   A. complete

   B. nurture

   C. cooperate

7. As a <u>recognized</u> leader in the biotechnology sector, ABC Corporation can provide Jeff with an ideal working environment in which he can contribute to the development of innovative medical scientific applications.

   A. disavowed

   B. accepted

   C. unrecompensed

8. As a recognized leader in the biotechnology sector, ABC Corporation can provide Jeff with an <u>ideal</u> working environment in which he can contribute to the development of innovative medical scientific applications.

   A. dissatisfaction

   B. facile

   C. exemplary

9. If successful in <u>securing</u> employment at your company, he will strive to enhance his research capabilities and professional knowledge.

   A. releasing

   B. relinquishing

   C. obtaining

10. If successful in securing employment at your company, he will <u>strive</u> to enhance his research capabilities and professional knowledge.

   A. aspire

   B. abdicate

   C. desist

Situation 3

1. Taiwan has become a <u>globally</u> leading manufacturing center, especially in computer-related products.

   A. regionally

   B. internationally

   C. locally

2. Although <u>imported</u> information systems are adopted extensively in manufacturing, analyzed information is typically insufficient to help staff to complete their tasks effectively.

   A. developed and manufactured domestically

   B. developed and manufactured regionally

   C. developed abroad

3. Although imported information systems are <u>adopted</u> extensively in manufacturing, analyzed information is typically insufficient to help staff to complete their tasks effectively.

   A. borrowed

   B. used

   C. gained

4. Although imported information systems are adopted <u>extensively</u> in manufacturing, analyzed information is typically insufficient to help staff to complete their tasks effectively.

   A. narrowly

   B. barely

   C. widely

5. Although imported information systems are adopted extensively in manufacturing, analyzed information is typically <u>insufficient</u> to help staff to complete their tasks effectively.

A. ample

B. inadequate

C. supple

6. Thus, overwork remains critical to <u>manufacturing</u> many products rapidly.

A. producing

B. relaying

C. retrieving

7. <u>Accordingly</u>, death due to overworking has been much discussed recently.

A. However

B. Thus

C. Finally

8. Individuals who grow up in such a <u>competitive</u> environment strive to work efficiently.

A. lagging

B. emulous

C. dormant

9. Individuals who grow up in such a competitive environment <u>strive</u> to work efficiently.

A. energize

B. collaborate

C. aim

10. Thus, methods of <u>upgrading</u> information systems to suit Taiwan's unique manufacturing processes and management culture are increasingly important.

A. decelerating

B. elevating

C. degrading

H Common elements in describing the field or industry to which one's profession belongs include:

1. Introducing a relevant topic with which one's profession is concerned

2. Describing the importance of the topic within one's profession

3. Complimenting the company on its commitment to excellence in this area of expertise

4. Stating anticipated contribution to company in this area of expertise if employed there

In the space below, describe the field or industry to which your profession belongs.

_____

_____

_____

_____

_____

_____

_____

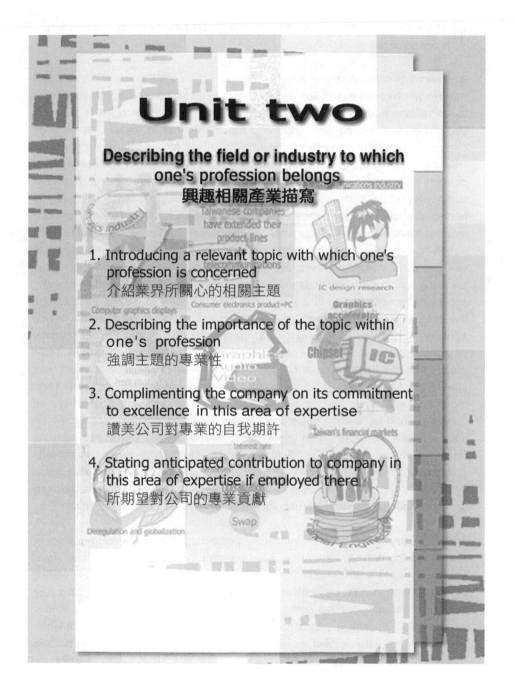

Unit two

Describing the field or industry to which one's profession belongs
興趣相關產業描寫

1. Introducing a relevant topic with which one's profession is concerned
   介紹業界所關心的相關主題

2. Describing the importance of the topic within one's profession
   強調主題的專業性

3. Complimenting the company on its commitment to excellence in this area of expertise
   讚美公司對專業的自我期許

4. Stating anticipated contribution to company in this area of expertise if employed there
   所期望對公司的專業貢獻

Look at the following examples of how to describe fields or industries to which professions belong.

◎Biotechnology companies and related academic institutions are actively researching ways in which to develop reagents for biochip, gene and protein applications. With the increasing number of human diseases, cancer and human genetics research disciplines have subsequently expanded rapidly. Meanwhile, many biotechnology companies are developing rapid diagnostic methods for such diseases. Proteins related to a test reagent, DNA, RNA, and siRNA are all involved in the development of such diagnostic methods. Human stem cell culture is an especially popular component. Many biotechnology companies are actively researching the use of human stem cells to treat diseases using the above applications. Drawn from bone marrow, the human stem cell is inserted in vitro culture for growth in a patient's body, subsequently healing injured organs. This cell can also be used to treat cardiovascular system diseases, Parkinson's disease, and spinal cord injury. Your company has aggressively engaged itself in developing a molecular testing reagent, especially through the use of a stem cell culture method that is considered among the best in the biotech sector. Your company has many stem cell types, having fulfilled the demand of laboratories in many scientific institutions or company laboratories. Additionally, your company's extensive laboratory resources would greatly facilitate my own research interests, which are hopefully in line with your current direction. Having frequently held large-scale public discussions on the latest biotechnology trends, your company has equipped itself with state-of-the art equipment and knowledge of pertinent issues for future development. Moreover, your company has adopted an integrated approach towards learning by adopting multi-disciplinary approaches. Such exposure would allow me to interact with professionals from different fields. The opportunity to work at your company would allow me to hopefully contribute to the development of the latest biotechnology products, hopefully furthering your company to unprecedented levels of growth.

◎Rapid industrial expansion, environmental pollution, and the increasing quantity of processed foods have all dramatically impacted individual lifestyles, leading to serious illnesses and carcinoma cancer. For instance, in Taiwan, roughly 34,000 individuals died in 2002 because of malignant diseases. Radiation therapy, surgery, and chemotherapy are three conventional means of treating cancer. 50% to 60% of all individuals diagnosed with cancer will require radiation therapy, some of which are for curative, while others are for palliation. For preoperative radiation therapy, radiation therapy attempts to reduce the size of the cancerous region, in which the cancer cell could be easily eliminated. In postoperative radiation therapy, residual cancer cells and peripheral lymph nodes are treated. Thus, radiation therapy is vital, as evidenced by the increasing number of hospitals that offer such therapy. Working in your hospital would hopefully allow me not only to pursue some of my above research interests, but also to contribute to the overall welfare of those patients seeking therapeutic treatment.

◎Despite the tremendous number of research personnel in the medical field, the role of image analysis in acute cerebral infarction as a viable therapeutic treatment requires further study, an area of research that I am deeply interested in. A patient's valuation is an essential starting point of investigation. Taiwan's current lack of instrumentation and trained personnel explains why no serial study has yet been performed island wide. After studying pertinent literature, I collaborated with a medical instrumentation company in adopting this simulation program. In addition to benefiting patients and increasing Taiwan's medical service level, such collaboration could significantly contribute to the status of Taiwan's renowned additives sector internationally. Given the rapid growth of technological advances in this field, my graduate school research emphasized the feasibility of using various computer programs to enhance the quality of MRI. With most hospitals using X-ray film of inverted PACS type, the knowledge acquired through work with simulation programs in this area has enabled me to serve hospital patients more professionally. I must hold myself to achieving this career aspiration. Your company offers an excellent working environment to pursue this path.

◎Following its rapid industrial development in recent decades, Taiwan has experienced an unusually high amount of natural calamities and emergency situations. For instance, the mortality rate for traffic accidents in Taiwan is around sixty two individuals out of 100,000 involved. Sustaining an injured victim's life prior to arrival at the hospital's emergency care unit is a pressing concern. Governmental organizations increasingly stress that medical treatment strategies (a) include an emergency medical first aid project, (b) augment professional knowledge of how to care for emergency patients, (c) promote the quality of a hospital's emergency medical services, and (d) enhance medical treatment administered in aircraft. Several efforts must be made to achieve the above governmental strategy, such as developing an emergency medical assessment system, enlarging the organizational framework of emergency medical services, establishing an emergency medical information system, and providing clear standards for ambulance management. Renowned for its efforts to remain abreast of governmental strategies and current trends, your hospital will establish a second medical center in Taipei County in the near future. I am most impressed that this new center will provide high quality medical treatment to more critical patients in a relatively short time. With my decade of experience in emergency care departments and graduate degree in Business Management, I believe that I can significantly contribute to efforts to train emergency care professionals and assess the process and preparation of emergency medical staff.

◎Taiwan's biotechnology sector currently focuses on developing both healthy foods, screen tests for particular diseases, cord blood banking and pharmaceuticals. Screen tests include those for cancer, infectious diseases and drug abuse. However, many Taiwanese researchers involved in developing screen tests lack clinical experience, subsequently preventing the commercialization of research products. Thus, both clinical experience and sufficient knowledge skills must be acquired simultaneously. As Taiwan aspires to become the biotechnology center of the Asian Pacific region, your company's research group has distinguished itself for its contribution to this field, especially in developing screen test technologies, While advancing my expertise in this area, I hope to work at your company in order to refine my skills in medicine science technology and knowledge of microbiology.

◎An increasing variation in known viruses has led to the onset of new diseases. Regardless of whether for the global or domestic market, developing a diagnostic reagent kit to examine new diseases is of high priority. Once diagnosed, diseases need appropriate drugs for therapeutic treatment. However, developing a diagnostic reagent kit for disease examination would first require a higher rate of accuracy in related examinations. Additionally, adequate medication would help ensure a bright prognosis for an ill patient. With this in mind, your company has spent considerable time in developing a new reagent to treat diseases, as evidenced by your recent collaboration with another company in quantifying the new reagent. In addition to benefiting patients, your company has significantly contributed to the entire medical treatment sector. If successful in securing employment at your company, I bring to your organization a strong scholastic background and practical knowledge, which will hopefully be in line with your company's innovative technological developments. As your employee, I will continuously upgrade my professional knowledge skills and technological expertise. I hope that my entry into your organization will ultimately contribute to increased commercial activity and profits.

◎I hope to contribute to your company's efforts to develop a lyase of availability by enzyme brightening, subsequently providing a highly value added product. Commercial use of this patented product will hopefully yield substantial profits for your company. This lyase can enable some waste byproducts of hard decompositions to carry on the decomposition, e.g., decomposition, protease, enzyme of fat - splitting of the fiber. This enzyme can be used in your company's development of shampoo products, daily consumer products, and health foods. Additionally, effective use of waste enzyme production can yield some useful materials, which will hopefully be commercially viable for your company. Moreover, your company's sound reputation can help me to attain my career aspirations of not only enhancing my technical expertise, but also working in a management capacity in the near future.

◎Biotechnology developments will continue to advance rapidly in the coming decades. Taiwan must strive to expand upon those developments to remain competitive globally. Integrating medicine and biotechnology into the recently emerging bio-medicine field requires professionals with knowledge of medicine and molecular biology for bio-medicine applications. As a leader in this field, your company offers an impressive number of wide ranging training courses for your employees so that they remain competent in the field. Working at your company would not only advance my professional capabilities, but also enhance my research and knowledge skills.

◎Rapid and highly accurate molecular biology procedures can facilitate efforts to investigate the properties of *V. parahaemolyticus*, thus necessitating the development of a method that uses a gene with a high specificity on the chromosome of *V. parahaemolyticus*. The appliance authenticates quickly in the PCR bacteria. Molecular biotechnology has been applied extensively in agriculture and medicine, e.g., fluorescence in situ hybridization (FISH), polymerase chain reaction (PCR), and restriction enzyme and donature gradient gel electrophoresis (DGGE). These applications have been integrated into the research of living creature processes for developing a revolutionary modern ear. The living creature methods that your company has developed are applied in areas more than just the medicine industry, including agriculture, food processing, environmental protection, energy and chemical products. All of these areas hold a large market share in Taiwan's output, with enormous commercial opportunities. As your company continuously develops, technological developments such as this rapid consultation method will usher in prosperity, not only for your company but society as well. This explains why I hope to join your corporate family as a researcher.

◎Given the accelerated development of radiation treatment technologies in recent decades, IMRT has become the conventional standard for use in radioncology. Taiwan's aspiration to join the World Heath Organization necessitates that medical workers continually upgrade their professional skills. In radiation treatment, radiotherapy has become increasingly important with the progressively rising cancer death rate. Radiotherapy is especially attractive since it is not injected into the patient, yet yields curative effects rapidly. The quite impressive training courses that your company offers for its employees reflect your excellence in leadership and commitment to staff excellence. If successfully employed at your corporation, I will dedicate my efforts to contributing to the success of the corporate family.

◎The healthcare industry is definitely a rising industry not only in Taiwan, but worldwide. Correspondingly, the biotech industry has recently emerged in Taiwan as well, which requires overcoming several obstacles to achieve success. However, adversity ultimately results in creativity within the biotech industry. Although twenty research centers have discovered the DNA sequence, the constitution of DNA is volatile and each DNA type represents the diversity within the human body. Consequently, biotechnology methods have important implications for an enterprise. As a leader in the biotechnology field, your company has combined commercial success with innovation. Your company has also distinguished itself in the health care sector. I am especially amazed by your company's creativity in using standard operating procedures to create state-of-the-art product technologies. Employment at your company would give me a valuable opportunity to contribute my background expertise in biotechnology to your innovative research efforts.

◎As the demand for medical image professionals in Taiwan outstrips the available supply, local educational institutions must devote more resources to equipping students with the necessary skills. This is especially true when using advanced technologies in the field, such as the picture archive connective system (PACS) and those that combine radiology technology, digital imagery and the Internet. With a long tradition committed to this profession, your hospital offers extensive training courses for technical staff to maintain competitiveness in all of the hospital departments. Working in your organization would definitely benefit my professional development.

◎Cancer-related deaths occur annually in the tens of thousands worldwide, posing major socioeconomic problems. The most effective therapeutic results can be ensured when treatment policy decisions are made by a multidisciplinary team rather than by an individual specialist. Thus, a radiation oncology department contains several kinds of professionals, including physicians, medical physicists, dosimetrists, therapists, and nurses. The physician in that department must discuss a patient's condition with physicians in interrelated ones and, then, decides what treatment approach and dose are the most appropriate. Once the treatment approach and dose are determined, the medical physicist is responsible for planning radiation treatment. Besides, the dosimetrist is responsible for calculating the treatment dose. Then, the therapists perform clinical treatment by using a linear accelerator. A notable example of quality healthcare is the Department of Radiation Oncology at Chang Hua Christian Hospital, which takes care of patients by integrating the efforts of several departments. Following this approach, a patient receives the most effective treatment outcome. With my experience as a dosimetrist in a radiation oncology department and recent completion of a master's degree in Medical Imagery, I bring to your organization a wide breadth of clinical and academic experiences that will definitely benefit those cancer patients under treatment.

◎A neutron leak incident occurred in the beginning of 2004 at Cheng Ching Hospital in Kaohsiung of southern Taiwan, causing heightened concern among radiology technology personnel. Therefore, both increasing work safety for technical personnel and patients and developing lower dose radiotherapy methods are of priority concern. Consequently, a medical physicist must regularly monitor radiation dose in the workplace and also assist the oncologist in designing radiotherapy planning, as well as devising a safety radiotherapy room. Your hospital's cancer center for tumor therapy is known for its strict adherence to quality standards, as well as its frequent journal publications on novel radiotherapy procedures and clinical experiences. If successful In securing employment at your hospital, I will offer my professional knowledge in areas such as detecting the radiation dose in the workplace, designing appropriate radiotherapy planning and devising appropriate shielding for a radiotherapy room. I hope that my contribution to your hospital will allow technical personnel to more naturally tend to the patients' needs, hopefully resulting in a positive therapeutic outcome.

◎Regardless of whether for medical situations or not, measuring radiation dosage levels and providing necessary protection are vital concerns. Radiation dose is also of priority concern for research or medical units handling radioactive materials. In a hospital, radiation is used mainly for diagnosing and providing therapy for tumor patients. Hospital staff must thus be extremely careful in not neglecting any aspect of handling radiation. I am especially concerned with measuring the appropriate radiation dosage level. Researching topics related to this dosage level not only contributes to the quality of therapy, but also ensures that technical staff will remain safe. Recent research investigations constantly describe efforts to develop enhanced therapeutic plans in order to elevate the quality of healthcare, an area I am highly interested in. Although carcinogenesis remains the tenth leading cause of mortality, physicians and medical staff continue to develop a more complete therapeutic strategy. If employed at your hospital, I will devote my professional knowledge of how to estimate the optimum dosage level for therapy on tumor patients. While at your hospital, I hope to develop a more efficient and flexible means of estimating radiation dosage levels without sacrificing accuracy.

◎In a macro environment, each industry is increasingly oriented towards strategic marketing rather than sole emphasis alone on manufactured products and services. The healthcare sector is no exception. With the popularity of the national health insurance scheme in Taiwan, patients can freely choose from an array of hospital-related services. Therefore, the inability to analyze consumer behavior accurately and the validity of marketing strategies for business will lead to a loss of patients and, ultimately, not only decrease the number of benefits available but also incur a high cost in attracting new patients. Your hospital highly prioritizes offering not only excellent medical quality to patients, but also on-the-job training for new employees, explaining why I most eager to secure employment at your hospital in a management-related position. Following the development of my expertise in business management during graduate school, I can contribute to efforts to increase managerial efficiency and to optimize the productivity of hospital personnel.

◎Rapid advances in information technologies and electronic financial services have become irresistible among consumers in recent years. For instance, local financial institutes have not only developed entirely new approaches and practices, but also face stiff international competition. Therefore, making information as available as possible is necessary to corporate survival. In this respect, in addition to continually upgrading its operational performance, safety and security, your company concentrates heavily on controlling the institute's property and centralizing traditional banking operation and data management practices. Those strategies have largely contributed to the solid management team at your company. If I am successful in gaining employment in your company, both my solid academic training and research on information system development will make me a strong asset in your efforts to upgrade e-business operations, such as in online queries, payments and account transferals. Moreover, your company's professional training program for new employees will equip me with the necessary skills to provide a diverse array of newly offered services to the community conveniently.

◎Governmental policy over Taiwan's National Health Insurance (NHI) scheme continuously changes. The explosive pace at which innovative medical policy appears in hospital administration never ceases to amaze I, explaining why I am eager to advance further in this field through employment in your organization. The diversity of hospital marketing projects and related departments demonstrates your hospital's commitment to implementing sound marketing strategies that are consumer-oriented. Having distinguished itself in the medical sector, your hospital heavily emphasizes adopting consumer-oriented marketing practices. Acquiring additional experience in this area would definitely benefit my professional development. Public relations in hospitals has declined even through physicians examines patients, nurses provide benevolent care and advanced instrumentation provides the most advanced diagnostic and therapeutic strategies. What is lacking is a well-defined role for hospital administrators in implementing marketing management practices. Hospital management expertise is vital in the intensely competitive healthcare environment. Through my previous work and academic experiences, I have acquired specialized skills that make me receptive to novel concepts and diversity in a workplace culture. As a member of your hospital staff, I would continuously promote these acquired skills in order to become more competent in daily work tasks. I am also confident that my previous work experience will enable me to more fully realize the consumer needs of patients and the nature of their turnover rates, an area which I understand that your hospital is especially concerned with.

◎Established for a decade, Taiwan's National Health Insurance (NHI) scheme is compulsory. Also requiring that individuals pay a monthly premium for coverage, the NHI received only 30% satisfaction with its services during the first year. Since then, the NHI has been able to continue by adjusting governmental policies and adopting widely implemented business models. The NHI strategy encompasses a diverse array of services, including care for those with prolonged illnesses, free childbirth, disease prevention for adults and related health care services, disease prevention for children and related health care services, and prenatal examinations. Consequently, public satisfaction with NHI has increased with the full realization of what it encompasses in the daily lives of the island's inhabitants. Unique worldwide in its operation, the NHI ensures the immediate treatment of the poor and emergency patients, with its medical resources extended all over Taiwan. A notable example of NHI's success was in the SARS crisis that struck last year. During the crisis, NHI staff united in spirit through a professional attitude and acted responsibly by dispatching physicians, other medical personnel and materials, e.g., masks and protection devices, to each hospital as well as accumulating hospital surveys to appraise the level of preparedness during the medical epidemic. I definitely believe that the NHI played a significant role in finally bringing the SARS disease under control in July. This event further affirmed public confidence in NHI and the vital role that it plays in the daily lives of common people. With its motto of public service, active role in the lives of Taiwan's residents, and innovation, the NHI must continually upgrade its knowledge skills to operate efficiently.

◎A large majority of medical fees are owing to the strong demand for advanced technology equipment and expertise, explaining why effectively controlling related medical expenses is of priority concern. Advanced technology in medicine comes in many forms. For instance, a computerized tomography (CT) scanner is universally adopted yet expensive. Properly using such medical resources in a timely manner requires accumulating pertinent data, e.g., patient's name, personal identification number and physician's name, over the Internet before an examination, which is confirmed with a scheduled appointment number. This data is then compared with other hospitals. Hospitals initially opposed this strategy since it increased work loading. However, this strategy was gradually accepted owing to its ability to determine the optimum conditions for using a CT scanner. Following a year of adopting this strategy, costs associated with use of CT decreased dramatically, as anticipated. This strategy also forced hospitals to deliberate carefully on the essentials of specific examinations in order to evaluate their quality in terms of technical efficacy, diagnostic accuracy, therapeutic effectiveness and patient recovery. Besides reducing medical expenditures, this novel approach has indirectly enhanced the quality of medical services. I believe that your hospital will find my experience in adopting different approaches to enhancing the quality of medical services as a valuable asset in any strategic planning that undertaken to increase your organization's quality of healthcare services in the intensely competitive medical sector.

◎Taiwan's elderly population of roughly 1,900,000 explains the serious demand for long-term care of this segment. According to World Health Organization (WHO) statistics, Taiwan has been an "aging society" since 1993. However, the island's health care sector for long-term care does not have an equitable standard, neither in service nor in service fees despite the tremendous amount of attention paid to this topic. Economic, cultural, and other societal problems have made it impossible to achieve a standard level of equitable care among Taiwan's elderly. Moreover, governmental privacy laws severely limit access to long term-care research data, documentation and commercial management practices, which are largely controlled by non-profit organizations involved with organizational management. Non-profit organizations heavily emphasize charity and volunteerism, often resulting in ineffective management and use of available resources that would be viewed as a loss of resources in a commercial enterprise. Adhering to the objectives of governmental law while remaining aware of its limitations as well as introducing commercial management practices to the long-term health care sector will help organizations to achieve sustainable management and provide high quality and relatively inexpensive services and products. Given my expertise in this area, I look forward to joining your company.

◎In 1998, owing to an imbalance between revenue and overhead costs, our hospital center unit began establishing bench marks, e.g., releasing patients in emergency unit stays after three days, releasing patients in general admission stays after fourteen days, as well as establishing a medicine ratio, asthma admission ratio, and long term health care strategy. I am responsible for analyzing medicinal expenses and asthma-related admissions Medicinal expenses have increased dramatically, with this expense often referred to as a hole because of its depth and vastness. Medicinal expenses include antibiotics, general medicine, outpatient use, and injection. For medicinal expenses that surpass the benchmarks, visits are made to area hospitals to reach a consensus on the logical growth ratio, while emphasizing the need for adequate medicinal resources. Most hospitals agree on the need to effectively control medicinal expenses. Although universal in nature, asthma-based admissions are uncommon. When the hospital's asthma admission ratio exceeds a certain level, we mandate that the ratio is lowered. Moreover, hospitals acting collaboratively can select medicines and negotiate for discounted prices. Another strategy that hospitals employ is to adopt a global budget. In my most recent work, I was also responsible for formulating internal communiqué among staff to ensure that hospital policies regarding medicinal expenses were implemented smoothly. My above work experiences will prove invaluable to your company's efforts to provide quality healthcare services.

◎The deadly SARS virus spread from southern China across the globe. When the epidemic initially struck, Singapore gained considerable praise for effectively responding by quarantining up to 1500 individuals who had close contacts with

SARS victims. The government even installed video cameras on the doorsteps of those individuals to discourage breaking the quarantine. When Taiwan's government accelerated efforts to contain the spread of SARS, Hsinchu Mayor Lin Cheng-Jer led several city council members in blocking an ambulance carrying three SARS patients from entering the Hsinchu Hospital. Panic and even hysteria over SARS spread as well, largely owing to ignorance about the new viral disease. Irresponsible media coverage also exacerbated the situation. This epidemic also witnessed several individuals lose their humanity, even physicians and nurses. This explains why my graduate school research focused on effectively managing customer relations in the medical profession. Given my academic background and relevant work experiences, I am confident of my ability to contribute to your hospital's administrative operations.

◎An enormous earthquake occurred in Taiwan in 1999, subsequently displacing me from my work owing to the damage that my work place incurred. During that period, I did not go back to school for further academic training; instead, I participated in job training courses established by the government for displaced workers to promote my professional skills. Among those courses most helpful included commercial pursuit dispatching and Internet archival design. Upon completion of the training courses, I began working in health insurance claims for the Puli Municipal Government in Nantou County of central Taiwan. Taiwan's national health insurance scheme has thus interested me since I began working in the Puli Municipal Government in Nantou County three years ago. I worked with the general public in handling problems over health insurance affairs. During that period, I became intrigued with how to enhance the national health insurance system, reduce related premiums, as well as research not only its impact on the quality of medical services, but how to help hospital employees to provide quality care to patients. Following a rigorous nationwide technical school examination, I gained entry to the Department of Healthcare Management at Yuanpei University of Science and Technology (YUST) and eventually completed a maser's in Business Administration at the same institution. I hope that you will find my above working and educational experiences conducive to the needs of your organization.

◎Taiwan's economy is developing rapidly. High employment has subsequently created anxiety among the general public. With an increasingly diminishing number of desirable work opportunities, even working diligently does not seem to yield a good outcome. I would thus like to clarify how pressure is vital to success. Leisure management can enable employees to go to work without increasing anxiety. I bring to your organization abundant academic and professional experiences in this area.

◎Although research of this topic initially began abroad, I attempted to extend those results and make them applicable to Taiwan's circumstances. All MRI and fMRI instrumentation is operated from a three-diffusion aspect to diagnose diseases in Taiwan's hospitals. Through my research, I discerned between a 360-degree water diffusion mode and a takeover water diffusion mode that occupies three times the amount of airspace. The integral diffusion value of a normal brain tissue could then be modified according to a simulation program, in which the values are used to adjust the map of a normal brain tissue. In addition to enabling physicians to accurately diagnose diseases, the simulation program can also determine the diagnostic values for patients. Given my expertise in this area, I feel equipped to serve as a researcher in the medical imagery fields, areas that your company has devoted considerable resources.

◎Given that a patient's valuation is an essential starting point of investigation, Taiwan's current lack of instrumentation and trained personnel explains why no serial study has yet been performed island wide. After studying pertinent literature, I collaborated with a medical instrumentation company in adopting this simulation program. In addition to benefiting patients and increasing Taiwan's medical service level, such collaboration can significantly contribute to the status of Taiwan's renowned additives sector internationally. As a member of your corporation, I would bring to your organization a wealth of technological expertise and experience in the above area.

◎Radiotherapy research involving tumors has received extensive attention in both Taiwan and abroad for several years. However, many abnormal proliferates of cellulose can be adequately controlled using certain methods. Therefore, developing a more effective means of controlling such proliferates is highly desired, as evidenced by the amount of related research currently underway both locally and overseas. Furthermore, radiotherapy research of tumors remains a vital topic as the number of cancer-related diseases increases despite societal advances. As cancer accounts for the tenth leading cause of mortality in Taiwan, radiotherapy in tumor patients cannot be neglected. A recent advance in radiotherapy in tumor patients is B neutron capture treatment (BNCT), having been researched in the United States and used experimentally. Importantly, effectively treating tumor patients largely hinges on adopting the latest instrumentation and closely collaborating with other research teams, both locally and abroad.

◎In modern society, the unimaginable has become reality, which occasionally appears to be out of control. Computer skills and the information industry have dramatically influenced daily lives worldwide at an unprecedented rate. Lifestyles are thus changing daily, as impacted by factors such as the global economy and cultural innovations. Taiwan will encounter many unforeseen calamities if the government can not remain attune of current healthcare trends, resulting in a gradual lowering of individual living standards. Many countries experience a gap in medical care between urban and rural areas. Although Taiwan has closely followed actions taken by European governments, governmental authorities in Taiwan can not effectively raise the welfare standards of its population. Occasional intervention in the island's health insurance scheme is ineffective. As a medical professional, I am concerned that political concerns will sacrifice individual health quality. If fortunate to become a member of your administrative team, I am interested in addressing some of the above issues

◎In the medical market, expensive medical care is a nightmare, especially for those whose financial resources are drained owing to an illness. Even countries with the most advanced medical instrumentation have an unequal distribution in health resources between urban and rural areas. Examples of effective medical instrumentation include nuclear medicine procedures, computer tomography, magnetic resonance, and positron emission tomography. Such effective yet expensive machinery is unequally distributed among urban and rural areas. For instance, patients wanting to make a diagnostic investigation can spend up to half of their median monthly salary. I believe that uniform and equitable medical care is a common right of all individuals. Additionally, progressive medicine can alleviate a patient's physical and mental suffering. Imagery medicine is a highly effective means of decreasing medical expenses. In addition to my normal work responsibilities, I successfully completed a master's degree in Medical Imagery, which enabled me to research the latest topics in advanced medical instrumentation As your organization has committed itself to providing quality medical services for several years, I am confident of my ability to contribute to your corporate goals.

◎Medical treatment methods are constantly developing, thus necessitating their continuous development to accurately identify and treat illnesses. As Taiwan's development of medical methods lags behind that of Europe and North America, technicians are frequently sent abroad to receive training on the latest technological developments and knowledge skills, thus elevating the island's quality of medical treatment. However, the level of medical treatment has decreased island wide since

Taiwan instituted the national health insurance scheme in 1993 owing to the strain placed on the limited resources of hospitals and physicians. For instance, a series of x-ray examinations patient may be delayed two or three times, not only wasting hospital resources but also delaying the accurate diagnosis and treatment of a disease. A precise and clear medical image is thus crucial for physicians to have the most accurate diagnostic information available. My most recent research focused on creating such a concise and clear medical image by adopting the latest computer programs and upgrading the operating technician's expertise. In particular, I become adept in using computer programs to enhance medical imagery in order to facilitate a physician's diagnostic capabilities. My gradual maturation as a proficient researcher in medical imagery will hopefully prove to be a valuable asset in your laboratory, allowing me to contribute significantly to any of your team's research efforts.

◎Taiwanese physicians heavily rely on medical images to diagnose and treat patients, thus necessitating a reliable and concise image. Using computers to process medical images is especially widespread island wide. For example, computer tomography (CT) is processed through a computer for calculation and analysis to create a precise image. Whereas medical images were printed on an x-ray film previously, such images are now displayed on a computer monitor. In addition to providing us with desired information, such a procedure can reduce the time to transfer data, decrease data storage capacity, as well as lower overhead costs and yield optimum results. Picture achievement computer system (PACS) is the latest medical imagery trend in Taiwan, with some hospitals even devoting entire buildings to its development In addition to use in individual institutions, PACS can also connect hospitals islandwide. For instance, for patients transferring from one hospital to another, their data can be transferred immediately without delay. As a leading medical center in Taiwan, your hospital would definitely benefit from my knowledge expertise in this field.

◎Medical imagery belongs to the larger medical technology sector. While Taiwan has focused on developing the semiconductor and OEM industries in recent decades, the question arises as from where the island's latest technological advancements will emerge. Restated, exactly where does Taiwan rank in the globalization scheme? With the rapidly elderly population worldwide, the long-term health sector will undoubtedly emerge as a leading industry. Given my rich academic background and professional experiences, I feel prepared to contribute to this area of development that your company has committed itself to.

◎The emerging trend of biotechnology in all facets of daily life reflects the increasing emphasis on health, as evidenced by an increasing elderly population globally. Regardless of whether materials or the human body is concerned, technological advances from the macro to micro level are increasing, e.g., nanometer technology. For human eyes, researching a phenomenon sized at the nanolevel is nearly impossible. However, auxiliary instruments can facilitate research into molecular-sized objects. The computer enables such an investigation. For instance, medical imagery is placed in a human organ microscopically and then investigated at a molecular size. For quite some time, I have researched topics related to nuclear medicine as an example of what molecular medicine can encompass. The medical imagery sector belongs to the long-term health care sector, an area that will undoubtedly play a pivotal role in science in the new century. Your hospital will find my professional training in this field to be a valuable asset in your highly respected organization.

◎With the recent emergence of Taiwan's biotechnology sector, many researchers have adopted biotechnology to develop vaccines and medicine to advance human health globally. Genomic research began with the Human Genome Project, with international research efforts aimed at determining the DNA sequence of the entire human genome. Genetic engineering has subsequently flourished in recent decades. My research has concentrated mainly on microbiology-related topics, especially with respect to how to apply biotechnology to solve medical care-related problems, e.g., resistant pathogenic bacteria. Your company's decision to pursue this line of product technology development is what attracts me, given my considerable technical expertise in this field.

◎Having devoted considerable resources to biotechnology development, many countries view this technology as a viable means of not only increasing the quality of life, but also enhancing competitiveness in global markets. My research in recent years has focused on diagnosing heredity illnesses, which are a source of confusion over their origin and why infant mortality occurs as a result. Graduate level training in this area greatly compensated for my lack of professional knowledge in this area. The ability to fully grasp biotechnology-related concepts allowed me to enhance my research skills considerable, which will make me a valuable asset to any research effort that I belong to, hopefully at your company.

◎Science and technology are continuously advancing, with agricultural developments to reach a new milestone. Restated, biotechnological applications will significantly transform agricultural production. Biotechnology has played a vital role in agriculture for thousands of years, with fermentation technology as a typical example. Modern biotechnology has focused on molecular biology, genetic engineering, and transduction, which involve the genetic substances of living organisms. Rather than depending only on simply breeding or fermentation procedures, agricultural production in the future will increasingly depend on biotechnology innovations such as genetic transduction to elevate living standards. by increasing the production level. My recent research emphasis on biotechnology applications in the agricultural sector has prepared me for the rigorous challenges that such a career pursuit demands. Your reputed biotech firm would provide me with the opportunity to further pursue my professional interests in the above area.

◎Although widely anticipated, Taiwan has not yet gained entry into the World Health Organization (WHO). Nevertheless, Taiwan's medical community remained vigilant during the SARS crisis. Such vigilance reflects Taiwan's capability and determination to participate in WHO. To contribute to Taiwan's efforts to gain recognition for its contributions to the international medical community, I conducted biotechnology research aimed at eradicating immunological diseases. Employment in your hospital would offer me a practical context for effectively addressing the island's community health-related issues.

◎With Taiwan's unprecedented growth in the biotech sector and ability to avoid economic turmoil island wide, the biotech sector has flourished although a self-examination of its strategy is necessary. Having focused on biological chemistry and microbiology studies, I adopted a systematic approach in my research to acquiring knowledge in these disciplines. In addition to biological chemistry and microbiology, my research delved into immunization and bioinformatics-related topics, all of which allowed me to remain abreast of the latest trends in the biotech sector. Working in your company would definitely further my technological expertise in the above areas.

◎Recent biotechnology developments in Taiwan have witnessed the commercialization of biological methods in diverse areas such as (a) genetic engineering, (b) cell fusion methods, (c) a bioreaction technology that incorporates fermentation technology, enzyme technology, and a bioreactor, (d) cell culture approaches, (e) gene recombination, (f) embryo transplantation methods and (g) nucleus transplantation approaches. To remain abreast of the latest market trends in biotechnology, I focused my research recently on applying cell fusion and cell culture approaches to human cell signal transduction. The Taiwanese biotechnology market includes many aspects of DNA technology, which can alleviate many genetic defects to enhance human health and provide employment opportunities. I look forward to joining your company for such an opportunity.

◎As an emerging global trend, biotechnology will provide novel medical treatment approaches that can be used to design highly effective medical procedures. Among Taiwan's many potential areas for biotechnology applications in the marketplace include agriculture, genetically modified food, and the industrial sector. Additionally, from a medical perspective, an increasing demand exists for biotechnology applications aimed at disease prevention. I have, for quite some time, devoted myself to this multidisciplinary field. I am confident of my ability to significantly contribute to Taiwan's efforts to scale new heights in this area of technology development through employment in a renowned biotech firm such as yours.

◎Biotechnology will lead the way among other emerging technologies in the new century, with genetics playing a major role in this field. Employment opportunities in this field are nearly saturated, explaining why I constantly strive in the laboratory to further enhance my fundamental skills in the biotechnology field. My research has so far brought me into contact with experiments involving signal transduction, molecular biochemistry, and medical microbiology. Hoping to gain a better theoretical and practical grasp of this discipline, I hope to join the talented research staff in your company's product development division.

◎Extensively studied in recent decades, biotechnological applications can especially be found in medical science, drug design, disease diagnosis, determination of lifeblood, and related industrial products. Whereas biotechnology was seldom researched in Taiwan just a few years ago, this multidisciplinary field is now actively researched island wide, as evidenced by its use in plants and animals for agricultural production. Biotechnology will continue to undergo tremendous growth in the future, such as in human cloning, genetic sequence, genomic DNA, transformation, and transduction. My commitment to pursuing a research career in this exciting field will hopefully allow me to significantly contribute to Taiwan's role in global technology development. Employment at your company would allow me to fully realize my career aspirations.

◎Biotechnology has, in recent years, focused on genome research. However, adopting genome research to develop living creature techniques has been problematic. Via biotechnology, several thousand genes can be quickly separated for authentication. Still, understanding the function of these genes is even more difficult. Resolving such problems would greatly facilitate efforts not only to detect the conversion of the genome, but also to determine how some proteins produced by a gene can be used for drug applications. The protein that wants these indoles can be used in DNA recombination for mass production. However, the protein of the bulk analysis is detected after enzyme production is taken through DNA recombination technique, making commercialization impossible. Your company is renowned for its efforts to adopt living creature techniques for use in synthetic antigen as treatment in both humans and animals for medicinal purposes. I am especially fascinated with how you have used strategic partners to adopt living creature techniques for commercialization, i.e., medicinal purposes. I am confident of my ability to rise to the challenges of the biotechnology profession, hopefully at your company in a managerial position.

◎Several shattering medical errors were made in Taiwanese health institutions at the end of last year. While a nurse in a Taipei Hospital gave the wrong injection that led to infant mortality, another inappropriate medication dosage was made in a Pingtung hospital in southern Taiwan. Our instructor thus assigned us the task of compiling a report on the exactitude of medical administration. Based on our study of the flow path in which patient medications are administered, we recommended measures that a hospital can adopt to avoid errors and ensure patient safety. In addition to completing this report, we observed the management models that the General Affairs Section adopts. This has fueled my interest in knowledge management. While the medical sector is a relatively closed system in terms of external factors, new strategies must be adopted such as in knowledge management, balance score card and the six sigma approach. While progress is relatively slow, aggressive efforts to promote the business aspect are underway. From this angle, I hope to propose new management models for hospitals. My above interests hopefully match the direction that your hospital is taking in increase the efficiency of its administrative affairs. With this in mind, I look forward to joining your organization.

Susan

promote cures

radiological technology
Breast Cancer

highly nutritious foods

Matt

medical professionals

excellent staff

ischemia or hemorrhaging

life expectancy ↑

Larry

computer information
systems

enhanced modified

school

某某大學

I Write down the key points of the situations on the preceding page, while the instructor reads aloud the script from the Answer Key.

Situation 4

_____

_____

_____

Situation 5

_____

_____

_____

Situation 6

_____

_____

_____

J Oral practice II
Based on the three situations in this unit, write three questions beginning with **Why**, and answer them. The questions do not need to come directly from these situations.

Examples

Why is there an increasing rate of cancer in the general population?

The hectic pace and pressure of daily life, as well as the consumption of some highly nutritious foods

Why is Susan quite impressed with the variety of research projects and departments within ABC Company?

Owing to its leading role in the medicine and pharmaceutical fields

1. _____

_____

2. _____

_____

3. _____

_____

K Based on the three situations in this unit, write three questions beginning with **What**, and answer them. The questions do not need to come directly from these situations.

Examples

What sort of medical professionals do Taiwan's hospitals severely lack?

Those with a biotechnology background

What may eventually obstruct societal progress and considerable resources if this problem is not solved?

Medical professionals with a biotechnology background

1. _____

   _____

2. _____

   _____

3. _____

   _____

L Based on the three situations in this unit, write three questions beginning with *How*, and answer them. The questions do not need to come directly from these situations.

Examples

How long has Larry devoted himself to developing computer information systems?
For over a decade

How did Larry attempt to identify accurately what aspects of an information system must be developed, enhanced or modified?
Through his experience as a researcher

1. _____

_____

2. _____

_____

3. _____

_____

M Write questions that match the answers provided.

Examples

What does Larry constantly strive to equip himself with?

Stronger analytical skills

Why must a system having gone online be continually enhanced or modified?

Because of corporate re-engineering, re-organization, ergonomic issues and consumer demand

Why must the end user always spend much time?

To modify functions that are related to practical operations

1. _____

   _____

   National Taiwan University Hospital

2. _____

   _____

   A solid academic background and practical expertise

3. _____

   _____

   An extremely difficult entrance examination

N Listening Comprehension II

Situation 4

1. What appears to be limitless?

   A. cancer

   B. opportunities in the technical and medical sectors of this field

   C. Susan's professional development

2. What did Susan gain expertise in during graduate school?

   A. medical imaging

   B. medicine and pharmaceutical fields

   C. therapeutic treatment of cancer

3. What would definitely promote Susan's professional development?

   A. advanced knowledge of radiological technology

   B. further graduate school education

   C. working at ABC Company

4. Other than benefiting society, what can ABC's reputation and technological capabilities do?

   A. increase corporate profits

   B. give Susan employment

   C. offer therapeutic treatment for cancer

5. What persists as the second leading cause of death among females with cancer?

   A. stomach cancer

   B. lung cancer

   C. breast cancer

Situation 5

1. What sort of background would Matt bring to National Taiwan University

Hospital?

   A. distinguished on

   B. a solid one

   C. a practical one

2. What sort of medical professionals do Taiwan's hospitals severely lack?

   A. those with a biotechnology background

   B. those with a clinical background

   C. those with a medical imagery background

3. What skills are Matt determined to improve upon?

   A. nuclear medicine-related ones

   B. medical imaging-related ones

   C. biotechnology-related ones

4. What does National Taiwan University Hospital have state-of-the-art instruments and expertise in?

   A. increasing the life expectancy of hospital patients

   B. handling stroke patients

   C. easily distinguishing ischemia from hemorrhaging

5. What is National Taiwan University Hospital respected for?

   A. training courses in biotechnology

   B. training courses in nuclear medicine

   C. training courses in medical imaging

Situation 6

1. What must the end user always spend much time to do?

   A. enhance functions that are related to practical operations

   B. modify functions that are related to practical operations

   C. implement information systems?

2. Why does Larry constantly strive to equip himself with stronger analytical skills?

A. to contribute significantly to any product development efforts

B. to be a valuable asset to ABC Corporation

C. to identify accurately what aspects of an information system must be developed, enhanced or modified

3. When did Larry mature as a proficient researcher?

A. during graduate school

B. while working at ABC Corporation

C. during undergraduate school

4. How long has Larry devoted himself to developing computer information systems?

A. for nearly a decade

B. for over a decade

C. just under a decade

5. What can not be implemented without problems?

A. corporate re-engineering

B. corporate re-engineering

C. an information system

O Reading Comprehension II
Pick the word or expression whose meaning is closest to the meaning of the underlined word or expression in the following passages.

Situation 4

1. The <u>hectic</u> pace and pressure of daily life, as well as the consumption of some highly nutritious foods, account for the increasing rate of cancer in the general

population.

A. slack

B. busy

C. relaxed

2. The hectic pace and pressure of daily life, as well as the <u>consumption</u> of some highly nutritious foods, account for the increasing rate of cancer in the general population.

A. usage

B. conservation

C. preservation

3. The hectic pace and pressure of daily life, as well as the consumption of some highly <u>nutritious</u> foods, account for the increasing rate of cancer in the general population.

A. unwholesome

B. alimentary

C. detrimental

4. Therefore, identifying adequate <u>therapeutic</u> treatments and prognostic factors is essential in the field of radiological technology; Susan has a particular interest in management in this field.

A. retrograde

B. regressive

C. curative

5. Breast cancer persists as the second leading cause of <u>death</u> among females with cancer.

A. existence

B. mortality

C. survival

6. Breast cancer <u>persists</u> as the second leading cause of death among females with cancer.

A. perseveres

B. relinquishes

C. abdicates

7. In <u>academia</u>, Susan has always been interested in identifying prognostic factors of breast cancer and especially those factors can that can promote cures for treated patients.

A. daily affairs

B. hi tech-related work

C. school-related work

8. In academia, Susan has always been interested in identifying <u>prognostic</u> factors of breast cancer and especially those factors can that can promote cures for treated patients.

A. introductory

B. predictive

C. prolific

9. Opportunities in the technical and medical sectors of this field appear to be <u>limitless</u>.

A. contracted

B. constrained

C. boundless

10. The variety of research projects and departments within ABC Company is quite <u>impressive</u>, and explains the company having taken a leading role in the medicine and pharmaceutical fields.

A. despondent

B. moving

C. desperate

Situation 5

1. Taiwan's hospitals <u>severely</u> lack medical professionals with a biotechnology background.

    A. amply

    B. austerely

    C. professionally

2. Taiwan's hospitals severely <u>lack</u> medical professionals with a biotechnology background.

    A. spurn

    B. need

    C. deny

3. This <u>shortage</u> may eventually obstruct societal progress and considerable resources may eventually have to be expended to solve unforeseeable problems.

    A. deficiency

    B. glut

    C. windfall

4. This shortage may eventually <u>obstruct</u> societal progress and considerable resources may eventually have to be expended to solve unforeseeable problems.

    A. allow

    B. access

    C. block

5. This shortage may eventually obstruct societal progress and considerable resources may eventually have to be <u>expended</u> to solve unforeseeable problems.

    A. wasted

    B. spent

C. conserved

6. This shortage may eventually obstruct societal progress and considerable resources may eventually have to be expended to solve <u>unforeseeable</u> problems.

   A. estimated

   B. unpredictable

   C. calculated

7. Matt is thus <u>determined</u> to improve his biotechnology-related skills for a career in medical imagery.

   A. ambivalent

   B. uncertain

   C. resolute

8. As evidenced by its highly <u>respected</u> training courses in nuclear medicine, National Taiwan University Hospital has state-of-the-art instruments and expertise in handling stroke patients.

   A. esteemed

   B. dysfunctional

   C. erratic

9. As evidenced by its highly respected training courses in nuclear medicine, National Taiwan University Hospital has <u>state-of-the-art</u> instruments and expertise in handling stroke patients.

   A. antiquated

   B. out-dated

   C. advanced

10. For instance, its excellent staff has perfected easily <u>distinguishing</u> ischemia from hemorrhaging.

   A. comparing

   B. differentiating

C. resembling

Situation 6

1. Having <u>devoted</u> himself to developing computer information systems for over a decade, Larry is well aware that no information system can be implemented without problems.

A. forsaken

B. committed

C. foregone

2. Having devoted himself to developing computer information systems for over a <u>decade</u>, Larry is well aware that no information system can be implemented without problems.

A. twenty years

B. five years

C. ten years

3. Having devoted himself to developing computer information systems for over a decade, Larry is well aware that no information system can be <u>implemented</u> without problems.

A. executed

B. aborted

C. abandoned

4. The end user must always spend much time to <u>modify</u> functions that are related to practical operations.

A. aggravate

B. alter

C. solidify

5. Even after a system has gone online, it must be continually <u>enhanced</u> or modified

because of corporate re-engineering, re-organization, ergonomic issues and consumer demand.

A. degraded

B. upgraded

C. deteriorated

6. Even after a system has gone online, it must be continually enhanced or <u>modified</u> because of corporate re-engineering, re-organization, ergonomic issues and consumer demand.

A. harden

B. congeal

C. varied

7. Even after a system has gone online, it must be continually enhanced or modified because of corporate re-engineering, re-organization, <u>ergonomic</u> issues and consumer demand.

A. social-related

B. work-related

C. organizational-related

8. Thus, Larry constantly <u>strives</u> to equip himself with stronger analytical skills to identify accurately what aspects of an information system must be developed, enhanced or modified.

A. travails

B. conjures

C. presents

9. Thus, Larry constantly strives to equip himself with stronger analytical skills to identify accurately what aspects of an information system must be developed, <u>enhanced</u> or modified.

A. demoted

B. downgraded

C. enriched

10. His <u>maturation</u> as a proficient researcher during graduate school will hopefully prove to be a valuable asset to ABC Corporation, allowing Larry to contribute significantly to any product development efforts.

A. deconstruction

B. development

C. reconstruction

Unit Three

Describing participation in a project that reflects interest in a profession

描述所參與方案裡專業興趣的表現

Vocabulary and related expressions 相關字詞

highly theoretical study
高度理論性的學習
squadron 一群
conscientious 憑良心的
extensive laboratory training
廣大的實驗室訓練
highly adept 高度內行的
disparate 不同的
theoretical concepts 理論性觀念
competence 能力
deep interest in 對……具高度興趣
actively participated in 積極參與
formation 形成
mechanism 機制
physicians 醫師
on-line promotional material 線上促銷

physical examinations 身體檢查
equipped 配備
military personnel 軍事人員
capacity 能力
research assistant 研究助手
large-scale operations 大規模的執行
valuable experiences 寶貴的經驗
comprehend 了解
arose 上升
applicable 可應用的
innovative 革新的
tasks at hand 在手邊的工作
implementing 實行的
fundamental concepts 基礎觀念
unique opportunity 難得的機會
hospital emergency patients 醫院急診病患

innovative product development
創新產品的研發
collaboration 合作
colleagues 同事
questionnaire 問卷調查
statistical capabilities 統計能力
active participation in 積極參與
collaborative project 合作的計畫
unique phenomena 獨特的現象
gain a competitive edge 獲得競爭力
paid considerable attention to
對……加以特別注意
sponsored research project
受贊助的研究計畫
extensive on-the-job training
大規模的在職訓練
adept 內行的
mastered 精通
research skills acquired 研究技能的培育
strong desire 強烈的慾望
reflect one's commitment
反映出某人的承諾
domestic and international journals
國內及國際期刊

as evidenced by 由……可證明
strategy 策略
responsible for 是……的原由
administration 行政
quality healthcare 優質的健康照顧
a valuable reference 有價值的參考
hospital administrators 醫院的行政人員
queries 醫學中心詢問處
emergency staff 緊急事件處理人員
National Science Council 國科會
played a leading role in 扮演帶頭的角色
subsequent 隨後的
Chinese herbal medicine 中國草藥
commitment to 承諾
build on 在……上建立
received praise from 受到……的讚美
curriculum development 課程設計
actively engaged in 積極的致力於
confident in 對……有信心
carefully analyzing 仔細分析
distinguish 區別
level of satisfaction 滿意度
marketing practices 市場經營
comprehensive training 綜合訓練

Jim

National Tsing Hua University

laboratory instuments

qualities

Jane

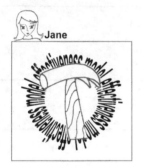

treat patients

product development

Sam

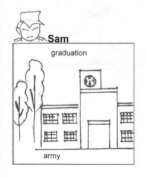

graduation

army

conducting

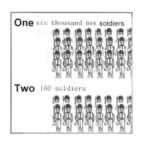

One six thousand new soldiers

Two 160 soldiers

Describing participation in a project that reflects interest in a profession
描述所參與方案裡專業興趣的表現

A Write down the key points of the situations on the preceding page, while the instructor reads aloud the script from the Answer Key.

Situation 1

_____

_____

_____

Situation 2

_____

_____

_____

Situation 3

_____

_____

_____

B Oral practice I
Based on the three situations in this unit, write three questions beginning with *How*, and answer them. The questions do not need to come directly from these situations.

Examples

How did the Department of Nuclear Science at National Tsing Hua University equip Jim with a solid background in independently conducting experiments?

The intellectual rigor of highly theoretical study

How has Jim's practical experience greatly increased his competence in the laboratory?

He learned not only how seemingly disparate fields are related to each other, but also how to succeed in complex projects that force him to apply theoretical concepts in a practical context.

1. _____

   _____

2. _____

   _____

3. _____

   _____

C Based on the three situations in this unit, write three
questions beginning with ***What***, and answer them.
The questions do not need to come directly from
these situations.

Examples

What motivated Jane's active participation in projects aimed at establishing a
humane leukemia disease model in zebrafish embryos?
A deep interest in technology

What did the experimental results in Jane's research study demonstrate?
The effectiveness of her proposed model

1. _____

_____

2. _____

_____

3. _____

_____

D Based on the three situations in this unit, write three questions beginning with *Why*, and answer them. The questions do not need to come directly from these situations.

Examples

Why did Sam have many opportunities not only to come into contact with hospital staff and physicians, but also to familiarize yourself with large-scale operations?
Because of the environment in the military hospital

Why can LMN Corporation provide Sam with a unique opportunity?
To build upon his previous experiences in the above areas

1. _____

_____

2. _____

_____

3. _____

_____

E Write questions that match the answers provided.

Examples

Who is this model a valuable reference for?

Physicians when they treat patients

How did Jane become interested in its innovative product development strategy and in its laboratory?

After carefully reading DEF Company's on-line promotional material

1. _____

   _____

   A professional soldier and officer

2. _____

   _____

   These valuable experiences

3. _____

   _____

   LMN Corporation

F Listening Comprehension I

Situation 1

1. What made Jim extremely conscientious and careful in using laboratory instruments?

   A. his competence in obtaining pertinent data

   B. his extensive laboratory training

   C. his undergraduate studies

2. What quality does Jim has in the laboratory?

   A. as a highly adept investigator

   B. as extremely conscientious and careful in using laboratory instruments

   C. possessing intellectual rigor of highly theoretical study

3. What forced Jim to apply theoretical concepts in a practical context?

   A. extensive laboratory training

   B. complex projects in the laboratory

   C. nearly four years in the Department of Nuclear-Science at National Tsing Hua University

4. Why is Jim competent in obtaining pertinent data and analyzing problems independently?

   A. practical experience as a research assistant in the Institute of Environmental Engineering

   B. as an undergraduate student in the Department of Nuclear-Science at National Tsing Hua University

   C. as an employee at ABC Corporation

5. What did National Tsing Hua University equip Jim with?

   A. how to succeed in complex projects

   B. a solid background in independently conducting experiments

C. how to apply theoretical concepts in a practical context

Situation 2

1. What have the projects that Jane participated in aimed to do?

    A. form a mechanism of use in other animal models

    B. provide a valuable reference physicians when they treat patients

    C. establish a humane leukemia disease model in zebrafish embryos

2. What did Jane carefully read?

    A. literature on how to establish a humane leukemia disease model in zebrafish embryos

    B. DEF Company's on-line promotional material

    C. literature on innovative product development strategy

3. What is responsible for DEF Company's leading role in its field?

    A. its innovative product development strategy

    B. its laboratory

    C. both A and B

4. How was Jane able to demonstrate the effectiveness of her proposed model?

    A. her experimental results

    B. her responsible attitude in the laboratory

    C. her interest in innovative product development strategy

5. What is Jane confident of?

    A. her active participation in biotechnology projects

    B. DEF's ability to give her the opportunity to build upon her previous experience

    C. the effectiveness of her proposed model

Situation 3

1. What was Sam initially responsible for in the army as a professional soldier and

officer?

A. managing the activities of nearly 160 soldiers

B. handling the administration of the physical examinations of six thousand new soldiers

C. familiarize himself with large-scale operations

2. What did Sam realize by applying his previous experiences to the tasks at hand?

A. why confusion often arises in a health-related environment

B. why health-care administration students become discouraged with many management methods that are neither applicable to practical business nor innovative

C. students lack experience in implementing various models and conducting operations in medium-sized and large-scale organizations

3. What can LMN Corporation provide Sam?

A. how to conduct operations in medium-sized and large-scale organizations

B. a unique opportunity to build upon his previous experiences in the above areas

C. the ability to comprehend why confusion often arises in a health-related environment

4. What did Sam's second job in the military involve?

A. managing the activities of nearly 160 soldiers

B. familiarizing himself with large-scale operations

C. being directly responsible to a general

5. How many military personnel were there in the large squadron that Sam was responsible for handling the administration of their physical examinations?

A. around five thousand

B. around ten thousand

C. around twenty thousand

G Reading Comprehension I
Pick the word or expression whose meaning is closest to the meaning of the underlined word or expression in the following passages.

Situation 1

1. The <u>intellectual</u> rigor of highly theoretical study over nearly four years in the Department of Nuclear Science at National Tsing Hua University equipped Jim with a solid background in independently conducting experiments.

   A. amateurish

   B. freshman

   C. scholarly

2. The intellectual <u>rigor</u> of highly theoretical study over nearly four years in the Department of Nuclear Science at National Tsing Hua University equipped Jim with a solid background in independently conducting experiments.

   A. feasibility

   B. toughness

   C. flexibility

3. The intellectual rigor of highly theoretical study over nearly four years in the Department of Nuclear Science at National Tsing Hua University <u>equipped</u> Jim with a solid background in independently conducting experiments.

   A. installed

   B. deposited

   C. instilled

4. During this period, his <u>extensive</u> laboratory training made him extremely conscientious and careful in using laboratory instruments, while ensuring timely completion of tasks.

A. partial

B. fragmentary

C. comprehensive

5. During this period, his extensive laboratory training made him extremely <u>conscientious</u> and careful in using laboratory instruments, while ensuring timely completion of tasks.

A. principled

B. unethical

C. unscrupulous

6. During this period, his extensive laboratory training made him extremely conscientious and careful in using laboratory instruments, while ensuring <u>timely</u> completion of tasks.

A. ill-timed

B. opportune

C. inconvenient

7. <u>Following</u> his undergraduate studies, he served as a research assistant in the Institute of Environmental Engineering at National Taiwan University.

A. after

B. before

C. previous

8. As a highly <u>adept</u> investigator in the laboratory, Jim learned not only how seemingly disparate fields are related to each other, but also how to succeed in complex projects that force him to apply theoretical concepts in a practical context.

A. inept

B. effective

C. reliable

9. As a highly adept investigator in the laboratory, Jim learned not only how seemingly <u>disparate</u> fields are related to each other, but also how to succeed in complex projects that force him to apply theoretical concepts in a practical context.

   A. relevant

   B. associated

   C. polar

10. As a highly adept investigator in the laboratory, Jim learned not only how seemingly <u>disparate</u> fields are related to each other, but also how to succeed in <u>complex</u> projects that force him to apply theoretical concepts in a practical context.

   A. facile

   B. intricate

   C. effortless

Situation 2

1. Owing to a <u>deep</u> interest in biotechnology, Jane has actively participated in projects aimed at establishing a humane leukemia disease model in zebrafish embryos.

   A. skin-deep

   B. shallow

   C. profound

2. Owing to a deep interest in biotechnology, Jane has actively participated in projects <u>aimed at</u> establishing a humane leukemia disease model in zebrafish embryos.

   A. focused on

   B. detracted from

C. relying on

3. Her experimental results <u>demonstrated</u> the effectiveness of her proposed model.

　　A. disproved

　　B. exhibited

　　C. refuted

4. Her experimental results demonstrated the <u>effectiveness</u> of her proposed model.

　　A. incapability

　　B. inadequacy

　　C. efficacy

5. This disease model provided a <u>formation</u> mechanism of use in other animal models.

　　A. establishment

　　B. eradication

　　C. replacement

6. This model is also a <u>valuable</u> reference for physicians when they treat patients.

　　A. finite

　　B. inestimable

　　C. calculable

7. After carefully reading DEF Company's on-line <u>promotional</u> material, Jane is especially interested in its innovative product development strategy and in its laboratory, which are responsible for the company's leading its field.

　　A. closing

　　B. publicity

　　C. reference

8. After carefully reading DEF Company's on-line promotional material, Jane is especially interested in its <u>innovative</u> product development strategy and in its laboratory, which are responsible for the company's leading its field.

A. basic

B. rudimentary

C. ingenious

9. She is <u>confident</u> of DEF's ability to give her the opportunity to build upon her previous experience in the above area.

A. optimistic

B. realistic

C. pessimistic

Situation 3

1. Following graduation from university, Sam <u>joined</u> the army as a professional soldier and officer.

A. departed

B. coalesced

C. retreated from

2. He was <u>initially</u> responsible for handling the administration of the physical examinations of six thousand new soldiers out of a large squadron of around ten thousand military personnel.

A. finally

B. ultimately

C. first

3. He was initially responsible for handling the <u>administration</u> of the physical examinations of six thousand new soldiers out of a large squadron of around ten thousand military personnel.

A. reorganization

B. management

C. execution

4. He was initially responsible for handling the administration of the physical examinations of six thousand new soldiers out of a large squadron of around ten thousand military <u>personnel</u>.

   A. employees

   B. subordinates

   C. management

5. In this <u>capacity</u>, he was directly responsible to a general.

   A. arrangement

   B. position

   C. corporation

6. The environment provided him with many opportunities not only to come into <u>contact</u> with hospital staff and physicians, but also to familiarize himself with large-scale operations.

   A. avoid

   B. avert

   C. interact

7. The environment provided him with many opportunities not only to come into contact with hospital staff and physicians, but also to <u>familiarize</u> himself with large-scale operations.

   A. become acquainted with

   B. distance oneself from

   C. supply oneself with

8. These valuable experiences enabled Sam to <u>comprehend</u> not only why confusion often arose in a health-related environment, but also why health-care administration students become discouraged with many management methods that are neither applicable to practical business nor innovative.

   A. neglect

B. perceive

C. avoid

9. These valuable experiences enabled Sam to comprehend not only why <u>confusion</u> often arose in a health-related environment, but also why health-care administration students become discouraged with many management methods that are neither applicable to practical business nor innovative.

A. peace

B. nirvana

C. hysteria

10. These valuable experiences enabled Sam to comprehend not only why confusion often arose in a health-related environment, but also why health-care administration students become <u>discouraged</u> with many management methods that are neither applicable to practical business nor innovative.

A. satisfied

B. appalled

C. enjoyed

H Common elements in describing participation in a project that reflects interest in a profession include:

1. Introducing the objectives of a project in which one has participated

2. Summarizing the main results of that project

3. Highlighting the contribution of that project to the company or the sector to which it belongs

4. Complimenting the company or organization, at which one is seeking employment, on its efforts in this area

Describe your participation in a project that reflects interest in a profession.

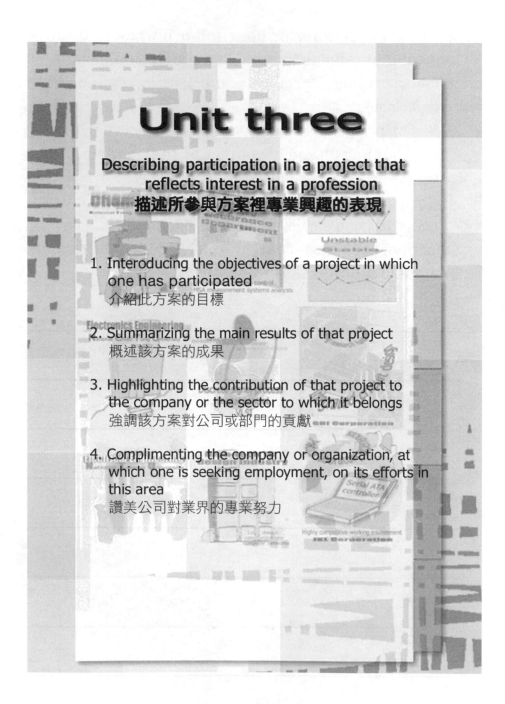

Unit three

Describing participation in a project that reflects interest in a profession
描述所參與方案裡專業興趣的表現

1. Interoducing the objectives of a project in which one has participated
   介紹此方案的目標

2. Summarizing the main results of that project
   概述該方案的成果

3. Highlighting the contribution of that project to the company or the sector to which it belongs
   強調該方案對公司或部門的貢獻

4. Complimenting the company or organization, at which one is seeking employment, on its efforts in this area
   讚美公司對業界的專業努力

Look at the following examples of how to describe your participation in a project that reflects interest in a profession.

◎Owing to my deep interest in biotechnology, I am especially interested in the practical applications of current cell culture methods. I am thus drawn to related topics of cytogenesis, cell physiology, cellular cycle, and cellular biology. My recent research focused on cellular signal transduction-related topics. I also investigated the presence of nitric oxide in the cell line of murine macrophage: a topic which I found interesting to understand how NO regulates different pathways. Besides attempting to determine what role the protein kinase C plays in the cell line of murine macrophage, I collaborated with others in discovering many physiological characteristics of this cell line. Our collaborative efforts also led to the discovery of a new nitric oxide regulation pathway, as well as many cytokine functions. Our results further allowed us to clarify how the murine macrophage cell line physiology, pathology, and immunity are related. Moreover, that research effort enabled us to understand more cellular functions through analysis of its characteristics, which is important in that histiocyte culture method is still widely implemented. I am well aware of your company's efforts to research antibodies and the suppression of cancer medicine research, thus highlighting the importance of the characteristics of cell physiology and culture methods. Based on my current research direction, I am optimistic of my ability to contribute to your company's efforts in developing cancer medicine.

◎Your company, a leader in this field of research, could greatly enhance my research capabilities in cellular-related topics in medical science. Given your company's considerable experience in developing biotechnology products, I am especially impressed with your ability to evaluate the potential commercialization of various related technologies. Confident of your company's future development, I hope to contribute my specialized knowledge to your research efforts with all of my energies.

◎My recent research effort examined the role of dose detection in relation to radiation security. In doing so, I became proficient in not only the use of many radiation detection methods, but also an understanding of how such methods can be applied in a clinical hospital setting. Effectively planning several radiation dose detection research efforts required that I read upon and thoroughly understand thermoluminescence dosimetry as well as familiarize myself with detection methods of neutron contamination or energy. Moreover, I thoroughly reviewed pertinent literature on radiation dose detection to comprehend how the unique features of a radiation detector can benefit my research. Acquiring the above knowledge skills enabled me to more creatively discuss current developments in my research with other collaborators. Your company can provide me with a unique opportunity to build upon my previous experiences in the above areas.

◎My recent research emphasis on magnetic resonance imaging (MRI) allowed me to grasp the theoretical and practical concepts related to this discipline as well as future trends. I once participated in a research group that conducted related experiments at the Veterans General Hospital in Taipei. In this project, physicians focused on researching topics related to functional Magnetic Resonance Imaging (fMRI), which left me responsible for most of the engineering portion of this project. Although extremely taxing, the project instilled in me a sense of confidence in meeting the rigorous challenges of such an undertaking. Your company would offer an excellent learning environment where I could contribute my expertise in MRI research.

◎Although research of this topic initially began overseas, I was able to extend those results and make them applicable to Taiwan's circumstances. All MRI and fMRI instrumentation is operated from a three-diffusion aspect to diagnose diseases in Taiwan's hospitals. My recent research enabled me to discern between a 360-degree water diffusion mode and a takeover water diffusion mode that occupies three times the amount of airspace. The integral diffusion value of a normal brain tissue was then modified according to a simulation program, in which the values were used to adjust the map of a normal brain tissue. In addition to enabling physicians to accurately diagnose diseases, the simulation program developed in my research can also determine the diagnostic values for patients. By constantly pursuing my research interests, I try to remain abreast of the latest developments in pertinent literature and strive diligently to grasp their practical implementations. Working at your hospital would allow me to apply my research findings in a practical context, enabling me to understand even further a patient's needs.

◎I have spent considerable time in project evaluation to reduce overhead costs in a hospital in order to avoid the risk of loss valuation. During that period, I scrutinized many patient bill charges to identify the losses incurred patient-related and material-related charges. Based on those results, hospital administrators made corresponding modifications to reduce overhead costs. Given my experience in this area, I would definitely contribute to your hospital's efforts to satisfy medical consumers demands while effectively controlling overhead costs. Please give me this opportunity.

◎My recent research largely focused on the natural transformation of Helicobacter pylori to determine whether gene HP1089 plays a role in Helicobacter pylori. I also wanted to identify what gene HP1089 functions on behalf of the used gene knockout, DNA sequence in order to facilitate the construction of a Helicobacter pylori mutation library. My research results ultimately obtained a gene HP1089 correlation between Helicobacter pylori natural transformation, NTUCH-1 Helicobacter pylori strain gene HP1089 DNA sequence size about 2.4 Kb different 26695 and 99 Helicobacter pylori strains. My research skills in the above area will allow me to significantly contribute to your company's product development efforts. More importantly, I offer to your company my specialization in biotechnology, which will hopefully have a substantial impact on your company's product innovativeness in contributing to the human genome project.

◎Given my commitment to this profession, I actively participated in graduate level research to prevent and treat the Epstein-Barr virus (EBV), having collaborated with others in related projects. Such collaborative efforts attest to my determination to pursue this career path. For instance, I collaborated with others in developing a deterministic and stochastic model for the signal transduction pathway to achieve active 25% cellular NF-κB. Our simulation model of EBV could ensure that CTAR1 the position obviously influences NF-κB signal transduction. During the development stage, EBV could be quickly distinguished to invade the pathway in the cell. Results of that research effort clarified the enhanced relation between EBV and NF-κB signal transduction in order to treat associated-EBV cancer. Your company provides an excellent work environment in the highly competitive biotech industry, as well as possesses many well-trained professionals on your staff. Working at your company would allow me to continuously upgrade my knowledge skills and own specialization. Moreover, your company provides a highly collaborative environment with other businesses in undertaking innovative EBV development projects.

◎As evidence of my strong interest in this specialized field, I actively participated in a project aimed at cloning a gene, serine hydroxylmethyltransferase gene (SHMT), in a zebrafish to more fully understand the major expression pattern of the SHMT gene with respect to its role during the embryo development process of zebrafish. The method developed in our laboratory involved successfully cloning a sequence of SHMT that can detect 400 base pair gene fragments through the electrophoresis analysis. The zebrafish has become a highly significant vertebrate mode in embryo development and genetics studies. In line with this research effort, genetics research can be used to detect hundreds of gene mutations. In this area of development, your company provides a highly competitive work environment and is home to highly skilled professionals. The opportunity to work in your organization would definitely strengthen my technological expertise and professional skills.

◎My undergraduate background in food science included knowledge of food processing, related analytical skills, microbiology and dietetics, as well as proficiency in using procedures such as examination of food microbes, food composition analysis and food additive analysis. My subsequent graduate school research in the Institute of Biotechnology at Yuanpei University of Science and Technology exposed me to molecular biology approaches. With the flourishing biotech industry, agricultural biotechnology has been actively promoted with respect to areas such as growth of seedlings, development of seafood products, use of animals for vaccine purposes, and use of living creature techniques for agrochemical purposes. Additionally, research in this area entails areas such as promoting gene medicine hygiene, utilizing gene development drugs, undertaking genetic diagnosis and preventive healthcare, conducting genetic therapy of the gene ketone body with protein drugs, studying Chinese herbal medicine applications, and performing patient trials of elixir. Employment at your biotechnology firm will hopefully allow me to undertake biotechnology and related application studies. Moreover, I hope to contribute to your company's efforts to enhance information exchange in the biotech industry, enhance product manufacturing on a global level to increase competitiveness abroad.

◎Given my strong devotion to this profession, I actively participated in a project aimed at identifying prognostic factors of breast cancer and subsequently developing an effective prognostic method to ultimately increase the survival rate of breast cancer patients. Those prognostic factors identified can provide a valuable reference for radiologists when devising a therapeutic treatment program for treating patients. The therapeutic treatment strategy can effectively terminate cancer cells while not affecting normal cells, explaining why identifying current and effective prognostic factors is essential. The prognostic factors identified in that research effort can also benefit the cancer patients in your hospital, an organization that is already reputed in the medical field and has gained international recognition for its own research advances. As a leading medical center in Taiwan, your department is renowned for its high quality medical services. The opportunity to work in your hospital would expose me to your physicians' abundant experiences in diagnosing and treating diseases. I look forward to joining your organization.

◎Given my strong desire to thrive within this profession, I collaborated with others in developing a novel imaging procedure for use in nuclear medicine - PET/CT - to provide follow up treatment for cancer patients. The results of that project confirmed the effectiveness of our procedure not only to evaluate precisely how nuclear medicine and radiology imager are related, but also to provide accurate imagery-related information to clinically diagnose cancer patients. Following that research effort, clinical efforts to detect cancer in the early stages have been significantly enhanced, thus improving the outcome of treating cancer patients. Your department offers state-of-the-art instrumentation and clinical training for those involved in researching PET/CT-related topics. Your laboratory, a leader in this field of research, offers a valuable opportunity for me to advance my knowledge skills.

◎My sincere commitment to elevating quality control standards in medical imagery, which is vital for patients severely affected by tumor-related diseases, is reflected in my active participation in our hospital's efforts to decrease the waiting time for diagnostic procedures. Specifically, I collaborated with my colleagues in producing an enhanced imagery slice by relying on the results obtained from the picture archiving communication system (PACS) in our Medical Imagery Department. Five years ago, a tumor patient would wait nearly half a day for confirmation of the results of the diagnostic procedure, with most of that time spent in waiting for the X-ray slides. However, with the assistance of PACS, physicians can now obtain the slides immediately and explain the diagnosis results in detail, subsequently attracting many patients to our hospital for diagnosis and curative treatment. In addition to providing a worry free environment for patients, our group attempted to model the efforts of other medical centers. Moreover, our efforts to enhance PACS facilitated the assessment of uncontrollable time periods to satisfy patients' requirements. As a leader in the medical quality field, your hospital would provide me with me with many collaborative opportunities to not only provide better medical care for patients through your solid training curricula, but also continually upgrade my knowledge expertise and research capabilities.

◎My profound interest in radiation detection explains my active participation in a project aimed at developing a novel method and promoting public awareness of radiation protection. Those project results confirmed the feasibility of using only a survey meter or TLD to obtain the precise neutron dose for a tumor patient. For clinical use, a value acquired from only a survey meter is then multiplied by a factor of the difference value between the survey meter and TLD. In addition to increasing work efficiency and decreasing human resource expenditures, more importantly, this project reduced patient's suspicions about the reliability of the results and enhanced the therapeutic prognosis. In this area, your department has distinguished itself in developing novel radiotherapy methods that have greatly benefited patients, as evidenced by your frequent publications in international journals. I look forward to the opportunity of working for your organization.

◎My deep interest in the radiotechnology profession led to my active participation in a project aimed at developing a more sound quality assurance system. While working closely with a medical team, I devised treatment plans for quality assurance purposes that could be delivered precisely to those patients. Treating tumor patients through radiation therapy is preferable over surgical procedures. A precise dose measurement can significantly enhance therapeutic treatment strategies, explaining why correlating such strategies with a patient's specific needs is of priority concern. In sum, developing a sound quality assurance system can ensure the reliability of therapeutic treatment and increase the efficiency of eradicating tumors. Your company offers comprehensive and challenging training for researchers of radiation therapy and protection. Such training could provide me with a marvelous opportunity to put my above knowledge expertise into practice.

◎My active participation in a project aimed at assessing the quality of a hospital's medical services reflects my avid interest in strategic marketing. This undertaking involved collaborating with other marketing planning personnel, quality management personnel and educational training personnel. A questionnaire on the level of service quality in the hospital was designed and distributed among patients to understand their attitudes towards the hospital's facilities, instrumentation and software capabilities, which are two important factors as to why they selected the hospital in the first place. In addition to revealing why patients selected the hospital, the results of that project indicated areas in which patients were dissatisfied with the hospital's facilities, instrumentation and software capabilities. Recommendations were made on what steps hospital administrators should take in remedying these areas of patient dissatisfaction. While customer satisfaction may not necessarily equate customer loyalty, they are directly related. Based on the results of that research effort, the hospital attempted to modify its services in order to increase its competence in the highly competitive medical sector. Related project experiences have greatly strengthened my independent research capabilities and statistical as well as analytical skills. Given my work experiences, your company offers a competitive work environment and highly skilled professionals: these ingredients are essential to my continually upgrading knowledge skills and expertise in the above area.

◎A proposal for a pharmaceutical firm that I wrote during graduate school attempted to organize an administrative unit that would encourage independent pharmacies to form a strategic alliance. In addition to effectively addressing specific problems that each independent pharmacy faces, the proposed unit attempted to execute joint purchases as well as acquire advanced information technologies that would greatly facilitate the operations of independent pharmacies. Those merits would enhance sales volume, reduce purchasing costs and identify areas of potential growth to gain a competitive edge. Moreover, this proposal examined the feasibility of adopting marketing methods, such as in promotion and advertising. Through proposal writing and my subsequent research focus on the pharmaceutical sector, I am confident of my ability to quickly adapt to your company's highly competitive environment. I am even more confident that I can significantly contribute to your franchise. While offering renowned medical product brands in the Taiwan market from the United States, your franchise highly prioritizes quality assurance and professionals in a diverse range of medical fields. Specifically, I hope to contribute to your marketing efforts, logistics management and medicine research — areas which are expected to expand in the future.

◎Owing to a deep interest in how to further strengthen my decision-making capabilities, I initiated a project aimed at developing an efficient product control system capable of monitoring the Work-in-Process (WIP) and dispatching the lot via Automated Material Handling Systems (AMHS). The results of that project confirmed the ability of our system not only to evaluate precisely bottlenecks in production, but also to evaluate immediately the manufacturing system's status with respect to re-scheduling WIP. According to our results, our hypothesis dispatching procedure increases the performance of AMHS. Additionally, the operation cycle time (OCT) and delivery time (DT) were reduced as well. Your company offers a competitive work environment and is home to highly skilled professionals. The comprehensive and challenging training for individuals involved in upgrading manufacturing technologies would continually upgrade my knowledge skills and expertise in the above area, if given the opportunity to work in your organization.

◎I recently participated in a cost-benefit analysis project for a hemodialysis unit in a hospital so that staff could enhance medical services while conserving overhead costs. My deep interest in the medical profession also explains my active participation in a project aimed at developing an efficient response surface method to optimize ordered categorical cost-benefit analysis in the medical sector. Whereas this project greatly added to my professional skills, the results of that project confirmed that the treatment of seriously ill patients requires a closer look at operating costs and work efficiency, thus highlighting the importance of cost-benefit analysis in cost reengineering. The novel scheme developed in that project can simplify the design of a hemodialysis unit, reduce the work load as well as overhead costs in a hospital. Your commitment to excellence in hospital innovation is reflected in your outstanding human resources and state-of-the-art medical instrumentation. I look forward to contributing to your hospital's commitment to providing quality healthcare.

◎As evidence of my commitment to the biotechnology profession, I participated in several biotechnology projects during graduate school. Specifically, I actively participated in a project aimed at developing an efficient protein production system. During this effort, I collaborated with others in developing a yeast transformation system that includes several factors obtained as experimental data. Importantly, that project developed a protein production system successfully, as well as utilized the amylase strength promoter of the Saccharomycopsis fibuligera; an efficient yeast transformation system was subsequently developed. A gene wanting to achieve expression into this system can use such a system to produce the target product. This system is highly promising for both academic and commercial purposes. Results of this project increased the protein safety and led to a successful yield, which is a major breakthrough. Your company's heavy emphasis on ensuring that each new target can reach its goal successfully is a major breakthrough in science and technology. This research can promote professional knowledge and advanced techniques for use in industry, eventually elevating the biotech industry's global competitiveness and benefiting society. I hope to secure employment in such a promising company as yours.

◎In 2001, I spearheaded a research project at Chung Kun Hospital on administrative expenses. This hospital is the only medical center in northern Taiwan with a police precinct office located on its premises. Chung Kun Hospital also has a ward capacity of 3500 beds, 4000 staff, and state-of-the-art medical equipment and facilities. To remain competitive in the tight medical services sector, the hospital also strives to achieve the latest medicinal technological advances by employing highly qualified physicians with diverse specialties. Of priority concern is the rapid increase in medicinal expenses, as evidenced by an annual growth ratio about of around 10%. In our research project, seventeen essential items were first analyzed: clinical expenses, ward room expenses, examination expenses (e.g., blood, urine, and sputum check), dietary expenses, X-ray expenses (CT or MRI), anesthesia expenses, surgery expenses, physical examination expenses, medicinal expenses, material expenses (e.g., syringes, intravenous hook up, and gypsum), and infant care expenses. Expenses in each item were then compared with those of a hospital of comparable size, e.g., National Taiwan University Hospital. That comparison revealed which expenses to be extraordinarily high, with that data subsequently sent back to the hospitals in the study for further analysis with respect to the histories of those patients involved in order to determine which expenses could be eliminate entirely or decreased incrementally. Next, the following areas at Chung Kun Hospital, i.e., internal medicine, external medicine, infant medicine, gynecology medicine osteological medicine, and other miscellaneous departments, were analyzed with respect to expenses, with those results subsequently compared to those from hospitals of a comparable size. Results of that project provided a valuable reference for hospital administrators in determining appropriate expense budgets for various departments, establishing goals for improvement, and acquiring essential data such as patient mortality and infection rates. Your hospital will hopefully find my above experiences to be a valuable asset as an employee in your highly regarded organization.

◎University provided me with the opportunity to work in a practicum internship at Chimei Hospital during summer vacation, where I assisted in personnel matters and administrative tasks. More recently, I served in a practicum at a Hsinchu-area hospital in which I participated in a hospital evaluation. This work allowed me to understand how a hospital evaluates its personnel and current policies. I also worked in a restaurant as well. Up until graduating from university, I also worked in the campus health care center. This interesting job focused on ways to combat smoking among students and how to properly orient the student body on its dangers. The target group also includes primary to high school students in Hsinchu City. The Health Care Center heavily prioritizes creating a nonsmoking environment on campus. My above experiences hopefully reflect what your organization is looking for in its staff.

◎As an undergraduate student, I completed a term project and subsequently submitted a research report under my teacher's guidance in a human resource management course. The project allowed me to probe the difficulties that businesses have in devising and implementing knowledge management strategies. The results of that project indicated that most employees enjoy developing their professional knowledge skills, but prefer not to share those knowledge skills with colleagues. Based on those results, we recommended that businesses adopting knowledge management practices must focus on creating a culture of sharing. Restated, employees must know whether if sharing their knowledge with other colleagues will lead to them mutually receiving knowledge from those same colleagues; doing so would increase work competence throughout the company. Moreover, successfully adopting knowledge management practices among employees will enhance the ability of company executives to interact with all employees. Such practices include encouraging teamwork to proceed with certain activities or discussing related topics on a regular basis - all with objective of enhancing business performance and employees' knowledge expertise. Given my previous experiences in this area, I look forward to joining your company's research staff

◎My academic advisor in graduate school arranged for me to conduct experiments in the Biochemistry and Tumor Laboratory in the Department of Medical Science at Chang Gung University over the winter break. By learning how to use the MASS spectrometer, I measured the purification of a protein. I also became adept in operating the MASS spectrometer since my analysis of the glycoprotein of Epstein-Barr Virus (EBV) concentrated on the cell surface. For instance, I analyzed the glycoprotein of EBV on the cell surface, e.g., gH, gL and gp42. However, the biological role of the gH protein of EBV had not yet been identified. During this period, I also enhanced my writing skills to submit a research paper to an international journal for publication. I hope that these laboratory skills are what your institute is looking for in its research staff.

◎I recently attended the 2003 Conference on Health Management held at Yuanpei University of Science and Technology, the major technical and scientific meeting of the academic year. The Conference contained several informative seminars that offered many research articles and information on the latest biotechnology trends. This forum allowed me to quickly obtain information rather than the conventional way of obtaining literature through a library search. I hope to present my research results orally in an upcoming seminar in the near future. The ability to closely interact with peers in my field will hopefully prove to be an asset for future employment, hopefully at your company.

◎While working in a practicum at Tri-Service General Hospital, I gained invaluable exposure to molecular biology related technologies, as well as their theoretical and practical applications. After conducting research for a period of time, I realized that only conducting an experiment is insufficient. Researchers must thoroughly understand all of the theoretical concepts involved and, then, compare them with the experimental ones. Only then can problems be identified and solved. Therefore, my recent research offered numerous opportunities to learn of the latest professional technologies to compensate for my limitations in the laboratory. The strong desire to continually upgrade my professional knowledge of the food science sector is hopefully what your company is looking for in its research staff.

◎I once participated in a research group that conducted related experiments at the Veterans General Hospital in Taipei. In this project, physicians focused on researching topics related to functional Magnetic Resonance Imaging (fMRI), which left me responsible for most of the engineering portion of this project. Although extremely taxing, the project instilled in me a sense of confidence in meeting the rigorous challenges of such an undertaking. This confidence will enable me to significantly contribute to collaborative research efforts that I engage in, hopefully at your highly prestigious company.

◎Additionally, while serving in five practicum internships or orientation training programs in a hospital, I acquired professional knowledge on the latest techniques in clinical and patient care. For me, patient care was the most important because the hospital environments that I worked in were full of frail patients in dire need of attention and respect. Medical personnel must thus be in tune with a patient's physical and mental well being to ensure a full recovery. Therefore I must be more attentive to patient care and apply the concepts taught in pertinent literature to my work place. I am confident that your company highly prioritizes the above attributes in your employees.

◎During undergraduate study, I worked in a practicum internship in the Department of Radiography at Tri-Service General Hospital, one of Taiwan's premier hospitals. In addition to orienting me on how to perform routine processing, e.g., chest, abdomen, liver, skull, computer tomography, MRI, and angiography, this practicum experience provided me with the fundamental skills required for advanced research. The six-month practicum internship equipped me with the necessary radiology skills necessary not only for treating patients humanely, but also for applying professional knowledge to perform a successful x-ray film examination. Following university graduation, I passed the rigorous radiologist examination to receive my license. My teacher then invited me to serve as a research assistant in the Department of

Radiology, where I was also a teaching assistant in a departmental course entitled "Radiology Experiments". Watching so many students successfully graduate from university, secure employment in hospitals and, eventually, receive their licenses to practice as radiologists has provided me with much personal satisfaction. I firmly believe that your hospital will find my academic and professional training to be a valuable asset in your highly respected organization.

◎Working in a practicum internship in a hospital definitely made me a more patient individual. During this period, I had more time to communicate with patients and learn how to remain calm under emergency situations, thus making me a more seasoned professional and able to empathize with others. I also learned how to more efficiently use my time and become more industrious when attempting to handle a large amount of daily tasks at work or resolve a bottleneck in an experiment or project. My gradual maturation as a proficient researcher will hopefully prove to be a valuable asset in your laboratory, allowing me to contribute significantly to your team's research efforts.

◎I worked as a research assistant at National Taiwan University following undergraduate school. Applying academic concepts taught in university to a practical work environment was an exciting challenge for me. More than acquiring work experience in academia, I acquired specialized knowledge skills. The professor that supervised me also encouraged me to continue with my academic studies. While aware that it will be a long and arduous journey, I am ready to immerse myself in administrative responsibilities. Regardless of the obstacles to be overcome, I am determined become an excellent manager. This explains why I am seeking employment in your organization for an administrative level position.

◎My practicum internships at Taipei Veterans General Hospital and Tri-Service General Hospital largely influenced my decision to study radiation and pursue a related career. I recall a shocking experience when working in a practicum internship in the Emergency Department at Taipei Veterans General Hospital. The ambulance brought in a severely mutilated patient who had a shattered mandible and was bleeding profusely. For a period of time, I carried a portable x-ray machine to all patients' rooms, where I saw many elderly men whom were lonely and in pain. Despite the misery and terrible human conditions, I have never been discouraged with this line of work. Therefore, I look forward to the challenges of working in your hospital's highly competitive environment.

◎Recent university graduates often enter society inexperienced and unaware of what to expect in the workplace. However, after working for a period of time, many individuals prefer conducting research to acquire more theoretical and practical experiences. I was fortunate to have worked with a research group at Academia Sinica, where I was exposed to the latest experimental techniques. I was also able to enhance my knowledge skills and expertise while conducting experiments. While at the Institute of Biological Chemistry, I became acquainted with a professor who was compiling a textbook on biochemistry related technologies for university students wanting to learn more about chemistry and the chemical industry. While recognizing my professional interest in these areas, this professor invited me to contributed to this body of work. I believe that my above capabilities are what your organization looks for in its research staff.

◎I served in a practicum internship in a transfusion center in Taipei during university. Exactly what is a transfusion center? While consisting of a transfusion sector, check routine sector, packing sector and service provider for hospitals, this public welfare organization strives to ensure the health of all patients. Working in this center allowed me not only to enhance my professional medical skills, but also to help others in need. Among the skills I learned included using an ulcer tissue to culture *Helicobacer pylori*, isolating chromosomal DNA from *Helicobacter pylori*, constructing a genomic library in the pILL570 vector, performing mutagenesis of 96 independent DNA inserts, learning about a gene colony, assaying natural competence in *Helicobacter pylori* and assaying gene expression. Exposure to this research environment reinforced my dedication to pursuing a career in the biotech sector, hopefully at your company.

◎Undergraduate studies exposed me to close collaboration with others on a medical technology project that involved different tasks and skills. I approached this project with both a deliberate attitude and solid logical skills. While in university, I also participated in some experiments that made me aware of how knowledge is infinite. Laboratory experiments greatly fostered my ability to solve problems rationally and methodologically. I continuously strive to acquire advanced skills in my field so that I am more independent in conducting independent research. Additionally, the more diligently I persist, the more benefits I will reap in the future. Although unfamiliar with how to perform an experiment at the outset, I persist until I not only successfully complete the experiment, but also understand the underlying theoretical and practical principles. Given my above background, I feel equipped to serve as a medical technology researcher, an area that your research institute is renowned.

◎My senior term project prior to university graduation focused on customer satisfaction in a hospital from a patient's perspective. As a recently emerging topic in the health sector, customer satisfaction belongs to the discipline of customer relationship management. This research project involved designing a questionnaire, interviewing study participants and analyzing data. Although this journey was an extremely arduous one, this experience offered me insight into the exciting challenges of becoming a researcher. The opportunity to work at your company would provide me with an excellent environment not only to fully realize my career aspirations, but also allow me to apply theoretical concepts taught in graduate school in the classroom to a practical work setting.

◎As evidence of the strong desire to strengthen my research fundamentals, I participated in a microbiology research project, in which fermentation was of primary emphasis. More specifically, our major concern was the oenology produced by vegetables. Previously, derivatives of saccharides were used to ferment wines. However, as well known, vegetables have many nutrients that offer beneficial and restorative functions to the human body. Therefore, our research examined the feasibility of using the flavor and probiolotic functions of vegetables to ferment wine. The skills that I acquired during this research project will prove to be a valuable asset for any research team that I belong to within your organization.

◎I spent the last seven years in nurturing my knowledge expertise in the medical technology field by immersing myself in life science-related research projects and their extensive applications. For instance, I participated in a National Science Council-sponsored research project on microbiology, which involved investigating how a hospital can adopt appropriate measures to combat infection. Additionally, I participated in several work practicum internships, including experiences at a teaching hospital and a biotechnology company. I am enthusiastic about studying many scientific and technological applications — both theoretical and practical ones. I have already been working in a hospital for three years now, offering much theoretical and practical knowledge of medical technology and biotechnology in the workplace. Securing employment at your highly prestigious biotech firm would allow me to contribute more significantly to society than I would be able to do so without such advanced knowledge expertise.

◎My recent collaborations have allowed me to gain immense exposure to salivary research-related topics. During graduate school, I received specialized training in medical education programs, including clinical laboratory experiences that sharpened my knowledge and professional skills. My graduate thesis advisor, a renowned professor from National Taiwan University, supervised my research while I received advanced training skills in his laboratory. The laboratory's high standards and heavy workload exposed me to many knowledge skills and technical expertise. My graduate school research focused on saliva hormone assay, i.e., an emerging field of clinical diagnosis. Acquiring knowledge of advanced techniques in this area along with background information made me confident of my standing both theoretically and practically. Experiences and knowledge acquired during graduate study and subsequent research definitely enhanced my knowledge of the field, hopefully enabling me to look beyond the role of assisting others in the laboratory to that of leading. The various seminars and conferences that I attended broadened my perspective dramatically. Additionally, the research articles that I co-authored during my study made me aware of the value of research and reviewing pertinent literature. Moreover, the many years in which I served as a technical assistant have provided me with valuable practical experiences. In sum, I will be in a better position not only to understand any changes that may occur in the field of clinical science, but also to find an answer to resolve the problem at hand. Exposure to research early on in my academic studies fostered my interest in graduate study and, ultimately, my decision to pursue a research career in this field of study, hopefully at your company.

◎A practicum training internship at Mackay Memorial Hospital equipped me with a solid clinical knowledge in medical technology and a strong ability to develop my problem-solving skills. As an undergraduate senior, I participated in a National Science Council-sponsored research project on analyzing the natural transformation ability of Helicobacter pylori. I often consulted with other research collaborators on how to solve bottlenecks in research and develop new laboratory procedures. Our results on the discovery of how some genes are associated with the natural transformation of Helicobacter pylori were eventually published in an international journal. Intensive laboratory training in molecular biology has refined my ability to think logically, respond effectively under stressful situations, accumulate relevant information, as well as analyze and solve problems. These strong personality traits will prove invaluable to your company's efforts to develop high quality biotechnology products.

◎While working in a practicum internship at the Tri-Service General Hospital, I gained invaluable exposure to molecular biology related technologies, as well as their theoretical and practical applications. My subsequent research at the same hospital attempted to elucidate the nature of antibiotic-resistant bacteria by investigating the feasibility of adopting various molecular biology approaches to identify the genotype of antibiotic-resistant bacteria. Results of this study were published in the journals of the Medical Technology Association of the Republic of China (R.O.C.) and the Microbiology Association of the R.O.C. Conducting research in practicum internships at both the Institute of Biological Chemistry of Academia Sinica and the Tri-Service General Hospital made me realize that merely performing experiments is not enough. Researchers must thoroughly understand all of the theoretical concepts involved and, then, compare them with the experimental ones. Having recently completed a Master's degree in Biotechnology from Yuanpei University of Science and Technology, I plan to earn a doctorate degree in a related field. However, before doing so, I would like to apply my strong theoretical and knowledge skills in a research institute as the beginning of my career path. I am especially interested in researching food science, microbiology and proteomics-related topics. Working in your research institute would expose me to the latest technological advances in my field as well as further refine my logical thinking skills. After conducting research in the hi-tech sector for a period of time, I eventually hope to teach in a university in the future after successful completion of my doctorate degree. Both my academic and professional experiences will prove invaluable for any research effort that I belong to in your institute, hopefully contributing to commercial opportunities that you are pursuing.

◎While pursuing a master's degree in Business Management, I worked at Ton-Yen General Hospital, which provided an excellent environment for me to conduct graduate-level research. Moreover, I have recently been involved in a Department of Health-sponsored project aimed at assisting visiting staff to teach the resident staff on how to enhance the quality of hospital services. This academic program has greatly added to my professional skills. The hospital is filled with many supportive colleagues whom have oriented me on these new surroundings. I am determined to learn as much as possible while contributing through any beneficial results that my graduate school research can generate. Employment at your hospital would allow me to build upon my previous academic training and professional experiences.

◎During university, in addition to consulting with several specialists in the medical field, I read many hospital management-related case studies in preparation for my senior thesis project. I once sought out a hospital administrator on the different methods and procedures that are adopted in daily operations. My subsequent graduate research heavily emphasized interviews with hospital administrators and staff to understand the practical applications of new management concepts in a practical setting. Strengthening my research skills is definitely a high priority for me. While academic study in a classroom is important for understanding fundamental concepts and theories, researching in an actual hospital is a whole new experience. I will strive my best to become a successful researcher in my own unique way, which is a friendly, contemplative and graceful one. Your medical center would definitely provide me the opportunity to further pursue my professional interests.

◎My most recent research focused on topics related to gH, a glycoprotein on Epstein-Barr Virus (EBV). EBV, a human herpes virus that may result in tumors. Results acquired so far have so far demonstrated that EBV induces either Burkitt's lymphoma or nasopharyngeal carcinoma. Additionally, EBV infect the B cell, causing the virus' glycoprotein gp 350 to combine with B cell's complement receptor type 2 (CR2). Results of my research will hopefully contribute to efforts to prevent and cure EBV-induced diseases. Internet search retrievals, library periodicals and news articles significantly enhanced my research capabilities. Additionally, the university's digital library greatly aided me in searching for electronic periodicals covering mainly virus-related topics. Additionally, I performed related experiments involving polymerase chain reaction (PCR) and cell culturing. While learning how to conduct experiments independently, I also acquired the latest information on advanced technologies by searching for periodicals online. Moreover, I occasionally attended seminars to remain abreast of the latest developments in the field. This acquired knowledge allowed me to thoroughly discuss the detailed contents of an experiment with my thesis advisor in the laboratory. If employed at your company, I hope that the above skills are what you are looking for in your product development efforts.

◎As a licensed medical technologist, I increased my clinical experiences and knowledge expertise, subsequently increasing my proficiency in conducting biotechnology experiments. While serving in a practicum internship in the Department of Medical Technology at Kuo Tai Hospital, the hospital oriented me on the latest advances in medical technology, I often visited the research center to acquire knowledge in advanced experimental technologies, as well as participated in medical technology symposiums. In addition to expanding my research capabilities and clinical knowledge, those activities greatly facilitated my research ambitions. As a member of your research staff, I bring to your company a wealth of knowledge expertise in biotechnology applications in the hi-tech sector.

◎My most recent experiments involved human genetics and proteins. I was fortunate to perform research under the supervision of a renowned scientist in this field. I also spent considerable time in the library accumulating data and, occasionally, perusing through international scientific journals such as *Nature*. I especially enjoy reading upon human DNA related research and, then in my spare time, I try to apply this knowledge to a laboratory experiment. I truly enjoy devoting my energies to researching different aspects of a cell for medical purposes. For instance, I often served in practicum internships in a hospital to gain exposure to the latest technologies and knowledge skills used in the workplace. The above experiences instilled in me a sense of originality that will definitely benefit my research on human DNA mutation and related diseases, hopefully at your research institute.

Max

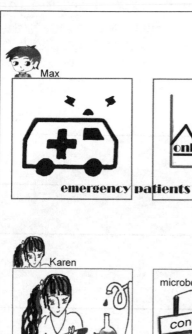

emergency patients

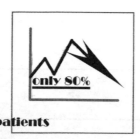

only 80%

standard

Karen

experiments

microbe development

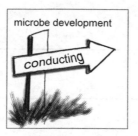

conducting

modification
food science sector

product development

Ellen

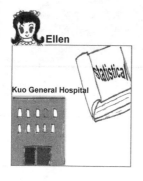

Kuo General Hospital

statistical

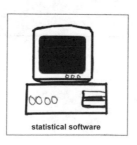

statistical software

marketing

effective hospital management

I Write down the key points of the situations on the preceding page, while the instructor reads aloud the script from the Answer Key.

Situation 4

_____

_____

_____

Situation 5

_____

_____

_____

Situation 6

_____

_____

_____

J Oral practice II

Based on the three situations in this unit, write three questions beginning with **What**, and answer them. The questions do not need to come directly from these situations.

Examples

What evidence does Max have of his concern with the needs and satisfaction of hospital emergency patients?

His recent collaboration with colleagues in a study that involved a questionnaire given to family members

What did the questionnaire given to family members contain?

125 queries on the level of treatment provided by physicians and emergency staff

1. _____

_____

2. _____

_____

3. _____

_____

K Based on the three situations in this unit, write three questions beginning with **Why**, and answer them. The questions do not need to come directly from these situations.

Examples

Why was Karen's participation in a National Science Council-sponsored research project productive?

It led to her subsequent graduate study of Chinese herbal medicine

Why did Karen receive praise from both teachers and students?

Because of her participation in developing an undergraduate enzymology curriculum

1. _____

   _____

2. _____

   _____

3. _____

   _____

L Based on the three situations in this unit, write three questions beginning with *How*, and answer them. The questions do not need to come directly from these situations.

Examples

How did participation in a collaborative project with an ophthalmologist at Kuo General Hospital benefit Ellen?

It strengthened her statistical capabilities.

How did Karen identify patients' particular needs in her project?

By using data mining approaches

1. _____

   _____

2. _____

   _____

3. _____

   _____

M Write questions that match the answers provided.

Examples

What is a notable example of IJK Corporation's commitment to quality excellence?

Extensive on-the-job training

1. _____

_____

Strengthen her statistical capabilities

2. _____

_____

Data mining approaches

3. _____

_____

That a hospital must distinguish itself from others by its marketing practices to gain a competitive edge

N Listening Comprehension II

Situation 4

1. Who did the results of the study that Max participated in provide a valuable reference for?

   A. emergency unit personnel

   B. hospital emergency patients

   C. hospital administrators

2. What is Max concerned with?

   A. the medical consumer's demand for quality healthcare

   B. the needs and satisfaction of hospital emergency patients

   C. comprehensive training and challenges that would greatly enhance his professional skills

3. What did Max's recent collaboration with colleagues in a study involve?

   A. the inability to satisfy the medical consumer's demand for quality healthcare

   B. how to increase the standard of care offered by public health personnel

   C. a questionnaire given to family members

4. What was the level of satisfaction with the emergency unit's treatment of patients?

   A. 80%

   B. 70%

   C. 90%

5. What could the medical center at the Veterans General Hospital in Taipei offer Max?

   A. collaboration opportunities with colleagues in a related study

   B. comprehensive training and challenges that would greatly enhance his professional skills

   C. satisfaction with the emergency unit's treatment of patients

Situation 5

1. What did Karen participate in developing while at undergraduate school?

    A. a National Science Council-sponsored research project

    B. a biotechnology-related career in the food science sector

    C. an undergraduate enzymology curriculum

2. What reflects Karen's commitment to pursuing a biotechnology-related career in the food science sector?

    A. her ability to contribute significantly to product development efforts

    B. her research skills acquired as an undergraduate in the Food Science Department and as a graduate student at the Institute of Biotechnology

    C. her participation in a National Science Council-sponsored research project

3. What did Karen become adept at while in graduate school?

    A. contributing significantly to product development efforts

    B. publishing her research findings in domestic and international journals

    C. conducting experiments on microbe development, genetic engineering and agent analysis

4. What reflects Karen's commitment to pursuing a biotechnology-related career in the food science sector?

    A. her research skills acquired as an undergraduate in the Food Science Department and as a graduate student at the Institute of Biotechnology

    B. her subsequent graduate study of Chinese herbal medicine

    C. having both participated in curriculum development and mastered several laboratory skills

5. What did the food science research that Karen actively engage in aim at?

    A. enzyme-related topics

    B. Chinese herbal medicine

    C. the genetic modification of microbes and analysis of related properties and agents

Situation 6

1. Why did Ellen's collaborative project use data mining approaches?

   A. to strengthen its statistical capabilities

   B. to identify patients' particular needs

   C. to distinguish itself from others by its marketing practices

2. What reflects Ellen's strong desire constantly to strengthen her statistical capabilities?

   A. her active participation in a collaborative project

   B. her considerable attention to effective hospital management

   C. her ability to make marketing-related decisions about the medical sector

3. What is a notable example of IJK Corporation's commitment to quality excellence?

   A. its ability to distinguish itself from other hospitals

   B. its leading role in the medical sector

   C. extensive on-the-job training

4. Why must a hospital distinguish itself from others by its marketing practices?

   A. to achieve quality excellence

   B. to gain a competitive edge

   C. to provide a valuable reference for administrators

5. What did carefully analyzing the data from Ellen's collaborative project reveal?

   A. patients' particular needs

   B. marketing practices to gain a competitive edge

   C. unique phenomena related to the hospital's particular circumstances

O Reading Comprehension II
Pick the word or expression whose meaning is closest to the meaning of the underlined word or expression in the following passages.

Situation 4

1. Max is concerned with the needs and <u>satisfaction</u> of hospital emergency patients, as evidenced by his recent collaboration with colleagues in a study that involved a questionnaire given to family members.

   A. displeasure

   B. indemnity

   C. disapproval

2. Max is concerned with the needs and satisfaction of hospital emergency patients, as <u>evidenced</u> by his recent collaboration with colleagues in a study that involved a questionnaire given to family members.

   A. proven

   B. negated

   C. denied

3. Max is concerned with the needs and satisfaction of hospital emergency patients, as evidenced by his recent <u>collaboration</u> with colleagues in a study that involved a questionnaire given to family members.

   A. autonomous work

   B. individual work

   C. synergy

4. Max is concerned with the needs and satisfaction of hospital emergency patients, as evidenced by his recent <u>collaboration</u> with colleagues in a study that involved a questionnaire given to family members.

A. superiors

B. peers

C. subordinates

5. It contained 125 queries on the level of <u>treatment</u> provided by physicians and emergency staff.

A. rehabilitation

B. disorder

C. malady

6. The level of satisfaction with the emergency unit's <u>treatment</u> of their relatives was only 80%, reflecting how public health personnel cannot satisfy the medical consumer's demand for quality healthcare.

A. disorder

B. therapy

C. infirmity

7. The level of satisfaction with the emergency unit's treatment of their relatives was only 80%, <u>reflecting</u> how public health personnel cannot satisfy the medical consumer's demand for quality healthcare.

A. echoing

B. rectify

C. redress

8. The results of that study provide a valuable reference for hospital <u>administrators</u> regarding how to increase the standard of care offered by public health personnel.

A. dependent

B. subservient

C. executives

9. The results of that study provide a valuable reference for hospital administrators regarding how to increase the <u>standard</u> of care offered by public health personnel.

A. random

B. criteria

C. disorganized

10. If Max were <u>employed</u> at the Veterans General Hospital in Taipei, the medical center would offer him comprehensive training and challenges that would greatly enhance his professional skills.

A. hired

B. laid off

C. fired

Situation 5

1. When at undergraduate school, Karen <u>participated in</u> a National Science Council-sponsored research project, which led to her subsequent graduate study of Chinese herbal medicine.

A. Refrained from

B. abstained from

C. engaged in

2. When at undergraduate school, Karen participated in a National Science Council-sponsored research project, which led to her <u>subsequent</u> graduate study of Chinese herbal medicine.

A. preceding

B. consecutive

C. prior

3. The <u>findings</u> of her research have been published in domestic and international journals.

A. discoveries

B. concealment

C. hidden

4. The findings of her research have been <u>published</u> in domestic and international journals.

   A. concealed

   B. proclaimed

   C. hidden

5. She has also participated in developing an undergraduate enzymology curriculum, which received <u>praise</u> from both teachers and students.

   A. condemnation

   B. commendation

   C. criticism

6. While researching enzyme-related topics in graduate school, she also became <u>adept</u> at conducting experiments on microbe development, genetic engineering and agent analysis.

   A. useless

   B. ineffectual

   C. effective

7. Having both participated in curriculum development and <u>mastered</u> several laboratory skills, Karen was also actively engaged in food science research aimed at the genetic modification of microbes and analysis of related properties and agents.

   A. decline

   B. conquered

   C. wane

8. Having both participated in curriculum development and mastered several laboratory skills, Karen was also actively <u>engaged</u> in food science research aimed at the genetic modification of microbes and analysis of related properties and

agents.

A. abstained

B. withheld

C. participated

9. Having both participated in curriculum development and mastered several laboratory skills, Karen was also actively engaged in food science research aimed at the genetic modification of microbes and analysis of related <u>properties</u> and agents.

A. characteristics

B. theories

C. hypotheses

10. In summary, her research skills <u>acquired</u> as an undergraduate in the Food Science Department and as a graduate student at the Institute of Biotechnology reflect her commitment to pursuing a biotechnology-related career in the food science sector.

A. ceded

B. relinquished

C. obtained

Situation 6

1. Ellen's strong <u>desire</u> constantly to strengthen her statistical capabilities is reflected by her active participation in a collaborative project with an ophthalmologist at Kuo General Hospital in analyzing medical data and storing them in a novel database for statistical software.

A. listless

B. lethargy

C. longing

2. Ellen's strong desire constantly to strengthen her <u>statistical</u> capabilities is reflected by her active participation in a collaborative project with an ophthalmologist at Kuo General Hospital in analyzing medical data and storing them in a novel database for statistical software.

    A. analytical

    B. theoretical

    C. hypothetical

3. Ellen's strong desire constantly to strengthen her statistical capabilities is reflected by her active participation in a <u>collaborative</u> project with an ophthalmologist at Kuo General Hospital in analyzing medical data and storing them in a novel database for statistical software.

    A. autonomous

    B. synergistic

    C. individual

4. Ellen's strong desire constantly to strengthen her statistical capabilities is reflected by her active participation in a collaborative project with an <u>ophthalmologist</u> at Kuo General Hospital in analyzing medical data and storing them in a novel database for statistical software.

    A. heart physician

    B. family physician

    C. eye physician

5. Carefully <u>analyzing</u> the data revealed unique phenomena related to the hospital's particular circumstances, providing a valuable reference for administrators who are making marketing-related decisions about the medical sector.

    A. emulating

    B. examining

    C. contending

6. Carefully analyzing the data revealed <u>unique</u> phenomena related to the hospital's particular circumstances, providing a valuable reference for administrators who are making marketing-related decisions about the medical sector.

   A. classical

   B. archetypal

   C. peerless

7. Carefully analyzing the data revealed unique phenomena related to the hospital's particular <u>circumstances</u>, providing a valuable reference for administrators who are making marketing-related decisions about the medical sector.

   A. trivialness

   B. events

   C. pettiness

8. The project involved the use of <u>data</u> mining approaches to identify patients' particular needs.

   A. statistics

   B. bogeyman

   C. phantom

9. The project involved the use of data mining approaches to <u>identify</u> patients' particular needs.

   A. misplace

   B. forfeit

   C. pinpoint

10. This project made Ellen <u>aware</u> that a hospital must distinguish itself from others by its marketing practices to gain a competitive edge.

    A. oblivious

    B. cognizant

    C. uncertain

Unit Four

Describing academic background and achievements relevant to employment

描述學歷背景及已獲成就

Vocabulary and related expressions 相關字詞

acquiring 獲得的
competent 有能力的
thrive 成功
theoretical and practical expertise
理論及實際的專業能力
exchange knowledge with
和……交換知識
statistical and analytical skills
統計分析能力
excellence 優秀
devising 設計
at the outset 開始
strives 努力
absorb 吸收
high pressure and demands
高度壓力及要求

advanced techniques 進階技能
emerging field 新興領域
perspectives 觀點
peers 同儕
potential solutions 可能的解決方法
co-authoring papers 和別人同寫的論文
implement 實行
publication and review process
發表及審核程序
matured 成熟
clinical science 臨床科學
innovative technology 創新科技
exposed 產品曝光
highly desirable 高度令人嚮往的
exposed 暴露的
publishing findings 結果發表

conducting original research
進行最初的研究
undoubtedly 肯定地
excel 優於
fully equip 裝備完整
diverse scientific interests
不同的科學興趣
conventional limits of a discipline
傳統紀律的限制
intensive training 密集訓練
strong desire for acquiring knowledge
對吸收知識有強烈慾望
collaborative effort 合作的努力
highly demanding 高度苛求的
enabled 使能夠
hypotheses 假設
in collaboration with 和……合作
cultivating friendships 和……培養友誼
broaden one's horizons 擴展視野
encompassed 包圍
seemingly unrelated fields
表面上無關的領域
multidisciplinary approach
有關各種學問的研究途徑
continual self-improvement 不斷自我進步
particular emphasis on 特別強調
clinical practices 開診
Animal Technology Institute of Taiwan
(ATIT) 動物科技研究所

fortunate 幸運的
high standards 高度水準
supervised by 由……監督
renowned 有名的
specialized training 專門的訓練
heavy workload 沉重的工作量
fully comprehend 完全理解
apply theoretical concepts 理論知識的運用
respond effectively 有效的回應
unforeseen 預料之外的
bottlenecks in research 研究瓶頸
love of challenges 愛好挑戰
heavy schedule 忙碌的行程
traced back to 追溯
first exposure to 首先見於
accumulated 累積
rigorous demands 嚴格的要求
distinguish 區別
contribute to society 對社會有貢獻
flexible 有彈性的
focused 集中的
fruitful results 豐富的結果
realize fully one's career aspirations
實現某人的求職志向
sufficient expertise 足夠的專業技術
complex models 複雜的模式
international conferences 國際研討會
fundamental and advanced research
capabilities 基礎及進階研究能力

Larry

graduate school training

concepts

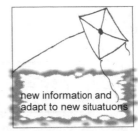

new information and adapt to new situatuons

Susan

renowned professor

saliva hormone assay

National Taiwan University

clinical science

Jerry

International journals

problem-solving

concepts

A Write down the key points of the situations on the preceding page, while the instructor reads aloud the script from the Answer Key.

Situation 1

_____

_____

_____

Situation 2

_____

_____

_____

Situation 3

_____

_____

_____

B Oral practice I

Based on the three situations in this unit, write three questions beginning with *How*, and answer them. The questions do not need to come directly from these situations.

Examples

How did Larry develop a strong commitment to the Business Management field?

By acquiring knowledge and skills through graduate school training

How did Larry learn how to adopt different perspectives when solving a particular problem during undergraduate training?

During undergraduate training

1. _____

   _____

2. _____

   _____

3. _____

   _____

C Based on the three situations in this unit, write three questions beginning with **Why**, and answer them. The questions do not need to come directly from these situations.

Examples

Why was Susan able to receive specialized training while writing her Master's thesis?

Because she was fortunate enough to be supervised by a renowned professor from National Taiwan University

Why was Susan able to learn many new skills and advanced techniques while working in the laboratory?

Because she adopted extremely high standards in the laboratory and handled a heavy workload

1. _____

   _____

2. _____

   _____

3. _____

   _____

D Based on the three situations in this unit, write three questions beginning with **What**, and answer them. The questions do not need to come directly from these situations.

Examples

What did graduate school expose Jerry to?

The high pressure and demands of conducting original research and publishing findings in international journals

What will enable Jerry to succeed in GHI Corporation's highly demanding product development projects?

His academic background, experimental and work experience in biotechnology, strong desire for acquiring knowledge and love of challenges

1. _____

_____

2. _____

_____

3. _____

_____

E Write questions that match the answers provided.

Examples

What did Jerry's undergraduate and graduate-level courses in biotechnology often include?

Term projects

When did Jerry receive intensive training?

While pursuing a Master's degree

1. _____

_____

The conventional limits of a discipline

2. _____

_____

Analyze problems, find solutions, and implement those solutions according to the concepts taught in class

3. _____

_____

Apply theoretical concepts in a practical context and develop problem-solving skills

F Listening Comprehension I

Situation 1

1. What did acquiring several statistical and analytical skills involve learning?

    A. how to devise marketing strategies for research purposes

    B. how to absorb quickly new information and adapt to new situations

    C. how to analyze problems, identify potential solutions, and implement those solutions according to concepts taught in the classroom

2. When does Larry strive to absorb quickly new information and adapt to new situations?

    A. when initially lacking expertise in a particular topic at the outset

    B. when trying to adopt different perspectives

    C. when acquiring knowledge and skills through graduate school training

3. What has Larry's commitment to the Business Management field done for him?

    A. made him competent academically

    B. allowed him to thrive in the workplace

    C. both A and B

4. When was Larry able to acquire several statistical and analytical skills?

    A. during undergraduate training

    B. during graduate school training

    C. while working in the Business Management field

5. What does Larry believe that ABC Company will find highly desirable?

    A. the ability to thrive in the workplace

    B. the ability to absorb quickly new information and adapt to new situations

    C. the ability to devise marketing strategies for research purposes

Situation 2

1. What has increased Susan's awareness of the latest developments in the field, both practical and theoretical?

   A. her specialized training in the laboratory of a renowned professor from National Taiwan University

   B. her acquired expertise in the laboratory

   C. her awareness of the detailed publication and review process

2. Why is Susan confident in her ability to contribute significantly to DEF Company's efforts to develop innovative technology products?

   A. because of the skillful use of the latest techniques in this field

   B. because of her extensive experience as a technical assistant

   C. because of her solid academic background

3. Why was Susan able to learn many new skills and advanced techniques?

   A. because she adopted extremely high standards in the laboratory and handled a heavy workload

   B. because of her extensive experience as a technical assistant that matured her as a researcher

   C. because of her supervision by a renowned professor from National Taiwan University

4. Why was Susan fortunate while writing her Master's thesis?

   A. She was exposed to a wide array of issues in salivary hormone research

   B. She was confident in both her theoretical and practical expertise in the laboratory

   C. She was supervised by a renowned professor from National Taiwan University

5. Why is Susan in a better position to understand and respond to the frequent changes that occur in clinical science?

   A. because of her skillful use of the latest techniques in the biotechnology field

B. because of her advanced training

C. because of her extensive experience as a technical assistant that matured her as a researcher

Situation 3

1. What allows Jerry to see beyond the conventional limits of a discipline?

A. his diverse scientific interests

B. his ability to apply theoretical concepts in a practical context and develop problem-solving skills

C. his ability to analyze problems, find solutions, and implement those solutions according to the concepts taught in class

2. What does Jerry love?

A. the high pressure and demands of conducting original research

B. his experimental and work experience in biotechnology

C. challenges

3. What did graduate school exposed Jerry to?

A. the high pressure and demands of conducting original research

B. publishing findings in international journals

C. both A and B

4. What does Jerry have a strong desire for?

A. developing problem-solving skills

B. acquiring knowledge

C. implementing solutions according to concepts taught in class

5. How does Jerry describe GHI Corporation's product development projects?

A. as highly challenging

B. as high pressured

C. as highly demanding

Unit Describing academic background and achievements relevant
Four to employment
描述學歷背景及已獲成就

G Reading Comprehension I
Pick the word or expression whose meaning is closest to the meaning of the underlined word or expression in the following passages.

Situation 1

1. Larry's strong <u>commitment</u> to the Business Management field has involved acquiring knowledge and skills through graduate school training.

   A. affliction

   B. tribulation

   C. obligation

2. Larry's strong commitment to the Business Management field has involved <u>acquiring</u> knowledge and skills through graduate school training.

   A. securing

   B. discarding

   C. disposing of

3. This commitment has not only made him <u>competent</u> academically, but also allowed him to thrive in the workplace.

   A. incapable

   B. skillful

   C. unqualified

4. This commitment has not only made him competent <u>academically</u>, but also allowed him to thrive in the workplace.

   A. socially

   B. athletically

   C. scholastically

5. This commitment has not only made him competent academically, but also

allowed him to <u>thrive</u> in the workplace.

A. excel

B. flop

C. sink

6. During undergraduate <u>training</u>, while learning how to adopt different perspectives when solving a particular problem, he acquired several statistical and analytical skills.

A. toil

B. travail

C. pedagogy

7. During undergraduate training, while learning how to <u>adopt</u> different perspectives when solving a particular problem, he acquired several statistical and analytical skills.

A. dump

B. utilize

C. throw out

8. During undergraduate training, while learning how to adopt different <u>perspectives</u> when solving a particular problem, he acquired several statistical and analytical skills.

A. viewpoints

B. goals

C. targets

9. During undergraduate training, while learning how to adopt different perspectives when solving a particular problem, he acquired several statistical and <u>analytical</u> skills.

A. rational

B. irrational

C. illogical

10. Doing so involved <u>learning</u> how to analyze problems, identify potential solutions, and implement those solutions according to concepts taught in the classroom.

A. dissipating

B. mastering

C. squandering

Situation 2

1. Graduate level research in biochemistry <u>exposed</u> Susan to a wide array of issues in salivary hormone research.

A. closed her to

B. opened her to

C. prevented her from doing something

2. Graduate level research in biochemistry exposed Susan to a wide <u>array</u> of issues in salivary hormone research.

A. nobility

B. highbred

C. range

3. While writing her Master's <u>thesis</u>, she was fortunate enough to be supervised by a renowned professor from National Taiwan University, allowing her to receive specialized training in his laboratory.

A. dissertation

B. plate

C. escape

4. While writing her Master's thesis, she was <u>fortunate</u> enough to be supervised by a renowned professor from National Taiwan University, allowing her to receive

specialized training in his laboratory.

A. disgraceful

B. deplorable

C. propitious

5. While writing her Master's thesis, she was fortunate enough to be <u>supervised</u> by a renowned professor from National Taiwan University, allowing her to receive specialized training in his laboratory.

A. lore

B. governed

C. myth

6. While writing her Master's thesis, she was fortunate enough to be supervised by a <u>renowned</u> professor from National Taiwan University, allowing her to receive specialized training in his laboratory.

A. looked down on

B. despised

C. illustrious

7. Susan adopted these <u>extremely</u> high standards in the laboratory and handled a heavy workload, so she learned many new skills and advanced techniques.

A. highly

B. slightly

C. rarely

8. Susan <u>adopted</u> these extremely high standards in the laboratory and handled a heavy workload, so she learned many new skills and advanced techniques.

A. exasperated

B. shuddered

C. embraced

9. Susan adopted these extremely high standards in the laboratory and handled a

heavy workload, so she learned many new skills and advanced <u>techniques</u>.

    A. perils

    B. procedures

    C. compasses

Situation 3

1. Graduate school exposed Jerry to the high pressure and demands of conducting <u>original</u> research and publishing findings in international journals.

    A. pioneering

    B. classical

    C. replicated

2. These <u>capabilities</u> will undoubtedly allow him to excel in the biotechnology field, as they more fully equip him with technical and professional expertise.

    A. competences

    B. constraints

    C. restraints

3. These capabilities will <u>undoubtedly</u> allow him to excel in the biotechnology field, as they more fully equip him with technical and professional expertise.

    A. questionably

    B. disputed

    C. absolutely

4. These capabilities will undoubtedly allow him to <u>excel</u> in the biotechnology field, as they more fully equip him with technical and professional expertise.

    A. descend

    B. outshine

    C. lower

5. These capabilities will undoubtedly allow him to excel in the biotechnology field,

as they more fully <u>equip</u> him with technical and professional expertise.

A. distill

B. instill

C. prepare

6. His <u>diverse</u> scientific interests allow him to see beyond the conventional limits of a discipline and fully comprehend how his field relates to others.

A. similar

B. variant

C. analogous

7. His diverse scientific interests allow him to see beyond the <u>conventional</u> limits of a discipline and fully comprehend how his field relates to others.

A. current

B. modern

C. traditional

8. Undergraduate and graduate-level courses in biotechnology often included term projects that allowed him to apply <u>theoretical</u> concepts in a practical context and develop problem-solving skills.

A. functional

B. hypothetical

C. serviceable

9. While <u>pursuing</u> a Master's degree, Jerry received intensive training. More specifically, he learned how to analyze problems, find solutions, and implement those solutions according to the concepts taught in class.

A. hiding

B. concealing

C. seeking

10. While pursuing a Master's degree, Jerry received <u>intensive</u> training. More

specifically, he learned how to analyze problems, find solutions, and implement those solutions according to the concepts taught in class.

A. spread out

B. diffused

C. concentrated

H Common elements in describing academic background and achievements relevant to employment include:

1. Summarizing one's educational attainment
2. Describing knowledge, skills and/or leadership qualities gained through academic training
3. Emphasizing a highlight of academic training
4. Stressing how academic background will benefit future employment

In the space below, describe your academic background and achievements relevant to employment.

_____

_____

_____

_____

_____

Unit four

Describing academic background and achievements relevant to employment
描述學歷背景及已獲成就

1. Summarizing one's educational attainment
   總括個人的學術成就

2. Describing knowledge, skills and/or leadership qualities gained through academic training
   描述學術訓練所獲得的技能及(或)領導特質

3. Emphasizing a highlight of academic training
   強調一個學術訓練的特定領域

4. Stressing how academic background will benefit future employment
   強調學術背景對未來求職的利處

Look at the following examples of describing academic background and achievements relevant to employment.

◎My graduate level research in the Institute of Biotechnology at Yuanpei University of Science and Technology focused on the role of cells and molecular biology in the signal transduction pathway and regulation of cell physiology. I especially concentrated on use of protein analysis methods, including protein expression, sequence analysis, protein purification and extraction, as well as determination of the molecular weight of proteins. I also entered a graduate student competition on related research topics presented at the Annual Meeting of the Society of Biology and Medical Science in Taiwan. My graduate thesis addressed how to regulate cellular proliferation and physiology functions of murine macrophage RAW 264.7 and J774 cell line in the endoplasmic reticular calcium pool. As for empirical studies of the cell culture, I investigated how the macrophage cell line induces nitro oxidation and then returns to the nitro oxide signal pathway. Additionally, our laboratory examined the signal pathways of TNF-α, NF-κB, and MAPK to more thoroughly understand not only cell-cell regulation, but also the role of different pathways. Based on our research results, I understood how different cell cycles are expressed in different protein types; these protein functions can also be used to determine cytogenesis or cell death. Moreover, I became adept in adopting intercellular DNA or RNA gene analysis methods to explore the unknown physiology functions of cells. In sum, graduate school instilled in me the need for harmony among research collaborators to achieve a desired outcome. I will apply the same responsible attitude towards any research effort that I belong to at your company.

◎As medical skills advance daily, medical professionals with a strong academic background in their profession gain much respect. This explains why I am committed to continuously upgrading my academic and professional skills so that I can be more proficient in my chosen career. With competitiveness among individuals increasing as society advances rapidly, strong analytical skills and the ability to solve problems logically in theory and practice are highly desirable attributes, explaining why I equally prioritize professional and academic experiences. For instance, I fully immerse myself in laboratory experiments to understand how theoretical topics from academic subjects can be applied in a realistic setting. Meanwhile, I constantly look for potential economic opportunities that could arise out of my integration of laboratory expertise and academic knowledge skills. Individuals must take advantage of their previous working experience as they apply their expertise to new technological settings. I would thus like to build upon my solid academic training and relevant work experiences by securing employment in your reputed medical organization. Your company's highly qualified staff and state-of-the-art facilities would allow me to become a distinguished researcher in my field.

◎The nature of my previous work led to my recent completion of a master's degree in Business Administration at Yuanpei University of Science and Technology, in which I diligently strived to identify what theoretical and academic principles can be applied to my workplace requirements. For instance, courses in Production and Operations Management provided valuable insight into the latest technological development trends, with a particular focus on commonly adopted management practices such as ERP and CRM. While a course in Statistics focused on how to analyze the effectiveness of the latest software applications, another course in English Writing oriented me on how to organize and write a research paper, as well as increase my academic reading comprehension. Oral presentations in class on my current research progress also increased my confidence in having the necessary skills for the workplace. The opportunity to work at your company would provide me with an excellent environment not only to fully realize my career aspirations, but also allow me to apply theoretical knowledge management concepts taught in graduate school to a practical work setting.

◎During graduate school, I learned how to effectively coordinate others in a concerted effort. Another personality trait that I developed was the ability to earnestly complete an assigned task. Instilled with a deep sense of responsibility since childhood, I have applied the same attitude to laboratory work. As experiments must be performed in detail and sequentially, I carefully write down the details of experimental steps to be followed. When the experiment is completed, I compare the data generated from the experiments with those results anticipated beforehand. However, bottlenecks in research are common and I must remain calm. Otherwise, experimental failure will occur if I become too anxious and try to rush the procedure, which would ultimately reduce the reaction time. As I am particularly concerned with this happening, occasional frustrations during the experimental process are natural. Nevertheless, I remain perseverant until success is achieved.

◎My academic work during the first two years of university was disappointing. Determined to change this situation, I challenged myself to improve my grade point average by striving more diligently with a clearer sense of my future direction. Hence, for the next two years of university, I received an improved grade point average higher than 80. I also performed related experiments under the supervision of my teacher. Following graduation, I could not find fulfilling employment, possibly owing to my lack of a master's degree. I firmly believe that my subsequent graduate school degree gave me a clearer direction of which career path to take. My academic advisor encouraged me tremendously, especially when I encountered difficulties during the academic year. This encouragement made me resolute to overcome the rigorous challenges of graduate study. This explains my confidence in persevering despite the intensely competitive nature of this field of research. A closely knit research group spells success for productive work. With one strategy, individual tasks must be carefully deployed to each member in order to ensure that the overall goal is achieved. I subsequently applied a more responsible attitude to my graduate study as well as more concentrated research efforts. My outgoing character and aggressiveness towards completing tasks completely will definitely prove to be assets in any research effort that I contribute to, hopefully at your company.

◎To achieve success in the laboratory, I often exchanged relevant theoretical knowledge and individual expertise with other research collaborators. I also attended several international conferences that addressed biotechnology-related issues to broaden my perspective on potential applications. Graduate school equipped me with much knowledge and logical competence so that I can devote all of my energies to further advancing Taiwan's biotechnology sector. Significant advances in biotechnology significantly impact our daily lives, explaining why many biotechnology firms are beginning to explore not only the importance of bone marrow in stem cell research for eradicating diseases, but also the role of cell culturing methods and protein analysis. I am absolutely confident that my strong academic background will prove invaluable to your company's highly demanding product development projects as a researcher who can effectively respond to the latest changes in the rapidly evolving biotechnology field.

◎Graduate school allowed me to increase my intellectual capacity by reading the latest medical publications, conducting experiments involving medical imagery, consulting with experts in the computer field, and familiarizing myself with advanced computer languages. Despite the obstacles of my limited experience in these areas, I was determined to strive for successful results. In addition to learning the mechanics of writing a research paper, graduate school made me aware of what I lacked to function properly in the workplace. I firmly believe that research skills such as designing a study, evaluating data, and communicating my results orally are essential for medical researchers in this field. Graduate school thus refined my writing and presentation skills while designing a research project. The opportunity to work at your company would provide me with an excellent environment not only to fully realize my career aspirations, but also to apply theoretical knowledge management concepts taught in graduate school to a practical work setting.

◎I received a Master's degree in Biotechnology from Yuanpei University of Science and Technology (YUST), focusing my research on the cell signal transduction pathway and its regulation. I was especially interested in DNA, RNA, and protein-related studies through the use of novel analysis procedures. Specifically, my graduate research focused on the regulation of cellular calcium ion and nitric oxide with respect to protein kinase C in different cells, thus enabling the investigation of cellular protein expression. I was also concerned with how protein kinase C isoform and nitric oxiderelated, which could be understood by comparing them. My reserved yet determined personality makes me suitable for a career as a researcher, hopefully at your institute. Having acquired substantial experience in analyzing cell cultures and protein purification through a research practicum, I am naturally curious in unknown scientific phenomena that require further exploration. I bring to your company the same level of intuitiveness when approaching bottlenecks in research during the product development phase.

◎I received a bachelor's degree in Chemical Engineering from National Taipei University of Technology, where the departmental curriculum at university sparked my interest into various directions. I especially became interested in medical imagery and radiotherapy in tumors, particularly for curative purposes. Several years of academic study have left me with the deep impression that study is more than not just for securing employment. This motivated me to adopt a more meaningful strategy towards learning, especially how different fields can be integrated and further my knowledge of science. Given my above background, I feel equipped to serve as a researcher in biotechnology or medical technology-related fields, areas that your research institute is renowned.

◎Having received a bachelor's degree in Atomic Science and a master's degree in Medical Imagery, I am well aware of the theoretical and practical issues involving radiation. My undergraduate studies in atomic physics enabled me to thoroughly understand how radiation affects materials. Radiation dosimetry oriented me on how to measure an actual dose from any radiation source, e.g., photons, electrons, neutrons, X-rays, and gamma rays. Moreover, radiation protection allowed me to realize that while radiation is extremely useful, workers or even the general public should remain aware of the potential dangers to avert irradiation harm. During graduate school, I frequently attended several academic conferences and occasionally published research articles. This exposure allowed me to expand the scope of my research activities as well as grasp many helpful concepts on the latest technological trends. As a leader in this field of research, your organization will provide an excellent environment for me to build on my above academic experiences so that I can not only more fully realize my career aspiration, but also significantly contribute to your research efforts.

◎My graduate school research in medical imagery allowed me to grasp the theoretical and practical concepts related to this discipline as well as future trends. I once participated in a research group that conducted related experiments at the Veterans General Hospital in Taipei. In this project, physicians focused on researching topics related to functional Magnetic Resonance Imaging (fMRI), which left me responsible for most of the engineering portion of this project. Although extremely taxing, the project instilled in me a sense of confidence in meeting the rigorous challenges of such an undertaking. Although research of this topic initially began overseas, I was able to extend those results and make them applicable to Taiwan's circumstances. All MRI and fMRI instrumentation is operated from a three diffusion aspect to diagnose diseases in Taiwan's hospitals. My graduate school research enabled me to discern between a 360-degree water diffusion mode and a takeover water diffusion mode that occupies three times the amount of airspace. The integral diffusion value of a normal brain tissue was then modified according to a simulation program, in which the values were used to adjust the map of a normal brain tissue. In addition to enabling physicians to accurately diagnose diseases, the simulation program developed in my research can also determine the diagnostic values for patients. My advanced knowledge expertise in this area hopefully matches your company's product development interests.

◎While pursuing a master's degree in Medical Imagery Technology at Yuanpei University of Science and Technology, I attempted to understand the nature of tumors in patients, especially the role of radiotherapy in eradicating tumors. Results of my research were published in an international journal, thus contributing to ongoing efforts to more effectively treat patients with tumors. During my graduate level research, I strengthened my fundamental knowledge of radiotherapy principles, including radiation physics, estimate-related topics, radiation curative physics, and nuclear medicine. Nevertheless, I am still unfamiliar with many aspects of this field. I am especially interested in modifying and improving upon current radiotherapy of tumors. This explains why I am eager to join your research institute, an organization that has significantly contributed to this field.

◎My graduate level research in magnetic resonance (MR) focused on digital image processing in hospitals so that I will have sufficient expertise to contribute significantly Taiwan's medical sector in the future. Under the guidance of three associate professors in the Institute of Medical Imagery, I wrote computer software programs to enhance the images quality during radiological examinations so that physicians can accurately diagnose ailments. At the Institute, a distinguished professor served as my graduate thesis supervisor at school, while a physician supervised my research in a local hospital and also helped me to screen patients for the study's control group. After collecting patient data, I analyzed that information through calculations and sorted through a large volume of data to ensure that my research findings were significant and had clinical value. Specifically, my research focused on acute infractions of brain tumor patients. In collaboration with the hospital physician, we discovered that screening of acute infract patients can be achieved for no longer than six hours; the initial diffusion-weighted image (DWI) examination can be performed as well. Subsequent experimental procedures involve performing DWI on the first, third, fifth, seventh days and one month after examination, measuring the B value infarct region, analyzing the frequency in which B value curve changes, identifying the proper medication time intervals and, finally, determining the therapeutic impact. I firmly believe that your hospital will find my above academic and professional training to be a valuable asset in your highly respected organization.

◎Following graduation from Mackay Medicine Nursing Junior High School in 1990 and successful completion of professional nursing training from Chang Gung Institute of Technology in 1992, I began working in the Emergency Care Unit of Chang Gung Memorial Hospital. After returning to school and receiving a bachelor's degree in Healthcare Management from Yuanpei University of Science and Technology (YUST) in 2003, I later matriculated into the Graduate Institute of Business Management in pursuit of a master's degree. The above academic training instilled in me the importance of enhancing one's professional knowledge and clinical nursing skills. For instance, the Department of Healthcare Management at YUST exposed me to financial management, cost-benefit analysis, human resources management, quality control and marketing management. Additionally, the Graduate Institute of Business and Management equipped me with the necessary research and analysis skills to solve problems logically and independently. In particular, customer relationship management and knowledge management-related skills acquired in graduate school have enabled me to become a proficient manager. Given my above background, I feel equipped to serve in a managerial position in your highly reputed medical center.

◎An undergraduate degree in Medical Technology and master's degree in Molecular Biology have paved the way for a career in researching gene cloning, gene expression and protein purification-related topics in the biotechnology field. My previous attempts to more clearly understand a gene's functions and characteristics have allowed me to publish those findings in international journals. Graduate school greatly strengthened my knowledge and professional skills through unique opportunities such as participating in seminar training where I could both learn and express my opinions. Besides my acquiring strong fundamentals in medical technology and molecular biology, graduate school and subsequent research strengthened both my writing skills to publish my findings in international journals and listening comprehension capabilities to fully engage in collaborative projects with overseas researchers. I hope that you will find these valuable assets conducive to the needs of your organization.

◎Graduate school oriented me on how to integrate simulation programs with the Internet and related technologies, thus favoring a patient's outcome immensely. Graduate school also enabled me not only to grasp the clinical implications of different diagnostic tests, but also to operate medical instrumentation appropriately. These knowledge skills have greatly aided me in ensuring that a patient receives an accurate diagnosis. While the routine work of a radiologist makes life occasionally monotonous and uneventful, I constantly strive to continually improve myself on a daily basis. As medical technologies and related knowledge skills advance daily, medical professionals must build upon their already strong academic backgrounds so that their professions are more meaningful and productive, especially when designing an experimental study, evaluating data and communicating those results. I believe that the above attributes are what your organization looks for in research staff.

◎I majored in Medical Technology during undergraduate studies at Yuanpei University of Science and Technology, and later received a master's degree in Biotechnology at the same institution. In addition to providing me with a strong theoretical knowledge of medical technology, the departmental curricula also equipped me with fundamental laboratory skills to conduct graduate level research. In addition to the departmental curricula, I fostered practical working skills to familiarize myself not only with the demands of my professional occupation, but also potential employment opportunities in the rapidly evolving medical sector, hopefully in a renowned corporation such as yours.

◎My graduate level research focused on protein engineering, which includes protein purification and extraction, protein expression, and protein sequence analysis. In addition to participating in several international conferences before graduation, I also learned how to establish a comprehensive framework for laboratory experiments and, in doing so, learned how to achieve individual goals to satisfy my master's thesis requirements through a concerted effort with other collaborating researchers. My research has so far brought me into contact with experiments involving signal transduction, molecular biochemistry, and medical microbiology. Through such contact, I acquired an advanced theoretical and practical grasp of this discipline. Moreover, extensive laboratory training greatly benefited my ability to define specific situations, think logically, collect related information, and analyze problems independently - skills which your company will find most valuable.

◎Biotechnology will lead the way among other emerging technologies in the new century, with genetics playing a major role in this field. Employment opportunities in this field are nearly saturated, explaining why I am pursuing a master's degree in Biotechnology to remain competitive in the marketplace. This explains why I am determined to further refine my fundamental biotechnology-related skills, hopefully at your company.

◎Graduate school research in the Institute of Biotechnology at Yuanpei University of Science and Technology enabled me to perform experiments involving both fermented slot and enzymes. In addition to conducting experiments involving living creatures, such as in the sampling DNA and PCRs, I learned how to independently operate 50 liters of fermentation for the above slot. My thesis research topic focused on repressing germs to experiment with potential Chinese herbal medicine applications. This research equipped me with the fundamentals of undertaking microorganism-related research, hopefully at your research institute. Graduate school also oriented me on procedural techniques involving living creature experiments, protein engineering, microbiology and biochemistry. Specifically, I became proficient in food hygiene examination and experimental procedures on living creature techniques, such as fluid matter examination, food pollutant examination, gene transformation, and fermentation for the mass production of food.

I believe that you will find my solid academic background and extensive laboratory experience a strong asset for your institute's research group.

◎My master's degree in Biotechnology prepared me for the stringent demands of conducting original research on zebrafish and, then, publishing those findings in international journals. Critical thinking skills developed during graduate studies enabled me not only to explore beyond the initial appearances of bio-medicine-related conferences and delve into their underlying implications, but also to conceptualize problems in different ways. Studying at Yuanpei University of Science and Technology highly motivated me to acquire advanced biotechnology-related knowledge skills. I learned how to analyze problems, identify viable solutions, and then implement them. In sum, graduate school equipped me with a significant amount of knowledge and logical competence to effectively address problems professionally. Moreover, extensive laboratory training enhanced my ability to define specific situations, think logically, collect related information, and analyze problems independently. Given the opportunity, I will contribute wholeheartedly to your company's product development efforts.

◎I received a junior college degree from the Radiology Technology Department of Yuanpei Junior College nearly two decades ago and have, recently, completed a Master's degree in Medical Imagery at Yuanpei University of Science and Technology. This study equipped me with the required knowledge skills and professional expertise for medical imagery training, in which I acquired many professional skills. After receiving a junior college diploma, I passed a rigorous nationwide examination to obtain my license to practice as a radiologist. While upgrading my expertise as an operating technician in clinical practice, I learned much about the latest radiological approaches, not only those related to medical technology, but also those involving the proper treatment of patients, including chest x-rays, abdomen x-rays, angiography, computer tomography, MRI, and sonography. I am absolutely confident that my nearly two decades of solid academic training, experimental and professional experiences in radiology technology will contribute to your hospital's widely recognized commitment to provide high quality medical services.

◎My interest in biotechnology can traced back to when I was first exposed to physiology, explaining why I completed a master's degree in Medical Imagery with an emphasis on biotechnology. Biotechnology-related information is extensively adopted throughout nearly all global industries. While in the laboratory, I accumulated much bio-informatics-related knowledge. While pursuing a master's degree in Medical Imagery from Yuanpei University of Science and Technology, I conducted biotechnology-related research at the Animal Technology Institute of Taiwan (ATIT). Graduate level research prepared me for the rigorous demands of generating experimental results and, then, publishing those findings in domestic and international journals. The fundamental and advanced researching capabilities acquired so far not only nurtured my talent in approaching biotechnology through a multidisciplinary approach, but also widened my scope of interest in order to fully grasp the latest biotechnology-related concepts. Moreover, my participation in research projects that encompassed other seemingly-unrelated fields reflects my willingness to absorb tremendous amounts of information and manage my time efficiently. As an employee of your corporation, I will bring the same level of commitment to your organization.

◎While serving as a research assistant in the Institute of Environmental Engineering at National Taiwan University, I learned how to coordinate different aspects of a research project, whether it be filling out weekly progress reports, managing financial affairs, or organizing regularly held seminars and report contents. Research projects in air pollution at Tahsi and Linyuan Industrial Park in Kaohsiung that I actively engaged in allowed our laboratory to closely collaborate with National Cheng Kung University in Tainan. In addition to providing me with several opportunities to corroborate what I had learned from textbooks in the classroom, this project allowed me to extend my knowledge skills to an entirely different field to achieve innovative solutions. Intensive training in my area of research interest has built upon what I lacked previously in creating a scientific hypothesis, analyzing data and closely collaborating with researchers in my field. Your organization would provide me with the opportunity to further pursue my professional interests.

◎A master's degree in Medical Imagery enabled me to acquire sufficient expertise that my profession demands for me to contribute effectively to society. Both my undergraduate and graduate training stressed close collaboration among researchers, where I also became adept in adopting various radiation detection methods. While graduate level research focused on detecting contamination dose during clinical practice, I familiarized myself with the underlying causes of contamination dose, the extent of injury caused to humans and to the wide array of preventive methods. As radiation detection and protection are essential in medicine and industry to safeguard employees and the general public, I aspire to be a medical physiologist in the radiation oncology department of a hospital, such as yours. I am

Unit Describing academic background and achievements relevant
Four to employment
描述學歷背景及已獲成就

confident of my ability to plan out radiological treatments, as well as implement radiation detection and protection strategies during therapeutic treatment, thus increasing a patient's curative rate and decreasing the likelihood of radiation injury. Securing employment at your hospital would definitely allow me to fully realize my career aspirations.

◎A strong academic background in Chemical Engineering at National Taipei University of Technology provided me with theoretical and practical knowledge skills in chemistry. Owing to my lack of interest in pursuing this career direction, I recently acquired a master's degree in Medical Imagery at Yuanpei University of Science and Technology. Graduate study equipped me with the required knowledge skills and professional fundamental expertise in medical physics and image processing. The graduate curriculum markedly differs from my undergraduate training, thus offering many opportunities for me to enhance my research fundamentals. For instance, the theoretical and practical concepts taught in the graduate curriculum nurtured my ability to solve problems logically and straightforwardly. Additionally, the theoretical knowledge and practical laboratory experiences from graduate school were equally important in allowing me to foster my fundamental research skills. In line with my professional interests, the opportunity to work in your hospital would allow me to follow this career path in medical physics.

◎Owing to my deep interest in radiotechnology for therapeutic purposes, I am committed to pursuing a career in medical imagery, largely owing to its ability to diagnose tumors and offer subsequent therapy, both of which are essential to a full recovery. Graduate school equipped me with much knowledge and logical competence to effectively address problems in the workplace, even though I may lack experience of a particular topic at the outset of a project. My professional knowledge will be able to directly facilitate the recovery of tumor patients undergoing therapy. I am confident about my solid academic background in radiology technology will prove to be an invaluable asset to your hospital.

◎I received my undergraduate and graduate training in the Healthcare Management at National Taipei College of Nursing (NTCN). Highly theoretical study and intellectual rigor at NTCN equipped me with strong research fundamentals and knowledge expertise of the medical sector. I later gained entry into the highly prestigious Master's degree program in the Institute of Business Administration at Yuanpei University of Science and Technology. My logical competence and analytical skills scaled to new heights during two years of intensive training. Solid training at this prestigious institute of higher learning equipped me with strong analytical skills and research fundamentals. Graduate courses in Marketing and Statistics often involved term projects that allowed me not only to apply theoretical concepts in a practical context, but also to refine my problem-solving skills. Working in your organization would give a practical context for the direction in which my career is taking.

◎While pursuing a graduate degree, I learned of advanced theories in my field and acquired practical training to enhance my ability to identify and resolve problems efficiently. Moreover, closely studying business practices in the medical sector during undergraduate and graduate school has equipped me with the competence to contribute to the development of management strategies in order to efficiently resolve unforeseeable problems. Medical and healthcare expenditures for each Taiwan household skyrocketed 5.4% to 11.5% of entire household income during the period 1991 to 2001. This trend reflects that the life span and health concerns of Taiwan's residents are increasing. Therefore, community pharmacies must strive to make consumer purchasing as convenient as possible. Additionally, this increasing trend in medical and healthcare expenditure offers potential profits for Taiwan's community pharmacies. As a community pharmacy chain, your franchiser has distinguished itself in overcoming operational difficulties and maintaining good discipline to effectively manage its business units. If I am successful in securing employment at your company, my strong academic and practical knowledge, curricular and otherwise, will enable me to contribute positively to your corporation.

◎I received my undergraduate and graduate training in management fields at Chia Nan University of Pharmacy and Science and Yuanpei University of Science and Technology, respectively. These institutions of higher learning prepared me for the rigorous challenges of business management and the expertise needed to thrive in this field. Their solid academic training not only equipped me with proficiency in numerous analytical skills, e.g., the gray forecasting of the gray theory, data envelopment analysis, and canonical correlation analysis, but also nurtured my problem-solving skills. In addition to becoming certified to perform cardiopulmonary resuscitation (CPR), I participated in a research project during graduate school under the close supervision of my academic advisor on how to conduct research independently. My graduate school research often focused on applying mathematical models to acquire sufficient and detailed information needed for data analysis that would facilitate managers to reach optimum decisions. In sum, graduate school equipped me with numerous analysis and excellent logical skills to

Unit Describing academic background and achievements relevant
Four to employment
描述學歷背景及已獲成就

resolve problems in the workplace efficiently. I believe that your organization offers an excellent environment to further pursue this career path.

◎Having devoted myself to developing information systems in the semiconductor industry for over a decade, I have developed a particular interest in enhancing work productivity via use of the latest information technologies. I have also spent considerable time in researching system integration for manufacturing applications on UNIX-based systems. Critical thinking skills developed during undergraduate and graduate training enabled me not only to explore beyond the initial appearances of manufacturing-related issues and delve into their underlying implications, but also to conceptualize problems in different ways. Notably, I initiated an intranet project as a section manager at MOSEL Corporation. This responsibility oriented me on how to lead a team and thoroughly understand various software development processes. While participating in several MOSEL group projects, I also learned how to address supply chain-related issues in order to broaden my perspective on potential applications of finance and decision making; these areas are now my main focus of interest. I am confident that my working experience in software development will equip me with the necessary competence to accurately address problems in the workplace. Moreover, my project management experience enabled me to carefully deal with others and resolve disputes efficiently. My love of challenges will enable me to satisfy constantly fluctuating customer requirements in information integration projects, hopefully at your company.

◎Undergraduate and graduate level training in Healthcare Management and Business Management, respectively, equipped me with the knowledge expertise necessary for a career in a medical-related profession. While university instilled in me a solid theoretical and professional knowledge of the healthcare sector, the departmental curricula oriented me on how to solve problems logically and efficiently. In addition to helping me acquire essential work place skills, university offered a theoretical and practical understanding of the latest concepts in my field. As a university sophomore, I worked in a practicum at a hospital. During that period, I acquired many knowledge skills, such as how to estimate operational costs to performing assay tests. My undergraduate study definitely equipped me with the skills necessary to conduct research independently in graduate school. During graduate school, the Institute's curricula fostered my analytical skills and advanced knowledge of the business management profession. Naturally curious, I enjoy learning new concepts. I am especially confident of my academic fundamentals and related work experiences — all of which will enable me to collect pertinent research data and analyze problems independently so that I can ultimately contribute to Taiwan's medical sector. My enthusiastic attitude explains why I am determined to complete an assigned task completely. I bring to your hospital this strong sense of determination in order to apply my above experiences to your staff's larger goals.

◎My undergraduate study in the Department of Radiology at YUST provided strong research fundamentals and professional work experience in a hospital through a practicum internship, which is a prerequisite before taking the nationwide examination to become a licensed radiologist. A theory-based curriculum at YUST was followed with practical training in hospitals throughout Taiwan. Such training definitely benefited my original intention to work in a radiology technology-related career. Following graduation, I passed our country's intensely competitive civil service examination for two consecutive years, which qualified me for higher levels of employment as member of a public affairs staff. To continually build upon my solid academic training and remain abreast of the latest technological practices in the workplace, I took courses at Yangming University on management in the medical sector, our country's National Health Insurance scheme and finance-related courses — all of which oriented me on how to enhance work productivity and initiate innovative practices in the workplace. Course training enabled me to evaluate work productivity and personnel, carefully plan administrative activities, establish and implement new methods at work, and conserve overhead costs in materials and personnel. My familiarity with how to adopt different strategies for various purposes allowed me to transfer to a new position in which I was responsible for simplifying administrative procedures and effectively managing personnel. I bring to your company a wealth of academic and professional experiences.

◎I received a bachelor's degree in Healthcare Administration from Chungtai Institute of Health Sciences and Technology in 1998. The departmental curricula included hospital administrative courses that instilled in me a solid understanding of professional knowledge within the medical sector, especially internal affairs and public relations、as well as external medical policies and customer relations management (CRM). While working in a practicum internship for a medical supply company, I found an actual working environment to be much more complex than what I was taught in the classroom. After retiring from professional military service of nearly four years, I decided to pursue business-related issues by further attending not only several introductory courses, but also many conferences that addressed topics in this field. Moreover, I served as a research assistant in the Society of Emergency Medicine, R.O.C., which allowed me not only to see the connection between theoretical knowledge and actual commercial practices, but also to realize how results from academic investigations can influence governmental medical policies. Your company definitely offers an excellent environment to further pursue this career path.

◎After receiving my junior college diploma from Yuanpei University of Science and Technology in 2001 and then passing a highly competitive nationwide university entrance examination, I gained entry to the Department of Hospital Administration at Chia Nan University of Technology, where I later graduated from in 2003. Having majored in Hospital Administration for seven years throughout junior college and undergraduate school, I fostered an interest in statistics, logical reasoning, hospital information systems and medical marketing. I also maintained a high grade point average in those subjects. While preparing for the graduate school entrance examination, I audited a course in occupational diseases, as offered by another department. The professional knowledge skills acquired during graduate school further equipped me for the intensively competitive work environment of your company.

◎I received my junior college diploma in Nursing from Chang Gung Institute of Technology in 1994. While working in the emergency room of a hospital for nearly a decade, I acquired my bachelor's degree in Business Management at Yuanpei University of Science and Technology this past May. I particularly enjoyed departmental courses in Management of Consumer Relations, while my senior term project was on cost management. Undergraduate school equipped me with strong analytical skills and research fundamentals for advanced study. From my experience in the emergency room, I submitted a journal article entitled "Assessing the Needs and Satisfaction Level of Families of Emergency Patients: Case Study in a Teaching Hospital in Taiwan." This publication received considerable praise from peers in my field. Highly interested in this area of research, I recently completed a master's degree in Business Management at the same university and look forward to continue on this career path in a reputable firm such as yours.

◎I received a bachelor's degree from the Healthcare Management Department at Yuanpei University of Science and Technology (YUST) in 2003. The departmental curricula provided me with a theoretical and practical understanding of management courses, especially on how to accumulate statistics and effectively manage sales and financial affairs While gathering statistics and effectively managing financial affairs proved to be most helpful for me during university, I realized that they were not especially difficult after diligently studying the topic at hand if I only remained attentive or diligently reviewed different briefs. I am especially interested in researching business process reengineering, which is interesting for me because I can understand how a business operates or how a hospital may lose its competitiveness. How to effectively solve problems involving a hospital's competitiveness is particularly intriguing. I am definitely interested in this aspect of quality management, an area that your company has devoted a considerable amount of resources.

◎While my work experience focused on collecting data and overseeing workflow control on a production line, my graduate school research allowed me to develop a database method that integrates data mining and knowledge management approaches. I am especially fascinated with how machine learning, statistics and visualization technologies can be adopted to identify and present knowledge that humans can easily comprehend. Given my area of interest, I will strive to effectively use software development technologies to ensure that an information system performs optimally. Combining academic concepts with my knowledge expertise from previous employment will enable me to rise to the arduous challenges of working in the intensely competitive hi-tech sector for a renowned corporation such as yours.

◎I graduated from Yuanpei University of Science and Technology in 2003, attaining a cumulative grade point average of 3.5/4.0. Undergraduate school fostered my interest in studying business management literature. Humans are destined to interact with each other and develop skills based on those interactions. The university's departmental curricula oriented me on how to solve problems logically and foster strong analytical skills. In addition to helping me to nurture skills necessary for the workplace, university instilled in me a theoretical and practical understanding of the latest concepts in my field. As a university sophomore, I worked in a practicum at a hospital. During that period, I acquired many knowledge skills, such as how to estimate operational costs to performing assay tests. My undergraduate study definitely equipped me with the skills necessary to thrive in the intensely competitive business management profession.

◎I received my bachelor's degree in the Department of Medical Technology from Kaohsiung Medical College in 1989. University life exposed me to medicine-related courses on image physiology and radiology. While immensely enjoying these courses, I had difficulty in seeing how these different disciplines could be integrated.

For instance, how can medical professionals enhance operational procedures for patients diagnosed with cancer? Some diagnostic methods for patients are necessary, including nuclear medicine diagnosis, computer tomography, and magnetite resonance imagery. Owing to the limited four years of undergraduate study, I lacked the professional skills necessary for pursuing a career in radiology. This explains why I subsequently pursued a master's degree to quench my thirst for academic and professional knowledge to more fully realize my career ambitions. Graduate school is essential for achieving such a goal. Fortunately, many excellent faculty members were available at Yuanpei University of Science and Technology to share their expertise. Until now, I still lack sufficient knowledge of biochemistry, nuclear medicine, imagery medicine, cellulogy — all of which I familiarized myself with during graduate school. In addition to remaining abreast of the latest advances in medicine science, researchers strive to know in the utmost details of their profession. Therefore, besides the basic theoretical and research fundamentals acquired during university, I want to fully emerge myself in advanced experiments that require the latest medical science-related skills. As for my academic interests, imagery medicine is one of my favorite subjects. Modern screening methods allow us to detect many previously unidentifiable diseases, such as lung cancer, sarcoma, cysts, and pyorrhea. In a hospital, an emergency rescue team must closely collaborate with each other to ensure that lives are saved and also that they are performing meaningful work. As a medical technologist in a hospital for nearly a decade, I feel that routine work makes life monotonous and uneventful. Therefore, how to continually improve myself on a daily basis is a rigorous challenge. With my above background, I feel equipped to serve as a researcher in biotechnology or medical technology-related fields, areas that your research institute is renowned.

◎I attended many other professional symposiums and annual meetings not only to strengthen my knowledge expertise, but also to present my research results in oral and written form. The latter included learning how to express myself during a lecture and making Power Point presentations with respect to lecture format and harmonious colors. Having spent much time in preparing a smoothly delivered presentation, each lecturer had his or her own unique style, which I immensely enjoyed listening to. Having definitely learned from their presentation delivery, I look forward to adopting some of these techniques in my own presentations in a hi-tech company such as yours.

◎During undergraduate school, I wrote an academic article that evaluated the procreation of fetuses in relation to bone mineral density, which I later submitted as a poster presentation at an annual meeting in Kaohsiung last year upon the recommendation of my teacher. While designing the contents of this poster, I realized the painstaking process of publishing one's research results. Additionally, I assisted my teacher who also served as the editor of a radiation medical technology publication in compiling research articles for publication. My work involved sending acceptance and receipt notices of submitted manuscripts as well as typesetting and formatting before publication. Despite the tedious nature of this work, I learned many aspects of the publication process, such as formatting an article and writing references, which proved invaluable for writing my master's thesis and other academic articles. I hope that my strong writing and presentation skills will prove to be valuable assets for your company's product development efforts.

◎I firmly believe that desiring more things and achieving more things go hand in hand. A notable example is my grade point average during university, which was below the average of my classmates. For instance, although deeply interested in biochemistry, I couldn't comprehend how to analyze the life cycle in cell division, such as understanding how various metabolic mechanisms function during laboratory experiments. After successfully passing an intensely competitive nationwide university entrance examination, I gained entry into Kaohsiung Medical College and studied medicine-related technologies. Despite my eagerness to fostering my fundamental academic skills, I was unsuccessful in grasping theoretical and practical concepts taught in the classroom. I therefore opted out of taking the undergraduate school entrance examination and completed a junior college degree instead. Academically, this may put me at a disadvantage with my other graduate school classmates since I lack their solid undergraduate training necessary for conducting advanced research. Nevertheless, the academic goals that I established attest to my ability to resolve medical problems. Despite my undistinguished academic performance during college, I remain confident of the expertise acquired through rigorous training of medical-related skills. After graduating from Kaohsiung Medical College with a major in Medical Technology over a decade ago, I feel that I have not made much progress in acquiring the latest technological concepts in the rapidly fluctuating medical sector. Whereas I did not concern myself with upgrading my skills for a long period, graduate study re-ignited my interest in positron emission tomography, i.e., the most effective means of diagnosing malignant tumors. Pursuing a master's degree has definitely enhanced my career aspirations. The professional knowledge acquired from graduate school will also strengthen my intellectual capacity to give me a clearer picture of my career path, hopefully at your company.

◎My graduate school research focused on studying PACS-related principles and how they could be applied to clinical practice. Correlating theoretical and practical results allowed our research group to extend the existing theory and explore potential applications. Graduate courses in Program Design, Digital Image Processing, Radiation Chemistry and Seminar greatly added to my expertise in this area. Through graduate school research, I contributed to efforts to elevate the quality of medical treatment in Taiwan and its related applications. I hope to continue this line of work upon employment in your organization.

◎To supplement my current knowledge of radiology, I entered the Graduate Institute of Medical Imagery at Yuanpei University of Science and Technology. While focusing my research on radiation therapy, I reviewed pertinent literature and presented my findings in weekly graduate seminars. My graduate school research attempted to contribute to efforts to help reduce the mortality rate of cancer patients by investigating related prognostic factors and eliminating obstacles to provide the most effective therapy as possible.

◎Like AIDS, cancer has no cure. Whereas physicians can only instruct individuals on how to avoid cancer, its cure still remains unknown, thus making therapy extremely critical. In particular, my research addressed how radiology therapy can facilitate a patients' diagnosis and recovery. Once patients are diagnosed as having cancer, radiology therapy is deemed essential. I hope that my research interests match those of your medical center.

◎As a junior high school student, I enrolled in a vocational arts course, which developed my interest in electronic devices. Aware how electronic devices significantly impact my daily life, I enjoyed studying electronic circuits from that moment. Upon graduation, I went to a public high school, where I acquired much knowledge about electronic devices, including electronic circuitry packaging, electronic parts, theoretical fundamentals of electronic circuitry, television operation and maintenance, transceivers, radio operation, as well as amplifier packaging and maintenance. During that period, I also obtained much information on the structure and theory of IC digital circuits, tube structure theory, and circuitry design. This early training explains why I majored in Electronics Engineering in both junior college and university.. My solid academic training reflects my commitment to working in a leading company in this field such as yours.

◎I participated in the 2003 Conference on Health Management held in our university.

The Conference largely focused on three-dimensional image reconstruction and image transfer. In the first part of the conference, a senior manager from AGFA lectured on imaging transfer and storage. This informative lecture taught me much about the importance of the transfer speed and computer capacity for storing data, as well as recent development trends and the necessity of network matching. In the second part of the Conference, Professor Liu demonstrated the reconstruction of three-dimensional images, while emphasizing design concerns. He also compared the merits and limitations of various imaging reconstruction methods. In the third part of the Conference, the Section Chief of the Department of Medical Imagery at Tzu-Chi Hospital shared his experience with us on using the picture archiving and communication system (PACS) in a teaching hospital. The lecture highlighted the numerous benefits of a filmless system, among which include its ability to increase the efficiency of imaging transfer, decrease storage space, and lower pollution levels in the surrounding environment. An increasing number of hospitals are thus adopting PACS. The final part of the conference consisted of practical training in imaging transfer in the university's computer classroom. The short training course provided much knowledge on data transferal. The Conference was extremely informative and I hope to participate in others like it in the near future

◎While majoring in Nuclear Science at Tsing Hua University, I pursued further education in management after schoolwork out of my desire-to-desire related skills so that my professional aims would be more complete. As for extracurricular activities during university, I actively participated in public affairs, such as serving as class chairman and a delegate of the student association. These experiences allowed me to more closely interact and collaborate with others. However, student life did not seem to yield practical benefits after graduating from university. Feeling somewhat unprepared for the demands of the workplace, graduate school allowed me to further strengthen my knowledge skills in management, thus enabling me to more effectively apply my strong academic background in order to enhance my work competence.

◎Despite my undistinguished grade point average during undergraduate school, I strived diligently to learn in order to compensate for what I lacked in knowledge of course work. Specifically, I often searched for the most efficient means of resolving problems, depending on how familiar I was with the topic at hand. This attests to my determination to strive for completeness when tackling a problem. Owing to my ability not only to identify the untapped market demand for a potential technology application, but also to resolve problems efficiently, a professor invited me to collaborate with him in a research project. The ability to remain abreast of popular trends in my field allowed me to fully engage in discussion with my professor to understand what research results must be generated in the laboratory to yield a successful outcome. Thus, I was highly confident of my ability to significantly contribute to research efforts in graduate school. However, doing so required that I continuously increase my knowledge skills to become a distinguished researcher in my field.

◎My studies in Medical Technology at Yuanpei University of Science and Technology over the past seven years concentrated mainly on microbiology, biochemistry, and ABO blood type-related topics. Delving further into these topics necessitated that I conduct graduate level research. Conducting research independently in my field depended on my ability to identify the bacterial growth curve. The experimental results that I obtained allowed me to attain this goal. However, many bottlenecks in research had to be overcome before I made progress. I firmly believe that remaining prepared ensures success. In this area I must strive more diligently.

◎Moreover, I am increasingly in tune with the latest technological developments in my chosen field of biotechnology and microbiology. Pertinent literature and international publications markedly enhanced my creativity and overall understanding as I realize the importance of English proficiency. As English is the common language worldwide, especially for scientific publications and communication, my language skills must be further strengthened to remain abreast of the latest scientific and technological trends. Furthermore, graduate school forced me to adapt to new environments. Despite my initial reluctance and the occasional frustrations that I face, I am resolved to persevere in the hopes of becoming successful one day.

◎Making advances in science and technology has become highly competitive for my generation, as evidenced by the seemingly endless applications in daily life. While majoring in Food Science during junior college, I enjoyed a wide array of topics such as Microbiology, Organic Chemistry, Analytical Chemistry, Biochemistry, and Biotechnology. My subsequent undergraduate study allowed me to further explore my interests in topics such as Molecular Biology and Biotechnology. These courses exposed me to the dynamic nature of biotechnology developments, both practical and theoretical ones. My strong analytical skills and a high cumulative GPA attested to my ability to fully grasp the concepts taught in these courses. This explains why, following university graduation, I strongly desired to gain entry into a renowned graduate school program that specializes in this field because I plan to thoroughly research the above topics in order to determine my future career direction. As an undergraduate student, I acquired many practical laboratory experiences and even participated in a biotechnology project, which exposed me to the latest technological advances in this field. Among the biotechnology developments that I learned over the past seven years included microorganism incubation and fermentation, strains screening and mutation, DNA extraction, PCR, gel electrophoresis, PAGE, and PFGE.

◎Under my teacher's instruction, I participated in the Annual Meeting of the Food Science Association of Taiwan while in junior college by helping in the accumulation of conference papers to be submitted during the event. From this event, I learned how to submit a conference paper and present those results in a formal oral presentation both concisely and clearly. As a freshman in university, I also attended the Conference on Health Management held at YUST. During this event, I attended the session on functional components of soybeans. The lecture provided me with a valuable opportunity to observe how to effectively publish one's research results orally, including the logical format of the presentation, its deliberate delivery, and unique perspectives that are adopted in approaching a research problem. Besides attending research symposiums, I worked in a biotech company during summer and winter vacations, where I applied my solid academic training to a practical working environment in order to acquire advanced knowledge skills necessary for the intensely competitive hi-tech sector.

◎My cumulative grade point average during junior college and undergraduate school exceeded 80, thus ranking me within the top ten of my graduating classes. Having maintained consistently good marks in my coursework, I focused on acquiring knowledge related to food processing in junior college; whereas, in undergraduate school, I concentrated on molecular biology-related topics. While food is inseparably related to humans, the food processing sector in Taiwan has reached its climax and is somewhat on the wane. Nevertheless, I strive to remain in tune with popular trends in the food processing sector and hope to identify ways in which the sector can adopt biotechnology practices to remain competitive globally. As biotechnology is an emerging trend globally that continues to expand its influence at an astonishing tempo, I hope to enhance my knowledge expertise in this field. Through my research, I am optimistic that I can significantly contribute to efforts to address human health issues efficiently.

◎I graduated from the Department of Medical Technology at Yuanpei University of

Science and Technology in 2003. The departmental curricula provided me with technical expertise and knowledge skills that will be invaluable for future employment opportunities, as well as strong analytical skills and practical laboratory experiences that will greatly benefit me in graduate school. Undergraduate school provided me with much medical knowledge, especially hematology, microbiology and molecular biology. Work in a hospital practicum two years ago balanced my academic skills with practical experiences. As academics play a crucial role in our highly competitive society, I decided to pursue a graduate degree in Biomechanics in order to increase my ability to solve problems logically.

◎My academic performance during university is a notable example of my diligence. My teacher and classmates can attest to my ambitious, responsible and trustworthy character. Other teachers commented on my ingenuity as well. When assigned an experiment, I quickly generate a schedule, record data and then proceed with an experiment. I will apply this responsible attitude towards graduate study and research efforts that I am involved in. When unforeseen experimental problems may produce and cause delays, these problems can be resolved. Moreover, I am confident that I can contribute positively to collaborative efforts by my classmates in graduate school. In addition to coursework, my personal actions reflect my desire to be a high achiever.

◎After receiving a junior college diploma from the Food Science Department of China College of Marine Technology and Commerce (CCMTC) in 1997, I entered the Department of Biomedical Technology at Yuanpei University of Science of Technology (YUST) in pursuit of a bachelor's degree. In addition to my solid academic training, I acquired a license in Chemistry and Food Inspection and Analysis from the R.O.C. Employment and Vocational Training Administration. Additionally, I served in a practicum internship in the Food Science Department at National Taiwan Ocean University in 1996. I was determined to apply my biotechnology knowledge skills and practical experimentation capabilities to enhance my competence in the workplace. Graduate school subsequently equipped me with a larger global picture, which emphasizes the importance of being bilingual in both written and oral skills. Since my graduate level training at YUST up until now, I have prepared myself for a career in biotechnology research by acquiring advanced knowledge skills and technical capabilities, as well as strengthening my coordination and bilingual skills during graduate school.

◎Following junior high school graduation, I studied in the Department of Medical

Technology of Yuanpei University of Science and Technology up until my recent graduation from university. As an undergraduate student, I never imagined continuing with graduate studies owing to the difficulty in acquiring new knowledge skills. However, my decision to pursue graduate studies is largely owing to my experience in conducting a monographic study that involved applying transgenic methods to the study of zebra fish, which fostered my interest in this research field. In my monographic research, I was responsible for cloning the genetic sequence of SHMT, which is a zebra fish gene. Besides participating in the monographic study, I also participated in a school-sponsored symposium and practicum internship in a hospital. During this period, I fully realized the importance of biotechnology as well as my desire to pursue a research career. This explains why I recently completed a master's degree in Biotechnology at the same institution. My graduate school research focused on purifying and characterizing a trypsin inhibitor. Given the preliminary nature of this research owing to its originality, I often encountered bottlenecks while conducting experiments, such as in handling packing gel, purification or SDS-PAGE. I often faced questions such as "What are the underlying principles of these experimental procedures?" and "Which experiment should I perform first?" Despite these questions, my graduate level training enabled me to conduct research independently, particularly functional analysis of purification proteins.

◎I received my bachelor's degree from the Department of Food Science at Yuanpei University of Science and Technology (YUST). Owing to my aspiration to acquire advanced knowledge skills in microbiology and molecular biology, I also recently completed a master's degree in Biomechanics at YUST. My most recent research involved extracting bacteriostasis from Chinese medicinal herbs and producing cellulases from gene manipulated *Streptomyces*. The graduate institute's curriculum was geared towards biomedical science, which makes the experimentation extremely complex. Practical laboratory experiences compensated for my lack of background knowledge in this field. In addition to biological chemistry and microbiology, I researched topics involving immunization and bioinformatics. The graduate curriculum definitely prepared me for the rigorous challenges of a career in the biotech sector. I am especially interested in researching the ability of Chinese herbal medicine to restrain bacterium growth. In particular, my experiments focused on restraining *Candida*, *S.aureus*, and *salmonalla* growth, which require a considerable amount of knowledge expertise and patience.

◎I studied in the Department of Medical Technology of Yuanpei University of Science and Technology since junior high school up until my recent graduation from university. The departmental curricula not only provided me with a theoretical knowledge of medical technology, but also equipped me with fundamental laboratory skills to conduct graduate level research. In addition to the departmental curricula, I fostered practical working skills in order to familiarize myself not only with the demands of my professional occupation, but also potential employment opportunities in the rapidly evolving field.

◎As an undergraduate student, I never imagined continuing with my studies after graduation because of the difficulty in acquiring new knowledge skills. However, my decision to pursue graduate studies is largely owing to my experience in conducting a monographic study with Dr. Chei, thus fostering my interest in this research field. Dr. Chei's research involved applying transgenic methods to the study of zebra fish. I was responsible for cloning one gene sequence, SHMT, the gene of a zebra fish. Besides participating in the monographic study, I also joined a school-sponsored symposium and practicum internship at a hospital. During this period, I fully realized the importance of biotechnology as well as my desire to pursue a research career. This explains why I subsequently received a master's degree in Biotechnology from the same institution.

◎During my academic studies, I searched for the most feasible solution to solve the problem at hand. Avidly reading biotechnology articles is an effective way of answering questions about the human DNA and RNA. I owe my discipline to my parents whom brought me up rather strictly. This explains why I cautiously approach new circumstances with a deliberate and clever attitude. During university, I concentrated on maintaining a good grade point average with the intention of becoming a high achiever in the biotechnology profession. I did so by remaining abreast of the latest trends in this field. I occasionally become overloaded with information and feel confused if I forget trivial figures. In such cases, I need to restore myself through sleep after returning home late from the laboratory.

◎Ample knowledge skills acquired from my work experience greatly facilitated my graduate school research. Despite the rigorous challenges of academic research, my professional experiences reinforce my dedication to laboratory work and ability to develop pertinent research questions and experimental designs, which facilitate data analysis. I especially became proficient in areas of enzyme immunoassay (EIA), radio immunoassay (RIA), cell culture, saliva analysis, extraction of Chinese herbal medicine, and DNA chip technology.

◎While I majored in Radiology Technology during undergraduate school, the classroom provided only theoretical knowledge. I wanted to acquire clinical experience first hand, explaining why I worked in a practicum internship in the radiology department of a hospital. Among the different hi-tech instruments and techniques that I was exposed to include computed tomography (CT), magnetic resonance (MR), ultrasound, x-ray tube, mammography, as well as angiography and fluoroscopy. In addition to determining the actual size and mode of examination requirements and operating conditions, operating these apparatuses allows me to closely interact with and assist patients. Becoming competent in the laboratory makes me confident of my future prospects. I am fortunate to have chosen such a worthy profession!

◎I often attend symposiums and workshops to remain abreast of emerging trends in medicine as well as further enhance my professional skills. For instance, I recently attended the 2003 Conference on Health Management the first of November, which was held at Yuanpei University of Science and Technology. While attending a session on image transmissions, I not only made new acquaintances with professionals in the field, but also learned how to present one's research results orally and make a poster presentation. I was fortunate to attend this conference. As my graduate school research topic was "Anisotropic of Brain Tissue in Diffusion-Weighted Image (DWI)", I was fortunate to have the opportunity to present my research results in English both in written form and orally. A week later, I attended a seminar on quality control of mammography examinations, where I learned how to inspect machinery to ensure quality control and a medical image's quality assurance.

◎Questions that commonly arise in the laboratory are questions such as "How does one proceed with an experiment when there is not much available data to reference to beyond a certain point of the process?" "What are the theoretical principles behind an experiment?" "How can experimental procedures be implemented smoothly?" and "What happens if my experimental results differ from data in previous literature?" When running into above difficulties, I strive diligently to find solutions, whether it is through reference books or publications in the library, data from the Internet or consultation with professors knowledgeable of this field of research. I am aggressive in searching for solutions and identifying which method is the most feasible to solve a given problem. Moreover, I feel that my greatest personal strength is the ability to closely collaborate with others. For instance, I can quickly accommodate myself to different groups and actively engage in the topic that they are discussing. This allows me to interact well with others, as evidenced by my enthusiasm and sense of humor, which helps lighten up tense situations and make others happy.

◎As a graduate student, I studied more than I did in undergraduate school in order to enhance my knowledge skills and expertise in the laboratory. I often attended research symposiums with other graduate school students. These symposiums shed light on the latest investigations in my field and allowed people undertaking similar research to come together and share their results. Attending individual sessions within a symposium strengthened my intellectual skills by allowing me to form and raise logical questions. These are important skills for my own research and investigative process. Discussing my research in an online environment, such as a chat room for a specific topic, also allows me to increase my English language skills, thus allowing me not only to acquire more knowledge about my field of research, but also try to become fluent in another language.

◎As an undergraduate student, I adopted a strict methodological approach towards my academic studies. For example, taking exhaustive notes both inside and outside of class and then constantly reviewing them largely explained my success in class.

◎In addition to providing me with a theoretical knowledge of medical technology, undergraduate studies equipped me with practical skills for working in a hospital. Besides mastering routine tasks in a hospital such as identifying blood type, performing urine analysis and stool-related experiments as well as monitoring blood slides, the university arranged a practicum internship in a hospital focused on refining students' professional skills. Of the several practicum internships that I served in at several hospitals, I was able to integrate my academic knowledge and clinical skills. These practical experiences fully complemented my academic coursework.

◎While pursuing a Master's degree in Biotechnology at Yuanpei University of Science and Technology (YUST), I gained immense exposure to salivary research. As a graduate from both the Department of Medical Technology and Institute of Biotechnology at YUST, I received specialized training in medical education programs, including clinical laboratory experiences that sharpened my knowledge and professional skills. My graduate thesis advisor, a renowned professor from National Taiwan University, supervised my research while I received advanced training skills in his laboratory. The laboratory's high standards and heavy workload exposed me to many new knowledge skills and technical expertise. My graduate school research focused on saliva hormone assay, i.e., an emerging field of clinical diagnosis. Acquiring knowledge of advanced techniques in this area along with background information made me confident of my standing both theoretically and practically. Experiences and knowledge gained during my study for a master's degree definitely enhanced my knowledge of the field, hopefully enabling me to look beyond the role of assisting others in the laboratory to that of leading other research collaborators. The various seminars and conferences that I had the opportunity to attend broadened my perspective dramatically. Additionally, the research articles that I co-authored during my study made me aware of the value of research and reviewing of papers. Moreover, the many years in which I served as a technical assistant provided me with valuable practical experiences. In sum, I am in a better position not only to understand any changes that may occur in the field of clinical science, but also to find answers on how to resolve the problem at hand.

◎I have immersed myself in food science since junior college at Cha-Yi University. Upon graduation, I gained entry to the Food Science Department at Yuanpei University of Science and Technology (YUST) in pursuit of a bachelor's degree. While the Department focused on molecular biology and biotechnology-related topics, I delved into those topics to identify exactly what I would be interested in researching. Having recently emerged as one of the leading scientific disciplines of the new century, biotechnology will provide humans with elevated living standards through genetic engineering. This explains why I recently completed my Master's degree in Biotechnology from YUST. While majoring in Food Science during junior college, I enjoyed a wide array of topics such as Microbiology, Organic Chemistry, Analytical Chemistry, Biochemistry, and Biotechnology. My subsequent undergraduate study allowed me to further explore my interests in topics such as Molecular Biology and Biotechnology. My strong analytical skills and a high cumulative GPA attest to my ability to fully grasp the concepts taught in these courses. Among the biotechnology-related developments that I have remained abreast of during the past seven years include microorganism incubation and fermentation, strains screening and mutation, DNA extraction, PCR, gel electrophoresis, PAGE, and PFGE.

◎As an undergraduate student, I joined Dr. Lee's laboratory research, where I was exposed to a wide array of advanced microbiology and molecular biology-related knowledge skills. This experience exposed me to different aspects of a project, including the writing of a research proposal. Additionally, I participated in a hygiene investigation of fish for consumption in Hsinchu City. From this research, I learned how to design experiments, analyze experimental results, and become proficient in basic experimental procedures. Subsequently, I participated in numerous experiments in this area. In addition to identifying the peka that forms using the fermentation procedures conventionally adopted in Taiwan, our investigation also isolated yeast strains in fermentation. Moreover, while using the conventional approach to identify these wine yeast strains, our investigation also adopted PCR and PFGE, which are common molecular biology methods. The results of our research significantly contributed to efforts to develop a rapid yeast strain identification method. I am absolutely confident that my academic background and experimental as well as professional experiences in food science and biotechnology will allow me to succeed in your company's many collaborative product development projects.

Mary

Tom

Taiwan's medical sector

Chang Gung Memorial Hospital

Laura

bio-informatics-related knowledge

221

I Write down the key points of the situations on the preceding page, while the instructor reads aloud the script from the Answer Key.

Situation 4

_____

_____

_____

Situation 5

_____

_____

_____

Situation 6

_____

_____

_____

J Oral practice II
Based on the three situations in this unit, write three questions beginning with *How*, and answer them. The questions do not need to come directly from these situations.

Examples

How did academic study enable Mary to search for sources of problems?

By gathering large amounts of data to offer hypotheses for her research

How was Mary able to cultivate many friendships during graduate school?

By performing many experiments in collaboration with her classmates

1. _____

_____

2. _____

_____

3. _____

_____

K Based on the three situations in this unit, write three questions beginning with *Why*, and answer them. The questions do not need to come directly from these situations.

Examples

Why did Tom emphasize developing radiochemistry-related analytical skills as well as becoming proficient in conducting laboratory experiments during graduate school?

To contribute significantly to Taiwan's medical sector

Why would working at Chang Gung Memorial Hospital enhance Tom's previous working experiences?

Because his experiences would allow him to be a valuable asset to any collaborative effort in which he is engaged

1. _____

_____

2. _____

_____

3. _____

_____

L Based on the three situations in this unit, write three questions beginning with ***What***, and answer them. The questions do not need to come directly from these situations.

What can Laura trace her interest in biotechnology back to?

Her first exposure to physiology

What did Laura emphasize in her research while completing a master's degree?

Biotechnology

1. _____

_____

_____

2. _____

_____

_____

3. _____

_____

_____

M Write questions that match the answers provided.

Examples

What reflects Laura's willingness to absorb tremendous amounts of information and manage her time efficiently?
Her participation in research projects that encompassed other seemingly unrelated fields

What prepared Laura for the rigorous demands of generating experimental results and publishing those findings in domestic and international journals?
Graduate-level research

1. _____

    _____

    The Animal Technology Institute of Taiwan (ATIT)

2. _____

    _____

    Yuanpei University of Science and Technology

3. _____

    _____

    ABC Company

N　Listening Comprehension II

Situation 4

1. How can Mary make her life more meaningful?

A. by seeing fruitful results of her work

B. by remaining conscientious, flexible and focused

C. by collaborating with her classmates

2. What will allow Mary to see fruitful results of her work?

A. Cultivating friendships through employment in JKL Corporation

B. Continual self-improvement through employment in JKL Corporation

C. Strengthening her English language skills through employment in JKL Corporation

3. How did Mary perform many experiments as a graduate student?

A. by taking many unique leadership opportunities

B. by distinguishing between theoretical and practical applications

C. by collaborating with her classmates

4. What will determine whether Mary can contribute to society?

A. whether she can handle a heavy schedule and perform many experiments

B. whether she can broaden her horizons and become a high achiever

C. whether she can remain conscientious, flexible and focused

5. How was Mary able to search for sources of problems during her academic study?

A. by allowing herself to broaden her horizons and become a high achiever

B. by gathering large amounts of data

C. by making her life more meaningful

Situation 5

1. How did Tom increase his exposure to the radiochemistry profession?

227

A. by learning a wide array of theoretical concepts associated with radiopharmaceutical synthesis

B. by attending several international conferences on radiology technology

C. by becoming proficient in conducting laboratory experiments

2. What did Tom's research at graduate school often involve?

A. deriving complex models and modifying clinical practices to meet research requirements

B. responding effectively to unforeseen bottlenecks in research

C. acquiring sufficient expertise to contribute significantly to Taiwan's medical sector

3. What did Tom focus on during his undergraduate training?

A. medical imagery

B. radiopharmaceutical synthesis

C. nuclear medicine and radiochemistry

4. What will Chang Gung Memorial Hospital will undoubtedly find Tom's experiences to be?

A. proficient in conducting laboratory experiments

B. a valuable asset

C. able to respond effectively to unforeseen bottlenecks in research

5. Where did Tom learn a wide array of theoretical concepts associated with radiopharmaceutical synthesis?

A. at several international conferences on radiology technology that he attended

B. during undergraduate and graduate-level courses in radiochemistry and medical imagery

C. in the Institute of Medical Imagery

Situation 6

1. How did Laura nurture her talent in biotechnology?

    A. by grasping fully the latest biotechnology-related concepts

    B. through a multidisciplinary approach

    C. by pursuing a Master's degree in Medical Imagery at Yuanpei University of Science and Technology

2. What has Laura acquired?

    A. advanced skills in conducting biotechnology-related research

    B. fundamental and advanced research capabilities

    C. sound theoretical knowledge management concepts

3. What did Laura accumulate while in the laboratory?

    A. much bio-informatics-related knowledge

    B. a multidisciplinary approach towards biotechnology

    C. the ability to manage her time efficiently

4. In addition to providing Laura with an excellent environment to realize fully her career aspirations, what would working at ABC Company allow her to do?

    A. to absorb tremendous amounts of information and manage her time efficiently

    B. to generate experimental results and publish those findings in domestic and international journals

    C. to apply theoretical knowledge management concepts taught in graduate school, in a practical work setting

5. What reflects Laura's willingness to absorb tremendous amounts of information and manage her time efficiently?

    A. her work at ABC Company

    B. her participation in research projects that encompassed other seemingly unrelated fields

    C. her biotechnology-related research at the Animal Technology Institute of

Taiwan (ATIT)

O Reading Comprehension II
Pick the word or expression whose meaning is closest to the meaning of the underlined word or expression in the following passages.

Situation 4

1. Mary's academic study <u>enabled</u> her to search for sources of problems by gathering large amounts of data to offer hypotheses for her research.

   A. disabled

   B. empowered

   C. disenfranchised

2. Mary's academic study enabled her to search for sources of problems by gathering large amounts of data to offer <u>hypotheses</u> for her research.

   A. erroneousness

   B. fallacy

   C. conjecture

3. As a graduate student, she handled a <u>heavy</u> schedule, performing many experiments in collaboration with her classmates, thereby many cultivating friendships.

   A. cumbersome

   B. light

   C. transparent

4. As a graduate student, she handled a heavy schedule, performing many experiments in <u>collaboration</u> with her classmates, thereby many cultivating friendships.

A. individuality

B. autonomy

C. cooperation

5. As a graduate student, she handled a heavy schedule, performing many experiments in collaboration with her classmates, thereby many <u>cultivating</u> friendships.

A. deconstructing

B. nourishing

C. decontaminate

6. In graduate school, Mary <u>strived</u> to distinguish between theoretical and practical applications to understand the global implications of her field.

A. averted

B. avoided

C. endeavored

7. In graduate school, Mary strived to <u>distinguish</u> between theoretical and practical applications to understand the global implications of her field.

A. balance

B. discriminate

C. parallel

8. In graduate school, Mary strived to distinguish between theoretical and practical <u>applications</u> to understand the global implications of her field.

A. inhibitions

B. preventions

C. implementations

9. In graduate school, Mary strived to distinguish between theoretical and practical applications to understand the global <u>implications</u> of her field.

A. undercurrents

B. generations

C. placate

10. Moreover, her <u>academic</u> activities allowed her not only to strengthen her English language skills, but also to take many unique leadership opportunities that allowed her to broaden her horizons and become a high achiever.

A. recreational

B. extracurricular

C. literary

Situation 5

1. Tom's undergraduate training in Radiotechnology and his Master's degree in Medical Imagery <u>enabled</u> him to acquire sufficient expertise to contribute significantly to Taiwan's medical sector.

A. prevented

B. permitted

C. blocked

2. He <u>focused</u> on nuclear medicine and radiochemistry, with a particular emphasis on developing radiochemistry-related analytical skills as well as becoming proficient in conducting laboratory experiments.

A. scattered

B. wandered

C. concentrated

3. He focused on nuclear medicine and radiochemistry, with a particular emphasis on developing radiochemistry-related analytical skills as well as becoming <u>proficient</u> in conducting laboratory experiments.

A. masterly

B. amateurish

C. novice

4. Undergraduate and graduate-level courses in radiochemistry and medical imagery taught him a <u>wide</u> array of theoretical concepts associated with radiopharmaceutical synthesis.

A. expensive

B. expansive

C. corrosive

5. Undergraduate and graduate-level courses in radiochemistry and medical imagery taught him a wide array of theoretical concepts <u>associated with</u> radiopharmaceutical synthesis.

A. opposed to

B. related to

C. in contrast to

6. Tom's research at graduate school often involved <u>deriving</u> complex models and modifying clinical practices to meet research requirements.

A. opening

B. deconstructing

C. inducing

7. Tom's research at graduate school often involved deriving complex models and <u>modifying</u> clinical practices to meet research requirements.

A. sustaining

B. retaining

C. mutating

8. He also <u>attended</u> several international conferences on radiology technology, increasing his exposure to the radiochemistry profession.

A. participated in

B. skipped

C. audited

9. Moreover, intensive laboratory training enhanced his ability to respond effectively to unforeseen <u>bottlenecks</u> in research.

A. solutions

B. problems

C. resolutions

10. Chang Gung Memorial Hospital will undoubtedly find Tom's experiences to be a valuable asset to any collaborative effort in which he is <u>engaged</u>.

A. overseeing

B. organizing

C. participating in

Situation 6

1. Laura's interest in biotechnology can be <u>traced back</u> to her first exposure to physiology.

A. returned back

B. trailed back

C. switched back

2. In the laboratory, she <u>accumulated</u> much bio-informatics-related knowledge.

A. retrieved

B. retracted

C. collected

3. While <u>pursuing</u> a Master's degree in Medical Imagery at Yuanpei University of Science and Technology, she conducted biotechnology-related research at the Animal Technology Institute of Taiwan (ATIT).

A. acquiring

B. tinkering with

C. puttering

4. Graduate-level research prepared her for the <u>rigorous</u> demands of generating experimental results and publishing those findings in domestic and international journals. She has acquired fundamental and advanced research capabilities.

   A. feasible

   B. facile

   C. stringent

5. Graduate-level research prepared her for the rigorous demands of <u>generating</u> experimental results and publishing those findings in domestic and international journals. She has acquired fundamental and advanced research capabilities.

   A. extracting

   B. yielding

   C. retracting

6. Graduate-level research prepared her for the rigorous demands of generating experimental results and publishing those findings in domestic and international journals. She has acquired fundamental and <u>advanced</u> research capabilities.

   A. right-wing

   B. orthodox

   C. progressive

7. She has only <u>nurtured</u> a talent in biotechnology through a multidisciplinary approach, but also widened her field of interest to grasp fully the latest biotechnology-related concepts.

   A. cultivated

   B. trained

   C. secured

8. She has only nurtured a talent in biotechnology through a <u>multidisciplinary</u> approach, but also widened her field of interest to grasp fully the latest

biotechnology-related concepts.

A. different positions

B. different examinations

C. different fields

9. Moreover, her participation in research projects that <u>encompassed</u> other seemingly unrelated fields reflects her willingness to absorb tremendous amounts of information and manage her time efficiently.

A. divest

B. expose

C. covered

10. Moreover, her participation in research projects that encompassed other <u>seemingly</u> unrelated fields reflects her willingness to absorb tremendous amounts of information and manage her time efficiently.

A. unobvious

B. apparently

C. conversely

Unit Five

Introducing research and professional experiences relevant to employment

介紹研究及工作經驗

Vocabulary and related expressions　相關字詞

initially 最初地
unfamiliar with 對……不熟悉
medical instrumentation 醫學儀器的使用
work flow 工作量
colleagues 同事
deepen one's knowledge of
加深某人的知識
interpersonal skills 人和人之間的技能
collaborative environment 合作的環境
comradeship 同伴友誼
empathizes with 使同情
welfare 福利
dependants 受撫養者
empathy 移情
accurately diagnosing 精準的診斷
disease symptoms 疾病的症狀

recommended 推薦
preside over 負責
annual convention 年會
overseas tour 海外旅遊
proficient 專家
confidence in 自信
firmly believes 堅定相信
tedium 單調無味的
quality control 品質管理
essential 必要的
challenges 挑戰
determined 已下決心的
vocation 職業
assigned a task 分配工作
flexible schedule 有彈性的行程
crisis 危機

acquired 養成的

theoretical knowledge 理論性知識

clinical experience 開業經驗

enhance one's research capabilities
加強某人的研究能力

collaborators 合作者

merits 優點

limitations 限制

clearly define objectives
清楚地為目標定義

solid academic background
堅固的學術背景

problems at hand 在手邊的問題

committed to 對……承諾

deep concern for 對……關心

patients' welfare 病人的福利

pursuing one's Master's degree
攻讀碩士學位

feel overwhelmed by 被……征服

emerge 出現

collaborate closely with others
和他人密切合作

successful in gaining employment
成功的獲得職位

assess the quality of
對……的品質加以評價

enhance one's academic knowledge
加強某人的學術知識

strengthens one's knowledge, skills and
expertise 強化某人的知識、技能及專業
能力

student association 學生公會

fostered 養育的

communicative skill 溝通技巧

benefited greatly from 由……大大獲益

analytical skills 分析技巧

pursuing a common goal 追求相同的目標

data collection capabilities 資料搜集能力

hands-on experience 實際的經驗

administrative department 行政部門

corroborate 證實

inefficiency 無效率

colleagues and superiors 同事及上司

practical training 實務訓練

problems analysis 問題分析

data evaluation 資料評估

collaboration 合作

commend 表揚

excellent environment 優良的環境

graduate-level research 研究所等級研究

absorbed 吸收

adopted 採用

remaining optimistic 保持樂觀

increasingly competitive 逐漸競爭

perspectives 觀點

unique manner 獨特的方式

contemplative 沉思的

repair 修理

dignity 尊嚴

basic quality of life 基本的生活水準

negotiate 談判

Alice

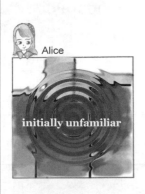

Max

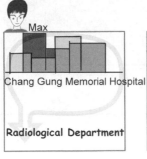

Margaret

A Write down the key points of the situations on the
preceding page, while the instructor reads aloud the
script from the Answer Key.

Situation 1

_____

_____

_____

Situation 2

_____

_____

_____

Situation 3

_____

_____

_____

B Oral Practice I

Based on the three situations in this unit, write three questions beginning with *How*, and answer them. The questions do not need to come directly from these situations.

Examples

How did Alice become familiar with the medical instrumentation, work environment and work flow that you were initially unfamiliar with?

By learning quickly and allowing her colleagues to help her to become more proficient

How is each individual to perform his or her task?

A strong sense of comradeship enables him or her to do so

1. _____

   _____

2. _____

   _____

3. _____

   _____

C Based on the three situations in this unit, write three questions beginning with *Why*, and answer them. The questions do not need to come directly from these situations.

Examples

Why did Max benefit greatly from his work at the Radiological Department at Chang Gung Memorial Hospital?

Because of the support of his colleagues

Why does Max firmly believe that quality control is essential for patients?

So that they can benefit from excellent medical services

1. _____

_____

2. _____

_____

3. _____

_____

D Based on the three situations in this unit, write three questions beginning with *What*, and answer them. The questions do not need to come directly from these situations.

Examples

What has fostered Margaret's communicative skills and ability to achieve accuracy and efficiency?

Her professional experience with the student association

What reflects Margaret's strong desire to identify the interests of individual collaborators while actively pursuing a common goal?

Her ability to use time effectively in meetings

1. _____

_____

2. _____

_____

3. _____

_____

Unit Introducing research and professional experiences relevant
Five to employment
介紹研究及工作經驗

E Write questions that match the answers provided.

Examples

What did Max represent at the hospital's Quality Control Convention?

The Radiological Department

What supports Max's belief that opportunities are presented to individuals for a
`
purpose?

His faith in God

1. _____

_____

The merits and limitations of various methods used in business, and the
need to clearly define objectives

2. _____

_____

Strong communicative, organizational and management skills

3. _____

_____

A flexible schedule that can be adjusted in case of a crisis or any need for
change

F Listening Comprehension I

Situation 1

1. How has Alice been able to use her empathy for patients?

    A. developing a collaborative environment among the staff

    B. by examining them thoroughly and accurately diagnosing disease symptoms

    C. by increasing work efficiency

2. How was Alice able to become familiar with the medical instrumentation at the hospital?

    A. Her colleagues helped her to become more proficient

    B. She acquired the theoretical knowledge she needed to combine with her clinical experience

    C. She developed her interpersonal skills

3. What did Alice's work expose her daily to?

    A. family and dependants of patients

    B. patients from all walks of life

    C. disease symptoms

4. How has Alice been able to enhance her research capabilities more effectively to help her patients?

    A. by learning quickly

    B. by examining them thoroughly and accurately diagnosing disease symptoms

    C. by acquiring the theoretical knowledge she needed to combine with her clinical experience

5. Why is Alice even more determined to serve sick people as an important part of her career?

    A. She empathizes with those in pain and is concerned with their welfare

    B. She considers her work to be almost a calling

C. She enjoys a collaborative environment among the staff

Situation 2

1. Why does Max believe that opportunities are presented to individuals for a purpose?

    A. because he benefited greatly from the support of his colleagues

    B. because individuals have the freedom to choose what they love

    C. because of his faith in God

2. How can patients benefit from excellent medical services?

    A. through quality control

    B. through confidence in their professional abilities

    C. the support of their colleagues

3. What did Max's colleagues recommend him to do?

    A. preside over all of the department's activities

    B. participate in the annual convention

    C. both A and B

4. Where did Max represent the Radiological Department?

    A. at the department's activities

    B. at the hospital's Quality Control Convention

    C. at the annual convention

5. What does Max believe that individuals should learn to do?

    A. benefited greatly from the support of their colleagues

    B. benefit from excellent medical services

    C. love the vocation that they have chosen

Situation 3

1. What has Margaret come to understand?

A. her strong desire to identify the interests of individual collaborators while actively pursuing a common goal

B. essential communicative skills in daily work

C. the merits and limitations of various methods used in business

2. What reflects Margaret's strong desire to identify the interests of individual collaborators while actively pursuing a common goal?

A. her strong communicative, organizational and management skills

B. her knowledge, skills and expertise

C. her ability to use time effectively in meetings

3. What has fostered Margaret's communicative skills and her ability to achieve accuracy and efficiency?

A. her solid academic background

B. her professional experience with the student association

C. her understanding of the merits and limitations of various methods used in business

4. What does Margaret believe is an essential communicative skill in daily work?

A. holding conferences

B. clearly defining objectives

C. understanding the merits and limitations of various methods used in business

5. Why does Margaret believe that carefully arranging a flexible schedule that can be adjusted is important?

A. to improve communicative, organizational and management skills

B. in case of a crisis or any need for change

C. to clearly define objectives

G Reading Comprehension I
Pick the word or expression whose meaning is closest to the meaning of the underlined word or expression in the following passages.

Situation 1

1. Although Alice has had several <u>practicum internships</u> at different hospitals during university, her current work is in a totally different area from the work she has been involved in previously.

   A. apprenticeship

   B. employment

   C. over time

2. Although Alice has had several practicum internships at different hospitals during university, her current work is in a <u>totally</u> different area from the work she has been involved in previously.

   A. partially

   B. absolutely

   C. entirely

3. Although <u>initially</u> unfamiliar with the medical instrumentation, work environment and work flow, she learned quickly, and her colleagues helped her to become more proficient.

   A. in the end

   B. at the outset

   C. on the outside

4. Although initially unfamiliar with the medical instrumentation, work environment and <u>work flow</u>, she learned quickly, and her colleagues helped her to become more proficient.

A. way of doing things socially

B. way of doing things in practice

C. way of doing things at work

5. Although initially unfamiliar with the medical instrumentation, work environment and work flow, she learned quickly, and her <u>colleagues</u> helped her to become more proficient.

A. collaborators

B. rivals

C. competitors

6. Although initially unfamiliar with the medical instrumentation, work environment and work flow, she learned quickly, and her colleagues helped her to become more <u>proficient</u>.

A. amateurish

B. novice

C. expert

7. <u>Interpersonal</u> skills are necessary in developing a collaborative environment among the staff and increasing work efficiency.

A. defensive

B. communicative

C. offensive

8. Interpersonal skills are necessary in developing a <u>collaborative</u> environment among the staff and increasing work efficiency.

A. synergetic

B. lone

C. autonomous

9. A strong <u>sense</u> of comradeship enables each individual to perform his or her task.

A. flushed

B. sensitivity

C. glowing

10. A strong sense of <u>comradeship</u> enables each individual to perform his or her task.

   A. strong-spirited

   B. individualism

   C. companionship

Situation 2

1. In March 2001, before graduation, Max began <u>working</u> at the Radiological Department at Chang Gung Memorial Hospital.

   A. screening

   B. laboring

   C. visiting

2. He benefited greatly from the support of his <u>colleagues</u>.

   A. target customers

   B. rivals

   C. co-workers

3. After three months, his colleagues <u>recommended</u> him to preside over all of the department's activities, to participate in the annual convention, and to make an overseas tour.

   A. opposed

   B. advocated

   C. objected

4. After three months, his colleagues recommended him to <u>preside over</u> all of the department's activities, to participate in the annual convention, and to make an overseas tour.

A. be aware of

B. be exempt from

C. be in charge of

5. After three months, his colleagues recommended him to preside over all of the department's activities, to participate in the <u>annual</u> convention, and to make an overseas tour.

A. every month

B. every year

C. every two years

6. These tasks <u>deepened</u> his knowledge of the disposition method and the interlocution mode.

A. stagnated

B. receded

C. further

7. These tasks deepened his knowledge of the <u>disposition</u> method and the interlocution mode.

A. temperament

B. feasible

C. motion

8. These tasks deepened his knowledge of the disposition method and the interlocution <u>mode</u>.

A. drop

B. method

C. association

9. In the following year, Max represented the Radiological Department at the hospital's Quality Control Convention, where he received first <u>prize</u> for his work.

A. restraint

B. demerit

C. accolade

10. This <u>accomplishment</u> greatly increased his confidence in his professional abilities.

   A. demission

   B. attainment

   C. renunciation

Situation 3

1. When assigned a task, Margaret carefully <u>arranges</u> a flexible schedule that can be adjusted in case of a crisis or any need for change.

   A. solicit

   B. lobby

   C. organize

2. When assigned a task, Margaret carefully arranges a <u>flexible</u> schedule that can be adjusted in case of a crisis or any need for change.

   A. malleable

   B. rigid

   C. strict

3. Professional <u>experience</u> with the student association has fostered her communicative skills and her ability to achieve accuracy and efficiency.

   A. green

   B. familiarity

   C. inexpert

4. For instance, holding conferences is an essential <u>communicative</u> skill in daily work, despite potential tedium and inefficiency.

   A. shy

B. introverted

C. extroverted

5. For instance, holding conferences is an essential communicative skill in daily work, despite potential <u>tedium</u> and inefficiency.

A. excitation

B. boredom

C. entertainment

6. For instance, holding conferences is an essential communicative skill in daily work, despite potential tedium and <u>inefficiency</u>.

A. incompetency

B. skillful

C. sufficient

7. Her ability to use time <u>effectively</u> in meetings reflects her strong desire to identify the interests of individual collaborators while actively pursuing a common goal.

A. ineffectual

B. inadequately

C. vigorously

8. Her ability to use time effectively in meetings reflects her strong desire to identify the interests of individual collaborators while actively pursuing a common <u>goal</u>.

A. clump

B. intention

C. clod

9. Such an approach <u>strengthens</u> her knowledge, skills and expertise.

A. toughen

B. exasperate

C. weaken

10. In particular, Margaret has come to understand the <u>merits</u> and limitations of

Unit Introducing research and professional experiences relevant
Five to employment
介紹研究及工作經驗

various methods used in business, and the need to clearly define objectives.

A. restrictions

B. restraints

C. virtues

H Common elements in introducing research and professional experiences relevant to employment include:

1. Introducing one's position and/or job responsibilities, beginning with the earliest position and ending with the most recent one

2. Describing acquired knowledge, skills and/or leadership qualities

In the space below, introduce your research and/or professional experiences.

_____

_____

_____

_____

_____

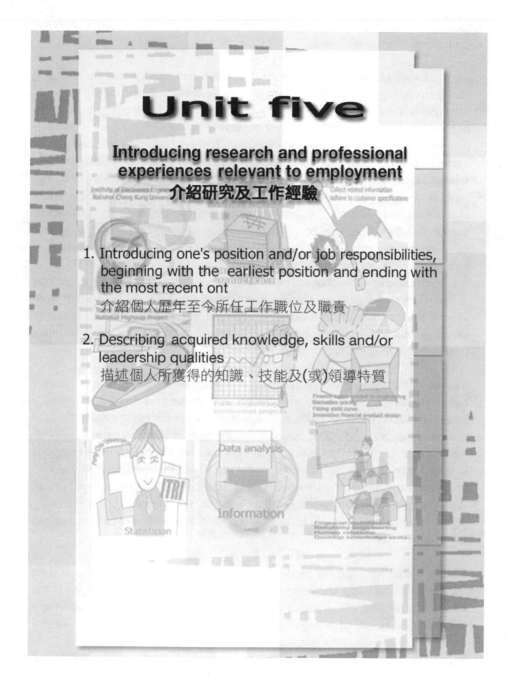

Unit five

Introducing research and professional experiences relevant to employment
介紹研究及工作經驗

1. Introducing one's position and/or job responsibilities, beginning with the earliest position and ending with the most recent ont
   介紹個人歷年至今所任工作職位及職責

2. Describing acquired knowledge, skills and/or leadership qualities
   描述個人所獲得的知識、技能及(或)領導特質

Look at the following examples of introducing one's professional and/or research experiences.

◎As a graduate student, I acquired much theoretical and practical training at Chang Gung University during the summer and winter breaks. Such training not only strengthened my resolve to remain abreast of the latest advances in this rapidly evolving field, but will definitely benefit my career direction. Serving as a research assistant in the Institute of Biotechnology of Yuanpei University of Science and Technology, I had many opportunities to come into close contact with biotechnology-related topics in different forms, including laboratory experiments, weekly progress reports, and regularly held seminars. I found those experiences to be highly stimulating and rewarding. Given my past academic performance and recent laboratory experiences, I am confident of my ability to significantly contribute to your research team's current efforts. Practical laboratory experiences corroborated what I had learned from textbooks and even extended my knowledge expertise. Equipped with such valuable experiences to become an adept researcher in the biotechnology sector, I am confident that the above experiences enhanced my skills which were lacking previously, such as evaluating data and collaborating within a research group. As a member of your company, I believe that these skills will prove most helpful in your research endeavors.

◎Intense laboratory and theoretical training in a hospital during the summer vacation before my senior year in undergraduate school motivated my decision to pursue a career in biotechnology research and remain abreast of the latest developments in this rapidly evolving field. The occasional frustrations of slow progress in research have strengthened my resolve to excel in the laboratory, making me more tenacious in spirit. Laboratory research definitely nurtured my skills that were previously lacking in experimental design, data evaluation and collaboration within a research group. Working in your company would hopefully allow me not only to pursue some of my above research skills, but also to contribute to the overall welfare of patients seeking therapeutic treatment.

◎I worked while receiving my professional nursing training, enabling me to acquire clinical and theoretical knowledge simultaneously. As a project manager in the emergency medical unit, I strived to reduce material and overhead costs without sacrificing the quality of emergency medical services. With my graduate research focusing on knowledge management in emergency medical units to facilitate knowledge sharing, I strive to apply those research findings to my current work requirements in order to upgrade my professional skills. This explains why I was recognized recently for leading the best emergency unit in our hospital. Besides my background in the nursing profession, I strive constantly to integrate my substantial management experiences with theoretical knowledge of science, making me more adept in making the correct strategic decisions in our hospital's emergency medical unit. If given the opportunity to work in your organization, I am confident of my ability to significantly contribute to your efforts to elevate the quality of healthcare management.

◎During my summer and winter breaks during university, I worked in a practicum at Mackay Memorial Hospital, as a research assistant at Dr. Chip Biotechnology Company, and also received intensive laboratory and theoretical training in biotechnology research at National Taiwan University College of Medicine. Despite the occasional frustrations of setbacks in my research, these experiences sharpened my observational skills in the laboratory, subsequently making me more perseverant in my efforts. While laboratory work familiarized me with use of advanced experimental procedures, I assumed an increasing amount of responsibility in the laboratory as I gradually learned how to conduct research independently. Hands-on experience in the laboratory provided me with numerous opportunities to apply textbook knowledge in a practical context. While closely collaborators with others to achieve desired research results, I learned how to evaluate a wide array of issues in biotechnology, molecular biology, medicine and even societal concerns. The opportunity to work at your company would allow me to hopefully contribute to the development of the latest biotechnology products by building upon my previous working experiences, hopefully furthering your company to unprecedented levels of growth.

◎Understanding the theoretical and practical concepts of radiation technology has allowed me to more easily adjust to the workplace. For instance, while working in a practicum internship in a hospital, I learned how to apply academic theory to perform an x-ray examination for the first time; I also learned of its value in clinical medicine. Upon completion of my undergraduate studies, I worked in a hospital to become a radiotechnologist. During that period, I conducted many clinical experiments. Although coming into contact with patients was initially a frightening experience, I gradually became accustomed to interacting with them. I later became involved in researching more advanced applications of clinical medicine. For instance, I felt a sense of achievement in my ability to identify lesions from x-ray films, which enabled physicians to diagnose illnesses and increase the prognosis rate for patients. If successful in securing employment at your hospital, I will strive to enhance my research capabilities and professional knowledge even further.

◎Since completing a Bachelor's degree in Radiology Technology and Master's degree in Medical Imagery from Yuanpei University of Science and Technology, I have worked as a radiology technician in a hospital's radiology department, which combines the use digital technologies and the Internet. The technical staff must adhere to stringent requirements when processing medical images for hospitals and medical instrumentation companies. Since vocational school up until graduate studies, I gradually improved upon my laboratory skills and knowledge of medical image processing by studying diligently. Interacting with the highly skilled professionals of your company will provide me with an excellent research environment, advanced equipment and related resources to enhance my research capabilities so that I can thrive in this dynamic profession.

◎As for my professional experiences, I have acquired much knowledge of molecular biology-related methods, especially with respect to the physiological functions of an organism and the DNA transition RNA process. Given my advanced knowledge of the latest biotechnology trends, I gradually assumed a leadership role in several research groups. Capable of objectively handling problems with an open mind of various alternatives to resole them, I absorbed the perspectives of other research collaborators. Besides, performing experiments allowed me to nurture my logical thinking skills by acquiring hands-on experience in a laboratory setting. Such a setting provided me with numerous opportunities to corroborate what I had learned from textbooks and, then, extend that knowledge to an independent search for innovative solutions. Given the way in which my vast laboratory experience allowed me to think independently and possess a responsible attitude towards work, I believe that your company will find my professional knowledge of biotechnology as a valuable asset to your innovative product research efforts.

◎After receiving my bachelor's degree and license as a radiotechnologist, I started working in the Radiology Department of the Veterans General Hospital in Taipei, where I received two years of rigorous training on how to operate the picture archive connective system (PACS), an advanced technology that combines radiation technology, digital networks, the Internet and clinical medicine. I am encouraged that my professional interests match your organization's direction in providing quality medical services.

◎I have acquired substantial work experience in my field over the past five years. During undergraduate school, I served as a research assistant in a biotechnology company. Among the many technology-related skills I learned involved DNA, RNA and protein chip manufacturing. I also learned of the underlying theoretical concepts that make product research possible. I also had the opportunity to serve as a medical technician in a hospital, which involved examining advanced medical technologies and performing clinical diagnosis. While at the hospital, I worked in outpatient services, responsible for administering urine, blood and stool examinations. I also participated in a cancer research project within the hospital, which made me proficient in using many cancer prognosis methods. Additionally, serving as a research assistant in several National Science Council-sponsored biotechnology projects oriented me on how a research laboratory should run smoothly, including weekly progress reports and regularly held seminars. I found this work highly stimulating and rewarding. Given my past academic performance and recent laboratory experiences, I am highly motivated to pursue a career in biotechnology research, hopefully at your company.

◎My enclosed curriculum vitae reflects extensive cell culture experience in the biotechnology field. After receiving a Master's degree in Biotechnology from Yuanpei University of Science and Technology, I worked in the product research division of a biotechnology firm. After rising from biotechnology assistant to departmental manager over a three year period, I was promoted to assistant manager of the genetic engineering department, becoming, adept in gathering information, evaluating data, and developing cell culture-related skills. The occasional frustrations of progress in research strengthened my resolve to excel in the laboratory. Additionally, I refined my ability to resolve bottlenecks in research, which required not only absorbing the perspectives of other research collaborators, but also learning how to think independently and deliberately. Extensive laboratory work also exposed me to advanced experimental techniques and significantly improved my analytical skills and data collection capabilities. I believe that your company will find the above work experiences to be a valuable asset to any research effort that I belong to.

◎Following university graduation in 2000, I began working in a hospital clinical laboratory, where I was largely responsible for collecting blood for diagnostic purposes. I eventually learned how to draw blood, a difficult task since the blood vessels of patients vary in size depending on their pathological state. I occasionally had to rely on my medical knowledge or intuition when having difficulty in locating a patient's blood vessel to draw blood. Then, for distribution of the blood specimens, I had to properly use different examination items such as assay tubes. Importantly, distribution of blood specimens into the wrong assay tubes would invalidate the analysis report. For example, examination items for serum-immunology and biochemistry must be sampled into the red bottle cap of the analysis tube since the entire blood clot must be centrifuged to obtain the serum specimen. Additionally, examining the hematological parameters requires sampling the blood specimen in a purple bottle cap of the analysis tube, which has an anti-coagulating agent that can enable a cell count of all of the blood making cells. Moreover, examining blood sugar requires using a gray cap bottle of the analysis tube, which contains NaF that avoids reduction of the sugar levels. In handling all of these assignments, I was initially assisted and supervised until I could do so independently. Notably, advanced instrumentation now allows laboratory technicians to obtain blood profiles and hematological parameters automatically.

◎Reliability of analysis results in a clinical laboratory must be confirmed, requiring that I am knowledgeable of the normal and pathological range of various hematological parameters. Such knowledge at work often required adding comments to automated reports so that a physician could accurately diagnose a patient's predicament. In contrast, laboratory work also required performing urine assays, which were easier to do so than blood sampling. The urine strip could analyze nine of the examination items, providing the urine chemistry data in only two minutes. Additionally, urine sediment assay had to be performed via microscopic examination to observe the urine components after centrifuging. Those components include cells, bacteria, yeasts, crystals, cast, and parasites. In sum, working as a clinical laboratory technician allowed me not only to contribute to the accurate diagnosis of illnesses, but also to appreciate the value of having a healthy life. Through the acquired technical skills of sampling and obtaining different samples to facilitate an accurate diagnosis of a particular disease or illness, I feel that I am well equipped for your hospital's challenging environment.

◎After completing our country's compulsory military service of nearly two years, I started working in an information-integrated company to start my career. The company's comprehensive operations broadened my horizons as to the dynamics of working in the hi-tech sector. I first learned how to maintain hardware, construct a network and, finally, learn the principles of how an information system is manufactured. Moreover, I participated in several MES projects on ensuring the software quality and bringing a new system to the production line. In addition to nurturing my problem-solving and basic knowledge skills in software engineering, this working experience exposed me to the complexity of interacting with individuals in an intensely competitive environment. I later served in the MIS Department of a semi-conductor manufacturer, coming into contact with the latest information systems at that time. After striving diligently to familiarize myself with the latest information technologies, e.g., programming skills, database management and UNIX environment, I was later promoted to section manager in 1999. While working in the semiconductor company, I not only kept the MIS system running smoothly without any crashes, but also expanded the system capacity to satisfy user's requests and reduce overhead costs. Based on principles of efficient development, easy maintenance, stable operations, and low operational costs, I spent half a year in developing a new Intranet system for the company. The software development of this Intranet exposed me to both objective-oriented analysis (OOA) and objective-oriented programming (OOP); I also became proficient in adopting related methods. After leaving the semiconductor industry, I began working for an information-integrated company again. As a project manager, I was responsible for performing systems analysis and negotiating with clients. More than integrating information technologies in the company through software development, I had to refine my interpersonal skills so that I could effectively lead a development team and achieve on-time delivery of our company's products and services.

◎Following graduation from Yuanpei University of Science and Technology (YUST) in 1991, I began working in a hospital. The solemn and occasionally depressing environment of the hospital left me uncomfortable with ill patients constantly waiting for treatment. After deciding to leave this environment, I prepared diligently for the governmental civil service examination, which subsequently qualified me for an administrative management position in the medical sector. With my lack of practical experience in this area, I find the data analysis especially complicated, despite my proficiency in administrative-related tasks. To compensate for this limitation, I studied diligently while pursuing a Master's degree in Business Administration at YUST.

◎When my university department established a continuing educational degree program in 2001, I worked during the daytime and went to class during the evenings. Despite the difficulty of holding down a job and pursuing a bachelor's degree simultaneously, I acquired much professional knowledge in areas such as biotechnology, molecular biology, immunology, microbiology and hereditary science. This rich combination of practical working experience and solid undergraduate training motivated me to enroll in the university's Master's degree program in Biotechnology in the fall of 2003.

◎After passing a nationwide examination that certifies professional radiation technologists, I obtained my license in diagnosis radiation, radiotherapy and nuclear medicine. After obtaining the license, I began working in the Radiation Department at Veterans General Hospital in Taipei, where I received rigorous training for two years on how to operate the picture archive connective system (PACS).

◎I worked in the Radiology Department of Zen Chi Hospital in 1997 as my first place of employment. Among the numerous skills I acquired while working there included operating bedside portable machinery, computer tomography (CT) and mammography. Although leaving the hospital a year later to pursue undergraduate studies, I continued working part time in a clinical practicum internship at Chun Pai Hospital. In addition to closely collaborating with other colleagues, I learned how to operate radiology diagnostic equipment and employ the latest radiation technologies. Upon completing my bachelor's degree, I gained entry into the Radiology Department of Taipei Veteran's General Hospital. While there, I learned how to care for critical patients and how to take professional x-ray films for emergency patients. I especially became familiar with picture archive communicating system (PACS), an advanced technology that combines radiation technology, digital networks, the Internet and clinical medicine. Via a light cable, PACS can connect local hospitals with those abroad, as well as transfer medical imagery and a patient's medical history and examination data. As a fundamental aspect of medical imagery, this technology played a pivotal role in my subsequent graduate school research.

◎As a medical professional, I am especially interested in processing and analyzing medical images of acute stroke patients. My work involves standardizing data for this stroke type so that physicians have sufficient information for patient consultation and therapeutic treatment. I must also measure the infarct field range within the order of severity level melt to ensure that acute infarct stroke patients can receive optimum treatment efficiently. Following appropriate therapy, patients can slowly recover and live independently once again. Research scholars will expand on previous results obtained from data of acute stroke patients and attempt to understand the implications for other diseases. For providing high quality diagnosis and treatment of stroke patients, your hospital has among the most advanced instrumentation in Asia. Your hospital has distinguished itself as well for providing a high degree of success in curative treatment for this unique population I believe that you will find that my professional experience and knowledge skills can easily blend into your professional team that is dedicated to producing accurate medical images for diagnostic purposes.

◎As for professional experience, I worked in a practicum at Shin Kong Wu Ho-Su Memorial Hospital. While this work offered many practical experiences, I became fascinated with how the Internet impacts all aspects of modern marketing. I also worked in the administrative unit of a hospital for my practicum internship during university. This valuable work experience provided me with a theoretical and practical understanding of hospital administrative occupations, especially in human relations and hospital development strategies. Additionally, I participated in a project aimed at planning a health-based community activity. During this period, I became fascinated with how to effectively plan and implement activities.

◎I participated in a non-profit scouting organization during the summer vacation before my final year in university. Responsible mainly for coordinating activities, I considered what the scouts were interested in and then those costs versus our allocated budget. Following agreement by all of the members, the plan was implemented harmoniously. The experience instilled in me the importance of planning in the early stages incorporation of all members' opinions in order to spur creativity. Volunteer work in this scouting organization greatly impacted my life by making me more conscious of others' needs and aware of my societal responsibilities.

◎After graduating from Yuanpei University of Science and Technology (YUST), I began working in a hospital, which I found extremely difficult to adapt to when dealing daily with ill patients, regardless of whether they were cancer victims, road accident victims or suicidal patients. Fortunately, I passed our government's civil service examination and found employment as an administrator at the National Health Insurance Office, where I was responsible for analyzing and auditing the administrative expenses of Chung Kun Memorial Hospital (the only medical center in northern Taiwan). In particular, our group analyzed the hospital's clinical expenses, ward room expenses, examination expenses (e.g., blood, urine, and sputum check), dietary expenses, X-ray expenses (CT or MRI), anesthesia expenses, surgery expenses, physical examination expenses, medicinal expenses, material expenses (e.g., syringes, intravenous hook up, and gypsum), and infant care expenses. Such a thorough analysis allowed us not only to identify unnecessary or unreasonable high medical expenses, but also to devise strategies to restrain the growth of medical fees. Inappropriate use of medical instrumentation or personnel strains available medical resources, ultimately lowering the quality of patient medical services. The analysis skills that I acquired in this hospital management-related position instilled in me the importance of uniformly distributing medical resources and seeking treatment opportunities that promote equality among all segments of society, thus ensuring that patients receive quality medical services.

◎My work as an administrative assistant in a construction company in Puli of central Taiwan, following my graduation from business vocational school, allowed me to apply theories taught in the classroom to actual working situations. I then worked in a small home appliances retail outlet for three years, where I was responsible for the accounting. During this period, I pursued a junior college diploma on the weekends. The devastating Chi-Chi earthquake occurred in Taiwan in 1999, subsequently displacing me from my work owing to the damage that my work place incurred. I participated in job training courses established by the government after this adverse event. Among those courses most helpful to me included Commercial pursuit dispatching and Internet archival design. Upon completion of the training courses, I began working in the health insurance claims office for the Puli Municipal Government in Nantou County of central Taiwan. I became especially interested in Taiwan's national health insurance scheme during that period, particularly how to enhance the overall scheme, reduce related premiums, as well as research not only its impact on the quality of medical services, but also help that hospital employees require to provide quality care to patients. Following a rigorous nationwide technical school examination, I gained entry to the Department of Healthcare Management at Yuanpei University of Science and Technology (YUST) and, later, entered the Graduate Institute of Business Management at YUST in pursuit of a master's degree. Numerous years of practical work experience have not only enabled me to closely interact with my peers, but also nurtured my mild temperament - skills which I think your company is looking for in employees who can yield an excellent performance in the workplace.

◎After graduating from Chung Jen Vocational High School of Nursing and Midwifery, I started working in an administrative position of an after school program to prepare students for the nationwide nursing college examination. After passing an intensely competitive examination, I gained entry to Fooyin University of Science and Technology (FUST). A year later, I worked part time in the FUST library, where I acquired more professional experiences and learned how to get along with individuals from diverse backgrounds. Roughly a year later, I transferred to the personnel department, where I performed administrative work involving civil servants. During my three years at FUST, I worked during the daytime and attended classes in the evenings. After graduating from the Healthcare Management at Yuanpei University of Science and Technology and passing an intensely competitive graduate school entrance examination, I gained entry to the Institute of Business Management at YUST.

◎While I consider myself a generous individual whom can easily accommodate to a larger group, I occasionally lose patience and must therefore strive to be more empathetic. My job demands that I closely interact with others, explaining why effective communication and a congenial attitude are essential.

◎My three summer vacations working for the Fortune Information Company enabled me to participated in three different projects: the first as a scanner operator for documenting images at the Ministry of Education, second as a technician responsible for quality control of document images at the National Science Council (NSC), and third as a project leader to control a planning schedule, also at the NSC. As an undergraduate senior, I also served as a research assistant in a National Health Research Institute-sponsored project on analyzing glaucoma-related data with an oculist. While finding this work highly stimulating and rewarding, I realized how unprepared I was for the rapidly emerging analytical skills that are necessary in the work place, particularly multivariate analysis. This explains why I returned to university for a graduate level education. After receiving a Master's degree in Business Management from Yuanpei University of Science and Technology, I acquired substantial experience in dealing with complex business collaboration opportunities. I also learned how to adeptly apply multivariate analysis in actual situations. In addition to refining my ability to coordinate related activities, these experiences enabled me to face rigorous challenges of the management sector. I believe that practical exposure to the health care sector and educational research environments have nurtured my skills that were previously lacking. These skills will prove valuable in any future research project in which I am involved, hopefully at your company.

◎After completing our country's compulsory military service of nearly two years, I began my career working in an information integration company, where I first learned how to maintain hardware systems and construct a network, followed by orientation with the different functions of manufacturing-oriented information systems. I also participated in several MIS projects aimed at ensuring the quality of company software and bringing a new system onto the production line. In addition to nurturing my problem-solving and basic knowledge of software engineering, the complexities of interacting with other information specialists profoundly impacted my career direction. I then started working in the information systems department of a semiconductor manufacturer, where I came into contact with the most advanced information systems at that time. While diligently striving to familiarize myself with state-of-the-art information technologies, including programming skills, database management and proficiency in the UNIX environment, I was eventually promoted to section manager in 1999, a role in which I became adept in accumulating information, evaluating data, negotiating prices, and reviewing budgets. Your company will hopefully find my above experiences to be in line with your current information system requirements.

◎After leaving the semiconductor industry, I returned to an information integration company, where I was responsible for system analysis as a project manager. By assuming such responsibilities, I acquired a breadth of experience in dealing with complex management issues. In addition to refining my ability to coordinate related activities, I became highly adaptive to change, responsive to sudden fluctuations in user requirements, and flexible in acquiring diverse skills demanded in a competitive corporate climate. I still felt somewhat unprepared for my career, particularly with the unpredictable nature of rapidly evolving information technologies and modern management practices, explaining why I returned to university for graduate study. Having recently fulfilled my graduate degree requirements, I look forward to applying my newly acquired knowledge and skills as an employee of a globally renowned corporation such as yours.

◎Following graduation from Chang Gung Institute of Technology where I received my professional nursing training, I worked in the Emergency Care Unit at Chang Gung Memorial Hospital, I acquired many clinical nursing care and related technology skills. As a medical center, this hospital receives more critically ill patients than regional hospitals do. After returning to clinical nursing in 1997 after a break of three years, I completed my undergraduate studies and continued with graduate studies in the Institute of Business Management at Yuanpei University of Science and Technology. I most recently served as the head nurse in an emergency care unit, where I was responsible for coordinating personnel, planning and teaching a nursing course in critical care, maintaining medical instrumentation, conducting inter-departmental activities to streamline the hospital's operational procedures, thus maintaining nursing quality in the emergency room. In addition to my nursing license, I am also professionally licensed in advanced cardial life support, basic life support license, emergency trauma technology and advanced pediatric life support.

Regardless of whether I am teaching nurses or training an ambulance staff, my personal working style is one in which I set high goals for myself, yet remain lenient towards others. Strategic decision making skills, clear headed thinking, the ability to convey my concerns through effective communication with college, and confidence in myself — all of these attributes will allow me to significantly contribute to your hospital's committed staff of highly trained professionals.

◎As evidence of my solid work experiences, I participated in a project to assess the quality of a hospital's medical services. This experience enhanced my academic-based knowledge and significantly improved my analytical skills as well as data collection capabilities. The hands-on experience in a hospital administrative department provided me with numerous opportunities to corroborate what I had learned from textbooks and, then, to extend that knowledge to an independent search for solving the problems at hand. The hospital's practical training definitely strengthened my research skills in areas that I was previously lacking, such as problems analysis, data collection, data evaluation and collaboration within a research group. By placing a large number of responsibilities on my shoulders, this project greatly matured me as an individual. These skills will now prove valuable in any future research project in which I am involved, hopefully at your company.

◎My three summer vacations working for the Fortune Information Company enabled me to participated in three different projects: the first as a scanner operator for documenting images at the Ministry of Education, second as a technician responsible for quality control of document images at the National Science Council (NSC), and third as a project leader to control a planning schedule, also at the NSC. As an undergraduate senior, I also served as a research assistant in a National Health Research Institute-sponsored project on analyzing glaucoma-related data with an oculist. While finding this work highly stimulating and rewarding, I realized how unprepared I was for the rapidly emerging analytical skills that are necessary in the work place, particularly multivariate analysis. This explains why I returned to university for a graduate level education. After receiving a Master's degree in Business Management from Yuanpei University of Science and Technology, I acquired substance experience in dealing with complex business collaboration opportunities. I also learned how to adeptly apply multivariate analysis in actual situations. In addition to refining my ability to coordinate related activities, these experiences enabled me to face rigorous challenges of the management sector. I believe that practical exposure to the health care sector and educational research environments have nurtured my skills that were previously lacking. These skills will now prove valuable in any future research project in which I am involved, hopefully at your company.

◎I most recently served as the head nurse in an emergency care unit, where I was responsible for coordinating personnel, planning and teaching a nursing course in critical care, maintaining medical instrumentation, conducting inter-departmental activities to streamline the hospital's operational procedures, thus maintaining nursing quality in the emergency room. In addition to my nursing license, I am also professionally licensed in advanced cardial life support, basic life support license, emergency trauma technology and advanced pediatric life support. Regardless of whether I am teaching nurses or training an ambulance staff, my personal working style is one in which I set high goals for myself, yet remain lenient towards others. Strategic decision making skills, clear headed thinking, the ability to convey my concerns through effective communication with college, and confidence in myself — all of these attributes will allow me to significantly contribute to your hospital's committed staff of highly trained professionals.

◎My postgraduate school research often involved deriving complex digital image processing models, which I learned how to do so through frequent participation in related workshops. Interacting with other researchers in my field allowed me to remain abreast of the latest developments in this area. Given the rapid technological advances in this field, my graduate school research emphasized the feasibility of using various computer programs to enhance the quality of MRI. With most hospitals using X-ray film of inverted PACS type, the knowledge acquired through work with simulation programs in this area has enabled me to serve hospital patients more professionally. I am optimistic that my research findings will contribute to the efforts of hospitals attempting to more fully serve their patients. As a member of your organization's highly qualified staff, I look forward to bringing my above research expertise to your hospital.

I Write down the key points of the situations on the
preceding page, while the instructor reads aloud the
script from the Answer Key.

Situation 4

_____

_____

_____

Situation 5

_____

_____

_____

Situation 6

_____

_____

_____

J Oral practice II

Based on the three situations in this unit, write three questions beginning with **Why**, and answer them. The questions do not need to come directly from these situations.

Examples

Why has Bill's colleagues and superiors commended him many times on your responsible attitude?

Because of his deep concern for patients' welfare

Why is Bill similar to most medical professionals?

Because he feels overwhelmed by the rapid rate at which new medical technologies emerge, and are adopted by hospitals

1. _____

   _____

2. _____

   _____

3. _____

   _____

K Based on the three situations in this unit, write three questions beginning with **How**, and answer them. The questions do not need to come directly from these situations.

Examples

How was Teresa able to enhance her academic knowledge and significantly improve your analytical skills and data collection capabilities?

By participating in a project to assess the quality of a hospital's medical services

How was Teresa able to corroborate what she had learned from textbooks?

From her hands-on experience in a hospital administrative department

1. _____

_____

2. _____

_____

3. _____

_____

L Based on the three situations in this unit, write three questions beginning with **What**, and answer them. The questions do not need to come directly from these situations.

Examples

What provided an excellent environment for conducting graduate-level research?

Ton-Yen General Hospital

What further developed May's professional skills and taught her how to collaborate closely with others?

Her work experience

1. _____

_____

2. _____

_____

3. _____

_____

M Write questions that match the answers provided.

Examples

What definitely strengthened Teresa's research skills in areas where she was previously lacking?

The hospital's practical training

How did the project greatly mature Teresa as an individual?

By requiring her to meet many responsibilities

1. _____

_____

Learn as much as possible while contributing any beneficial results that can be generated by research at her workplace

2. _____

_____

How carefully to negotiate with others, while maintaining the dignity of each collaborator

3. _____

_____

In her unique manner

N Listening Comprehension II

Situation 4

1. Why does Bill want to continually increase his expertise?

   A. to remain optimistic when interacting with others

   B. to ensure that his patients can maintain a basic quality of life

   C. to repair nuclear medicine machinery

2. Why has Bill's colleagues and superiors commended him many times on his responsible attitude?

   A. commitment to his many patients

   B. knowledge of how to repair nuclear medicine machinery

   C. because of his deep concern for patients' welfare

3. What kind of attitude do Bill's colleagues and superiors believe that he has?

   A. an optimistic one

   B. a responsible one

   C. a competitive one

4. What does Bill believe is important for his patients to maintain?

   A. an optimistic attitude

   B. a responsible attitude

   C. a basic quality of life

5. What profession does Bill belong to?

   A. the medical profession

   B. the hi tech profession

   C. the biotechnology profession

Situation 5

1. What has definitely strengthened Teresa's research skills?

A. hands-on experience in a hospital administrative department

B. the hospital's practical training

C. numerous opportunities to corroborate what she had learned from textbooks

2. What has greatly matured Teresa as an individual?

A. knowledge to solving independently the problems at hand

B. research skills in areas where she were previously lacking

C. participation in a research project

3. How was Teresa able to assess the quality of a hospital's medical services?

A. by participating in a project

B. by collecting data

C. by analyzing problems

4. How did Teresa apply the knowledge learned from textbooks?

A. to find employment at DEF Corporation

B. to solve independently the problems at hand

C. to assess the quality of a hospital's medical services

5. What did Teresa acquire in a hospital administrative department?

A. managerial experience

B. administrative experience

C. hands-on experience

Situation 6

1. What will May strive to do if successful in gaining employment at ABC Corporation?

A. collaborate closely with others

B. contribute to the organization in her unique manner

C. carefully to negotiate with others, while maintaining the dignity of each collaborator

2. What definitely supports May's aspiration to become a healthcare management professional?

   A. her dignity

   B. her strong research capabilities, knowledge and expertise

   C. her previous work experience

3. Why was Ton-Yen General Hospital an excellent environment for May?

   A. for her to become a healthcare management professional

   B. for her to conduct graduate-level research

   C. for her to contribute to the organization

4. How could one describe May's unique manner?

   A. contemplative

   B. determined

   C. careful

5. What did May's work experience teach her?

   A. how to become a healthcare management professional

   B. how to collaborate closely with others

   C. how to carefully negotiate with others

O Reading Comprehension II
Pick the word or expression whose meaning is closest to the meaning of the underlined word or expression in the following passages.

Situation 4

1. Bill is <u>committed</u> to his many patients.

   A. oblivious

   B. neglected

C. devoted

2. His deep <u>concern</u> for patients' welfare has led his colleagues and superiors to commend him many times on his responsible attitude.

   A. consideration

   B. disregard

   C. oversight

3. His deep concern for patients' welfare has led his colleagues and superiors to <u>commend</u> him many times on his responsible attitude.

   A. criticize

   B. compliment

   C. censure

4. His deep concern for patients' welfare has led his colleagues and superiors to commend him many times on his <u>responsible</u> attitude.

   A. accountable

   B. remiss

   C. derelict

5. Like most medical professionals, he feels <u>overwhelmed</u> by the rapid rate at which new medical technologies emerge, and are adopted by hospitals.

   A. prevailed

   B. deluged

   C. undercurrent

6. Like most medical professionals, he feels overwhelmed by the <u>rapid</u> rate at which new medical technologies emerge, and are adopted by hospitals.

   A. sluggish

   B. tardy

   C. accelerated

7. Bill must therefore <u>continually</u> increase his expertise to ensure that his patients

can maintain a basic quality of life.

A. cessation

B. ceaselessly

C. standstill

8. For instance, he must know how to <u>repair</u> nuclear medicine machinery. He also believes that remaining optimistic when interacting with others is essential, especially as people become increasingly competitive.

A. smash

B. annihilate

C. mend

9. For instance, he must know how to repair nuclear medicine machinery. He also believes that remaining <u>optimistic</u> when interacting with others is essential, especially as people become increasingly competitive.

A. dismal

B. rose-colored

C. gloomy

10. For instance, he must know how to repair nuclear medicine machinery. He also believes that remaining optimistic when interacting with others is <u>essential</u>, especially as people become increasingly competitive.

A. paltry

B. trivial

C. vital

Situation 5

1. Teresa <u>participated in</u> a project to assess the quality of a hospital's medical services. This experience enhanced her academic knowledge and significantly improved her analytical skills and data collection capabilities.

A. curtailed

B. abstained from

C. engaged in

2. Teresa participated in a project to <u>assess</u> the quality of a hospital's medical services. This experience enhanced her academic knowledge and significantly improved her analytical skills and data collection capabilities.

A. overlook

B. appraise

C. afterthought

3. Teresa participated in a project to assess the quality of a hospital's medical services. This experience enhanced her <u>academic</u> knowledge and significantly improved her analytical skills and data collection capabilities.

A. agrarian

B. agricultural

C. scholastic

4. Teresa participated in a project to assess the quality of a hospital's medical services. This experience enhanced her academic knowledge and significantly improved her analytical skills and data <u>collection</u> capabilities.

A. emancipation

B. accumulation

C. liberation

5. Her <u>hands-on</u> experience in a hospital administrative department provided her with numerous opportunities to corroborate what she had learned from textbooks and, then, to apply that knowledge to solving independently the problems at hand.

A. hypothetical

B. theoretical

C. practical

6. Her hands-on experience in a hospital <u>administrative</u> department provided her with numerous opportunities to corroborate what she had learned from textbooks and, then, to apply that knowledge to solving independently the problems at hand.

A. subservient

B. managerial

C. subordinate

7. Her hands-on experience in a hospital administrative department provided her with numerous opportunities to <u>corroborate</u> what she had learned from textbooks and, then, to apply that knowledge to solving independently the problems at hand.

A. confirm

B. deny

C. cancel

8. Her hands-on experience in a hospital administrative department provided her with numerous opportunities to corroborate what she had learned from <u>textbooks</u> and, then, to apply that knowledge to solving independently the problems at hand.

A. expenses

B. curricula

C. tuition

9. Her hands-on experience in a hospital administrative department provided her with numerous opportunities to corroborate what she had learned from textbooks and, then, to apply that knowledge to solving independently the <u>problems at hand</u>.

A. repeating problems

B. recurrent problems

C. current problems

10. The hospital's <u>practical</u> training definitely strengthened Teresa's research skills in areas where she were previously lacking, including problems analysis, data collection, data evaluation and collaboration within a research group.

Unit Introducing research and professional experiences relevant
Five to employment
介紹研究及工作經驗

A. functional

B. conjectural

C. abstract

Situation 6

1. While pursuing her Master's degree, May continued to work at Ton-Yen General
   Hospital, which was an <u>excellent</u> environment for conducting graduate-level
   research.

   A. substandard

   B. first-rate

   C. inferior

2. Her work experience further <u>developed</u> her professional skills and taught her how
   to collaborate closely with others.

   A. waned

   B. deconstructed

   C. fostered

3. In so doing, she not only <u>absorbed</u> colleagues' perspectives, but also learned how
   carefully to negotiate with others, while maintaining the dignity of each
   collaborator.

   A. assimilated

   B. preoccupy

   C. excoriate

4. In so doing, she not only absorbed colleagues' perspectives, but also learned how
   carefully to <u>negotiate</u> with others, while maintaining the dignity of each
   collaborator.

   A. concede

   B. bargain

C. cede

5. In so doing, she not only absorbed colleagues' perspectives, but also learned how carefully to negotiate with others, while maintaining the <u>dignity</u> of each collaborator.

A. prestige

B. squalor

C. foulness

6. If <u>successful</u> in gaining employment at ABC Corporation, May will strive to contribute to the organization in her unique manner, which is friendly, contemplative and graceful.

A. dereliction

B. failure

C. accomplished

7. If successful in gaining employment at ABC Corporation, May will strive to contribute to the organization in her unique <u>manner</u>, which is friendly, contemplative and graceful.

A. difficulty

B. style

C. ease

8. If successful in gaining employment at ABC Corporation, May will strive to contribute to the organization in her unique manner, which is friendly, <u>contemplative</u> and graceful.

A. extroverted

B. outspoken

C. reflective

9. If successful in gaining employment at ABC Corporation, May will strive to contribute to the organization in her unique manner, which is friendly,

contemplative and <u>graceful</u>.

A. pathetic

B. elegant

C. rueful

10. Her previous work experience <u>definitely</u> supports her aspiration to become a healthcare management professional.

A. chancy

B. certainly

C. dubious

Unit Six

Describing extracurricular activities relevant to employment

描述與求職相關的課外活動

Vocabulary and related expressions　相關字詞

student associations 學生社團
actively involved in 積極參與
largely responsible 主要負責
distributed 分配
supervised 監督
consultation 諮商
large-scale events 大規模的事件
campus events 校園事件
people from diverse backgrounds
來自不同背景的人們
subordinates 部下
devote one's energies to
把某人的精力貢獻給……
campus mountaineering group
校園的登山團
spiritual well being 心理健康

trial-and-error procedure 試誤程序
patient 病患
administrative tasks 行政任務
accumulated experiences 累積的經驗
a well-rounded person 多才多藝的人
as evidenced by 由……可證明
extracurricular activities 課外活動
experimentation 實驗法
complex task 複雜的工作
administrative skills 行政能力
planning a framework 計畫一個架構
implementing operations 實行工作
assertive personality 獨斷的個性
capacity 能力
persevering 堅忍的
punctual 準時的

unforeseen circumstances
對付不可知的情勢
natural habitats 天生的習慣
collaborated with peers 和同儕合作
outdoor entertainment 戶外娛樂
broaden one's horizons 擴展視野
physical challenges 體能挑戰
undergraduate school 大學部
diverse educational activities
不同的教育活動
cycles up to Yang Min Mountain
騎車到陽明山
converse and interact with someone
和某人相互交談
balance one's academic and
extracurricular activities 學業及課外活動
的平衡
concentrate closely on unforeseen
circumstances 集中注意不可知的情境

organisms 有機體
basic etiquette 基礎的禮儀
diligent 勤奮的
class-related activities 和課程相關的活動
interact with 和……交互作用
in one's spare time 在某人的空閒時間
mental relaxation 心理放鬆
necessary balance 必要的平衡
recalls 回憶
an outing 戶外活動
academic interests 學術興趣
personal investments 個人投資
a diverse array of interests 不同的興趣
a broad perspective 寬廣的觀點
strengthened and broaden one's
professional knowledge base 強化專業技能
基礎
professional meetings 專業會議
journals 期刊

Shelly

three years SAC

improved

organizational skills and ability to handle crises

John

table tennis

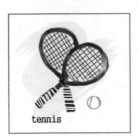

tennis

with people
patient and persevering

Lisa

well-rounded person

goal
accomplish

assign tasks to subordinates

A Write down the key points of the situations on the preceding page, while the instructor reads aloud the script from the Answer Key.

Situation 1

_____

_____

_____

Situation 2

_____

_____

_____

Situation 3

_____

_____

_____

B Oral Practice I

Based on the three situations in this unit, write three questions beginning with *How*, and answer them. The questions do not need to come directly from these situations.

Examples

How was Shelly involved in extracurricular activities at university?

By participating in several student associations

How did Shelly learn to write proposals and use a wide array of skills?

From her position at SAC

1. _____

_____

2. _____

_____

3. _____

_____

C Based on the three situations in this unit, write three questions beginning with *What*, and answer them. The questions do not need to come directly from these situations.

Examples

What kind of person does John consider himself to be?

A friendly and diligent one

What activities did John participate in while at university?

Several student association activities, including table tennis, tennis and other class-related activities

1. _____

   _____

2. _____

   _____

3. _____

   _____

D Based on the three situations in this unit, write three questions beginning with *Why*, and answer them. The questions do not need to come directly from these situations.

Examples

Why is Lisa a well-rounded person?

Because of her participation in numerous extracurricular activities in which she has acquired numerous professional skills

Why is Lisa able to estimate, plan and act efficiently when given the opportunity?

Owing to her assertive personality

1. _____

_____

2. _____

_____

3. _____

_____

E Write questions that match the answers provided.

Examples

What did experimentation make John?

A more patient and persevering individual

What allowed John more closely to interact with people?

By participating in sports

1. _____

_____

Individuals who collaborate with each other

2. _____

_____

According to their strengths

3. _____

_____

Accomplish her goals

F Listening Comprehension I

Situation 1

1. What did Shelly's position at SAC offer her many opportunities to do?

   A. hold small-scale activities

   B. plan a framework and implement operations

   C. come into contact with people from diverse backgrounds

2. How did Shelly become aware of the importance of writing skills and related administrative skills?

   A. because she came into contact with people from diverse backgrounds and used a wide array of skills.

   B. because SAC's approach to planning a framework and implementing operations closely resembles academic research methods

   C. because she cooperated with the governmental sector to hold small-scale activities

3. How did Shelly became aware of the importance of writing skills and related administrative skills?

   A. through much of her experience while at university

   B. through much of her experience of serving in SAC

   C. through much of her experience of serving in the Society of Emergency Medicine, R.O.C.

4. In what capacity did Shelly serve as a student association leader during university?

   A. She wrote proposals and used a wide array of skills

   B. She cooperated with the governmental sector to hold small-scale activities

   C. She coordinated the administrative activities of 65 student associations at Chungtai Institute of Health Sciences and Technology

5. How did Shelly's position as student association leader affect her?

   A. It made her an active individual

   B. It made her a persevering and punctual individual

   C. It made her an aggressive individual

Situation 2

1. What kind of person does John consider himself to be?

   A. patient and persevering

   B. friendly and diligent

   C. experienced and opportunistic

2. How did serving as class leader improve John?

   A. It improved his ability to coordinate and execute administrative tasks

   B. It improved his ability to conduct experiments

   C. It improved his ability to participate in class activities

3. What will definitely benefit John's future?

   A. close interaction with people

   B. his coordination and execution skills

   C. his accumulated experience

4. When did John conduct experiments?

   A. during undergraduate school

   B. during his spare time

   C. during graduate school

5. Where did John participate in several student association universities?

   A. at university

   B. at ABC Corporation

   C. in graduate school

Situation 3

1. More than a communicator, what must an excellent manager do?

    A. estimate plans efficiently

    B. act effectively and efficiently

    C. perform complex tasks with a minimum of staff and resources

2. What sort of communication skills does Lisa have?

    A. strong ones

    B. well-rounded ones

    C. excellent ones

3. How does Lisa assign tasks to subordinates?

    A. according to their experiences

    B. according to their seniority

    C. according to their strengths

4. What does Lisa believe that she has an excellent capacity to do?

    A. concentrate

    B. collaborate with others

    C. act effectively and efficiently

5. What do individuals who collaborate with each other depend on?

    A. an excellent capacity to concentrate

    B. communication and action

    C. a minimum of staff and resources

G Reading Comprehension I

Pick the word or expression whose meaning is closest to the meaning of the underlined word or expression in the following passages.

Situation 1

1. At university, Shelly <u>participated</u> in several student associations. For instance, she was actively involved in the student activity center (SAC) for three years.

   A. eluded

   B. shunned

   C. partook

2. At university, Shelly participated in several student associations. For instance, she was <u>actively</u> involved in the student activity center (SAC) for three years.

   A. dynamically

   B. acquiescent

   C. submissive

3. SAC was largely <u>responsible for</u> coordinating the administrative activities of 65 student associations at Chungtai Institute of Health Sciences and Technology.

   A. responsible to

   B. in charge of

   C. under one's supervision

4. It <u>distributed</u> funds, supervised and supported activities, provided consultation and sponsored large-scale events. At SAC, Shelly was in charge of furnishing and operating stage lighting and acoustics for campus events.

   A. exposed

   B. introduced

   C. disseminated

5. It distributed funds, supervised and supported activities, provided consultation and <u>sponsored</u> large-scale events. At SAC, Shelly was in charge of furnishing and operating stage lighting and acoustics for campus events.

A. outsourced

B. patronized

C. ransack

6. It distributed funds, supervised and supported activities, provided consultation and sponsored large-scale events. At SAC, Shelly was in charge of <u>furnishing</u> and operating stage lighting and acoustics for campus events.

A. giving up

B. sacrificing

C. providing

7. This <u>position</u> not only offered her many opportunities to come into contact with people from diverse backgrounds, but also to write proposals and use a wide array of skills.

A. organization

B. placement

C. agency

8. This position not only offered her many opportunities to come into contact with people from <u>diverse</u> backgrounds, but also to write proposals and use a wide array of skills.

A. heterogeneous

B. homogeneous

C. run-of-the-mill

9. This position not only offered her many opportunities to come into contact with people from diverse backgrounds, but also to write proposals and use a wide <u>array</u> of skills.

A. area

B. limit

C. scope

10. Through much of her experience of <u>serving</u> in the Society of Emergency Medicine, R.O.C., Shelly became aware of the importance of writing skills and related administrative skills because SAC's approach to planning a framework and implementing operations closely resembles academic research methods.

A. planning

B. working

C. creating

Situation 2

1. John considers himself to be friendly and <u>diligent</u>.

A. shiftless

B. industrious

C. sluggish

2. At university, he <u>participated</u> in several student association activities, including table tennis, tennis and other class-related activities.

A. abstain

B. refrain

C. indulge

3. Participating in sports allowed him more closely to <u>interact with</u> people.

A. avoid

B. come into contact with

C. avert

4. He conducted experiments in his <u>spare</u> time, which required hard work since they often involved trial-and-error procedures.

A. free

B. hectic

C. filled up

5. Such <u>experimentation</u> has made him a more patient and persevering individual.

A. production

B. trial

C. error

6. Such experimentation has made him a more <u>patient</u> and persevering individual.

A. irritation

B. impatient

C. forbearing

7. Additionally, serving as class leader has improved his ability to <u>coordinate</u> and execute administrative tasks.

A. arrange

B. randomly place

C. mess up

8. John <u>firmly</u> believes that every opportunity is an opportunity for learning. His accumulated experiences will definitely benefit his future.

A. wobbling

B. wavering

C. solidly

9. John firmly believes that every opportunity is an opportunity for learning. His <u>accumulated</u> experiences will definitely benefit his future.

A. dispersed

B. collected

C. distributed

Situation 3

1. Lisa is a <u>well-rounded</u> person, as evidenced by her participation in numerous extracurricular activities in which she has acquired numerous professional skills.

   A. aggressive

   B. contemplative

   C. balanced

2. Lisa is a well-rounded person, as <u>evidenced</u> by her participation in numerous extracurricular activities in which she has acquired numerous professional skills.

   A. disputed

   B. proven

   C. refuted

3. Lisa is a well-rounded person, as evidenced by her participation in numerous extracurricular activities in which she has <u>acquired</u> numerous professional skills.

   A. dispensed

   B. obtained

   C. created

4. She also believes that she has an excellent <u>capacity</u> to concentrate.

   A. place

   B. ability

   C. company

5. She will <u>devote</u> her energies to accomplish her goals.

   A. abandon

   B. renounce

   C. dedicate

6. She will devote her <u>energies</u> to accomplish her goals.

   A. fragility

   B. strengths

C. infirmity

7. She has an <u>assertive</u> personality, as proven by her ability to estimate, plan and act efficiently.

A. feeble

B. frail

C. emphatic

8. She has an assertive <u>personality</u>, as proven by her ability to estimate, plan and act efficiently.

A. disposition

B. humor

C. hilarious

9. Moreover, she believes that she is a leader in the sense that she can perform a <u>complex</u> task with a minimum of staff and resources.

A. facile

B. convoluted

C. fluid

10. She can also <u>assign</u> tasks to subordinates according to their strengths.

A. designate

B. relieve

C. boost

H Common elements in describing extracurricular activities relevant to employment include:

1. Introducing an extracurricular activity in which one has participated

2. Highlighting the acquired knowledge, skills or leadership qualities that are relevant to employment

In the space below, describe your extracurricular activities that are relevant to employment.

_____

_____

_____

_____

_____

_____

_____

_____

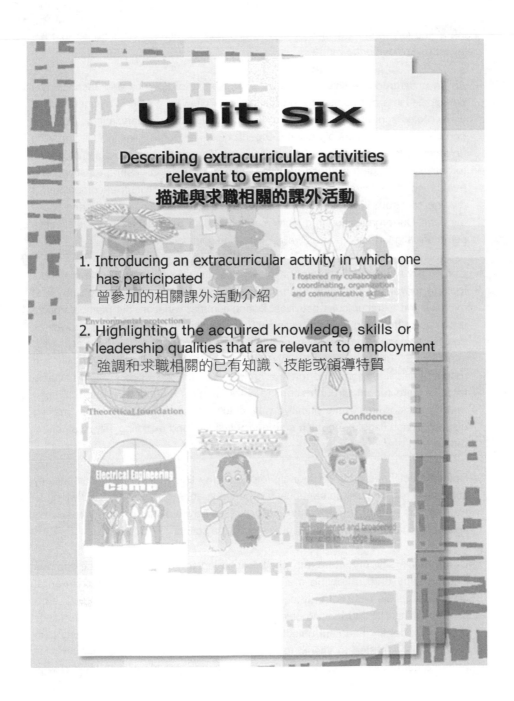

Unit six

Describing extracurricular activities relevant to employment
描述與求職相關的課外活動

1. Introducing an extracurricular activity in which one has participated
   曾參加的相關課外活動介紹

2. Highlighting the acquired knowledge, skills or leadership qualities that are relevant to employment
   強調和求職相關的已有知識、技能或領導特質

Look at the following examples of how to describe extracurricular activities that are relevant to employment.

◎As an undergraduate student at Yuanpei University of Science and Technology, I participated in a campus scouting organization. Following a year of stringent drills, I was elected scoutmaster. In addition to academic study, organizational activities occupied a large amount of my time. Organizational responsibilities included drawing up a schedule for scouting and engineering-related activities, encouraging members to actively participate in those activities, leading discussions during meetings and evaluating the success of our activities. Our scouting activities encompassed a diverse spectrum, including outdoor survival skills, community service, and social etiquette. Our organization frequently met to discuss various topics such as effective communication, democracy, as well as legal and spiritual concerns.

◎Community service is an integral aspect of scouting activities, with club members looking forward to activities such as working with area youth through physical exercise and extracurricular activities. During summer vacation, our members guide a cub scout troupe in learning skills such as survival and CPR training, as well as how to get along with others harmoniously. Outdoor program activities are especially intriguing. Scouts learn how to camp, run、cross country, track wildlife, identify and respect one's limitations and reach a consensus with one's peers. Such valuable lessons were taught through scouting skills such as mountain rescue attempts, making outdoor fires in the primitive way, outdoor cooking without utensils, making distress signal, flags, performing emergency first aid, and exploring Taiwan's natural resources.

◎Scouting activities have profoundly impacted my life, making me more socially conscious, responsible, courageous, independent, aggressive, honest and willing to help others. All of these traits will prove to be invaluable to any research collaboration that I am involved in during graduate school.

◎During university, my interest in photography led to participation in the campus photography club, allowing me to closely interact with many departmental classmates. This club not only equipped me with much knowledge expertise on photographing still and moving objects, but also instilled in me an aesthetic quality on how to identify beautiful objects in daily life. To do so, the photography club occasionally ventured to scenic resorts during the holidays. During that period, I became genuinely interested in others and how to get along with them. I was responsible for collecting and managing photography-related documents, which greatly strengthened my computer skills. Owing to my administrative tasks, this experience enabled me to more easily grasp management concepts taught in class. I am indebted to the teacher supervising the photography club as well as my upper classmates for their valuable guidance.

◎Among the many extracurricular activities that I participated in during university, I immensely enjoyed the campus kickboxing organization as a freshman. I especially recall a friendly match with National Chiao Tung University, in which my opponent had already acquired a black belt, whereas I was only a novice. Although I lost, I learned how to persevere — even against seemingly unbeatable odds. I continued with kickboxing until my physical education instructor recruited me into the volleyball team I was fascinated with how agile my classmates were while playing. Through daily continuous exercise, not only did I make many close acquaintances, but I also became interested in extracurricular activities. During the same period, I participated in the department's student association. As the section chief of document compilation, I was responsible for accumulating and organizing academic journals and departmental newsletters. Again, I made many acquaintances with classmates through these activities, and we remain in touch until now. Additionally, participation in the departmental association exposed me to the private sector. I recall one occasion in which I successfully negotiated a lower price for printing a journal with a publisher. University also provided me with many opportunities to identify and deliberate upon which plan is the most appropriate for a given situation.

◎In addition to equipping me with strong organizational and management skills, the above experiences have enabled me to systematically apply logical reasoning to solve academic problems, such as in operations research, statistics and econometrics. Moreover, I learned to easily adjust to new environments. Extracurricular activities definitely nurtured many of my personal qualities.

◎I enjoy watching English language movies to strengthen my listening comprehension. Learning and effectively using a second language is a must for university students, explaining why I often listen to radio programs on ICRT, read both English language newspapers and *Time* magazine, and watch international news on the television such as CNN. While my roommates are occasionally surprised with my near obsession to strengthen my English language skills, I explained that nearly all international scientific publications are in English. With my realization since junior high school that bilingual competence in both Chinese and

English is essential, I decided to devote my efforts to learning English, specifically in writing, listening and reading. I was determined to achieve a language level in which I could express my opinions just like a native speaker even though my English level is still inadequate. Nevertheless, I remain perseverant. I recall when I attended an English language camp during university to strengthen my vocabulary skills. I felt embarrassed when an attractive girl from the United States complemented me on my language skills and wanted to make friends with me. However, partly out of nervousness and partly out of my limited language ability, I could not express myself well. From this experience, I learned that one must constantly practice English daily if any progress is to be made, regardless of whether it is speaking, writing, reading or listening. As for extracurricular activities during university, I spent nearly all my spare time in reading English language books and periodicals. Realizing that I needed to study diligently in order to fulfill my ambitions, I felt that my language skills must not fall behind those of my other classmates in graduate school. The investment that I made during university is starting to pay off in my graduate studies. For instance, I feel confident when expressing my opinions about what I have read in scientific articles in English. I never feel ashamed of expressing myself in English that is below the standard of others. And neither am I ashamed of the fact that while my roommates are in deep sleep, I am actively listening to English language broadcast programs on ICRT. Moreover, actively participating in numerous language study camps provided me with several unique leadership opportunities. I firmly believe that strengthening ones language skills is an effective means of going beyond one's surrounding environment to see the larger global picture. Actively writing, reading, listening and speaking in another language is important for me to see the connection between theory taught in class and practice in the real world. In sum, no deadline restricts us to the things that we can learn in life as long as we remain determined. Language is a vital part of our life's experiences, something that I am devoted to in my leisure time in order to build upon my solid academic background and to acquire a better position at work. As I have practiced English daily in some form for the past decade, I am interested in learning how to more efficiently study in order to further strengthen my interest in language learning.

◎Since elementary school, although my math scores were low, I have always had an excellent memory. I also served as class chairperson for three years during junior high school. My classmates regarded me as a congenial leader. Until reaching college, I devoted myself to work, study, and family simultaneously. I was therefore unable to fully immerse myself in academia, which is a common dilemma among Chinese students. The teacher generally spoon feeds education while students learn passively. My graduate studies allowed me to change these patterns so that I can more actively engage in my studies.

◎As for my extracurricular activities, I participated in campus wide anti-smoking activities sponsored by Taiwan's Bureau of Health Promotion Department. In addition to offering general orientation on the dangers of smoking, the activities also inform students on tobacco manufacturers' deceptive motives and marketing approaches. These activities profoundly impacted me to the point that my graduation thesis addressed how marketing is used in this area. As for my personality, I am easy to get along with. During university, although my academic marks were undistinguished, I always strived to study diligently despite my personal limitations. When working on a specific task, I always act quickly to efficiently resolve problems. I am also able to function well under pressure, making me a direct individual who does not evade pertinent questions with confidence. Above qualities make me receptive to learn new concepts, which will prove to be valuable assets when conducting graduate school research and completing my thesis.

◎Most extracurricular activities I participated in were medical-oriented out of concern to keep my academic scholarship for studies in medical technology. For instance, I often attended medical imagery or radiological technology symposia. I recently participated in a symposium on image reconstruction and transmission of three-dimensional images, as held by the Institute of Medical Imagery at YUST. This symposium greatly facilitated my understanding of image transmission, as well as implementation and storage in a hospital. More importantly, this symposium made me aware of the infinite possibilities of medical imagery in scientific and technological developments. Our dependence on science and technology became apparent to me during this symposium as well.

◎I always remain abreast of the latest governmental policies and economic trends by reading several newspapers and magazines regularly. I also discussed with my friends on their career developments, including helpful ideas or technologies, especially on how to enhance existing information systems. Besides, I enjoy reading Chinese ancient literature, such as *The Art of War* by Sun Tzu and *Tao Teh Jing* by Lao Tzu, authors whom are distinguished for Chinese philosophy worldwide and often inspire me in tackling management issues. In addition to reading many of their writings, I often search for information that is not available on Internet search engines. In addition to deriving much pleasure from reading, I participated in a martial arts school. This discipline not only regulates my health, but also cultivates my inner spirit.

◎While certain individuals may view me as being overanxious to assimilate much information, I constantly distinguish between academic/work reading and pleasure reading. I also enjoy sharing what I have learned with my friends. Sharing with others can supplement my knowledge and cultivate interpersonal and communication skills. In an era in which individuals are over loaded with information, I believe that effective collaboration is essential to success, explaining why I am always fascinated with management issues and recently completed a graduate school degree in Business Management.

◎I participated in a campus Chinese music club while studying in vocational school. That involvement led to my entry into the Chinese Music Association of the Taichung County Culture Center, in which I performed in many places. However, I did not participate in extracurricular activities at YUST out of concern that my academic studies would suffer. However, I enthusiastically partook in class activities, such as barbecues in Neiwan and Christmas caroling.

◎Getting along with others, especially with classmates in the university's extracurricular activities, was a large part of my daily campus life, regardless of whether I was collaborating on a project or spending leisure time with others. Although innocent in nature, getting along with others in school is good training for what I can expect in society. As a university freshman, my classmates and I participated in cheerleading events, which involved aerobics and acrobatics with upper classmates after school. Although we were often injured during exercise, being part of a group effort in which all were striving for the same common goal was a unique experience. I also formed tight bonds with upper classmates and different age groups. Those activities were a microcosm of what society is like in the real world.

◎I participated in a non-profit scouting organization during the summer vacation before my final year of university. Responsible mainly for coordinating activities, I considered what the scouts were interested in and then those costs versus our allocated budget. Following agreement by all of the members, the plan was implemented harmoniously. The experience instilled in me the importance of planning in the early stages so as to incorporate all members' opinions in order to spur creativity. Volunteer work in this scouting organization greatly impacted my life by making me more conscious of others' needs and aware of my societal responsibilities.

◎As for civic activities, I often donate blood to the Chinese Blood Foundation via a mobile blood bank that frequents Tungmun Circle in downtown Hsinchu. During the SARS crisis, many donors were afraid to donate blood at the blood bank out of fear of entering enclosed public spaces. This fear could have led to a shortage in blood supply, which could be fatal to hemodialysis patients. Nevertheless, I felt it was my social responsibility and did so.

◎My classmates elected me monitor, which is a unique leadership opportunity that increased my self-confidence in leadership skills while striving for harmony among classmates and coordination with the classroom instructor. I could also apply some human resource management concepts. Additionally, my classmates elected me as a candidate for the university's exemplary student award. The above extracurricular activities and recognition greatly added to me character, thus equipping me for the challenges of graduate school and ability to more fully grasp human resource management concepts.

◎Realizing the importance of health in the success of my career, I enjoy sports such as a track and field team that I once participated in. I also joined a local tennis tournament after receiving my junior college diploma, even meeting many sports celebrities. As an avid outdoorsman, I have climbed over ten of Taiwan's Hundred Mountains, such as Snow Mountain, Yu Mountain, Yang Tou Mountain, Liu Shun Mountain, Qi Cai Hu, Ta Ba Jian Mountain, He Huan mountain ranges, and Pei Ta Wu Mountain. These stringent tests of physical strength have definitely enabled me to cope with the most difficult assignments at work. From the above activities, I learned that patience, perseverance and reflection are essential to continuous learning throughout life.

◎I tried to balance my academic studies with extracurricular activities during university. Joining the campus mountaineering team required rigorous physical training to closely work with my climbing partner in tasks such as making a makeshift shelter, fire, rope, and sling. This unique opportunity broadened my personal horizons both physically and mentally. Additionally, I took many lessons in using a personal computer such as fabricating computer hardware, setting up a network and using basic computer software. Mastering the use of my computer for research purposes was essential for graduate school research in the Institute of Medical Imagery. When used efficiently, the Internet is especially attractive for accessing a significant amount of data and communicating through word, images and even voice. The Internet has definitely given me a larger perspective. Moreover, I have participated in mental calculation contests to increase my memory retention. Mental calculation requires a strong logical conception ability. In sum, the above activities reflect my interest in strengthening my academic and intellectual skills through diverse ways.

◎As evidence of my friendly, responsible and communicative nature, I participated in our department's volleyball team during university. While training with many classmates from diverse backgrounds, I learned how to easily accommodate myself within a group to contribute to a team effort. As for my responsible character, I was responsible for maintaining our class' public health by sanitizing the classroom and laboratory. I also have a strong sense of responsibility for my own actions, as evidenced by diligence in class attendance and submitted homework. I am also confident of my communicative skills, especially while working in the hospital. Regardless of whether I am communicating with patients, physicians, nurses or my superiors, I believe that effective communication can enhance the quality of medical treatment as well as resolve disagreements.

◎I participated in numerous extracurricular activities during undergraduate school. These activities nurtured my communicative skills by requiring that I closely collaborate with other club members to ensure that everything ran smoothly. Such collaboration undoubtedly broadened my horizons. One event that left a deep impression on me when I was in the department's student association at Tsing Hua University. During the annual Meichu sports competition between Tsing Hua University and Chiao Tung University, a riot almost ensued over a referee's controversial call. Fortunately, careful coordination among the student delegates led to a satisfactory resolution of the situation That event was a turning point in my decision to pursue a MBA degree. Coordinating activities to greet new arrivals at a camp was another unique leadership experience. As camp leader, I incorporated the opinions of the camp volunteers and then supervised others to ensure that all tasks were implemented smoothly. As a leader, I learned how to realize the discrepancy between theory and practice as well as the necessary balance between authority and responsibility.

◎Besides listening to music, I enjoy reading novels and writing for pleasure. Another activity that I will never forget was when I participated in a mountaineering trip during senior high school. The higher I climb, the less exhausted I feel. While the human body has its limitations, I am able to exceed those limitations through my willpower and determination. Although occasionally thinking about giving up, I convince myself to push forward. Once reaching the mountaintop, I have a deep sense of personal satisfaction. I firmly believe that individuals should test their limits to understand how successful they can become. I am resilient when it comes to facing obstacles and remaining perseverant. With this self-confidence, I do not flinch from difficult situations. In sum, learning allows me to see the world more deeply and clearly, as if I had just reached a mountaintop after a long hike. For those whom are determined to pursue their dreams, training is necessary to thrive in our highly competitive society.

◎As for my extracurricular activities, I enjoy singing to release pressures from school. Individuals need an outlet for expressing their spiritual side and remove themselves from the weariness of daily work. I also like to watch television programs, such as those on the *Discovery* and *Science* channels, as well as Japanese programs. These programs keep me up-to-date on the latest scientific and technology development trends. When short-tempered, I enjoy listening to classical music to temper any negative feelings. I also enjoy seeking out my teachers and friends for consultation and personal advice. If in a group of three, I believe that at least one of the other two has valuable advice to offer. The sea also has a calming effect on me when I go to the beach to think contemplatively, allowing me to release daily pressures and put my problems in a more realistic perspective.

◎Among the different extracurricular activities that I participated in during junior college included the campus harmonica club, computer science club, the Yu Noun service club that focuses on building character, and a scouting organization. The harmonica club orients members on becoming more aware musically, nourishing one's own musical specialty and teaching basic music literacy so that novice learners can appreciate its psychological meaning. The computer science club attempts to increase members' information technology skills and network capabilities in practical areas such as the Internet and handling of Word, Excel, Power point documents as well as other Windows functions. Finally, my participation in both the Yu Noun service club that focuses on building character and a scouting organization allowed me to more effectively improve my personal management as well as interpersonal skills through various group activities. Doing so often included drill activities and the learning of outdoor survival skills. The above experiences not only developed my self-reliance skills, but also strengthened my ability to handle personal crises. Moreover, above extracurricular activities offered diverse educational experiences and opportunities to apply knowledge skills and acquire leadership opportunities that gave me a broader perspective on the larger global picture.

◎Among the different extracurricular activities I enjoy during my leisure time include listening to music, going to the cinema, shopping, eating out, singing and painting. These activities take my mind off of the pressures in graduate school. The only activities related to study are watching English language television programs (such as the Discovery Channel, National Geographic Channel, Animal Planet Channel, and the Knowledge Channel), leaning English conversation and using the Internet. Extracurricular activities that are not directly related to graduate school still benefit my graduate studies. That is, such activities supplement my studies by providing simper and more interesting ways of learning that are not so serious and occasionally drab as academic papers can be. English learning is important because I often read from international periodicals in order to prepare for seminar.

◎During university, I joined several activities, such as camping and painting. These camping activities fostered our conversational, communicative and collaborative skills. As a leader, I initiated innovative ways of keeping the interest of others participating in campus events. This unique leadership opportunity was one of the most rewarding experiences of my undergraduate years and also enabled me to successfully complete a master's degree as a well-rounded individual.

◎I am interested in strengthening my English language skills, explaining why I constantly listen to the English language radio station, ICRT. My daily reading of biotechnology literature enhances both my knowledge of this field and origins of the research problem at hand. In addition to research-related courses, I took several elective courses to supplement my master's thesis investigation. Despite increasing pressure to fulfill the requirements of graduate study, I remained confident of my ability to succeed. More than just an academic pursuit, studying for a master's degree was a test of my determination and perseverance.

I Write down the key points of the situations on the preceding page, while the instructor reads aloud the script from the Answer Key.

Situation 4

_____

_____

_____

Situation 5

_____

_____

_____

Situation 6

_____

_____

_____

J Oral practice II

Based on the three situations in this unit, write three questions beginning with *How*, and answer them. The questions do not need to come directly from these situations.

Examples

How does a natural environment benefit Bruce?

It benefits his physical stamina and spiritual well being

How did Bruce participate in campus extracurricular activities while in university?

By participating in a campus mountaineering group

1. _____

_____

2. _____

_____

3. _____

_____

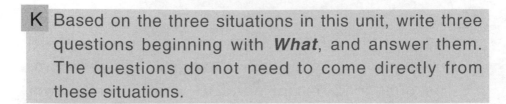

K Based on the three situations in this unit, write three questions beginning with *What*, and answer them. The questions do not need to come directly from these situations.

Examples

What did the many extracurricular activities in that Susan participated at undergraduate school give her?

The necessary balance between helping others and determining what path she should take in pursuing a career in research

What organizations was Susan involved in during your undergraduate studies?

Medical technology ones

1. _____

   _____

2. _____

   _____

3. _____

   _____

L Based on the three situations in this unit, write three questions beginning with *Why*, and answer them. The questions do not need to come directly from these situations.

Examples

Why did Jerry have to leave his home at 7 am and cycle up to Yang Min Mountain?
For his volunteer work with mentally challenged individuals

Why does Jerry feel that being responsible for such a large group is physically and mentally draining?
Because he had to concentrate closely on the mentally challenged individuals and anticipate any unforeseen circumstances

1. _____

_____

2. _____

_____

3. _____

_____

M Write questions that match the answers provided.

Examples

What is personally satisfying for Jerry?

Volunteer work

What did Jerry learn from attending a conference on personal investments?

Much about risk control

1. _____

   _____

   A natural environment

2. _____

   _____

   Balance his academic and extracurricular activities

3. _____

   _____

   Prepare outdoor events

N Listening Comprehension II

Situation 4

1. How did Bruce's mountaineering activities broaden his horizons?

    A. by allowing him to relax his mind

    B. by allowing him to take advantage of the unique leadership opportunities provided

    C. by allowing him to keep his mind clear

2. How has Bruce been able to more effectively to balance his academic and extracurricular activities?

    A. by seeing various organisms in their natural habitats

    B. by working more diligently

    C. by both the physical challenges and mental relaxation associated with mountain climbing

3. In addition to relaxing the mind, what have Bruce's extracurricular activities enabled him to do?

    A. to balance his academic and extracurricular activities

    B. to prioritize physical stamina and health

    C. to take advantage of the unique leadership opportunities provided

4. How has Bruce collaborated with peers?

    A. in preparing outdoor events

    B. in relaxing their minds

    C. in see various organisms in their natural habitats

5. What is Bruce able to do by keeping his mind clear?

    A. undertake serious mountaineering events

    B. collaborate with peers

    C. work more diligently

Situation 5

1. What did Susan occasionally do in her involvement with several medical technology organizations?

  A. collaborate with overseas researchers

  B. participate in professional meetings

  C. participate in extracurricular activities

2. What has prioritizing the improvement of her English language communication skills enabled Susan to do?

  A. increase her awareness of various medical issues

  B. improve her knowledge, skills and expertise

  C. collaborate with overseas researchers

3. What is of great interest to Susan?

  A. her diverse educational activities

  B. her English language communication skills

  C. library resources, including the latest medical journals

4. When did Susan participate in many extracurricular activities?

  A. during her graduate studies

  B. at undergraduate school

  C. while attending professional meetings

5. What type of journals is Susan interested in?

  A. medical ones

  B. educational ones

  C. English as a second language ones

Situation 6

1. How does being responsible for such a large group make Jerry feel?

  A. invigorated

B. physically and mentally draining

C. powerful

2. What sort of perspective does Jerry still try to attain?

A. a broad one that covers various fields

B. a specific one that covers a limited range of interest

C. a narrow one that covers only one topic

3. What did Jerry learn much about while attending a conference on personal investments?

A. mentally challenged individuals

B. risk control

C. serving in a group

4. How does Jerry feel about volunteer work?

A. It is personally fulfilling

B. It is risky

C. It is challenging

5. Who did Jerry occasionally volunteer to work with?

A. investors

B. graduate students

C. mentally challenged individuals

O Reading Comprehension II
Pick the word or expression whose meaning is closest to the meaning of the underlined word or expression in the following passages.

Situation 4

1. At university, Bruce <u>participated</u> in a campus mountaineering group.

   A. disclaimed

   B. engaged

   C. repudiate

2. A natural environment benefits his physical <u>stamina</u> and spiritual well being.

   A. staying power

   B. reluctance

   C. averseness

3. His activities have allowed him to see various organisms in their natural <u>habitats</u>.

   A. internship

   B. vacation

   C. stamping ground

4. When <u>called upon</u>, he has collaborated with peers to prepare outdoor events.

   A. asked to do something

   B. asked to refrain

   C. asked to abstain

5. When called upon, he has collaborated with <u>peers</u> to prepare outdoor events.

   A. subordinate

   B. superior

   C. equal

6. Close collaboration has allowed them to undertake <u>serious</u> mountaineering events

that have provided great outdoor entertainment.

A. earnest

B. light-hearted

C. comical

7. Moreover, these activities have <u>broadened</u> his horizons in other ways, such as allowing him to take advantage of the unique leadership opportunities provided.

A. cramp

B. confining

C. widen

8. Moreover, these activities have broadened his <u>horizons</u> in other ways, such as allowing him to take advantage of the unique leadership opportunities provided.

A. answers

B. perceptions

C. resolutions

9. Both the physical <u>challenges</u> and mental relaxation associated with mountain climbing have allowed Bruce more effectively to balance his academic and extracurricular activities.

A. provocation

B. sink

C. pit

10. Both the physical challenges and <u>mental</u> relaxation associated with mountain climbing have allowed Bruce more effectively to balance his academic and extracurricular activities.

A. physical

B. physiological

C. psychological

Situation 5

1. The many extracurricular activities in which Susan participated at undergraduate school gave her the necessary <u>balance</u> between helping others and determining what path she should take in pursuing a career in research.

   A. variable

   B. erratic

   C. parallel

2. The many extracurricular activities in which Susan participated at undergraduate school gave her the necessary balance between helping others and determining what <u>path</u> she should take in pursuing a career in research.

   A. entrance

   B. exit

   C. roadway

3. She <u>was involved with</u> several medical technology organizations, occasionally participating in professional meetings to improve her knowledge, skills and expertise.

   A. abstained from

   B. participated in

   C. refrained from

4. Additionally, library resources, including the latest medical journals are of great <u>interest</u> to her.

   A. disregard

   B. concern

   C. neglect

5. Her <u>diverse</u> educational activities have strengthened and broadened Susan's professional knowledge base and increased her awareness of various medical issues.

A. redundant

B. similar

C. varied

6. Her diverse educational activities have <u>strengthened</u> and broadened Susan's professional knowledge base and increased her awareness of various medical issues.

A. languish

B. fortified

C. wane

7. Her diverse educational activities have strengthened and broadened Susan's professional knowledge <u>base</u> and increased her awareness of various medical issues.

A. foundation

B. shifting

C. swamp

8. She <u>prioritizes</u> improving her English language communication skills, enabling her to collaborate with overseas researchers.

A. not consider important

B. heavily emphasizes

C. plays down

Situation 6

1. Jerry <u>occasionally</u> volunteers to work with mentally challenged individuals.

A. often

B. frequently

C. periodically

2. He recalls last summer vacation, when he volunteered to <u>serve</u> in a group that took

some of these adults and children on an outing to Yang Min Mountain.

   A. avoid

   B. wait upon

   C. prevent

3. A <u>typical</u> schedule for such an activity is as follows.

   A. atypical

   B. infrequent

   C. commonplace

4. He leaves his home around 7 am and <u>cycles</u> up to Yang Min Mountain.

   A. rides

   B. drives

   C. walks

5. The adults and children start <u>arriving</u> by school bus at 8 am to prepare for the day's activities.

   A. leaving

   B. disappearing

   C. showing up

6. After taking them to the toilet individually, he <u>instructs</u> them on basic etiquette during their journey to the Park.

   A. teaches

   B. leads

   C. guides

7. After taking them to the toilet individually, he instructs them on basic <u>etiquette</u> during their journey to the Park.

   A. discourteous

   B. impoliteness

   C. decorum

8. He must <u>concentrate</u> closely on the mentally challenged individuals and anticipate any unforeseen circumstances.

   A. retract

   B. focus

   C. draw away

9. Being <u>responsible</u> for such a large group is physically and mentally draining. In addition to watching out for them, Jerry must converse and interact with them.

   A. reckless

   B. accountable

   C. irresponsible

10. Nevertheless, volunteer work is personally <u>satisfying</u>. While pursuing his Master's degree, he had little time for extracurricular activities.

   A. not up to scratch

   B. below par

   C. fulfilling

Answer Key

解　答

Answer Key
Expressing interest in a profession
表達工作相關興趣

A

Situation 1

Susan's recent research interests have not only provided her with a sound theoretical knowledge of medical technology, but also allowed her to develop advanced expertise in conducting independent research. In pursuing these interests, she has acquired many professional skills to become familiar not only with the demands of her chosen career path, but also with potential employment opportunities in the rapidly evolving medical technology field. As for the specifics of her research involvement, Susan has conducted experiments to purify trypsin inhibitors from seeds and characterize the trypsin inhibitor assay. She will apply her professional and academic knowledge in a biotechnology or bioscience-related career, hopefully at the Industrial Technology Research Institute, commonly known as ITRI. She is confident in her ability to design and implement a research plan, allowing her to contribute significantly to the advancement of Taiwan's medical technology sector. She hopes that ITRI will find these valuable assets conducive to its organizational needs.

Situation 2

Tom's interest in information technology stems from his first contact with this field in undergraduate computer classes. The Internet especially fascinates him, with its ability not only to provide seemingly unlimited information that can be conveniently accessed anywhere, but also to help him cut down on expenses that he might otherwise spend on textbooks or other literature. Although the Internet is his information source, Tom occasionally peruses the latest technology magazines at the bookstore. Information technologies have definitely transformed living standards globally, as new innovations seem to appear daily. This fact explains why almost everyone is eager to learn how to use the latest computer programs and acquire as many knowledge-based skills as possible. Besides his strong interest in information technologies, Tom has acquired much valuable research experience through graduate studies in the Institute of Business Management at Yuanpei University of Science and Technology. These two ingredients are crucial for his fully realizing his career aspirations. He can further refine his skills if employed at ABC Corporation. The opportunity to work at ABC Corporation would provide Tom with an excellent environment not only to actualize his potential in a career, but also allow him to apply theoretical knowledge-management concepts taught in graduate school in a practical work setting.

Situation 3

Mary was first exposed to hospital management during undergraduate school, where she read many hospital management-related case studies in preparation for her senior thesis. Changes in Taiwan's national health insurance system have posed serious challenges for hospitals, requiring that they employ skilled management professionals. Becoming aware of an individual hospital's needs has shown Mary the importance of hospitals establishing feasible strategies for remaining competitive. Additionally, frequently coming into contact with hospitals has allowed her to spend considerable time to learn about their unique organizational culture and research related topics. For instance, she once consulted a hospital administrator on the various practices adopted in daily operations. Such experiences made her aware of how novel management concepts can be applied in a practical setting. Moreover, Mary is committed to strengthening her research capabilities. Doing so will make her a more competent professional, allowing her to face unforeseeable obstacles more effectively. As a researcher, she strives to distinguish herself from other collaborators while remaining congenial and approachable. For her, working in a management position in a hospital involves many exciting challenges, and the opportunity to work at Chang Gung Memorial Hospital would allow her to realize her career aspirations fully. Mary is determined to learn as much as possible while contributing any beneficial results that she can generate. Chang Gung Memorial Hospital would be an excellent learning environment in which Mary could wholeheartedly contribute her knowledge and expertise.

B

1. What have your recent research interests enabled you to do?

2. What professional skills have you acquired while developing your recent research interests?

3. What area do you hope to apply your professional and academic knowledge?

4. What are you confident in your ability to do?

5. What are the specifics of your research involvement in the biotechnology field?

6. What has allowed you to contribute significantly to the advancement of Taiwan's medical technology sector?

7. What are the potential employment opportunities in the rapidly evolving medical technology field?

8. What advanced expertise did you develop in conducting independent research?

9. What did you develop a sound theoretical knowledge of while conducting independent research?

10. What valuable assets would you offer to ITRI that would be conducive to its organizational needs?

C

1. How did your interest in information technology stem from your contact with this field in undergraduate computer classes?

2. How has the Internet helped you cut down on expenses when exploring your

research interests?

3. How has the Internet provided you with seemingly unlimited information that can be conveniently accessed anywhere?

4. How have technologies in your field transformed living standards?

5. How have you acquired much valuable research experience in your field?

6. How have you come to fully realize your career aspirations?

7. How are you able to apply theoretical concepts taught in university to a practical work setting?

8. How did you become interested in information technology?

9. How would you be able to further refine your skills if employed at ABC Corporation?

10. How would the opportunity to work at ABC Corporation provide you with an excellent environment for fully realizing your research interests?

D

1. When were you first exposed to hospital management?

2. When did you become aware of an individual hospital's needs?

3. When did you realize the importance of hospitals establishing feasible strategies for remaining competitive?

4. When did you become aware of how novel management concepts can be applied in a practical setting?

5. When did you learn about the unique organizational culture of hospitals and research related topics?

6. When did you consult a hospital administrator on the various practices adopted in daily operations?

7. When did you become committed to strengthening your research capabilities?

8. When did you learn how to distinguish yourself from other collaborators while

remaining congenial and approachable?

9. When were you able to realize your career aspirations fully?

10. When did you become determined to learn as much as possible while contributing any beneficial results that you can generate?

E

1. What has becoming aware of an individual hospital's needs shown Mary?

The importance of hospitals establishing feasible strategies for remaining competitive

2. What does Mary's work in a management position in a hospital involve?

Many exciting challenges

3. What would be an excellent learning environment in which Mary could wholeheartedly contribute her knowledge and expertise?

Chang Gung Memorial Hospital

F

Situation 1

1. B 2. C 3. A 4. C 5. A

Situation 2

1. B 2. C 3. A 4. B 5. B

Situation 3

1. B 2. C 3. A 4. B 5. C

G

Situation 1

1. B 2. A 3. C 4. A 5. B 6. C 7. B 8. C 9. A 10. B

Situation 2

1. B 2. B 3. C 4. B 5. A 6. A 7. C 8. B 9. C 10. A

Situation 3

1. B 2. B 3. A 4. B 5. C 6. B 7. C 8. B 9. A 10. C

I

Situation 4

The prevalence of many diseases increases as human civilization progresses. For instance, the incidence of human cancer is on the rise. With his research interest in cancer and the human immune system, John hopes to participate in a learning module where he can work further on this fascinating topic. With the recent emergence of biotechnology as a significant area of scientific development, his expertise gained at graduate school will hopefully enable him to contribute significantly to society as he strives to discover new scientific applications. To achieve his professional aspirations, John hopes eventually to obtain a doctorate degree in a related field. As scientific and technological breakthroughs are made daily, biotechnology appears to have limitless potential applications, necessitating the aggressive research efforts. Hoping to contribute to society to alleviate the suffering of those with diseases, John believes that DEF Company offers an excellent working environment in which to pursue a research career in the intensely competitive biotech sector.

Situation 5

Human relations have intrigued Lisa since childhood. Each individual has his or her own unique way of communicating. Finding the most effective way to communicate one's intended meaning is essential. Lisa's fascination with this endeavor led her to continue to research human relations after completing undergraduate school. A management course in which she enrolled during her senior year at university totally challenged her previous ways of thinking. During that period, she decided to pursue a Master's degree in Business Management. Her work experience after she received undergraduate and graduate level training increased her desire to grasp management principles more fully. Theoretical knowledge has little value without work experience. Several years of practical work experience and solid determination have prepared Lisa for a management level position in a reputed company such as GHI Corporation.

Situation 6

Taiwan's national health insurance scheme was instituted in 1995 to integrate insurance and medical treatment throughout the island. All Taiwanese residents participate in the health insurance scheme, by the deduction of a certain amount from their monthly income. They are thus entitled to hold an insurance card for hospital outpatient or admissions services, paying only a small fraction of the entire cost. This health insurance scheme provides a valuable service, especially for those in poverty and for the elderly. However, an increase in monthly premium costs has led to many individuals' excessively using medical treatment resources, straining the system's finances. Therefore, Jerry is interested in formulating an indicator to monitor the financial strain experienced by a hospital. He is encouraged that his professional interests match Mackay Memorial Hospital's specialization in providing quality medical services.

J

1. What do you hope to eventually to do in order to achieve your professional aspirations?

2. What is on the rise?

3. What do you believe that DEF Company can offer?

4. What has recently emerged as a significant area of scientific development?

5. What appears to have limitless potential applications?

6. What do you hope to contribute to society?

7. What company would offer an excellent working environment in which to pursue a research career in the intensely competitive biotech sector?

8. What expertise did you gain at graduate school that will hopefully enable you to contribute significantly to society?

9. What degree do you hope to eventually obtain?

10. What does the intensely competitive biotech sector offer?

K

1. How were you totally challenged in your previous ways of thinking?

2. How did you learn to grasp management principles more fully?

3. How did you become prepared for a management level position in a reputed company such as GHI Corporation?

4. How did you reach a decision to pursue a Master's degree in Business Management?

5. How did your work experience increase your desire to grasp management principles more fully?

6. How has several years of practical work experience and solid determination prepared you for a management level position?

7. How did you find the most effective way to communicate your intended meaning?

8. How does each individual communicate in his or her own unique way?

9. How have your previous ways of thinking been challenged?

10. How many years of practical work experience do you have in preparation for a management level position?

L

1. Why was Taiwan's national health insurance scheme instituted in 1995?

2. Why can all Taiwanese residents participate in the health insurance scheme?

3. Why do Taiwanese pay only a small fraction of the entire cost of health-related expenses?

4. Why is the health insurance scheme especially good for those in poverty and for the elderly?

5. Why have many individuals began excessively using medical treatment resources?

6. Why have the national healthcare system's finances become strained?

7. Why are you interested in formulating an indicator to monitor the financial strain experienced by a hospital?

8. Why do your professional interests match the specialization of the company that you are seeking employment?

9. Why are you interested in Taiwan's national health insurance scheme?

10. Why has there been an increase in monthly premium costs in the national health insurance scheme?

M

1. What encourages Jerry?

That his professional interests match Mackay Memorial Hospital's specialization in providing quality medical services

2. What does this health insurance scheme provide?

A valuable service

3. What has led to an increase in monthly premium costs?

Many individuals excessively using medical treatment resources

N

Situation 4

1. C 2. A 3. C 4. B 5. C

Situation 5

1. A 2. C 3. A 4. C 5. A

Situation 6

1. C 2. B 3. A 4. B 5. C

O

Situation 4

1. B 2. C 3. B 4. A 5. C 6. B 7. C 8. B 9. A 10. C

Situation 5

1. A 2. B 3. C 4. B 5. A 6. C 7. B 8. C 9. B 10. A

Situation 6

1. B 2. C 3. B 4. A 5. C 6. A 7. C 8. B 9. C 10. B

A

Situation 1

Taiwan has positioned itself as "Green Silicon Island" following its swift industrial development in recent decades. Besides scientific, technological and societal advances, international marketing and management are essential. However, Taiwan's information industry severely lacks international marketing and management personnel. The integration of IT with marketing or management science has recently emerged in Taiwan as an important area of research. Although the Taiwanese information sector has access to state-of-the-art technologies, few related products have been exported. Moreover, few Taiwanese products have brand recognition abroad. Thus, local companies that seek for their products to have international appeal require personnel with international marketing and management backgrounds. As a leader in the information technology sector, DEF Corporation is renowned for its state-of-the-art products and services, as well as outstanding product research and technical capabilities. Tom hopes to become a member of the DEF corporate family; his expertise developed in graduate school and his strong academic knowledge and practical skills will definitely make him an asset to any collaborative product development effort. Offering more than just technical expertise, Tom is especially interested in how DEF Corporation's marketing and related management departments make strategic decisions. Employment at DEF Corporation will undoubtedly expose him to new fields, as long as he remains open and does not restrict himself to the range of his previous academic training.

Situation 2

While biotechnology has emerged in Taiwan in recent years, the island severely lacks biotechnology professionals with management backgrounds, preventing Taiwan from keeping up with recent global trends in research and development.

Biotechnology has the potential to integrate seemingly polar disciplines to create new applications, methods and market sectors in Taiwan. Taiwan's biotech sector has the potential to develop medical applications. As a recognized leader in the biotechnology sector, ABC Corporation can provide Jeff with an ideal working environment in which he can contribute to the development of innovative medical scientific applications. If successful in securing employment at this corporation, he will strive to enhance his research capabilities and professional knowledge. Employment at ABC Corporation will undoubtedly provide Jeff with a practical context for his graduate school training, ensuring that he will not restrict himself to the scope of his previous research.

Situation 3

Taiwan has become a globally leading manufacturing center, especially in computer-related products. Although imported information systems are adopted extensively in manufacturing, analyzed information is typically insufficient to help staff to complete their tasks effectively. Thus, overwork remains critical to manufacturing many products rapidly. Accordingly, death due to overworking has been much discussed recently. Individuals who grow up in such a competitive environment strive to work efficiently. Thus, methods of upgrading information systems to suit Taiwan's unique manufacturing processes and management culture are increasingly important. An excellent system depends not only on information technology but also on the appropriate consideration of management issues. Therefore, following her completion of a graduate degree in Business Management and several years of work experience in the information sector, Amy hopes to further her expertise in this area through employment in a globally renowned corporation, such as GHI Corporation. She is confident in her ability to pursue a research career in this field and, in so doing, to contribute significantly to society.

B

1. How has Taiwan positioned itself as "Green Silicon Island"?

2. How did DEF Corporation become a leader in the information technology sector?

3. How have local companies sought to export products with an international appeal?

4. How did DEF Corporation become a leader in the information technology sector?

5. How will your expertise developed in graduate school and strong academic knowledge and practical skills make you an asset to any collaborative product development effort?

6. How do hope to contribute as a member of the DEF corporate family?

7. How can you offer more than just technical expertise in your position at DEF Corporation?

8. How will employment at DEF Corporation expose you to new fields?

9. How has DEF Corporation distinguished itself in product research?

10. How has Taiwan's information industry responded to the severe lack of international marketing and management personnel?

C

1. What has emerged in Taiwan in recent years?

2. What prevents Taiwan from keeping up with recent global trends in research and development?

3. What has the potential to integrate seemingly polar disciplines to create new applications, methods and market sectors in Taiwan?

4. What kind of ideal working environment can ABC Corporation provide you with?

5. What will you strive to do if you are successful in securing employment at ABC Corporation?

6. What corporation is a recognized leader in the biotechnology sector?

7. What corporation would provide you with a practical context for your graduate

school training?

8. What sort of professionals with management backgrounds does Taiwan lack?

9. What potential applications can Taiwan's biotech sector develop?

10. What innovative applications do you hope to contribute to the development of?

D

1. Why has Taiwan become a globally leading manufacturing center, especially in computer-related products?

2. Why is staff often unable to complete their tasks effectively?

3. Why has this topic been much discussed recently?

4. Why do individuals who grow up in a competitive environment strive to work efficiently?

5. Why are methods of upgrading information systems increasingly important?

6. Why are Taiwan's unique manufacturing processes and management culture suitable for such methods?

7. Why do you hope to further your expertise in this area of development?

8. Why would this globally renowned corporation allow you to further your expertise in this area of development?

9. Why are you confident in your ability to pursue a research career in this field?

10. Why are you confident in your ability to contribute significantly to society?

E

1. What is increasingly important?

   Methods of upgrading information systems to suit Taiwan's unique manufacturing processes and management culture

2. What has Taiwan become?

   A globally leading manufacturing center

3. What are adopted extensively in manufacturing in Taiwan?

Imported information systems

F

Situation 1

1. B 2. C 3. B 4. A 5. C

Situation 2

1. B 2. C 3. A 4. C 5. B

Situation 3

1. B 2. C 3. B 4. A 5. C

G

Situation 1

1. C 2. B 3. A 4. A 5. C 6. C 7. A 8. B 9. B 10. C

Situation 2

1. C 2. A 3. C 4. A 5. C 6. B 7. B 8. C 9. C 10. A

Situation 3

1. B 2. C 3. B 4. C 5. B 6. A 7. B 8. B 9. C 10. B

I

Situation 4

The hectic pace and pressure of daily life, as well as the consumption of some highly nutritious foods, account for the increasing rate of cancer in the general population.

Therefore, identifying adequate therapeutic treatments and prognostic factors is essential in the field of radiological technology; Susan has a particular interest in management in this field. Breast cancer persists as the second leading cause of death among females with cancer. In academia, Susan has always been interested in identifying prognostic factors of breast cancer and especially those factors that can promote cures for treated patients. Opportunities in the technical and medical sectors of this field appear to be limitless. The variety of research projects and departments within ABC Company is quite impressive, and explains the company having taken a leading role in the medicine and pharmaceutical fields. Working at ABC Company would definitely promote her professional development. Having gained medical imaging expertise in graduate school, Susan believes that her solid academic training and practical knowledge will contribute to ABC Company's efforts to improve its reputation and technological capabilities, not only benefiting society but also increasing corporate profits.

Situation 5

Taiwan's hospitals severely lack medical professionals with a biotechnology background. This shortage may eventually obstruct societal progress and considerable resources may eventually have to be expended to solve unforeseeable problems. Matt is thus determined to improve his biotechnology-related skills for a career in medical imagery. As evidenced by its highly respected training courses in nuclear medicine, National Taiwan University Hospital has state-of-the-art instruments and expertise in handling stroke patients. For instance, its excellent staff has perfected easily distinguishing ischemia from hemorrhaging. If successful in securing employment at National Taiwan University Hospital, Matt will bring to this organization a solid academic background and practical expertise that will hopefully increase the life expectancy of hospital patients. Moreover, having passed an extremely difficult entrance examination taken by medical professionals in his field, he believes that his knowledge of medical imaging will be an asset to any clinical department to which he belongs.

Situation 6

Having devoted himself to developing computer information systems for over a decade, Larry is well aware that no information system can be implemented without problems. The end user must always spend much time to modify functions that are related to practical operations. Even after a system has gone online, it must be continually enhanced or modified because of corporate re-engineering, re-organization, ergonomic issues and consumer demand. Thus, Larry constantly strives to equip himself with stronger analytical skills to identify accurately what aspects of an information system must be developed, enhanced or modified. His maturation as a proficient researcher during graduate school will hopefully prove to be a valuable asset to ABC Corporation, allowing Larry to contribute significantly to any product development efforts.

J

1. Why is there an increasing rate of cancer in the general population?

2. Why is identifying adequate therapeutic treatments and prognostic factors essential in the field of radiological technology?

3. Why does breast cancer persist as the second leading cause of death among females with cancer?

4. Why do opportunities in the technical and medical sectors of this field appear to be limitless?

5. Why are you quite impressed with the variety of research projects and departments within ABC Company?

6. Why has this the company taken a leading role in the medicine and pharmaceutical fields?

7. Why would working at ABC Company definitely promote your professional development?

8. Why were you able to gain medical imaging expertise in graduate school?

9. Why are you confident in your ability to contribute to ABC Company's efforts to improve its reputation and technological capabilities?

10. Why is your solid academic training and practical knowledge essential for employment at ABC Company?

K

1. What sort of medical professionals do Taiwan's hospitals severely lack?

2. What may eventually obstruct societal progress and considerable resources if this problem is not solved?

3. What skills are you determined to improve upon for a career in medical imagery?

4. What evidence is there that National Taiwan University has highly respected training courses in nuclear medicine?

5. What state-of-the-art instruments and expertise does National Taiwan University Hospital have in handling stroke patients?

6. What skills has the excellent staff at National Taiwan University Hospital perfected?

7. What can you bring to this organization if successful in securing employment at National Taiwan University Hospital?

8. What evidence demonstrates that you are qualified to be a medical professional in his field?

9. What knowledge expertise do you have that will be an asset to any clinical department to which you belong?

Unit Two   Answer Key
Describing the field or industry to which one's profession belongs
興趣相關產業描寫

10. What was the level of difficulty in the entrance examination that you passed?

L

1. How long have you devoted yourself to developing computer information systems?

2. How did you become aware that no information system can be implemented without problems?

3. How does the end user modify functions that are related to practical operations?

4. How does corporate re-engineering, re-organization, ergonomic issues and consumer demand affect a system having gone on-line?

5. How do you attempt to identify accurately what aspects of an information system must be developed, enhanced or modified?

6. How have you matured as a proficient researcher in your field?

7. How do you hope prove to be a valuable asset to ABC Corporation if successfully employed there?

8. How will you contribute significantly to any product development efforts at ABC Corporation?

9. How have you equipped yourself with stronger analytical skills that are necessary for the workplace?

10. How have computer information systems changed over the past decade?

M

1. Where does Matt hope to secure employment?

National Taiwan University Hospital

2. What does Matt bring to National Taiwan University Hospital?

A solid academic background and practical expertise

3. What did Matt pass?

An extremely difficult entrance examination

N
Situation 4

1. B 2. A 3. C 4. A 5. C

Situation 5

1. B 2. A 3. C 4. B 5. B

Situation 6

1. B 2. C 3. A 4. B 5. C

O
Situation 4

1. B 2. A 3. B 4. C 5. B 6. A 7. C 8. B 9. C 10. B

Situation 5

1. B 2. B 3. A 4. C 5. B 6. B 7. C 8. A 9. C 10. B

Situation 6

1. B 2. C 3. A 4. B 5. B 6. C 7. B 8. A 9. C 10. B

Answer Key
Describing participation in a project that reflects interest in a profession
描述所參與方案裡專業興趣的表現

A

Situation 1

The intellectual rigor of highly theoretical study over nearly four years in the Department of Nuclear Science at National Tsing Hua University equipped Jim with a solid background in independently conducting experiments. During this period, his extensive laboratory training made him extremely conscientious and careful in using laboratory instruments, while ensuring timely completion of tasks. Following his undergraduate studies, he served as a research assistant in the Institute of Environmental Engineering at National Taiwan University. As a highly adept investigator in the laboratory, Jim learned not only how seemingly disparate fields are related to each other, but also how to succeed in complex projects that force him to apply theoretical concepts in a practical context. This practical experience greatly increased his competence in obtaining pertinent data and analyzing problems independently. ABC Corporation will hopefully find these qualities to be invaluable to any research in which he is involved.

Situation 2

Owing to a deep interest in biotechnology, Jane has actively participated in projects aimed at establishing a humane leukemia disease model in zebrafish embryos. Her experimental results demonstrated the effectiveness of her proposed model. This disease model provided a formation mechanism of use in other animal models. This model is also a valuable reference for physicians when they treat patients. After carefully reading DEF Company's on-line promotional material, Jane is especially interested in its innovative product development strategy and in its laboratory, which are responsible for the company's leading its field. She is confident of DEF's ability to give her the opportunity to build upon her previous experience in the above area.

Situation 3

Following graduation from university, Sam joined the army as a professional soldier and officer. He was initially responsible for handling the administration of the physical examinations of six thousand new soldiers out of a large squadron of around ten thousand military personnel. In this capacity, he was directly responsible to a general. The environment provided him with many opportunities not only to come into contact with hospital staff and physicians, but also to familiarize himself with large-scale operations. These valuable experiences enabled Sam to comprehend not only why confusion often arose in a health-related environment, but also why health-care administration students become discouraged with many management methods that are neither applicable to practical business nor innovative. His second job involved managing the activities of nearly 160 soldiers. Applying his previous experiences to the tasks at hand, Sam realized how students lack experience in implementing various models and conducting operations in medium-sized and large-scale organizations. His experiences have allowed him to understand fundamental concepts of importance to any professional in the health care and management sector. LMN Corporation can provide him with a unique opportunity to build upon his previous experiences in the above areas.

B

1. How did the Department of Nuclear Science at National Tsing Hua University equip you with a solid background in independently conducting experiments?

2. How did your extensive laboratory training make you extremely conscientious and careful in using laboratory instruments?

3. How were you able to complete laboratory tasks on time?

4. How did you learn how seemingly disparate fields are related to each other?

5. How did you learn to succeed in complex projects that forced you to apply

theoretical concepts in a practical context?

6. How did you become a highly adept investigator in the laboratory?

7. How has your practical experience greatly increased your competence in the laboratory?

8. How did you learn to increase your competence in obtaining pertinent data and analyze problems independently?

9. How did you perform as a research assistant in the Institute of Environmental Engineering at National Taiwan University?

10. How did the highly theoretical study in the Department of Nuclear Science at National Tsing Hua University benefit your subsequent work as a research assistant?

C

1. What motivated your active participation in projects aimed at establishing a humane leukemia disease model in zebrafish embryos?

2. What did the experimental results in your research study demonstrate?

3. What are the merits of your proposed model?

4. What sparked your deep interest in biotechnology?

5. What sparked your interest in working at DEF Company?

6. What literature is available on DEF Company's innovative product development strategy?

7. What can DEF Corporation give you the opportunity to do?

8. What is DEF Company renowned for?

9. What proof do you have to demonstrate the effectiveness of your proposed model?

10. What promotional material does DEF Corporation offer to introduce its innovative products?

D

1. Why did you wait to join the army until after graduating from university?

2. Why did you have many opportunities not only to come into contact with hospital staff and physicians, but also to familiarize yourself with large-scale operations?

3. Why are you able to comprehend why confusion often arises in a health-related environment?

4. Why did the environment that you worked in allow you to familiarize yourself with large-scale operations?

5. Why do students lack experience in implementing various models and conducting operations in medium-sized and large-scale organizations?

6. Why have your experiences allowed you to understand fundamental concepts of importance to any professional in the health care and management sector?

7. Why are you able to apply your previous experiences to the tasks at hand?

8. Why are you confident in LMN Corporation's ability to provide you with a unique opportunity to build upon your previous experiences?

9. Why do you believe that your previous experiences will enable you to thrive at LMN Corporation?

10. Why did your responsibilities in the army change over time?

E

1. What did Sam join the army as?

   A professional soldier and officer

2. What enabled Sam to comprehend why confusion often arises in a health-related environment?

   These valuable experiences

3. What can provide Sam with a unique opportunity to build upon his previous experiences in the above areas?

LMN Corporation

F

Situation 1

1. B 2. A 3. B 4. A 5. B

Situation 2

1. C 2. B 3. C 4. A 5. B

Situation 3

1. B 2. C 3. B 4. A 5. B

G

Situation 1

1. C 2. B 3. C 4. C 5. A 6. B 7. A 8. B 9. C 10. B

Situation 2

1. C 2. A 3. B 4. C 5. A 6. B 7. B 8. C 9. A

Situation 3

1. B 2. C 3. B 4. A 5. B 6. C 7. A 8. B 9. C 10. B

I

Situation 4

Max is concerned with the needs and satisfaction of hospital emergency patients, as evidenced by his recent collaboration with colleagues in a study that involved a questionnaire given to family members. It contained 125 queries on the level of treatment provided by physicians and emergency staff. The level of satisfaction with the emergency unit's treatment of their relatives was only 80%, reflecting how public health personnel cannot satisfy the medical consumer's demand for quality healthcare. The results of that study provide a valuable reference for hospital administrators regarding how to increase the standard of care offered by public health personnel. If Max were employed at the Veterans General Hospital in Taipei, the medical center would offer him comprehensive training and challenges that would greatly enhance his professional skills.

Situation 5

When at undergraduate school, Karen participated in a National Science Council-sponsored research project, which led to her subsequent graduate study of Chinese herbal medicine. The findings of her research have been published in domestic and international journals. She has also participated in developing an undergraduate enzymology curriculum, which received praise from both teachers and students. While researching enzyme-related topics in graduate school, she also became adept at conducting experiments on microbe development, genetic engineering and agent analysis. Having both participated in curriculum development and mastered several laboratory skills, Karen was also actively engaged in food science research aimed at the genetic modification of microbes and analysis of related properties and agents. In summary, her research skills acquired as an undergraduate in the Food Science Department and as a graduate student at the Institute of Biotechnology reflect her commitment to pursuing a biotechnology-related career in the food science sector. Karen is confident in her ability to contribute significantly to product development efforts at GHI Corporation, to create healthy food and medicine.

Situation 6

Ellen's strong desire constantly to strengthen her statistical capabilities is reflected by her active participation in a collaborative project with an ophthalmologist at Kuo General Hospital in analyzing medical data and storing them in a novel database for statistical software. Carefully analyzing the data revealed unique phenomena related to the hospital's particular circumstances, providing a valuable reference for administrators who are making marketing-related decisions about the medical sector. The project involved the use of data mining approaches to identify patients' particular needs. This project made Ellen aware that a hospital must distinguish itself from others by its marketing practices to gain a competitive edge. Having paid considerable attention to effective hospital management, IJK Corporation has played a leading role in the medical sector. Extensive on-the-job training is a notable example of its commitment to quality excellence. Such training could provide Ellen with the latest knowledge required to build on her previous experiences in the above area.

J

1. What evidence do you have of your concern with the needs and satisfaction of hospital emergency patients?

2. What did the questionnaire given to family members contain?

3. What was the level of satisfaction with the emergency unit's treatment of the patients' relatives?

4. What reflects the inability of public health personnel to satisfy the medical consumer's demand for quality healthcare?

5. What did the results of that study provide?

6. What would employment in the medical center at the Veterans General Hospital in Taipei offer you?

7. What would greatly enhance your professional skills at the Veterans General Hospital in Taipei?

8. What line of work are you in?

9. What is your level of satisfaction with the work that you are currently involved?

10. What aspect of quality healthcare are you involved?

K

1. Why was your participation in a National Science Council-sponsored research project productive?

2. Why did your graduate study of Chinese herbal medicine originate from your work in undergraduate school?

3. Why did you receive praise from both teachers and students?

4. Why did you become became adept at conducting experiments on microbe development, genetic engineering and agent analysis?

5. Why did your food science research aim at the genetic modification of microbes and analysis of related properties and agents?

6. Why do your research skills reflect your commitment to pursuing a biotechnology-related career in the food science sector?

7. Why are you confident in your ability to contribute significantly to product development efforts at GHI Corporation?

8. Why would your employment at GHI Corporation benefit the company?

9. Why were you interested in participating in a National Science Council-sponsored research project at undergraduate school?

10. Why did you participate in curriculum development during graduate school?

L

1. How did participation in a collaborative project with an ophthalmologist at Kuo

General Hospital benefit you?

2. How did your research provide a valuable reference for administrators who are making marketing-related decisions about the medical sector?

3. How did you identify patients' particular needs in your project?

4. How did you become aware that a hospital must distinguish itself from others by its marketing practices to gain a competitive edge?

5. How has IJK Corporation played a leading role in the medical sector?

6. How has IJK Corporation demonstrated its commitment to quality excellence?

7. How could training at IJK Corporation provide Ellen with the latest knowledge required to build on her previous experiences?

8. How did you develop your strong desire to strengthen your statistical capabilities?

9. How did you become involved in a collaborative project aimed at analyzing medical data and storing them in a novel database for statistical software?

10. How do administrators make marketing-related decisions about the medical sector?

M

1. What does Ellen have a strong desire constantly to do?

Strengthen her statistical capabilities

2. What did Ellen's project involved the use of?

Data mining approaches

3. What is Ellen aware of?

That a hospital must distinguish itself from others by its marketing practices to gain a competitive edge

N

Situation 4

1. C 2. B 3. C 4. A 5. B

Situation 5

1. C 2. B 3. C 4. A 5. C

Situation 6

1. B 2. A 3. C 4. B 5. C

O

Situation 4

1. B 2. A 3. C 4. B 5. A 6. B 7. A 8. C 9. B 10. A

Situation 5

1. C 2. B 3. A 4. B 5. B 6. C 7. B 8. C 9. A 10. C

Situation 6

1. C 2. A 3. B 4. C 5. B 6. C 7. B 8. A 9. C 10. B

A

Situation 1

Larry's strong commitment to the Business Management field has involved acquiring knowledge and skills through graduate school training. This commitment has not only made him competent academically, but also allowed him to thrive in the workplace. During undergraduate training, while learning how to adopt different perspectives when solving a particular problem, he acquired several statistical and analytical skills. Doing so involved learning how to analyze problems, identify potential solutions, and implement those solutions according to concepts taught in the classroom. Larry's excellence in these areas proved especially effective in devising marketing strategies for research purposes. When initially lacking expertise in a particular topic at the outset, he strives to absorb quickly new information and adapt to new situations. He believes that ABC Company will find this quality highly desirable.

Situation 2

Graduate level research in biochemistry exposed Susan to a wide array of issues in salivary hormone research. While writing her Master's thesis, she was fortunate enough to be supervised by a renowned professor from National Taiwan University, allowing her to receive specialized training in his laboratory. Susan adopted these extremely high standards in the laboratory and handled a heavy workload, so she learned many new skills and advanced techniques. Her graduate research focused mainly on saliva hormone assay, an emerging field of clinical diagnosis. Becoming skillful in the use of the latest techniques in this field made her confident in both her theoretical and practical expertise in the laboratory. This acquired expertise has greatly increased her awareness of the latest developments in the field, both practical and theoretical, allowing her eventually to take a leading role in laboratory activities. Additionally, the various seminars and conferences in which Susan participated increased her opportunity to acquire and exchange knowledge with peers in various ways. Co-authoring papers as a graduate student made her aware of the detailed publication and review process. Combined with her extensive experience as a technical assistant that matured her as a researcher, her advanced training will place her in a better position to understand and respond to the frequent changes that occur in clinical science. Given her solid academic background, Susan is confident in her ability to contribute significantly to DEF Company's efforts to develop innovative technology products.

Situation 3

Graduate school exposed Jerry to the high pressure and demands of conducting original research and publishing findings in international journals. These capabilities will undoubtedly allow him to excel in the biotechnology field, as they more fully equip him with technical and professional expertise. His diverse scientific interests allow him to see beyond the conventional limits of a discipline and fully comprehend how his field relates to others. Undergraduate and graduate-level courses in biotechnology often included term projects that allowed him to apply theoretical concepts in a practical context and develop problem-solving skills. While pursuing a Master's degree, Jerry received intensive training. More specifically, he learned how to analyze problems, find solutions, and implement those solutions according to the concepts taught in class. He is absolutely confident that his academic background, experimental and work experience in biotechnology, strong desire for acquiring knowledge and love of challenges will enable him to succeed in GHI Corporation's highly demanding product development projects.

B

1. How did you develop your strong commitment to the Business Management field?

2. How has your commitment to the Business Management field made you competent academically?

3. How has your commitment to the Business Management field allowed you to thrive in the workplace?

4. How did you learn how to adopt different perspectives when solving a particular problem during undergraduate training?

5. How did you learn how to identify potential solutions, and, then, implement those solutions according to concepts taught in the classroom?

6. How did your excellence during undergraduate training prove effective in devising marketing strategies for research purposes?

7. How do you respond when you lack expertise in a particular topic at the outset?

8. How can you absorb new information quickly and adapt to new situations when you are unfamiliar with a new topic?

9. How receptive will ABC Company be to your expertise in this field?

10. How did undergraduate training prepare you for work in a research laboratory?

C

1. Why did graduate level research in biochemistry expose you to a wide array of issues in salivary hormone research?

2. Why were you able to receive specialized training while writing your Master's thesis?

3. Why were you able to learn many new skills and advanced techniques while working in the laboratory?

4. Why is saliva hormone assay an emerging field of clinical diagnosis?

5. Why are you confident in both your theoretical and practical expertise in the laboratory?

6. Why were you eventually able to take a leading role in laboratory activities?

7. Why did you become increasingly aware of the latest developments in your field?

8. Why did the various seminars and conferences in which you participated increase your research opportunities?

9. Why did you become aware of the detailed publication and review process when submitting an article?

10. Why will your advanced training place you in a better position to understand and respond to the frequent changes that occur in clinical science?

D

1. What did graduate school expose you to?

2. What capabilities will allow you to excel in the biotechnology field?

3. What capabilities learned in graduate school will equip you with technical and professional expertise in your chosen field?

4. What undergraduate courses allowed you to apply theoretical concepts in a practical context and develop problem-solving skills?

5. What experiences have allowed you to receive intensive training in your field?

6. What concepts taught in class oriented you on how to analyze problems, find solutions, and implement those solutions?

7. What will enable you to succeed in GHI Corporation's highly demanding product development projects?

8. What experience do you have in seeing beyond the conventional limits of a discipline and fully comprehending how your field relates to others?

9. What experience do you have in publishing your research findings in international journals?

10. What technical and professional expertise did you acquire during graduate school?

E

1. What does Jerry's diverse scientific interests allow him to see beyond?

   The conventional limits of a discipline

2. What did Jerry learn how to do while pursuing a Master's degree?

   Analyze problems, find solutions, and implement those solutions according to the concepts taught in class.

3. What did Jerry's term projects in undergraduate and graduate-level courses allow him to do?

   Apply theoretical concepts in a practical context and develop problem-solving skills

F

Situation 1

1. C 2. A 3. C 4. A 5. B

Situation 2

1. B 2. C 3. A 4. C 5. B

Situation 3

1. A 2. C 3. C 4. B 5. C

G

Situation 1

1. C 2. A 3. B 4. C 5. A 6. C 7. B 8. A 9. A 10. B

Situation 2

1. B 2. C 3. A 4. C 5. B 6. C 7. A 8. C 9. B

Situation 3

1. A 2. A 3. C 4. B 5. C 6. B 7. C 8. B 9. C 10. C

|

Situation 4

Mary's academic study enabled her to search for sources of problems by gathering large amounts of data to offer hypotheses for her research. As a graduate student, she handled a heavy schedule, performing many experiments in collaboration with her classmates, thereby cultivating many friendships. In graduate school, Mary strived to distinguish between theoretical and practical applications to understand the global implications of her field. Moreover, her academic activities allowed her not only to strengthen her English language skills, but also to take many unique leadership opportunities that allowed her to broaden her horizons and become a high achiever. Whether she can contribute to society depends on whether she can remain conscientious, flexible and focused. Continual self-improvement through employment in JKL Corporation will allow Mary to see fruitful results of her work and, in so doing, make her life more meaningful.

Situation 5

Tom's undergraduate training in Radiotechnology and his Master's degree in Medical Imagery enabled him to acquire sufficient expertise to contribute significantly to Taiwan's medical sector. He focused on nuclear medicine and radiochemistry, with a particular emphasis on developing radiochemistry-related analytical skills as well as becoming proficient in conducting laboratory experiments. Undergraduate and graduate-level courses in radiochemistry and medical imagery taught him a wide array of theoretical concepts associated with radiopharmaceutical synthesis. Tom's research at graduate school often involved deriving complex models and modifying clinical practices to meet research requirements. He also attended several international conferences on radiology technology, increasing his exposure to the radiochemistry profession. Moreover, intensive laboratory training enhanced his ability to respond effectively to unforeseen bottlenecks in research. Chang Gung Memorial Hospital will undoubtedly find Tom's experiences to be a valuable asset to any collaborative effort in which he is engaged.

Situation 6

Laura's interest in biotechnology can be traced back to her first exposure to physiology. She thus completed a master's degree with an emphasis on biotechnology. In the laboratory, she accumulated much bio-informatics-related knowledge. While pursuing a Master's degree in Medical Imagery at Yuanpei University of Science and Technology, she conducted biotechnology-related research at the Animal Technology Institute of Taiwan (ATIT). Graduate-level research prepared her for the rigorous demands of generating experimental results and publishing those findings in domestic and international journals. She has acquired fundamental and advanced research capabilities. She has not only nurtured a talent in biotechnology through a multidisciplinary approach, but also widened her field of interest to grasp fully the latest biotechnology-related concepts. Moreover, her participation in research projects that encompassed other seemingly unrelated fields reflects her willingness to absorb tremendous amounts of information and manage her time efficiently. Working at ABC Company would provide Laura with an excellent environment not only to realize fully her career aspirations, but also to apply theoretical knowledge management concepts taught in graduate school, in a practical work setting.

J

1. How did academic study enable you to search for sources of problems?

2. How were you able to cultivate many friendships during graduate school?

3. How did you attempt to understand the global implications of your field?

4. How did your academic activities allow you to strengthen your English language skills?

5. How did your academic activities allow you to broaden your horizons and become a high achiever?

6. How do you hope to contribute to society through your profession?

7. How can you remain conscientious, flexible and focused in your profession?

8. How will continual self-improvement through employment in JKL Corporation benefit you?

9. How do you hope to make your life more meaningful through your work?

10. How can English language skills increase your employment opportunities?

K

1. Why are you able to contribute significantly to Taiwan's medical sector?

2. Why did you emphasize developing radiochemistry-related analytical skills as well as becoming proficient in conducting laboratory experiments during graduate school?

3. Why were you able to acquire a wide array of theoretical concepts associated with radiopharmaceutical synthesis during undergraduate school?

4. Why did your research requirements often involve deriving complex models and modifying clinical practices?

5. Why did attending several international conferences on radiology technology increase your exposure to the radiochemistry profession?

6. Why were you able to enhance your ability to respond effectively to unforeseen

bottlenecks in research?

7. Why would Chang Gung Memorial Hospital find your experiences to be a valuable asset to any collaborative effort in which you are engaged?

8. Why would working at Chang Gung Memorial Hospital enhance your previous working experiences?

9. Why is it important for you to acquire sufficient expertise in Medical Imagery?

L

1. What can you trace your interest in biotechnology back to?

2. What did you emphasize in your research while completing a master's degree?

3. What institute did you work at while conducting biotechnology-related research for your master's degree?

4. What did graduate-level research prepare you for?

5. What fundamental and advanced research capabilities did you acquire while in graduate school?

6. What multidisciplinary approaches did you adopt to nurture your talent in conducting biotechnology-related research?

7. What were some of the latest biotechnology-related concepts that you were able to grasp fully in order to widen your field of interest?

8. What research projects did you participate in encompassed other seemingly unrelated fields?

9. What allowed you to absorb tremendous amounts of information and manage your time efficiently during graduate school?

10. What sort of environment would working at ABC Company provide you with?

M

1. Where did Laura conduct biotechnology-related research at?

The Animal Technology Institute of Taiwan (ATIT)

2. What university did Laura pursue a Master's degree in Medical Imagery?

Yuanpei University of Science and Technology

3. What company would provide Laura with an excellent environment not only to realize fully her career aspirations?

ABC Company

N

Situation 4

1. A 2. B 3. C 4. C 5.B

Situation 5

1. B 2. A 3. C 4. B 5. B

Situation 6

1. B 2. B 3. A 4. C 5. B

O

Situation 4

1. B 2. C 3. A 4. C 5. B 6. C 7. B 8. C 9. A 10. C

Situation 5

1. B 2. C 3. A 4. B 5. B 6. C 7. C 8. A 9. B 10. C

Situation 6

1. B 2. C 3. A 4. C 5. B 6. C 7. A 8. C 9. C 10. B

Answer Key

Introducing research and professional experiences relevant to employment
介紹研究及工作經驗

A

Situation 1

Although Alice has had several practicum internships at different hospitals during university, her current work is in a totally different area from the work she has been involved in previously. Although initially unfamiliar with the medical instrumentation, work environment and work flow, she learned quickly, and her colleagues helped her to become more proficient. Interpersonal skills are necessary in developing a collaborative environment among the staff and increasing work efficiency. A strong sense of comradeship enables each individual to perform his or her task. Alice's work has also exposed her daily to patients from all walks of life; she empathizes with those in pain and is concerned with their welfare, as well as that of their family and dependants. She has been able to use this empathy in examining them thoroughly and accurately diagnosing disease symptoms. As a graduate school student, Alice acquired the theoretical knowledge she needed to combine with her clinical experience to enable her to enhance her research capabilities more effectively to help her patients. She considers her work to be almost a calling, making her even more determined to serve sick people as an important part of her career.

Situation 2

In March 2001, before graduation, Max began working at the Radiological Department at Chang Gung Memorial Hospital. He benefited greatly from the support of his colleagues. After three months, his colleagues recommended him to preside over all of the department's activities, to participate in the annual convention, and to make an overseas tour. These tasks deepened his knowledge of the disposition method and the interlocution mode. In the following year, Max represented the Radiological Department at the hospital's Quality Control Convention, where he received first prize for his work. This accomplishment greatly increased his confidence in his professional abilities. He firmly believes that quality control is essential for patients to benefit from excellent medical services. Additionally, his faith in God supports his belief that opportunities are presented to individuals for a purpose. Despite the challenges of working in the radiology technology profession, Max is determined to succeed. Moreover, he believes that individuals have the freedom to choose what they love, and should learn to love the vocation that they have chosen.

Situation 3

When assigned a task, Margaret carefully arranges a flexible schedule that can be adjusted in case of a crisis or any need for change. Professional experience with the student association has fostered her communicative skills and her ability to achieve accuracy and efficiency. For instance, holding conferences is an essential communicative skill in daily work, despite potential tedium and inefficiency. Her ability to use time effectively in meetings reflects her strong desire to identify the interests of individual collaborators while actively pursuing a common goal. Such an approach strengthens her knowledge, skills and expertise. In particular, Margaret has come to understand the merits and limitations of various methods used in business, and the need to clearly define objectives. In addition to a solid academic background, a good manager should have strong communicative, organizational and management skills. Margaret is confident that she possesses such qualities.

B

1. How did you become familiar with the medical instrumentation, work environment and work flow that you were initially unfamiliar with?

2. How important are interpersonal skills in developing a collaborative environment

371

among the staff and increasing work efficiency?

3. How is each individual enabled to perform his or her task?

4. How do you empathize with those patients in pain in the workplace?

5. How are you able to accurately diagnose the disease symptoms of your patients?

6. How did acquiring the theoretical knowledge you needed to combine with your clinical experience enable you to enhance your research capabilities?

7. How did you become even more determined to serve sick people as an important part of your career?

8. How did you come into contact with different hospitals during university?

9. How did you become more proficient in your work?

10. How is your current work totally different from the work you were involved in previously?

C

1. Why did you benefit greatly from your work at the Radiological Department at Chang Gung Memorial Hospital?

2. Why did your colleagues recommend you to preside over all of the department's activities?

3. Why did you he receive first prize at the hospital's Quality Control Convention?

4. Why do you firmly believe that quality control is essential for patients?

5. Why do you believe that opportunities are presented to individuals for a purpose?

6. Why are you determined to succeed in the radiology technology profession?

7. Why do you believe that individuals have the freedom to choose what they love?

8. Why do you believe that individuals should learn to love the vocation that they have chosen?

9. Why did your colleagues have confidence in your managerial skills?

10. Why did departmental tasks deepen your knowledge of administrative

operations?

D

1. What has fostered your communicative skills and ability to achieve accuracy and efficiency?

2. What is an essential communicative skill in daily work?

3. What reflects your strong desire to identify the interests of individual collaborators while actively pursuing a common goal?

4. What has strengthened your knowledge, skills and expertise?

5. What have you come to understand as important in your work?

6. What should a good manager have?

7. What sort of experience do you have with the student association?

8. What needs to be clearly defined when using various methods in business?

9. What is required of a manager when individual collaborators are actively pursuing a common goal?

10. What aspects of various methods used in business need to be understood?

E

1. What has Margaret come to understand?

The merits and limitations of various methods used in business, and the need to clearly define objectives

2. What should a good manager have?

Strong communicative, organizational and management skills

3. What does Margaret carefully arrange when assigned a task?

A flexible schedule that can be adjusted in case of a crisis or any need for change

F

Situation 1

1. B 2. A 3. B 4. C 5. B

Situation 2

1. C 2. A 3. C 4. B 5. C

Situation 3

1. C 2. C 3. B 4. A 5. B

G

Situation 1

1. A 2. C 3. B 4. C 5. A 6. C 7. B 8. A 9. B 10. C

Situation 2

1. B 2. C 3. B 4. C 5. B 6. C 7. A 8. B 9. C 10. B

Situation 3

1. C 2. A 3. B 4. C 5. B 6. A 7. C 8. B 9. A 10. C

I

Situation 4

Bill is committed to his many patients. His deep concern for patients' welfare has led his colleagues and superiors to commend him many times on his responsible attitude. Like most medical professionals, he feels overwhelmed by the rapid rate at which new medical technologies emerge, and are adopted by hospitals. Bill must therefore continually increase his expertise to ensure that his patients can maintain a basic quality of life. For instance, he must know how to repair nuclear medicine machinery. He also believes that remaining optimistic when interacting with others is essential, especially as people become increasingly competitive.

Situation 5

Teresa participated in a project to assess the quality of a hospital's medical services. This experience enhanced her academic knowledge and significantly improved her analytical skills and data collection capabilities. Her hands-on experience in a hospital administrative department provided her with numerous opportunities to corroborate what she had learned from textbooks and. then, to apply that knowledge to solving independently the problems at hand. The hospital's practical training definitely strengthened Teresa's research skills in areas where she was previously lacking, including problems analysis, data collection, data evaluation and collaboration within a research group. By requiring her to meet many responsibilities, this project greatly matured her as an individual. These skills will now prove valuable in any future research project in which she is involved, hopefully at DEF Corporation.

Situation 6

While pursuing her Master's degree, May continued to work at Ton-Yen General Hospital, which was an excellent environment for conducting graduate-level research. Her work experience further developed her professional skills and taught her how to collaborate closely with others. In so doing, she not only absorbed colleagues' perspectives, but also learned how carefully to negotiate with others, while maintaining the dignity of each collaborator. If successful in gaining employment at ABC Corporation, May will strive to contribute to the organization in her unique manner, which is friendly, contemplative and graceful. Her previous work experience definitely supports her aspiration to become a healthcare management professional. Given her strong research capabilities, knowledge and expertise, May is determined to learn as much as possible while contributing any beneficial results that can be generated by research at her workplace.

J

1. Why have your colleagues and superiors commended you many times on your responsible attitude?

2. Why are you similar to most medical professionals?

3. Why are you committed to your many patients?

4. Why must you continually increase your expertise?

5. Why are you deeply concerned for your patients' welfare?

6. Why do new medical technologies emerge at a rapid rate?

7. Why are you able to remain optimistic when interacting with others?

8. Why is your expertise essential to ensure that your patients can maintain a basic quality of life?

9. Why do you feel overwhelmed by the rapid rate at which new medical technologies emerge?

10. Why must you know how to repair machinery in your workplace?

K

1. How were you able to enhance your academic knowledge and significantly improve your analytical skills and data collection capabilities?

2. How did you become involved with this project?

3. How were you able to corroborate what you had learned from textbooks?

4. How were you able to apply knowledge from textbooks to solve independently the problems at hand?

5. How has the hospital's practical training strengthened your research skills?

6. How has this project greatly matured you as an individual?

7. How will the skills that you have learned prove valuable in any future research project in which you are involved?

8. How has your hands-on experience in a hospital administrative department benefited you in the workplace?

9. How have you improved upon your research skills in areas where you were previously lacking?

10. How will DEF Corporation be able to employ your skills?

L

1. What provided an excellent environment for conducting graduate-level research?

2. What further developed your professional skills and taught you how to collaborate closely with others?

3. What allowed you to absorb colleagues' perspectives and learn how to carefully negotiate with others?

4. What will you strive to do if successful in gaining employment at ABC Corporation?

5. What is the best way to describe your unique manner?

6. What has supported your aspiration to become a healthcare management professional?

7. What assets do you bring to this profession?

8. What do you hope that research at your workplace can contribute?

9. What do you aspire to become?

10. What contribution have you made to your organization?

M

1. What is May determined to do?

   Learn as much as possible while contributing any beneficial results that can be generated by research at her workplace

2. What did May learn from her work experience

   How carefully to negotiate with others, while maintaining the dignity of each collaborator

3. How will May strive to contribute to the organization?

   In her unique manner

N

Situation 4

1. B 2. C 3. B 4. C 5. A

Situation 5

1. B 2. C 3. A 4. B 5. C

Situation 6

1. B 2. C 3. B 4. A 5. B

O

Situation 4

1. C 2. A 3. B 4. A 5. B 6. C 7. B 8. C 9. B 10. C

Situation 5

1. C 2. B 3. C 4. B 5. C 6. B 7. A 8. B 9. C 10. A

Situation 6

1. B　2. C　3. A　4. B　5. A　6. C　7. B　8. C　9. B　10. B

Answer Key

Describing extracurricular activities relevant to employment
描述與求職相關的課外活動

A

Situation 1

At university, Shelly participated in several student associations. For instance, she was actively involved in the student activity center (SAC) for three years. SAC was largely responsible for coordinating the administrative activities of 65 student associations at Chungtai Institute of Health Sciences and Technology. It distributed funds, supervised and supported activities, provided consultation and sponsored large-scale events. At SAC, Shelly was in charge of furnishing and operating stage lighting and acoustics for campus events. This position not only offered her many opportunities to come into contact with people from diverse backgrounds, but also to write proposals and use a wide array of skills. Through much of her experience of serving in the Society of Emergency Medicine, R.O.C., Shelly became aware of the importance of writing skills and related administrative skills because SAC's approach to planning a framework and implementing operations closely resembles academic research methods. During university, she also served as a student association leader, in which capacity she cooperated with the governmental sector to hold small-scale activities. This position not only improved her organizational skills and ability to handle crises, but also made her a persevering and punctual individual who can cope with unforeseen circumstances.

Situation 2

John considers himself to be friendly and diligent. At university, he participated in several student association activities, including table tennis, tennis and other class-related activities. Participating in sports allowed him more closely to interact with people. He conducted experiments in his spare time, which required hard work since they often involved trial-and-error procedures. Such experimentation has made him a more patient and persevering individual. Additionally, serving as class leader has improved his ability to coordinate and execute administrative tasks. John firmly believes that every opportunity is an opportunity for learning. His accumulated experiences will definitely benefit his future.

Situation 3

Lisa is a well-rounded person, as evidenced by her participation in numerous extracurricular activities in which she has acquired numerous professional skills. She also believes that she has an excellent capacity to concentrate. She will devote her energies to accomplish her goals. She has an assertive personality, as proven by her ability to estimate, plan and act efficiently. Moreover, she believes that she is a leader in the sense that she can perform a complex task with a minimum of staff and resources. She can also assign tasks to subordinates according to their strengths. Finally, Lisa has strong communicative skills. Individuals who collaborate with each other depend on communication and action. More than a communicator, an excellent manager acts effectively and efficiently.

B

1. How were you involved in extracurricular activities at university?
2. How is SAC responsible for extracurricular activities at Chungtai Institute of Health Sciences and Technology?
3. How did you become in charge of furnishing and operating stage lighting and acoustics for campus events?
4. How did your position in the school's extracurricular activities offer you many opportunities to come into contact with people from diverse backgrounds?
5. How did you learn to write proposals and use a wide array of skills?
6. How did your work experience in the Society of Emergency Medicine, R.O.C. make you aware of the importance of writing skills and related administrative

skills?

7. How did you cooperate with the governmental sector to hold small-scale activities while serving as a student association leader?

8. How did your position as a student association leader improve your organizational skills and ability to handle crises?

9. How did your position as a student association leader make you a persevering and punctual individual who can cope with unforeseen circumstances?

10. How did you learn to distribute funds, supervised and support activities, provide consultation and sponsor large-scale events?

C

1. What kind of person do you consider yourself to be?

2. What activities did you participate in while at university?

3. What allowed you to more closely interact with people?

4. What did you do in your spare time?

5. What often involves trial-and-error procedures in the laboratory?

6. What has made you a more patient and persevering individual?

7. What kind of individual have you become?

8. What has improved your ability to coordinate and execute administrative tasks?

9. What do you believe will definitely benefit your future?

10. What opportunities have you had for learning?

D

1. Why are you a well-rounded person?

2. Why did you acquire numerous professional skills while participating in extracurricular activities?

3. Why do you have an excellent capacity to concentrate on what you need to

accomplish your goals?

4. Why are you able to estimate, plan and act efficiently when given the opportunity?

5. Why are you able to perform a complex task with a minimum of staff and resources?

6. Why do you believe that you have strong communicative skills?

7. Why do individuals who collaborate with each other depend on communication and action?

8. Why did your participation in numerous extracurricular activities in university benefit others?

9. Why is an assertive personality important to estimate, plan and act efficiently?

10. Why should a manager assess subordinates according to their strengths?

E

1. Who depend on communication and action?

   Individuals who collaborate with each other

2. How does Lisa assign tasks to subordinates?

   According to their strengths

3. What will Lisa devote her energies to?

   Accomplish her goals

F

Situation 1

1. C 2. B 3. C 4. B 5. B

Situation 2

1. B 2. A 3. C 4. B 5. A

Situation 3

1. B 2. A 3. C 4. A 5. B

G

Situation 1

1. C 2. A 3. B 4. C 5. B 6. C 7. B 8. A 9. C 10. B

Situation 2

1. B 2. C 3. B 4. A 5. B 6. C 7. A 8. C 9. B

Situation 3

1. C 2. B 3. B 4. B 5. C 6. B 7. C 8. A 9. B 10. A

I

Situation 4

At university, Bruce participated in a campus mountaineering group. A natural environment benefits his physical stamina and spiritual well being. His activities have allowed him to see various organisms in their natural habitats. When called upon, he has collaborated with peers to prepare outdoor events. Close collaboration has allowed them to undertake serious mountaineering events that have provided great outdoor entertainment. Moreover, these activities have broadened his horizons in other ways, such as allowing him to take advantage of the unique leadership opportunities provided. Both the physical challenges and mental relaxation associated with mountain climbing have allowed Bruce more effectively to balance his academic and extracurricular activities. While relaxing the mind, extracurricular activities enable physical stamina and health to be prioritized. By keeping his mind clear, he is able to work more diligently.

Situation 5

The many extracurricular activities in which Susan participated at undergraduate school gave her the necessary balance between helping others and determining what path she should take in pursuing a career in research. She was involved with several medical technology organizations, occasionally participating in professional meetings to improve her knowledge, skills and expertise. Additionally, library resources, including the latest medical journals are of great interest to her. Her diverse educational activities have strengthened and broadened Susan's professional knowledge base and increased her awareness of various medical issues. She prioritizes improving her English language communication skills, enabling her to collaborate with overseas researchers.

Situation 6

Jerry occasionally volunteers to work with mentally challenged individuals. He recalls last summer vacation, when he volunteered to serve in a group that took some of these adults and children on an outing to Yang Min Mountain. A typical schedule for such an activity is as follows. He leaves his home around 7 am and cycles up to Yang Min Mountain. The adults and children start arriving by school bus at 8 am to prepare for the day's activities. After taking them to the toilet individually, he instructs them on basic etiquette during their journey to the Park. He must concentrate closely on the mentally challenged individuals and anticipate any unforeseen circumstances. Being responsible for such a large group is physically and mentally draining. In addition to watching out for them, Jerry must converse and interact with them. Nevertheless, volunteer work is personally satisfying. While pursuing his Master's degree, he had little time for extracurricular activities. However, he continued to participate in seminars, not all of which were related to his academic interests. He once attended a conference on personal investments. This event taught him much about risk control. While many of his friends and relatives have encouraged him to focus entirely on his professional field, he tries to have a diverse array of interests. Jerry still tries to attain a broad perspective that covers various fields.

J

1. How does a natural environment benefit Bruce?

2. How did you participate in campus extracurricular activities while in university?

3. How did mountaineering activities broaden your horizons?

4. How did you take advantage of the unique leadership opportunities provided in your mountaineering activities?

5. How have you been able to more effectively balance your academic and extracurricular activities?

6. How do you handle the physical challenges and mental relaxation associated with mountain climbing?

7. How have extracurricular activities enabled you to prioritize physical stamina and health?

8. How do you relax your mind while participating in extracurricular activities?

9. How have others called upon you to collaborate with them in the past?

10. How did you become involved in a campus mountaineering group at university?

K

1. What did the many extracurricular activities in which you participated at undergraduate school give you?

2. What organizations were you involved with during your undergraduate studies?

3. What did the professional meetings that you attended help you improve upon?

4. What skills did you acquire from the professional meetings that you participated

in?

5. What resources in the library are of great interest to you?

6. What activities have strengthened and broadened your professional knowledge base?

7. What did you increase your awareness of through the diverse educational activities that you participated in?

8. What skills have you prioritized improving upon?

9. What have your English language communication skills enabled you to do?

L

1. Why did you have to leave your home around 7 am and cycle up to Yang Min Mountain?

2. Why is being responsible for such a large group physically and mentally draining?

3. Why do you enjoy volunteering to work with mentally challenged individuals?

4. Why did the adults and children require instruction on basic etiquette?

5. Why do you find volunteer work to be personally satisfying?

6. Why did you have little time for extracurricular activities while pursuing your Master's degree?

7. Why are all of your interests not necessarily related to academic work?

8. Why have you to have a diverse array of interests?

9. Why have many of your friends and relatives encouraged you to focus entirely on your professional field?

10. Why have you attained a broad perspective on life that covers various fields?

M

1. What benefits Bruce's physical stamina and spiritual well being?

A natural environment

.

2. What has mountain climbing allowed Bruce to do more effectively?

Balance his academic and extracurricular activities

3. What did Bruce collaborate with peers to do?

Prepare outdoor events

N

Situation 4

1. B 2. C 3. B 4. A 5. C

Situation 5

1. B 2. C 3. C 4. B 5. A

Situation 6

1. B 2. A 3. B 4. A 5. C

O

Situation 4

1. B 2. A 3. C 4. A 5. C 6. A 7. C 8. B 9. A 10. C

Situation 5

1. C 2. C 3. B 4. B 5. C 6. B 7. A 8. B

Situation 6

1. C 2. B 3. C 4. A 5. C 6. A 7. C 8. B 9. B C

About the Author

Born on his father's birthday, Ted Knoy received a Bachelor of Arts in History at Franklin College of Indiana (Franklin, Indiana) and a Master's in Public Administration at American International College (Springfield, Massachusetts). He is currently a Ph.D. student in Education at the University of East Anglia (Norwich, England). Having conducted research and independent study in New Zealand, Ukraine, Scotland, South Africa, India, Nicaragua and Switzerland, he has lived in Taiwan since 1989 where he is a permanent resident.

Having taught technical writing in the graduate school programs of National Chiao Tung University (currently in the College of Management) and National Tsing Hua University (currently in the Department of Computer Science and Institute of Life Science) since 1989, Ted is a full-time instructor in the Foreign Languages Division at Yuanpei University of Science and Technology. He is also the English editor of several technical and medical journals and publications in Taiwan.

Ted is the author of *The Chinese Technical Writers'Series*, which includes <u>An English Style Approach for Chinese Technical Writers</u>, <u>English Oral Presentations for Chinese Technical Writers</u>, <u>A Correspondence Manual for Chinese Technical Writers</u>, <u>An Editing Workbook for Chinese Technical Writers</u>, and <u>Advanced Copyediting Practice for Chinese Technical Writers</u>. He is also the author of *The Chinese Professional Writers'Series*, which includes <u>Writing Effective Study Plans</u>, <u>Writing Effective Work Proposals</u>, <u>Writing Effective Employment Application Statements</u> and <u>Writing Effective Career Statements</u>.

Ted created and coordinates the Chinese On-line Writing Lab (OWL) at http://www.cc.nctu.edu.tw/~tedknoy, as well as the Online Writing Lab (OWL) at Yuanpei University of Science and Technology at www.owl.yust.edu.tw.

389

Acknowledgments

Thanks to the following individuals for contributing to this book:

元培科學技術學院　經營管理研究所
許碧芳(所長)　王貞穎　李仁智　陳彥谷　胡惠眞　陳碧俞　王連慶　蔡玟純
高青莉

元培科學技術學院　影像醫學研究所
王愛義(所長)　周美榮　顏映君　林孟聰　張雅玲　彭薇莉　張明偉　李玉綸
聶伊辛　黃勝賢

元培科學技術學院　生物技術研究所
陳媛孃(所長)　范齡文　彭姵華　鄭啓軒　許凱文　李昇憲　陳雪君　鄭凱暹
尤鼎元　陳玉梅

Thanks also to Wang Chen-Yin for illustrating this book and Wang Lien Ching for providing technical support. Graduate students at Yuanpei University of Science and Technology in the Institute of Business Management, the Institute of Biotechnology and the Institute of Medical Imagery are also appreciated. My technical writing students in the Department of Computer Science and Institute of Life Science at National Tsing Hua University, as well as the College of Management at National Chiao Tung University are also appreciated. Thanks also to Seamus Harris and Russell Greenwood for reviewing this workbook.

精通科技論文（報告）寫作之捷徑
An English Style Approach for Chinese Technical Writers （修訂版）

作者：柯泰德（Ted Knoy）

內容簡介

使用直接而流利的英文會話

讓您所寫的英文科技論文很容易被了解

提供不同形式的句型供您參考利用

比較中英句子結構之異同

利用介系詞片語將二個句子連接在一起

萬其超 / 李國鼎科技發展基金會秘書長

　　本書是多年實務經驗和專注力之結晶，因此是一本坊間少見而極具實用價值的書。

陳文華 / 國立清華大學工學院院長

　　中國人使用英文寫作時，語法上常會犯錯，本書提供了很好的實例示範，對於科技論文寫作有相當參考價值。

徐　章 / 工業技術研究院量測中心主任

　　這是一個讓初學英文寫作的人，能夠先由不犯寫作的錯誤開始再根據書中的步驟逐步學習提升寫作能力的好工具，此書的內容及解說方式使讀者也可以無師自通，藉由自修的方式學習進步，但是更重要的是它雖然是一本好書，當您學會了書中的許多技巧，如果您還想要更進步，那麼基本原則還是要常常練習，才能發揮書的精髓。

Kathleen Ford, English Editor,Proceedings(Life Science Divison), National Science Council

　　The Chinese Technical Writers Series is valuable for anyone involved with creating scientific documentation.

※若有任何英文文件修改問題，請直接與柯泰德先生聯絡：（03）5724895

特　　　價	新台幣300元
劃　　　撥	19419482 清蔚科技股份有限公司
線上訂購	四方書網 www.4Book.com.tw
發 行 所	華香園出版社

作好英語會議簡報
English Oral Presentations for Chinese Technical Writers

作者：柯泰德（Ted Knoy）

內容簡介

本書共分十二個單元，涵括產品開發、組織、部門、科技、及產業的介紹、科技背景、公司訪問、研究能力及論文之發表等，每一單元提供不同型態的科技口頭簡報範例，以進行英文口頭簡報的寫作及表達練習，是一本非常實用的著作。

李鍾熙／工業技術研究院化學工業研究所所長

> 一個成功的科技簡報，就是使演講流暢，用簡單直接的方法、清楚表達內容。本書提供一個創新的方法（途徑），給組織每一成員做爲借鏡，得以自行準備口頭簡報。利用本書這套有系統的方法加以練習，將必然使您信心備增，簡報更加順利成功。

薛敬和／IUPAC台北國際高分子研討會執行長
國立清華大學教授

> 本書以個案方式介紹各英文會議簡報之執行方式，深入簡出，爲邁入實用狀況的最佳參考書籍。

沙晉康／清華大學化學研究所所長
第十五屆國際雜環化學會議主席

> 本書介紹英文簡報的格式，值得國人參考。今天在學術或工商界與外國接觸來往均日益增多，我們應加強表達的技巧，尤其是英文的簡報應具有很高的專業水準。本書做爲一個很好的範例。

張俊彥／國立交通大學電機資訊學院教授兼院長

> 針對中國學生協助他們寫好英文的國際論文參加國際會議如何以英語演講、內容切中要害特別推薦。

※若有任何英文文件修改問題，請直接與柯泰德先生聯絡：（03）5724895

特　　　價　新台幣250元
劃　　　撥　19419482 清蔚科技股份有限公司
線上訂購　四方書網 www.4Book.com.tw
發 行 所　工業技術研究院

英文信函參考手冊
A Correspondence Manual for Chinese Technical Writers

作者：柯泰德（Ted Knoy）

內容簡介

本書期望成為從事專業管理與科技之中國人，在國際場合上溝通交流時之參考指導書籍。本書所提供的書信範例（附磁碟片），可為您撰述信件時的參考範本。更實際的是，本書如同一「寫作計畫小組」，能因應特定場合（狀況）撰寫出所需要的信函。

李國鼎 / 總統府資政

我國科技人員在國際場合溝通表達之機會急遽增加，希望大家都來重視英文說寫之能力。

羅明哲 / 國立中興大學教務長

一份表達精準且適切的英文信函，在國際間的往來交流上，重要性不亞於研究成果的報告發表。本書介紹各類英文技術信函的特徵及寫作指引，所附範例中肯實用，爲優良的學習及參考書籍。

廖俊臣 / 國立清華大學理學院院長

本書提供許多有關工業技術合作、技術轉移、工業資訊、人員訓練及互訪等接洽信函的例句和範例，頗爲實用，極具參考價值。

于樹偉 / 工業安全衛生技術發展中心主任

國際間往來日益頻繁，以英文有效地溝通交流，是現今從事科技研究人員所需具備的重要技能。本書在寫作風格、文法結構與取材等方面，提供極佳的寫作參考與指引，所列舉的範例，皆經過作者細心的修訂與潤飾，必能切合讀者的實際需要。

※若有任何英文文件修改問題，請直接與柯泰德先生聯絡：（03）5724895

特　　價　新台幣250元
劃　　撥　19419482 清蔚科技股份有限公司
線上訂購　四方書網 www.4Book.com.tw
發　行　所　工業技術研究院

科技英文編修訓練手冊
An Editing Workbook for Chinese Technical Writers

作者：柯泰德（Ted Knoy）

內容簡介

要把科技英文寫的精確並不是件容易的事情。通常在投寄文稿發表前，作者都要前前後後修改草稿，在這樣繁複過程中甚至最後可能請專業的文件編修人士代勞雕琢使全文更為清楚明確。

本書由科技論文的寫作型式、方法型式、內容結構及內容品質著手，並以習題方式使學生透過反覆練習熟能生巧，能確實提昇科技英文之寫作及編修能力。

劉炯明 / 國立清華大學校長

「科技英文寫作」是一項非常重要的技巧。本書針對台灣科技研究人員在英文寫作發表這方面的訓練，書中以實用性練習對症下藥，期望科技英文寫作者熟能生巧，實在是一個很有用的教材。

彭旭明 / 國立台灣大學副校長

本書為科技英文寫作系列之四；以練習題為主，由反覆練習中提昇寫作反編輯能力。適合理、工、醫、農的學生及研究人員使用，特為推薦。

許千樹 / 國立交通大學研究發展處研發長

處於今日高科技時代，國人用到科技英文寫作之機會甚多，如何能以精練的手法寫出一篇好的科技論文，極為重要。本書針對國人寫作之缺點提供了各種清楚的編修範例，實用性高，極具參考價值。

陳文村 / 國立清華大學電機資訊學院院長

處在我國日益國際化、資訊化的社會裡，英文書寫是必備的能力，本書提供很多極具參考價值的範例。柯泰德先生在清大任教科技英文寫作多年，深受學生喜愛，本人樂於推薦此書。

※若有任何英文文件修改問題，請直接與柯泰德先生聯絡：（03）5724895

特 價	新台幣350元	
劃 撥	19419482 清蔚科技股份有限公司	
線上訂購	四方書網 www.4Book.com.tw	
發 行 所	清蔚科技股份有限公司	

科技英文編修訓練手冊【進階篇】
Advanced Copyediting Practice for Chinese Technical Writers

作者：柯泰德（Ted Knoy）

內容簡介

本書延續科技英文寫作系列之四「科技英文編修訓練手冊」之寫作指導原則，更進一步把重點放在如何讓作者想表達的意思更明顯，即明白寫作。把文章中曖昧不清全部去除，使閱讀您文章的讀者很容易的理解您作品的精髓。

本手冊同時國立清華大學資訊工程學系非同步遠距教學科技英文寫作課程指導範本。

張俊彥 / 國立交通大學校長暨中研院院士

對於國內理工學生及從事科技研究之人士而言，可說是一本相當有用的書籍，特向讀者推薦。

蔡仁堅 / 前新竹市長

科技不分國界，隨著進入公元兩千年的資訊時代，使用國際語言撰寫學術報告已是時勢所趨；今欣見柯泰德先生致力於編撰此著作，並彙集了許多實例詳加解說，相信對於科技英文的撰寫有著莫大的神益，特予以推薦。

史欽泰 / 工研院院長

本書即以實用範例，針對國人寫作的缺點提供簡單、明白的寫作原則，非常適合科技研發人員使用。

張智星 / 國立清華大學資訊工程學系副教授、計算中心組長

本書是特別針對系上所開科技英文寫作非同步遠距教學而設計，範圍內容豐富，所列練習也非常實用，學生可以配合課程來使用，在時間上更有彈性的針對自己情況來練習，很有助益。

劉世東 / 長庚大學醫學院微生物免疫科主任

書中的例子及習題對閱讀者會有很大的助益。這是一本研究生必讀的書，也是一般研究者重要的參考書。

※若有任何英文文件修改問題，請直接與柯泰德先生聯絡： （03）5724895

特　　價　新台幣450元
劃　　撥　19419482 清蔚科技股份有限公司
線上訂購　四方書網 www.4Book.com.tw
發 行 所　清蔚科技股份有限公司

有效撰寫英文讀書計畫
Writing Effective Study Plans

作者：柯泰德（Ted Knoy）

內容簡介

本書指導準備出國進修的學生撰寫精簡切要的英文讀書計畫，內容
包括：表達學習的領域及興趣、展現所具備之專業領域知識、敘述
學歷背景及成就等。本書的每個單元皆提供視覺化的具體情境及相
關寫作訓練，讓讀者進行實際的訊息運用練習。此外，書中的編修
訓練並可加強「精確寫作」及「明白寫作」的技巧。本書適用於個
人自修以及團體授課，能確實引導讀者寫出精簡而有效的英文讀書
計畫。

本手冊同時為國立清華大學資訊工程學系非同步遠距教學科技英文
寫作課程指導範本。

于樹偉／工業技術研究院主任

《有效撰寫讀書計畫》一書主旨在提供國人精深學習前的準備，包括：
讀書計畫及推薦信函的建構、完成。藉由本書中視覺化訊息的互動及練
習，國人可以更明確的掌握全篇的意涵，及更完整的表達心中的意念。
這也是本書異於坊間同類書籍只著重在片斷記憶，不求理解最大之處。

王　玫／工業研究技術院、化學工業研究所組長

《有效撰寫讀書計畫》主要是針對想要進階學習的讀者，由基本的自我
學習經驗描述延伸至未來目標的設定，更進一步強調推薦信函的撰寫，
藉由圖片式訊息互動，讓讀者主動聯想及運用寫作知識及技巧，避免一
味的記憶零星的範例；如此一來，讀者可以更清楚表明個別的特質及快
速掌握重點。

※若有任何英文文件修改問題，請直接與柯泰德先生聯絡：（03）5724895

特　　　價　新台幣450元
劃　　　撥　19419482 清蔚科技股份有限公司
線上訂購　四方書網 www.4Book.com.tw
發 行 所　清蔚科技股份有限公司

有效撰寫英文工作提案
Writing Effective Work Proposals

作者：柯泰德（Ted Knoy）

內容簡介

許多國人都是在工作方案完成時才開始撰寫相關英文提案，他們視撰寫提案為行政工作的一環，只是消極記錄已完成的事項，而不是積極的規劃掌控未來及現在正進行的工作。如果國人可以在撰寫英文提案時，事先仔細明辨工作計畫提案的背景及目標，不僅可以確保寫作進度、寫作結構的完整性，更可兼顧提案相關讀者的興趣強調。本書中詳細的步驟可指導工作提案寫作者達成此一目標。 書中的每個單元呈現三個視覺化的情境，提供國人英文工作提案寫作實質訊息，而相關附加的寫作練習讓讀者做實際的訊息運用。此外，本書也非常適合在課堂上使用，教師可以先描述單元情境而讓學生藉由書中練習循序完成具有良好架構的工作提案。書中內容包括：1.工作提案計畫（第一部分）：背景 2.工作提案計畫（第二部分）：行動 3.問題描述 4.假設描述 5.摘要撰寫（第一部分）： 簡介背景、目標及方法 6.摘要撰寫（第二部分）： 歸納希望的結果及其對特定領域的貢獻 7.綜合上述寫成精確工作提案。

唐傳義／國立清華大學資訊工程學系主任

本書重點放在如何在工作計畫一開始時便可以用英文來規劃整個工作提案，由工作提案的背景、行動、方法及預期的結果漸次教導國人如何寫出具有良好結構的英文工作提案。如此用英文明確界定工作提案的程序及工作目標更可以確保英文工作提案及工作計畫的即時完成。對工作效率而言也有助益。

在國人積極加入WTO之後的調整期，優良的英文工作提案寫作能力絕對是一項競爭力快速加分的工具。

※若有任何英文文件修改問題，請直接與柯泰德先生聯絡：（03）5724895

特　　價　新台幣450元
劃　　撥　19735365 葉忠賢
線上訂購　www.ycrc.com.tw
發 行 所　揚智文化事業股份有限公司

有效撰寫求職英文自傳
Writing Effective Employment Application Statements

作者：柯泰德（Ted Knoy）

內容簡介

本書主要教導讀者如何建構良好的求職英文自傳。書中內容包括：1.表達工作相關興趣；2.興趣相關產業描寫；3.描述所參與方案裡專業興趣的表現；4.描述學歷背景及已獲成就；5.介紹研究及工作經驗；6.描述與求職相關的課外活動；7.綜合上述寫成精確求職英文自傳。

有效的求職英文自傳不僅必須能讓求職者在企業主限定的字數內精確的描述自身的背景資訊及先前成就，更關鍵性的因素是有效的求職英文自傳更能讓企業主快速明瞭求職者如何應用相關知識技能或其特殊領導特質來貢獻企業主。

書中的每個單元呈現三個視覺化的情境，提供國人求職英文自傳寫作實質訊息，而相關附加的寫作練習讓讀者做實際的訊息運用。此外，本書也非常適合在課堂上使用，教師可以先描述單元情境而讓學生藉由書中練習循序完成具有良好架構的求職英文自傳。

黎漢林／國立交通大學管理學院院長

我國加入WTO後，國際化的腳步日益加快；而企業人員之英文寫作能力更形重要。它不僅可促進國際合作夥伴間的溝通，同時也增加了國際客戶的信任。因此國際企業在求才時無不特別注意其員工的英文表達能力。

柯泰德先生著作《有效撰寫求職英文自傳》即希望幫助求職者能以英文有系統的介紹其能力、經驗與抱負。這本書是柯先生有關英文寫作的第八本專書，柯先生教學與編書十分專注，我相信這本書對求職者是甚佳的參考書籍。

※若有任何英文文件修改問題，請直接與柯泰德先生聯絡：（03）5724895

特　　價　新台幣450元
劃　　撥　19735365 葉忠賢
線上訂購　www.ycrc.com.tw
發 行 所　揚智文化事業股份有限公司

The Chinese Online Writing Lab
【 柯泰德線上英文論文編修訓練服務 】
http://mx.nthu.edu.tw/~tedknoy

您有科技英文寫作上的困擾嗎？
您的文章在投稿時常被國外論文審核人員批評文法很爛嗎？以至於被退稿嗎？
您對論文段落的時式使用上常混淆不清嗎？
您在寫作論文時同一個動詞或名詞常常重複使用嗎？

您的這些煩惱現在均可透過柯泰德網路線上科技英文論文編修
服務來替您加以解決。本服務項目分別含括如下：

1. 英文論文編輯與修改
2. 科技英文寫作開課訓練服務
3. 線上寫作家教
4. 免費寫作格式建議服務，及網頁問題討論區解答
5. 線上遠距教學（互動練習）

另外，為能廣為服務中國人士對論文寫作上之缺點，柯泰德亦
同時著作下列參考書籍可供有志人士為寫作上之參考。

＜1.精通科技論文（報告）寫作之捷徑
＜2.做好英文會議簡報
＜3.英文信函參考手冊
＜4.科技英文編修訓練手冊
＜5.科技英文編修訓練手冊（進階篇）
＜6.有效撰寫英文讀書計畫

上部分亦可由柯泰德先生的首頁中下載得到。
如果您對本服務有興趣的話，可參考柯泰德先生的首頁標示。

柯泰德網路線上科技英文論文編修服務
地址：新竹市大學路50號8樓之三
TEL:03-5724895
FAX:03-5724938
網址：http://mx.nthu.edu.tw/~tedknoy
E-mail:tedaknoy@ms11.hinet.net

國家圖書館出版品預行編目資料

有效撰寫英文職涯經歷 = Writing effective career
statements / 柯泰德(Ted Knoy)著. -- 初版. --
台北市：揚智文化, 2005[民94]
　　面；公分. --（應用英文寫作系列；4）

ISBN 957-818-700-9（平裝）

1. 英國語言 — 應用文 2. 履歷表

805.179　　　　　　　　　　　　　　93024012

有效撰寫英文職涯經歷　　　　應用英文寫作系列04

著　　　者／柯泰德（Ted Knoy）

出 版 者／揚智文化事業股份有限公司

發 行 人／葉忠賢

總 編 輯／林新倫

登 記 證／局版北市業字第1117號

地　　　址／台北市新生南路三段88號5樓之6

電　　　話／(02)2366-0309

傳　　　眞／(02)2366-0310

E - m a i l／service@ycrc.com.tw

網　　　址／http://www.ycrc.com.tw

郵撥帳號／19735365

戶　　　名／葉忠賢

印　　　刷／鼎易印刷事業股份有限公司

法律顧問／北辰著作權事務所　蕭雄淋律師

初版一刷／2005年1月

定　　　價／新台幣480元

ＩＳＢＮ／957-818-700-9